379/

THE DRAGON'S MOUTH

THE DRAGON'S MOUTH

LASELLE GILMAN

William Sloane Associates, New York

They can only set free men free . . .
And there is no need of that:
Free men set themselves free.

—James Oppenheim, *The Slave*

CONTENTS

THE DRAGON'S MOUTH

Imprimis

A red splendor lit the scene of fading battle, but the doctor was so close to the point of exhaustion that the eyes he turned to it saw only nightmare. It was very cold outside the cellar from which he had stumbled for a breath of air, and it would have been the cold and dark of midnight on an empty northern plain, except for the ring of fires. They leaped from a dozen burning villages along the horizon and the sparks whirled upward to rival the winter stars, and the glow of them was crimson on the icy pools. Near the ruined farmhouse where he stood there were watch fires and men lounging about them, warming themselves, the flames gleaming on pinched faces the color of orange peel and glinting on their weapons, and glinting too on the bright pinpoints of their eyes that turned toward the strange doctor, who was not one of them and therefore something to be wondered about and watched. Beyond them were other lights from long moving lines of trucks and carts and gun carriages, lurching southward across the flat plain. And still beyond all that, beyond the blazing villages there was yet a farther scarlet glow cast upward into the sky, and it flickered with the relentless rise and fall of massed batteries, their thunder rolling back over the plain and penetrating the frozen earth deep into the cellar the doctor had just left.

The air bit into his lungs like pure ether, but it was a relief from the smoke-clogged atmosphere in the cellar, with its reek of disinfectant and blood and vomit and garlic and putrescent decaying flesh, and he lingered a moment longer, blinking at the red horizon and listening to the pound of the guns. Down in his makeshift operating room he had been steadily at work over the smashed and mangled bodies of men for more than twenty hours; before that he had had three hours of drugged sleep on a dirty tarpaulin and before that eighteen hours at the operating table under the acetylene lamps. He was huddled into a quilted jacket and wore a fur cap, but his hands with the square hard fingers were still bare, and the skin of his face was only a stiff white blob behind flaps, collar and yellow beard-stubble.

A man detached himself from one of the closer fires and came up and peered into the doctor's face, his breath making a little cloud of steam between them, and he brought cigarettes out of his thick robe and gave the doctor one and lit it. In the light of the match he inspected the foreigner curiously.

"When did you eat?" he asked.

The doctor looked at him. "I don't know," he said, his voice hoarse and speaking the northern dialect common to this army. "I'm all right, we have things we can take to keep going. I have some pills."

The officer nodded. "I've given orders no more wounded shall be brought here—they must go to other field stations. There are eighty litter-beds in that house back there, partly protected by the thatch, and all the rest are stacked in the courtyard. Do you know how many casualties have been brought here since three days ago, here alone? Six hundred and seventy-three, the orderlies tell me. But it's nearly over now."

The guns rumbled, the glow brightened. "Nearly over," the doctor repeated as if to himself. "Well, it's better now, Colonel. When the machine guns and mortars are so near, the auscultation is difficult." He used the single English word, looked at the officer, and added, "The listening to the heartbeat."

"Anyway," the colonel said, "we have the victory." He carefully pinched out the end of his cigarette. "I don't know how many thousands are dead, or how many tens of thousands are wounded. The tallies aren't in yet, at headquarters. But the enemy is in flight below the Huai. In my opinion, it's decisive and he'll never stand and fight again. Not as he fought here, with his cumbersome mechanized armies against our massed guerrilla columns." He clapped the doctor on the padded shoulder. "Do you know, he's now like a great plodding buffalo, staggering away to the river in the south, blind and bleeding and dazed by our swift attack!"

"A buffalo," the doctor said, still repeating. "Harried by a pack of ravening wolves until it sinks to its knees and dies."

The colonel laughed, but stared at him narrowly. "Wolves and buffalo were evenly matched in strength, but not in intelligence. I tell you, Doctor, that in the number of men committed here by both sides, this was one of the great battles of all history—not only the history of this nation but of all the world! Six million men, Doctor! And besides the number involved, it was one of the significant battles of all time. The buffalo was prodded out into the open and forced to fight. He came disdainfully, bellowing that he would annihilate us, pawing the ground and shaking his great horns. And we flanked him and bore him down!"

"Another obscure battle fought in an unknown Chinese plain," the doctor said stubbornly. "The world will hear very little of it, if it hears at all, and will care less."

"That's the world's loss, then, if it's so deaf and stupid. This battle has shaped our destiny, and it may affect the destiny of many others far away."

The doctor pointed toward the west, where dying flames marked the funeral pyre of a small town at a crossroads on the plain, a town that had been of some importance and had been bitterly defended the previous day. It had a high mud-block wall around it, perhaps built in medieval times.

"I watched them storm that place, Colonel," the doctor said. "Your troops took it with the aid of wooden scaling ladders they brought up on rollers. The same method by which the barbarian hordes took your cities in the old invasions. And as I watched, I remembered that it was more than three years ago that an atomic bomb was used against Hiroshima."

The colonel laughed again, shortly and without humor. "That's the way we conquer," he said. "By improvising, by fluid maneuver against fixed strong points, by adapting our hard-learned Red guerrilla tactics." He looked at the white face of the doctor again. "If a long ladder wins a town, what do we need of your atomic bomb? You machine-minded Westerners—"

He checked himself. The doctor was very tired, and the colonel was truly fond of him. He was an alien, a lonely and unwilling outlander, and the colonel had picked him up many months ago in an isolated field hospital and impressed him for service, bringing him along to the war as a matter of expediency, without regard for his personal views or desires. He was a good man, this Doctor Fallon, for all his obvious indifference to the dialectic, and he had been invaluable not only to the unit but to the colonel himself. There was no need to start an argument now, at the moment of a glorious and lasting triumph. Sometime in the future, when the victory was consolidated and they had entered the great cities on the coast, perhaps he would offer this reluctant physician his freedom, his choice of remaining or departing, as his reward for service. But this was not the time, not here on the black frozen Huaihai.

"Never mind," the colonel said. "I'll try to send one of our battalion medical men from some other station to relieve you and you can get some sleep. We'll move forward out of this purgatory in a day or two."

He started to turn away toward the fires but the doctor laid a hand on his arm.

"Colonel Li, you think this is the end of the Civil War?"

"If you must call it that, yes. Nearly so."

"But it isn't the end of the fighting, I'm afraid. Has it occurred to you that now you've won, your greedy friends from the steppes may not only want a share in the spoils, but also may demand that you fight other battles for them?"

The colonel frowned. "What are you talking about?"

"The term in my own language for him is, the bear who walks like a man."

The guns muttered and flickered, more distantly. "We are seizing power by our own right, with only token aid from others," the colonel said coldly.

"I was thinking tonight of a man, a schoolmaster, whom I treated for a gunshot wound at Anyang a few months ago," the doctor said as if he had not heard. "He was a learned old fellow and he told me a parable from the ancient time of the warring kingdoms. It seems the king of Chao intended to make war on the king of Yen and asked advice of his counselor— Hmm, that schoolmaster later died of his wound, I recall."

"This is no time for parables and legends," the colonel said. "What was the counselor's advice?"

"Why, the counselor had just passed a stream where a crane had tried to thrust its beak into a clam lying in the sand, and the clam had shut itself up on the beak. Neither could get away, the clam was dying for water, the crane for food. Then a fisherman came along and caught them both. The counselor told the king about it and remarked that if the two kingdoms were locked in war and became exhausted, both would be easy victims for the savage Chin invaders from the north. So the king wisely gave up the campaign of extermination."

The colonel lit a cigarette and shrugged impatiently. "I'm a soldier, not a scholar, and a good thing too, or I'd be wasting my time on stuff like that. You'd best stop eating those pills, my friend, and get some food and rest."

He walked off to the watch fire and his comrades, shaking his head. "Clams and cranes and doddering old philosophers!" he said aloud, half in anger. "That's what comes when these foreigners get a smattering of our learning."

The doctor watched the glow reddening the night sky for a time, and then went back into his dugout abattoir.

The Wheel

I

It was enough to infuriate a brass image, and the doctor's face was stiff with anger. He stood before the assistant medical director, holding the cooling beaker in his hand, and brought his other fist down on the surface of the desk with such emphasis that the man's record books, fountain pen, table lamp and framed photo of The Chairman jumped. The assistant medical director jumped also, his fleshy body bouncing in the chair.

"What was that again?" the doctor demanded.

The assistant director's jaw set and his little almond eyes grew cold behind thick lenses. "I repeat," he said in his careful English, "the anesthetic has been disinfected at my orders."

"Disinfected! Do you mean you boiled it?"

"You can see for yourself, Dr. Fallon. The nurses are now boiling all anesthetics for three minutes to rid them of bacteria. There is a shortage and we cannot waste our supply." A hint of faint derision crept in. "A man of your experience, with the hospital at Anyang and all, should realize that. Even here in Shanghai, our people's institutions are not supported by your Rockefeller Foundation, you know."

"You damn fool, you can't disinfect procaine by—by cooking the stuff! All you've done is hydrolize it. It's worthless now, it's nonanesthetizing, it'd no more relieve pain than a cupful of river water. Rid it of bacteria! Did you think this up with your own head?"

The director straightened his white jacket and drew in his thick lips. "The procedure is contained in a directive from the Department laboratory," he said calmly. "It is quite possible, Doctor, that you are not up to date these days, since you are not in general practice and do not receive our publications. We are making rapid advances in every line of research, including ways and means of conserving pharmaceutical reserves. We do not have drugs and compounds to throw away in these times of the national emergency."

"What emergency?"

"The war in Korea. Remember?"

"There's a truce. The war's over in Korea."

"Perhaps."

Dr. Fallon put the beaker on the desk. "If you use that dose on your next patient before operating, Dr. Chu, you may as well give him a lead bullet to bite down on—chance of surviving shock will be better."

Two giggling nurses were grinning together outside the door and the director glared, aware that a point of face was involved here. He opened the desk drawer, selected a card from a file, and sat frowning portentously over it, stroking his chins.

"In the first place, Fallon," he said, "I don't believe it is any of your affair. You have been given the privileges of the stockroom for what supplies you think you need, at the request of your Colonel Li, but you're not on the resident staff here and we haven't sought your advice. Let me ask you something, to bring my records up to date. You've been using the hospital facilities now for about four years, I see—ever since we came into the city and took over the administration. You're attached to Li's bureau across the creek as an alien internee?"

Fallon looked down at him wearily. "You know all that. Just reminding me of it again?"

"Just for my file." Chu's small eyes glittered. "Actually, I've wondered how out of date you might be in your field. You haven't been in private practice for some time, I believe?"

"I was in private practice here in the Settlement for a year, after the war. Too much inflation and uncertainty to get a foothold. So I took a job upcountry with the field hospitals."

"A missionary endeavor, I take it."

"No. An international relief outfit, as you know quite well."

"Ah. Perhaps that, who can say? And then I gather you were—er—

drafted by the Red Army. In other words, it's been some seven years since you were practicing briefly here before. Now, I know you were in a prison camp down in the Philippines during the war, and some sort of a ship's surgeon before that. But tell me, Fallon: why did you come to China at all when you were liberated in the islands? You could have been repatriated."

Fallon set his mouth. "Why does anybody go anywhere to work for a living? And what's the object of this quiz? I've been put through the mixer by experts, Chu, many times. It's all in the Security dossier, if you want it."

"I'm sure it is. In fact, I've seen some of it. Unregenerate is the loose translation of one of the terms. I'm only surprised you're permitted to run at large. Colonel Li's fatuity, I suppose. Well, I merely wish to remind you of your rather precarious position."

"I haven't forgotten it," Paul Fallon said. "I haven't forgotten my basic chemistry, either, when it comes to boiling anesthetics."

He went out of the hospital into the hard blinding heat, across the littered and untended garden on which the English sisters had once lavished great care, into the crowded street along the creek. He was still flaming with righteous indignation, a bonfire of small annoyances and frustrations that had become his daily lot. But gradually he relaxed, as he had learned to do after such senseless clashes. And by the time he reached the bridge his bitter humor had reasserted itself. He stopped, leaning over the concrete balustrade for a moment to stare absently at the busy scene below, and suddenly he laughed aloud.

He was not laughing so much at Dr. Chu and his cooked procaine, for therein lay only a symbol of the vast human tragedy. With the top of his mind he was laughing at the frantic efforts of a boatman and his wife to retrieve and clean their naked son and heir, a top-knotted toddler who had fallen overboard into the debris of the muddy creek and drifted aft to the end of his rope. The baby was fished out, dripping oily scum but smiling with dignified aplomb at the harassed shrieks of his mother. And the tragedy was submerged by the comedy of the moment, the reliance and practical good nature of the river people on their floating home.

If that had been a foreign kid, Fallon thought, he'd probably be having hysterics now and be dead of fever tomorrow. But this one will survive to become another credit to his country.

He glanced around, hearing a murmuring and shuffling behind him, and realized with a start of self-consciousness that his loud guffaw had attracted attention. The bridge was massed with pedestrians, heavy hand-drawn carts and pedicabs, jammed, as were all streets and bridges at every hour of the day and night here in the heart of the city, and these burdened travelers passing in his vicinity had halted to look at him, not only because they were no longer accustomed to see among themselves the tall strange *yang-kweitze* with their big noses and red faces, but because they did not often hear the unfamiliar sound of laughter any more, especially from the diminishing colony of foreigners. These were earnest trying times unproductive of even simple amusement; the life of unremitting toil did not feed the risibilities.

Fallon met their curious stares equably, being inured to it, but only one returned a fleeting smile, an old and emaciated man in the ragged blue long-gown that was the uniform of the proletariat when it could not afford semimilitary tunic and trousers. He stood by the railing and had witnessed the rescue of the child, a commonplace occurrence in the kaleidoscopic existence along the waterway.

"That small man will benefit from his experience," the oldster murmured, "by learning that pitfalls await the one who strains beyond his tether."

"The pitfall held no terror for him," Fallon said. "He enjoyed the bath, though he emerges dirtier than before."

A twinkle appeared in the other's dark eyes and his leathery cheeks crinkled. "Dirtier and wiser," he agreed. He looked at Fallon in speculation, noting the long lean frame in washed and unpressed whites, the strong-fingered hands resting on the balustrade, the gaunt brown face with a touch of gray in the clipped mustache and at the temples, and the mild blue eyes beneath bleached-out hair. "You speak as a Northerner, perhaps one of Shantung," he said.

"I learned it imperfectly in Hopeh and Shansi," Fallon nodded.

"You are no Russian. Are you an Englishman?"

"America is my native place."

"Ah, *Meikuo-jen!*" the old man muttered, and light flared in his eyes and was shuttered. He coughed. In the crowd at the foot of the bridge two green-clad figures were approaching, their leather boots crunching above the whisper of scores of cloth slippers. Fallon also saw the patrolling People's Police, and recognized the mixed puzzlement and caution in the elder's face.

"You'd better go," he said. "Doesn't do to be seen with us."

"Yes." The man began to move away but still hesitated. "Formerly I knew many Americans and other Western folk, when I tutored in a business language school here," he added swiftly, his voice pitched low. "I was a scholar, and now am a government clerk, and they are nearly all gone. There have been many changes. I—I wish you fortune."

He melted into the moving procession and disappeared, leaving only the warming phrase with Fallon. It had been a long time since a stranger on the street had wished him anything good; he was accustomed to the shouted *"Hui lo! hui lo!"* of jeering urchins, the raucous invitation to get out and go home, and he was used to hostile glances and scowling silences and apprehensive withdrawals. The police were coming near and he began to walk on ahead of them toward his goal across the bridge, wishing to avoid another catechism. It was only a ten-minute stroll from the hospital, but already that morning he had twice presented his pass and other documents for inspection. He was tired of explaining himself to zealous constables.

The house where he was quartered stood just off the embankment beyond the span, segregated by its own compound wall. From the street it was hardly visible behind the wall and the thick foliage of a small garden; from the gate it loomed upward in its mounting three stories so near that one could hardly encompass the astonishing mass with its false stone front, its shuttered rows of windows, its unexpected cupolas and obtruding gables and haphazard balconies. It was an architectural monstrosity, but happily its gloomy seclusion concealed it from the casual eye.

Approaching it now, he was struck anew by realization that this unlovely structure was in the strict tradition of its hybrid surroundings in the center of the metropolis. It had been built probably forty years ago at the time of the first Revolution, and its style reflected the confusion of that chaotic era. There was a garden bench just inside the gateway, and he stopped for a moment before entering, and sitting there he thought he detected the underlying stink of the ancient marshland beneath.

He stared up at the building with mixed distaste and amusement. If he had been an archaeologist now, he decided, it might be interesting to dig into the floor levels and sunken basements, down to the sedimentary layers at the bottom beneath the rotting pilings. There, doubtless, would be traces of some rude fisherman's hut that had stood on this river mud flat in centuries past. For the cloying scents seemed to impregnate the damp walls of the house: above the shards there would be faint odors of sandalwood, teas and spices and opium, remnants of furs, cottons, silks and porcelainware. That would be the hong layer where one of the opulent foreign ghettos had risen a hundred years ago, its godown filled with riches from the hinterland, swapped in the face of a continent's stubborn disapproval.

The rice fields of the odorous foreshore were long gone, the compradors and wealthy refugee merchants who had haggled over this land as the settlement expanded were now with their ancestors. There might be a hint of incense here, but it was blanketed by the suspected smell of

Yorkshire pudding and exiles' borsch, for any observant digger and gleaner of refuse could find that the fortunes of this house had declined and its indigenous relics were topped by those of British and Russian household cultures. Once, indeed, it had served as a pension for Customs clerks. And in a period of war and occupation it had been a Japanese Naval Officers' Mess—the pungency of pickled daikon still seemed to linger. But in the tumultuous years following the war the crumbling shelter had become a roost for a bitter Greek harridan and her troupe of jaded but dextrous ladies.

Fallon grinned at the recollection. For when Colonel Li and his staff had entered the city four years ago and requisitioned this structure as a headquarters for the new Southeast Asia Bureau, the girls had been summarily ousted. There was a definite overlay of musk left in the rooms by the departed artists. And better, he thought as he rose from the bench, that rank lush reminder of the honest brothel than the stench of what was now cooking under this roof.

2

Fallon went into the hall, where light lay dim on faded elegance that had been the atmosphere of that last social layer. The colonel's staff had apparently been unaware of the incongruity, being mostly countrymen of humble origins and overwhelmed in those early days of the occupation by the strange richness and comforts of their surroundings, and the colonel himself had only inspected it with tolerance and then ignored it in the rush of organizing his peacetime affairs. Indeed, Fallon recollected now from that dimming period, the colonel had been forced to overrule his enthusiastic adjutant's plan to retain the bordello on the premises, including its nationalized merchandise. The girls had been packed off, vociferously protesting, to share the fate of other unwanted foreigners in less comfortable barracks.

He stood for a moment listening. It lacked an hour to lunchtime and he heard staccato voices from the kitchen in the rear, and a clatter of crockery bowls and chopsticks in the mess hall. He sniffed but had no appetite. From the adjutant's office behind the stairway came the pecking of a typewriter; above there was stillness.

After a short hesitation he plodded up to the dingy third floor room he had to himself, placed on his table the package of medicaments he had obtained at the hospital, and peeled off his damp jacket. The room was hot, but the house was cooler than more modern and pretentious buildings in the neighborhood and he better understood now why Colonel Li had chosen it, when he had the pick of towering apartments and hotel suites. Number 68 Soochow Road might be a moribund heap of stone and plaster, but its builder had insulated it against the city's tympany and the delta's extremes of climate. After years of itinerant warfare, the colonel yearned for quiet and tranquillity, and found a measure of it in the midst of the biggest and noisiest community in Asia.

Fallon got his pipe but could not find the new box of strong Weihsien tobacco he had left beside his cot. He smelled it, however, and followed the aroma down the hall to the cluttered room, blue with smoke, occupied by his compatriot.

Thorpe Albany was hunched over a desk by the window, scribbling in a notebook and so intent that he did not hear Fallon's step on rubber soles. The doctor stood for a moment in the door, watching him. Albany performed all functions with a sealed concentration, one of his few qualities Fallon acknowledged as enviable. Whatever he did, whenever he moved or spoke, it was with a catlike suppression of energy that could be permitted only one outlet at a time. Albany did, in fact, sometimes remind Fallon of a great dark cat with the disordered brush of black hair falling over his alert face and the muscles of his powerful body and limbs flowing smoothly under the hairy skin. He moved in that swift, coordinated manner now, sensing the doctor's presence and turning his watchful gaze behind thick spectacles toward the door.

Then he nodded, moving the hand-rolled cigarette to the side of his mouth. He closed the notebook and slid it into a desk drawer.

"You surprised me, Doc," he said, his words guarded and his tone easy. "You're as bad as the Security sleuths." At the same time his hands continued to move over the desk, gathering up stray bits of paper and pushing them into the drawer and closing it.

Fallon took the tobacco box and filled his pipe. "Privacy's a hard thing to come by around here. As hard as private property." He touched a match to the bowl and met Albany's suspicious glance.

"I'll have to get a key for this room. Didn't they teach you to knock on doors, back in your medical school?"

"I'm sure you're not writing anything in that book you'd not want me or the colonel or even Captain Kuo to see, are you?"

"Anybody's welcome to read my stuff any time," Albany said, shrugging. "Cops included. Part of my work, no thrills and all routine. Like in your own journal—I suppose you keep one. A lot of clinical gibberish on the colonel and his staff and me."

"You'd be surprised what I put in my journal," Fallon said. He smiled, watching Albany's glint of interest. Actually, Fallon kept no diary nor any private records, knowing the curiosity of his associates, and he sent and received no letters. He added, "Hope nobody finds the loose floor board where I hide it." And his grin widened as he speculated on how many hours might elapse before Albany would be prowling the doctor's quarters with professional zeal, prying at the floors and wainscoting.

He turned away so that the dislike he increasingly felt for Thorpe Albany should not show too plainly in his eyes. The irreconcilable antagonisms between them were still there, they grew by the day and the week, fed by such petty verbal fencing, but the outright clashes verging on blows were things of the past. At least, they both attempted to avoid those scenes that had embittered their first year or so of enforced fellowship in Number 68. Quarrels were fruitless, they annoyed the colonel and endangered the limited freedom, and were set aside in the interests of near-harmony on the third floor. A truce existed but was always threatened by a basic incompatibility both recognized; their lives were restricted to parallels inside this house, but there resulted no intimacy such as grows effortlessly between denizens of a prison. For Fallon was the only prisoner; Albany, if not a free agent, was at least a privileged trusty. Fallon refused to brood over the charged relationship, sloughing it off with as much good humor as he could muster and calling it shack fever. Albany's introspective nature, warped and deepened with the passing months, was something the doctor had no desire to study. He had little interest in psychoneurotic therapy.

But as he went to the door the old animosity rose again in his gorge and he looked back.

"My small privileges at the hospital don't extend to the tobacco supply," he said. "I have to scrounge what I get. I don't have a salary or expense account in this jail. I don't subscribe to sharing the wealth, either. You've got access to the best at your Information Bureau—why don't you provide your own smokes?"

Albany's pupils contracted. "Ah, I've been under the weather and haven't been out of the house since yesterday," he said, his voice sullen. "I ran out. For Christ sake, I wasn't stealing your poisonous stuff!" He threw his dead cigarette on the floor.

"There's nothing wrong with you a good cathartic won't cure," Fallon said. "You ought to get out in the air and take a walk. The junk you sit in here reading and writing is enough to clog up anybody's system."

"Keep your cracks and your nostrums to yourself, Fallon! Go treat the colonel's worms or whatever's the matter with him this week. Go bleed his stupid girl friend. What I read and write doesn't concern you."

"You're right, most of it. Nauseating tripe. But you got out of your depth the other day with that piece you wrote in the Information Bulletin your bureau issues. The bit about the germ warfare confessions. D'you really believe our fliers dropped cans of bugs over North Korea last year?"

Albany bridled. "I suppose we should have asked your aid as medical consultant! What makes you think I wrote it, anyhow?"

"Know your style, boy. The end justifies any vicious distortion. But I could have set you straight on certain elementary points about bacteriological warefare. Where'd you get that crap about your own countrymen —you call 'em the enemy!—spreading smallpox and typhus right up to the time of the ceasefire?"

"Maybe you can disprove it? It's a sworn statement from our own Red Army doctors in the field. When were you near Korea?"

"Neither of us has been any nearer Korea than right here in Shanghai. But I worked in mission hospitals in the north before your friends took over and shoved me into their field units. Epidemics like that are common enough. They have amoebic dysentery from polluted water supplies. They have typhus from hordes of rats. They have malaria and encephalitis from mosquitoes. War just intensifies disease, and your damned Red Army butchers did nothing to help. They only allowed starvation to be added to the list. Then to divert the guilt they started yelling germ warfare and dragging forced confessions from prisoners. Common sense should tell you that much, or stop you from adding your ignorance to the big lie."

"Common sense should tell you you'll get your neck in a sling if you go sticking your nose into this. Don't forget your status."

"That's the second time today I've been reminded of it and threatened. I learned to keep out of it long ago when I saw I was shouting against a blank wall. Maybe you've heard of the wholesale executions of liberal native doctors in this country, along with the others they call reactionaries."

"I suppose the aggressors did something to check those epidemics?"

"You mean the Allies? Certainly. Mass inoculations, spraying against contagion, research in developing new antibiotic techniques and formulas. Caring for millions of refugees, teaching 'em simple sanitation."

Albany looked grim. He said, "Go ahead, Doc, talk long enough and put your big foot in it. You've sneered at me before about being a propagandist. But that muck you're quoting is just imperialist propaganda. You got a private source of information, maybe, about what's going on over there?"

Fallon snorted. "This may sound trite to you, but truth sometimes leaks into the darkest corners. Our people—my people, I should say—have compassion in a country that's flat on its back. Your friends don't give a damn. Just another difference between two systems."

For a moment Albany stared at him, then hunched a shoulder. "You're mixed up, Fallon—you're the one who doesn't seem to give a damn. You may be held here in a sort of detention but you've got a pretty soft berth with the colonel. He thinks he needs you and he isn't ready to let you go. But you keep your mouth shut and hang onto it and later you'll probably be released. At least, you aren't in the calaboose, and you could do worse than pill-rolling for a few party whips and their pals, you know."

"Sure," Fallon said. "I could be a turncoat."

"You've called me that before," Albany said wearily. "Sticks and stones, Doc. You're pretty awful noble, but you won't feel so noble if Kuo and his Security kids get tired of your lip and take you away from your colonel and protector and toss you in the clink with the others. You've played it smart so far, why spoil it?"

Fallon felt suddenly drained and turned to the door. "I don't know," he said. "I get fed up with the pretense, I guess, and the slop I take from you and the rest. At least, the colonel knows I'm not here from choice, and so does Captain Kuo."

"And I am!" said Albany. "Well, it's a free choice. You go on doing your forced labor, Doc, and let me do my own work. For the greater glory."

3

In the night the shrill lament of a steam tug, whistling for the bridge on the creek, penetrated Fallon's troubled dreams. He heard the wind's uneasy strumming in the garden bamboos, and when it rose in a gust to blast the waterfront a few hundred yards away he began to mumble in an unintelligible patois of English and Chinese. His own words wakened him and he lay in darkness, hearing the lash of rain against his window. The storm beat upon the house, sweeping in across the coast with titanic force and bursting over the sprawling and unprotected city, the first gale of the season. It shook his bed but did not account for the specters. The white dial of his watch showed the hour before dawn.

Go, man, go! Run—run, man, run for your life! There's the whistle, there's the ship, there's the river down to the sea. So near, man! What are you waiting for, fool! The words the same, crowding in in mandarin or his native Maine: they spilled out at him from a stale knocking in his temples, they hurried before the dark dread rising over the ragged edge of his mind. *Go, man! Run now, while you still can run. . . .*

Fallon lay immobile on the bed, half-asleep and fumbling for one of the cigarettes he had rolled in the evening, and listened to the storm and the words. He looked up at the glowing tip of the cigarette in the forsaken moment before watery daylight and heard the distant crash of a wind-tipped chimney pot. There was that tireless old man talking nonsense again, perched like a weight upon his chest. What crazy counsel was this, after four empty years of restraints and restrictions! Where did you go, where did you run? Down the river to the mud-stained sea? The old man was getting senile in his thirty-seventh year, he was losing his grip at last, growing as ragged and erratic as Albany snoring there through the wall of the room, as irresponsible as the jumpy adjutant downstairs, Major Huang. As nervous and unpredictable as the boss, that Red Army's most celebrated hypochondriac, Colonel Li Han-tsen.

Li was impatient over the unresolved and indecisive truce in Korea, in which he had no part. Four years sitting in this city gnawing his impatience and nagging about his health, running the Southeast Asia Bureau and fretting through three of those years about Korea where he thought he belonged. Li had been another man entirely in that bitter winter battle nearly five years ago on the Huai, and even in the later busy season when he had finally swung into the city, one of the conquerors.

The memory of that time rose like another jumbled dream now, and then Fallon dismissed it. What the hell, it was all becoming indistinct, the drive south and the triumphant entry into the central coast metropolis and all the rest of it. The Big Takeover. The power play. The replacement of one corruption by another corruption.

Gray light was beginning to spread across the streaming windows, and reluctantly Fallon realized that he was wide awake for the day, with a headache. He rose, moving about the room in the sad morning gleam, his own footsteps plucking at his nerve ends. He brewed himself a pot of tea on a little spirit lamp. He shaved and lit another cigarette, noticing the deep nicotine stains on his fingers. The tea he made was strong and his mind began to turn over. The rain and wind had stopped abruptly a few moments before and he went to the window and flung it up.

Go, man, go! There's the river, there're the ships. . . .

This window at the corner overlooked a mass of verdure below and gave him an impressive view of the crenelated tiers of the emporium along the Bund, and the quays downriver beyond the creek mouth. Beneath was a jigsaw pattern of wet tiled rooftops, marked by narrow twisting lanes. Over them was the broad harbor of the curving river, cluttered with moored shipping. A flat shaft of sunlight pierced the fleeing tatters of the storm, striking the towers of the foreshore, the chocolate stream and the docks of Pootung beyond. The disordered scene of crowded tenements, slim spires, jumbled wharves and busy maritime activity, set upon the desolate and naked morning glitter of the flat delta, struck him full in the eyes. He squinted, picking out the masonry pile of the Customs House, the hotel where the Information Bureau now occupied an upper suite, the iron network of the bridge beside the park, and beneath it the swarm of bumbling sampans and cargo lighters venturing out on the heels of the wind to resume their loading of ships.

Out in the stream a squat, rusted freighter swung to a buoy, taking cargo aboard from the boats, hoisting crates and bales on faintly clanking booms. Her funnel markings proclaimed her a British vessel, up from Hongkong. He had seen many of her kind here in the past four years, but it was always hard to realize that there was still ordinary trade, ordinary commerce going up and down the river like this, under his nose. It was hard to remember that there were still Europeans moving about freely in these closed ports and cities, somehow hanging on from the time of unequal treaties, extrality, concessions, consular courts and gunboats. Now and then about the streets he saw a rare and dispirited white face. Men also segregated but living comparatively free lives in their homes, going to their offices, carrying on their dwindling business. Exiles, pale dyspeptic ghosts, a few "Old Hands," the last of the vanished race, walking anachronisms.

Fallon turned abruptly from the scene and poured the rest of his cooling tea into a cup. There was no point dragging such thoughts up again: you didn't escape from the inescapable dungeon. You might not be in solitary confinement, but Security had ten million watchful eyes. Ships came and went; it meant nothing. Yet he glanced out again at the freighter, and again saw the panorama upon which countless spectators from the Western world had gazed in the century now ended, both resident and transient. It gave him an odd feeling to remember that they were no longer here in their famed and cherished Paris of the East. The cycle had made a full turn. The city, like the majestic ruins of Angkor, remained, but those who had built it and made it rich were gone and only a few such incidental stragglers as himself and that ship lurked in the shadows. The ship would be gone tomorrow.

He looked around the shabby room. His life seemed always to have been channeled between this house and that block of hospital buildings across the creek, with occasional minor excursions through the town. And when he walked there he was alone in the blue-clad anonymous mass padding in the streets. He was given no activity but his work, not much freedom outside the bounds of his occupation, no casual relaxations, no theaters or clubs to attend, little to read but brochures, no one to talk to but Thorpe Albany, who talked like a brochure, nothing to listen to but the radio blatting excerpts from brochures and exotic orchestral recordings.

Run, man, run! Oh, he'd tried it before. He'd tried gambling with the bureau staff, for instance, but he had no luck and no money for losing. He'd tried getting drunk but his instincts and body revolted as his mind clouded. He'd tried women with the same unsatisfactory result. The raw liquors released by the State were sickening, and the raw peasant girls, oiled and chunky and matter-of-fact in their emancipation from ancient restraints, were little different and discouragingly intense and dedicated. He had no taste for them.

All right, Fallon thought, *a man should try anything once. Seek escape not vicariously but in direct physical action. Go, man!*

There had been a time when he had gone, gone hard and fast. He hadn't always existed behind this mask of passive serenity, this outward equanimity in the face of war and destruction, personal bad fortune, prolonged captivity, sometimes hunger and thirst. The colonel and the others, Albany included, thought he was resigned to this empty decay. But he could run, man, and struggle. God knew he'd had enough of it in the early and destitute years at medical school back home, in the long periods of wandering as a shipboard physician and plantation medico, in the relentless guerrilla warfare of the Samar jungle and the ensuing torment of the Japanese prison camp. What he hadn't learned he'd picked up later in the relief camps and field hospitals of the North China plain, and at the start of this endless internment.

He dressed, watching the British ship in the stream, and went down the stairs to the mess hall in search of some sort of breakfast, and found it deserted. It was still too early for most of the colonel's staff. A scowling cook glared at him through the door and brought him congee, rice cakes and tea. He ate the tasteless food in solitude, feeling the climbing morning heat, and was bemused by his unexpected waking reflections.

Fallon suddenly pushed back his bowl. *Somebody's going to run, somebody's going to go damned soon!* he thought. He felt the stubborn determination twisting and swelling in his mind. Over four years, that was enough of this half-deadness in a rotting city. A thing could be endured if there were reason for it, but the reason was gone with the hope, and he'd never shared the faith.

He was rising in decision from the table when the adjutant trotted in. Major Huang was still in his sleeping robe and appeared, as usual, harassed.

"Ah, Doctor!" he exclaimed. "Here you are! I looked in your room. The colonel, Doctor. Immediately, please."

"He's sick again?" Fallon said mildly.

"No, no, not sick today." He hesitated, apologetic. "You know his way. Peculiar working hours. So early, eh? I am afraid it is a discipline for you. Ai-yah! One of those bad days, one supposes."

4

The break of the equinoctial storms had already brought an oppressive heat. Its film shimmered over the gray towers and rose from the crevices of the streets. The charged atmosphere lay heavily on the delta, on the sullen coils of the river and on the irritable mass of humanity packed into the city, building up into thunderheads of tension.

Fallon concealed the annoyance he felt as he climbed to Colonel Li's suite. He resented the intrusion of the colonel's aches and pains and wakeful habits upon his own half-formed plans and wished he had skipped breakfast and gone to the hospital, where he always had the excuse of special patients sent to that institution from the bureau. He wished the deluge would continue and wash away the accumulated dirt, stench and bad temper, all reflected in full measure in Number 68.

He loitered on the stairs, rolling a cigarette. Sometimes he thought of this establishment as the House of Usher. Once he had referred to the hospital across the waterway as the Temple of Ten Thousand Abominations, and the colonel had been vaguely amused, though Albany had been present and frowned at the disparagement.

Number 68 contained eight large rooms on its two upper floors, four rooms to each level, and the permanent residents occupied these. In the time when it had been a pension, during the prosperous decade between the rise of the Kuomintang and the outbreak of the Japanese war, two low wings had been added, each divided into a number of apartments, and these were now reserved for the staff of planners of the Southeast Asia Bureau. Fallon seldom saw those gentlemen except when they fell ill, and since they largely ignored him as an infidel, there was little friction between them.

The rooms on the top floor had been set aside for Fallon and Albany, the colonel's adjutant, Major Huang, and the colonel's special consultant, Gregor Efremov. Fallon, by some fluke, had drawn the large front room overlooking the road and the creek. Perhaps it had been because the adjutant, in assigning quarters, had regarded Fallon in this changing and topsy-turvy world as the colonel's favorite protégé. Albany had the adjoining space, befitting a man of his importance in the Information Bureau. He did not rightly belong in the house at all since he was not under the colonel's jurisdiction, but there was a great scarcity of living room in the neighborhood and it was convenient to his office. Albany resented being herded into such close association with the doctor, conscious of the prison stigma of that floor, but Major Huang dourly lumped him in the category of an outlander, regardless of creed.

The adjutant had turned the second floor over to Colonel Li. There the colonel directed the affairs of his bureau from a large and pleasant office that had formerly been the Greek madame's boudoir. He had his living quarters attached, with a kitchen and personal cook at the rear.

The remaining room in this suite, connected with Li's own sanctum, was reserved for the only other foreign member of the ménage, Judith Markham. Since Mrs. Markham had no official status in the bureau, being linked with it only through a tenuous and private relationship with Colonel Li, Fallon saw very little of her. She emerged at irregular intervals to stroll alone on the creek embankment.

Major Huang had done the best he could with the disposal of personnel through the house and had received the colonel's approving nod. He would have liked to eject Albany, whom he regarded as a square peg who must be handled delicately because of his connections. And as for the Englishwoman, the major had a closed mind; he put her where he was instructed and left her entirely alone. He did not like his assignment as major-domo of Number 68, he bickered with the household staff, and kept out of the way as much as possible.

Fallon knocked at the colonel's door and an orderly admitted him. Colonel Li was at his desk, wearing a most unmilitary and luxurious robe of blue tribute silk. The room was hazy with smoke and aromatic with the scent of the colonel's special tea. Judith Markham was not in evidence at this hour, but Fallon saw that he was not the colonel's first visitor of the day, and the discovery brought an unpleasant flavor to his tongue. Sitting beside the desk, alert and immobile in his chair, was Captain Kuo Liang of the Security Bureau.

Captain Kuo was not properly a resident of the establishment but he sometimes seemed to be, so frequent and unscheduled were his arrivals and departures at odd hours. No cordial welcome was ever extended to him, least of all by the colonel, but Captain Kuo was unconcerned with hostile attitudes or cool receptions. His right to come and go was unquestioned and among his many shadowy duties he kept a close and watchful eye on the internal affairs of the Asia Bureau headquarters because of its foreign occupants, whom he distrusted without exception.

In the morning light from the window the colonel's bulk was indistinct, but Kuo's face was like aluminum-shaded parchment, the sharp planes paneling the gleam, and his ironic eyes, the shape and shine of ripe olives, were steady on Fallon as the doctor entered. He was a strong wiry man with a narrow jaw under wide cheekbones; he wore the distinctive uniform of the police. Fallon nodded and Kuo lifted his arm in a mocking salute.

"You sent for me?" Fallon asked.

The colonel smiled in deprecation, his mouth unhappy. He was never at ease in Captain Kuo's presence and obviously this call had taken him unawares. Then he affirmed his well-being. His health, he said, was excellent today, oddly enough. It was another matter, and he hesitated. Kuo waited, expectant. And it occurred to Fallon that the Security officer had come to continue his periodic interrogations. He put them all through the grinder occasionally, despite Li's impotent fuming and protests. Even the Russian consultant and the colonel's lady. These sessions had resulted in some highly emotional scenes in earlier days. But lately Kuo had contented himself with spaced and routine visits, reducing the indignation but reminding all, even Soviet guests and other alien friends, that they were always answerable to their hosts.

"Captain Kuo has received a complaint from the hospital," the colonel added lamely. He looked at a written report on his desk, and looked at Kuo, but Kuo said nothing. Obviously the captain had already delivered the complaint and now left it up to Li to deal with it. Li shifted uneasily in his chair and did not meet Fallon's gaze.

"A complaint from Dr. Chu?" Fallon said with interest. A moment or an hour before he had been tired and reluctant to renew his running fight with the assistant medical director, but now that it had been brought out into the open he became restless and eager, and grinned at the Security officer. His reaction brought a flicker of doubt to Kuo's eyes, the captain appeared off balance, and Fallon's spirits rose. "Well, Colonel, Dr. Chu has made it clear that I'm not welcome on the wards, if that's what is meant. The cooperation of his staff is grudging."

"There should be no friction," Colonel Li said, his words uncertain. The colonel leaned heavily on the medical services and on his personal physician. He was not only diabetic but suffered the agony of stomach ulcers. In wet weather, old wounds pained unbearably, in hot weather as now he was stricken with migraine, and he frequently took to his bed with recurrent attacks of both malaria and dysentery. Fallon saw him here in his suite nearly every day and often was called by the orderly in the night to give intravenous quinine injections or doses of stovarsol.

"I hope then that there's no difficulty in obtaining drugs from Dr. Chu," Li said.

"No," Fallon said promptly. "Aside from the usual shortages, there's never any trouble getting drugs, in a crisis. Especially for party members. The shortages, however, are due to mismanagement and bureaucratic delays. So only party members and soldiers get the benefits and ordinary patients get charcoal or anti-acid pills. Party members at the hospital have meat and vegetables in their diet, ordinary patients have vegetables and rice, the poorest have only millet and a little bean curd. A party official gets plenty of sulfadiazine for a small boil on his neck, such as you had last week, but there's no medication for a peasant kid with a purulent inflammation of the middle ear, such as I treated yesterday. That's progress."

Colonel Li said nothing, but he glanced anxiously at a bottle of neoarsphenamine that stood upon his desk. He pinned his only abiding faith on it, and Fallon's outburst passed unnoticed. That divine stuff, Li had often declared, had almost as many uses as bamboo. It had cured him of syphilis, and of blackwater fever. He was anemic and it seemed to stimulate his bone marrow. Colonel Li did not genuflect before the benign countenance of the Buddha nor before the scowling images of the Eighteen Lohan, he did not even nod to the huge framed photo of the balding Chairman that hung on the wall behind his desk. He burned incense instead to Neosalvarsan.

But Captain Kuo's face had become dark and swollen. This was heresy, not to be tolerated even from a bold alien dog-doctor whose only protection was the colonel's sloppy sentimentality.

"Dr. Chu is correct," the captain said in his flat harsh northern voice, "when he declares that we've dispensed with the stupid humanitarian viewpoint that lavishes valuable time and material on useless dregs of humanity just because they're sick. Doctors have only one interest and duty, and that's to keep fit those who are of value to the future of the State, and to them should be given the best of care!"

Fallon was still standing, looking down at them both. He said with contempt, "Dr. Chu has complained to you about me and would bar me from his hospital because I criticize his procedure. Twenty years ago he received an expensive medical education in America on a scholarship. Today he permits septic and aseptic cases to be handled at the same time. All the instruments are boiled together in one sterilizer. No changes of gowns or gloves are allowed because of cost. So most cases become infected. Now the wards are crowded, because typhoid is endemic and there has been an increase lately. The wards are filthy and patients are dying of abscesses and necrosis. Bandages go unchanged, orderlies handle patients with dirty hands. The other day the nurse assisting me admitted she'd just gone to the delivery room barehanded after treating a suppurating wound. Operating rooms are not cleaned between operations. In that bloody litter I have handled a foot amputation, an adenomatous goiter big as a grapefruit, and—"

Kuo rose swiftly. "Fah On I-sheng," he said, speaking formally and giving Fallon his phonetic equivalent and title, "perhaps you are not aware that we have an epidemic. You know of the typhoid?"

"The city has a fine British-built waterworks," Fallon shrugged. "It turns the river into a harmless liquid humans can drink. But people still drink untreated water from canals and creeks, as they have always done. If Dr. Chu is content with primitive methods, he can save you money by resorting to buffalo-dung plasters on wounds, and opium for a painkiller. To clear up the typhoid you can save on all that costly chemical purification and just dump a few barrels of raw whisky every day into the reservoirs." He grinned wryly at the thought. "It'd at least improve the disposition of the people and take some of that stuffy purposefulness out of all of you."

"I'll tell you what's probably been dumped into the reservoirs," Captain Kuo said, his voice rising. "They may have been sabotaged. If Dr. Chu's staff finds typhoid bacilli in the sample tests they are running, we will know."

Fallon's shoulders drooped. These people, at least the ones like Chu and Kuo, chose blind suspicion deliberately and there was no point in the argument. There may have been a minor typhoid scare, it was even possible that the water supply had been accidentally contaminated.

"Do you think there has been some senseless act of sabotage simply to discredit the administration?" he demanded. "At the risk of killing off the city's population?"

"It is not so absurd as you try to make it sound," said Kuo, furious now. "A laboratory investigation is being conducted. The underground is capable of making such a dangerous gesture."

"You make it sound subtle and sinister. It sounds idiotic to me. The brainstorm of a minor official in the Sanitary Department, perhaps?"

"There are plenty of dissidents and deviationists on the loose!" Kuo shouted. "They bubble up from the underground opposition. They might dump poison into the mains from pure spite."

Fallon grunted. That Kuo should even admit the existence of opposition was victory enough. This might be the surface disturbance of another of those constant and poorly concealed struggles that rived the body politic; everyone was sensitive to them. When a party composed of some two per cent of the people dictated the methods by which should be purified a vast reservoir of some five hundred million automatons, carrying out its decrees through the Army, there was bound to be a kickback.

Colonel Li had been listening to them in a sort of shocked silence, but when Kuo turned toward him he held up his hand.

"You are going to demand again that this doctor be detained, or put under house arrest. I know, I know, he sounds deranged, but he is harmless, Captain. I am responsible; possibly it is the weather."

Outside the window the sun was hot and the grass and shrubs of the garden steamed, and a thin vapor rose from the flowing water below the embankment. The colonel had set himself to be diplomatic, but he gave Kuo a short satirical nod. He was back in his usual good form.

The Security officer said nothing more; he slapped his cap on his head and stalked out. Fallon watched him go, saw the stiffness of his shoulders. Once, in another of their stormy encounters, Fallon had denounced Kuo to his face. He had called him a policeman of the regime of oppression, regimentation, brutality and mindless hate, plus all the evils they attributed to their enemies and predecessors, and more. Remembering that now, he thought he had done a rather astute job of it. Probably Kuo believed the doctor had jumped his trolley. But he bore Fallon a deeper malice than any of the others.

5

The orderly came with more tea as the day grew, and put cigarettes in a box on the desk. There was still no sign of Mrs. Markham, nor any sound from her inner quarters. The colonel's speculative gaze rested on the doctor, who had seated himself at last and was sipping the tea, and there was mild curiosity in the long-jaundiced eyes.

"You are becoming most indiscreet, I-sheng," Li said finally. "The captain is not a person to offend. He has much authority, even here over my own staff. If you antagonize him, I shall lose my physician."

"You don't need a physician. Dr. Chu would do."

"I neither like nor trust Dr. Chu. My feelings are the same toward Captain Kuo. That is also indiscreet, but I can say it to you."

"Yes."

Fallon glanced at the man who had conscripted him in the field five years before, indentured and defended him ever since. The colonel was an old soldier and his erect, powerful, military physique belied the inner decay. Like Fallon, he came from a rock farm, though his own had been a tenant-holding in Szechwan and the crop had been poppies. He had spent thirty years at his trade, rising from a gawky and starving rifleman to high command. He had fought warlords, both rebel and government battalions, splintered recalcitrants and Japanese invaders. He had switched sides several times to better his fortunes. He had marched on foot at the head of troops from one end of the country to the other, though he had never crossed a frontier. He had been married three times and his third wife now lived in the south. He had had six sons and three daughters and knew the whereabouts of none of them, for they had vanished in the wars. He was stern and driving with Major Huang and his staff, gentle and amused with Judith Markham, whom he had also taken under his wing, on guard with Albany and Efremov, and, like a complaining child, sought surcease from his ills with Dr. Fallon.

When Fallon first met Colonel Li in the receiving station at Anyang, long before the memorable and decisive battle on the Huai, the officer had been commanding a regiment. Now his regiment was on the Manchurian border and he commanded no troops. His staff people were not fighting men, but planners and strategists on a scale so broad that Fallon had no clear concept of their work. Their weapons were ceiling-high wall maps and file cabinets crammed with detailed confidential reports, and their troops were scattered.

Those forces they commanded wore no uniforms; they were couriers and agent-provocateurs, observers and organizers. They were seamen and rice merchants, political commissars with guerrilla units, supply-truck drivers, dealers in tin and rubber, traders whose stocks were explosives and ammunition, consular officials, small planters and the operators of modest mines in key areas. They were spotted carefully from Manila through Hanoi and Bangkok to Singapore and Rangoon, and as deep into the salient as Jakarta and Macassar, and at many lesser points between on steamship routes, railway lines and trans-border highways. They formed an unbroken network across Southeast Asia. Colonel Li did not think of them in any such dramatic terms as spies or terrorists or merchants in betrayal. They were commonplace gatherers of necessary information, liaison officers and activists; they formed the point, the advance guard.

The information they collected was channeled through Colonel Li, sifted and analyzed by his bureau, checked and coordinated, and passed on for whatever use the Command might have for it. It came in the form of ordinary mail or cable, or in the valises of travelers who constantly shuttled back and forth with untiring industry. They found their way in an endless stream to Number 68 Soochow Road, deposited their burdens and departed. At times when there were major activities in the

south—a drive in Laos, an outburst in Malaya, rioting in the Shan States
—the house hummed like a giant beehive. It was delicately attuned to
the nuances of distant unrest, violence or nihilist chaos, all in the rising
symphony of conquest.

These things Fallon understood very imperfectly, although Colonel
Li often confided in him. There were few persons to whom Li was
required to explain any of his actions; his bureau was not an army
section in the regional command, and Li was the authority for it himself.
What directions he received came from Peking, and his reports went
there. This immunity baffled and embittered Captain Kuo, who insisted
that all things be made clear to him. Li disregarded his demands and
protected the staff from Security pressures. Kuo was, at least, persistent
in his efforts to undermine the doctor's position.

Now Li drank from his tea glass, gazing reflectively over it at Fallon,
and said, "What's the matter with you, I-sheng? Are you ill?"

"Yes," Fallon said. "I'm fed up. I want you to release me."

"How can I release you? Kuo would only be too happy to arrest you
the moment you left my command, and jail you with the others."

Fallon accepted that. The few foreign pariahs remaining now in the
shell of this renowned entrepôt were as bleary and down-at-heel as the
city had become. He knew virtually none of the survivors. Many of
them, he was aware, were established in special detention centers, and
there were those unhappy ghosts who resided without hope in district
jails.

"You can deport me."

"That is not in my authority. That is for Security to say. After what
you have told Captain Kuo, I doubt if he would recommend it."

"I can escape, then!"

Li shrugged. "You can try. Fah On, I like and respect you, I sympathize
sometimes with you. If you try I should not interfere. We are friends
even though you are blind to your opportunities. Politically, I mean."

"I'm not interested in them politically. You know that. If I were I'd be
like Albany. The opportunities I am not blind to are closed to me by
Dr. Chu and his like. I told you long ago I'm here only for medical
reasons."

"Perhaps. But those opportunities are limitless."

"I used to think so," Fallon said. "The surgical work I did in your
field hospitals was with wounded men. Since you brought me here I've
engaged in a sort of socialistic general practice—smallpox, cholera, the
dysenteries, diphtheria, malaria. An endless variety of scabies and tra-
choma. Serving this staff and half a dozen associated bureaus and agen-
cies."

"Then you have gained knowledge. The time has not been entirely wasted."

"No, not wasted." Fallon's eyes returned to the window. Through it came the subdued sounds of noonday; the swarms were pausing in their labors for a meal. They were moving past on the creek and roadway, on boats, in cars and ricshas and pedicabs, on foot carrying burdens or pulling the big carts. Black clouds had again piled high in the east, rising out of the China Sea to overwhelm the flat coast and the city; soon more rain would fall.

"Not wasted entirely," he repeated. "I've studied, for instance, the old immunities of your race to the ravages of diseases. I suppose I've also developed a sort of sixth sense in symptomatic diagnosis, mainly because I'm barred from the hospital laboratory. I've spent a lot of time with obstetric cases, fighting brutal and dirty midwives. I've been repeatedly astonished at the lack of septic manifestations among most of their victims—probably the patients are so full of germs that a few billion more make no impression. I might now be called an authority on the complications of gastroenterostomy; every second or third case coming to my attention seems to be involved with intestinal parasites. I've concluded that worms and protozoa are the main obstacles to any more progress or development out here. In fact, I think the only real victory in the battle for Asia will be won finally against the filth and prejudice. And the ignorance and superstitions. Not in my time, though."

He stopped, drawing a deep breath, and returned the colonel's grin. It had been a long speech for Fallon and one only partly understood by his mentor, since many of the terms had no counterpart in the colonel's own language. But the officer was nodding and smiling.

"Then don't worry about Dr. Chu," Li said. "You have gained something, but you cannot right wrongs in his hospital. If you are wise you will go behind the good and evil, perhaps do nothing. Inaction is often wisdom. One can mold life without striving, we say."

"A fine thought for a soldier!" Fallon retorted. "It makes all war pointless, you know. Men try to interfere with the order of things and they bungle it, where nature would settle the problem anyway without all the bloodshed. Is that it?"

Li did not acknowledge that he had been caught out, but he still grinned.

"It is possible," he said. "Ever since man invented civilization he has been trying to alter the natural course of affairs. With disastrous results, I often think."

"So you advise me to sit here and wait, doing nothing, hoping things will change of their own accord."

The colonel had begun to dress; he paused in the act of pulling on a boot.

"The Law, my friend, turns endlessly on its great Wheel."

"And you think I should turn endlessly with it, going nowhere?" Fallon got up and punched out his cigarette. "Well, I'm tired of the empty circle. The Wheel gets noplace."

"Westerners," said Li, "are impetuous. Where do you wish to go that is so much better than where you are, or have been? When I first saw you, Fah On, you were serving as a field physician with the international hospitals when we overran the northern areas. You were restless in the time after the war. Our armies came and went, and you went with us. You told me a man has to do something useful; you might as well go with us. And you did, to the Huai."

And to this dead end as well. Fallon seemed to have been the classic innocent bystander who happened to get in the way, though of course he had to admit he was standing in a rather exposed position in the first place. And it hadn't taken much persuasion. One could make any specious excuse now, after so long. Perhaps it had been bad judgment, or an overdeveloped curiosity about what would happen, or merely a deep admiration for the pioneering Dr. Bethune. It didn't matter; he was here today. Just as he used to be in the ship surgeon's office on transpacific liners, just as he had once become absorbed in tropical diseases and wound up in the employ of a Manila corporation as a plantation medical director at Villareal. One thing led to another, as Villareal had led to the hit-run guerrilla operations against Japanese columns in the Samar hills, and that, in order, had led to the barbed wire barracks at Cabanatuan . . .

"My opportunities for any real service ended at the Huai," Fallon said. "Since then I've done nothing that a male nurse couldn't do. The Chus and Kuos won't allow it, and nothing will change, except for the worse. I could be doing better even back on Samar."

Li had been watching him closely, but his laugh was casual.

"How can we know what is better, what is worse? I don't, I am not a sage, but don't let your dissatisfaction with the turning of the Wheel get you into trouble, I-sheng. It could be most unpleasant for you." He buttoned his tunic. "As your friend, I only warn you."

The gong for the mess hall was sounding; there was a stir from Mrs. Markham's quarters and a plaintive murmur. Fallon hesitated, and then went out and up the steps toward his room, hearing rain gurgling once more in the roof-drains.

6

He had determined to run for it.

In the early evening Fallon sat in his room listening to the whisper of the rain on the roof and debating whether to wait for a break before the turning of the tide; ships sailed from river moorings on the ebb. He waited, with an eye to his watch, and idly fiddled with the dials of his desk radio, a standard set he had found in a pile of loot from an abandoned foreign home. It would not tune to the short waves but it brought in the local stations and the ones up and down the coast all too clearly. He rarely listened to them. But sometimes through meteorological caprices he could hear music and voices from Tokyo and Seoul, Taipeh and Hongkong and even Manila. Ordinary radios would not usually receive such distant stations and it was forbidden to tune to them anyway. Still, through this set Fallon had managed to keep track of the seesaw conflict on the thumb of land to the northeast and listened these nights to the echoes of the uneasy truce that prevailed there. He knew of the march of events abroad, both in his homeland and elsewhere. He did not depend on the taunting voices that snarled in the dark from transmitters along this coast.

Tonight, though, the storm howled and moaned in the speaker and brought only sad cries of torment from the outer blackness, through which there rose and faded the cheerful drawl of a transplanted Missourian in Tokyo, commenting unintelligibly on some aspect of the argument over prisoner-of-war repatriation. He meant, of course, those battalions of miserable uniformed men who had been taken in the roar and smoke of battle. He did not refer to the faceless unidentified civilians who were isolated behind walls of stone and silence. There were probably few enough of the latter on the official lists, and a nation in crisis is relatively unconcerned with such stragglers and a little resentful that they should have lingered too long, allowing themselves to get into a predicament from which their government could not easily extricate them. Why should it? They had been warned; if they were so blind or stubborn that they fell into a trap it was their own fault and they could stew there until the diplomats and generals eventually got around to them.

Fallon had recently heard a voice from Hongkong declare that there were probably no more than a hundred-odd nationals definitely known as internees; most of them were missionaries concentrated in Chinese prisons. He was quite sure that neither he nor Albany was on the roster.

He speculated on what certain persons in Washington might know about Albany, but he himself had never thought to register with any consulate. He was a cipher.

He flipped off the radio, put on the battered felt hat and the old raincoat, and glanced around the utilitarian quarters once more before turning off the reading lamp. The room contained only the bed and desk, an instrument cabinet, a wardrobe stand and a sagging red plush armchair. Fallon had learned long ago that a peripatetic medico must do without, and his personal possessions were of a spartan character. He had started adult life with nothing beyond the inheritance of that New England rock farm, the sale of which had launched him at medical school, and he had acquired very little since in the way of material things. His instruments and reference books had been with him in many compact ship's cabins, the trunks of secondhand cars, the sleeping quarters of tropical clinics and army ambulance vans. They bore traces of ravaging rusts and molds but were still treasured and serviceable. He regretted abandoning them now, but it was necessary. And very little else had rubbed off on him, particularly money. He had only a few cash dollars in his wallet to offer for passage. There was no clothing to carry; the wardrobe stand in the corner was a mockery and stage dressing, having last been used to hold the gowns of a Eurasian queen.

There was a pint of whisky in the cabinet, obtained from the hospital as medical supplies. He thrust it into the raincoat pocket and went out into the empty hall and down the stairs. On the landing he saw a crack of light under the colonel's door and heard the rapid clicking of mahjong. It was a capitalist vice to which Colonel Li and his privileged staff were addicted and the doctor was often asked to play with them. He heard Major Huang speaking casually in the resonant Shantung dialect, and he heard Judith Markham's unamused laughter. The mahjong games sometimes continued all night in Li's suite. Fallon had dodged the sessions when he could, being inexpert and unable to concentrate. Li and the others played very rapidly, feeling the carved ivory faces of the tiles with the balls of their fingers and throwing out the unwanted pieces without needing to look at them. They drank tea or rice wine and talked of inconsequential things as they played. It was all beyond Fallon's abilities.

The lower hall was quiet and he encountered no one as he let himself out into the garden and the wet darkness. If he had, he should only have said that he was going to the hospital; he often did when the phone service was erratic. His departure was simple and uncomplicated, as he had known it would be. In the road he turned his steps toward the river. The street was all but deserted in the rain, with dim lights flickering on poles at long intervals. Where the creek emptied into the larger stream he entered a small bit of parkway near the bridge, followed along the embankment under dripping plane trees, and heard only his solitary footsteps crunching on a winding path among unweeded flower beds.

There was no wind, and from the park he could see the misty lights of shipping in the port. They sparkled along the massive sweep of the Bund and from the flat teeming factory districts of Pootung on the opposite shore. The park was a tiny oasis of blackness and silence in the city. A thin vapor rose from the flowing velvety water below the stone banking.

Standing in the drizzle, he stared out for a moment toward where the ship lay. He did not know her name but he knew the position and could pick out her riding lights and something of the black bulk of her. She hung on the breast of the stream with the stark silhouette of the godowns rising from wharves behind her. The loading had stopped and the small boats had gone. He listened; he heard no sound of motors on the river, no indication of the prowling patrol boats that he knew must be there, though perhaps they were lying now in shelter.

He looked over the edge of the embankment and saw several small sampans tied to rings set in the stones. They were always there, waiting for chance passengers going down to the wharves and ships, and now they were huddled in together like a flock of ducks in the lee of the parkway. Fallon called down softly and in a moment was answered. A drowsy boatman put his head out from under the curving sampan roof. When the man understood what Fallon wanted, and saw that he was a foreigner, he became more wakeful. He put on his conical rain hat and the rough straw rain cape and came out on deck like a sleepy bear. He often took foreign seamen out to the ships and they paid well if they were not quarrelsome drunk. Fallon stepped down into the sampan and crouched under the mat shelter, and the *laodah* cast off his line and seized his sweep and they slid smoothly out of the creek mouth into the river.

The boat dropped down rapidly with the swift tide, the boatman heaving against the sweep, and in five minutes they were nosing alongside the high iron wall of the ship. Fallon's tension eased. There had been no other small craft in view, no purr of engines, no challenge. As he gripped the rung of the ladder and began to climb, he could have shouted with amazed exhilaration. He had not anticipated the simplicity of this short journey across the wide gap.

The deck, where he came up over the rail into the waist, was unlighted but there was a dim glow above on the bridge. His arrival aboard, however, was not unobserved. A gray wraith moved against him, a hoarse voice spoke in his face in the lilting rise and fall of the Cantonese tongue which he did not understand. But he knew it was a query or a challenge, probably from a watchman, perhaps from the bo'sun, and he replied as best he could, asking for the captain or the mate. The seaman appeared to study him, then beckoned and led the way up the steep ladder to the bridge.

The light was from the charthouse, but the officer on watch was standing in the outboard corner of the wing, as indistinct a figure as the first had been. When Fallon approached he knew that the man had been lounging there, out in the wet, in order to look down into the waist and alongside, and thus had watched him come aboard. But the figure was silent, only turning slightly against the rail to present a pale blob of face. Then the charthouse light revealed him dimly, a tall and bulging man of middle age with a ragged black mustache, wearing grease-stained khakis, the shirt unbuttoned, the cap set back on a balding head. A strong aura of gin hung about him.

"I'm looking for the captain," Fallon said after an awkward moment.

The man watched him with eyes that were clouded and secret. "Well?" he said at length.

"Are you—"

"I'm the captain. What d'you want?"

The tone was of forced belligerence, uncompromising, roughed by a thickened tongue. Unfriendly and on guard, but unmistakably British. Suddenly Fallon had to grope for words in the English language, realizing with a small inner shock that he had been using this medium so rarely that phrases came slowly from his mind and would be transmitted with even more difficulty when he spoke. He did something he had never done before, thinking in the easier Chinese, translating as he went.

"I want passage to wherever you're going. It's Hongkong, isn't it?"

The captain continued to regard him with his peculiar blank stare. Then he said, "Who're you?"

"My name's Fallon. I'm a doctor. I want to get out of here."

The other nodded as though now understanding for the first time. "Another perishin' missionary, eh? American, by the sound."

"American, yes. Not a missionary, a doctor."

"Same bloody thing. Why d'you come to me?"

"Well, you're a British ship. I don't know your name, but—"

"Are your papers in order?"

"I've identification. But no exit permit."

"I thought so! Thought so when I saw you coming up the ladder! Here's another of 'em, I thought. They come every trip I'm in this port, or any other damned port up or down the coast. They always come holding out their hand. 'Take me out of here,' they say. Why in bloody hell didn't they get out when they had the chance, three or four years ago? Why didn't you?"

Fallon's jaw set and tightened, his shoulder hunched under the wet coat, and he felt his nails biting into his palms. But he pressed down on his temper; this was no time to lose it.

"I was upcountry in the hospitals," he said evenly. "That's neither here nor there. Can you take me?"

"D'you have passage money?"

"I have funds in Hongkong and Manila, and solvent friends in both places."

"There you are again! No money, no papers, and asking me to risk my neck and my ship! I've had 'em come to me and ask it God knows how many times. D'you all take me for a blithering fool?"

Fallon involuntarily stepped toward him and the captain quickly drew back.

"I don't know now what I take you for," Fallon said. "Will you give me passage or not?"

"No!" the other said.

7

They stood staring at one another in the dimness of the bridge wing. Fallon's back was to the charthouse and his face was in shadow, but the face of the captain was still turned to the faint light, pastily blotched and lumpy, and Fallon was nearly overwhelmed by his desire to strike out at it, smash the puffy lips and dull heavy-lidded eyes. He stepped forward again, the other retreated another pace into the corner, and the hostility of his expression was replaced by a flash of fear.

"Why not?" Fallon demanded, halting. "What's wrong with you, what're you afraid of? What do you mean, risking your neck and ship?"

He knew that the stocky bo'sun stood nearby, behind him, waiting for the shipmaster's word to intervene, and in that moment he realized that there were others present too: someone had opened the charthouse door wider so that the light was increased, and there was a slow shuffle of steps on the bridge ladder. In the gloom around them members of the Cantonese crew had stopped their activities to listen. He had been on ships at night often enough, at anchorages such as this, to know and recognize the slight sounds presaging a sailing, and could hear the urgent tide chuckling against the straining hull. They had been preparing to cast off; now their routine was interrupted.

The captain braced himself against the rail. "You've got a damned lot of cheek, asking me on my own vessel what I'm afraid of!" But his voice was less certain, more blustery. "Barging aboard without leave, demanding I carry you free. I've half a mind to have you thrown overboard!"

But his eyes wavered and he did not give the signal to those who Fallon sensed were poised and watching.

"I asked you a civil question," Fallon said. "If you won't take me I'll get off again, but I'd like an answer. You needn't threaten."

"All right. It's none of your mucking business, but I'll tell you, just as I tell all the others. I've had to tell it till I'm sick of it. How in the devil do I know who you are? Or them? Russians in mufti come aboard these days with the Customs people and the police and all the rest of the snoopers. I doubt you're one—a man can see that well enough, I suppose. But it doesn't change matters. How long d'you think I'd last in this stinking trade if I smuggled refugees out of port every trip? Tell me that, mister!"

"It isn't smuggling—"

"The hell it isn't! They'd say it was, quick enough. I might get you down the river, down the coast, clear away before they found out. But d'you think they'd let me and my ship come back here again after that, or back anywhere else? And then what d'you think my firm in the Colony'd be saying, eh? What they've said to two or three other chaps of my certain knowledge already, skippers who were soft in the head and listened to your yarns. They're on the beach today, and I'd be there with 'em tomorrow, and my managers'd be justified. Is that clear enough?"

"They'd not have to know."

"Oh, no? Do you think I can trust this blasted crew not to spread the tidings? It's riddled with agents and delegates. The whole lot of 'em rush ashore in these ports to go to union meetings and to cheer at rallies, while the damned river police sit here watching me and my officers to see we don't try to blow up the bank, eating up our stores and intimidating the contract stevedores. Insolent sods! Suppose I took you—very likely that bo'sun there'd signal a patrol boat before we got past Woosung and they'd have the lot of us locked up and my ship impounded. And there's blockade vessels outside to think of, too. I'm not in this trade for health or pleasure, mister. It's legal so far but it's a rough go. There's top pay in it—a few more runs and I can afford to be out of it and into something decent, and bugger all of 'em!"

As he spoke he was edging around Fallon, and getting clear of the wing he sidled away toward the charthouse door. Fallon followed slowly, knowing as he listened that there wasn't a chance for further argument.

He might have seen that before exposing himself. The man was in almost as bad a corner as he himself. The gall of this defeat rose in his throat, doubly bitter because of the blithe assurance he had felt only a few minutes previously when he climbed over the rail. But he swallowed it as his face came up into the light and he grinned stiffly.

"All right," he said. "That's plain enough. I just didn't know. If my boat's still alongside I'll go."

The bo'sun understood him and muttered something, and the captain shook his head. The sampan was gone. The master's face seemed older and infinitely weary. "I've standing instructions to signal a river police patrol launch in cases like this," he said in a tired voice from which the indignation had drained. "Devil I will—they'd put you in quod for sure, and likely twist your tongue out on the way. Come along in and have a drink, I'll think of something."

He led the way down to his musty uncleaned cabin at the foot of the bridge ladder, and fished an unopened bottle of gin from a case under his bunk. He rinsed two tumblers, poured the spirits into them, and drank deep without further formality, as though he needed it. Then he looked at Fallon gloomily.

"How in hell did you manage to get yourself into such a balls-up? You say you're no missionary? But a medical missionary, p'raps?"

"Not even that," Fallon said, getting the gin down with an effort but feeling better for it. "I've been asked the question before and still haven't any good answer."

"A journeyman sawbones, eh? Haw!" But there was no laughter in the skipper's guffaw. He squinted and winked. "Just went along with the Commies for a bit, like? And got a bellyful? Never mind, man, I've seen a lot of 'em. Fugitives from the comrades. Things are getting thicker in this bloody benighted country every time I come in. Expect in time they won't even be able to stand each other—then watch out!"

Fallon considered. There was no real use explaining, or trying to explain, himself to this shipmaster, no obligation to do so; they'd never see each other again. But he couldn't let it stand as it was.

"I went along with them at first because there was a job to do for a doctor," he said. "There's still a job—a job so big all the doctors in the world couldn't make a dent in it—but they want to do it their way. And their way won't work. So it's time I got out. I can work somewhere else and maybe do a little good."

But he saw, by the captain's eyes, that the man was unconvinced, and he didn't particularly care. The arrival of the squat bo'sun in the door relieved them of further sparring.

After the seaman had spoken, the master said, "The last lot of stevedores is going ashore now—they've been topping off. Their foreman says you can nip along with 'em. Dunno how he knew about you at all, but you can't keep anything from any of these bastards. Want to chance it?"

"Sure," Fallon said. The chance, he knew, was whether the stevedores would deliver him to the first patrol boat they met in the stream or set him ashore without ado. He'd have to take it unless he wished to swim.

They went on deck and saw the cargo coolies disappearing over the side, going down into a waiting lighter. One of their number stood by the rail and looked at Fallon carefully as he came up. The foreman, a thickset and dark-skinned man wearing the rags and tatters of his profession, nodded without expression and gestured down toward the boat.

"I'm sorry," the captain said suddenly, and put out his hand. "But blast it—! Anyway, good luck to you, lad!" The first awkwardness returned; Fallon shook the hand and went down the ladder with the foreman after him. The boat shoved off, drifting swiftly away in the dark toward the Bund.

Fallon sat on a pile of sacks amidships, feeling no special emotion now. He did not look back at the ship again. He pulled up the collar of his coat against the thin rain and felt the bump of the pint bottle in his pocket. The gin was still warm in his stomach and he didn't want it to go, along with everything else warm and promising. He took out the bottle and tilted it, letting the whisky run down his throat to wash away the lingering taste of gall. Then he saw that the stevedore foreman had come and seated himself beside him on the sacks and he offered the bottle in payment.

The foreman accepted it, sniffed, and drank. He passed it back but Fallon motioned for him to keep it, and he nodded and slid it under his ragged jacket. The others of the gang, squatting in the boat ahead of them, were talking together in low voices, but Fallon heard only enough to know that it was some of the riverfront argot that none but these people used. The foreman was listening; presently he spoke sharply and one replied and he spoke again, louder, and they became silent. The lighter was nearing shore.

The foreman leaned closer. "They are wondering about you, I-sheng," he said in a voice covered by the slap of water under the short counter. "They were uncertain where to take you. I told them. Here at this landing stage ahead you will be only a short distance from home. Go alone, as if you had never been away. It is not so late that you could not be returning from your duties."

Fallon did not look at him directly, but he said, "You know me?"

"I know you," the man said. "These others do not. I have seen you at the hospital and in the street. You are a good person, they say. You could be one of us."

"Who says I am a good person?"

"My friends, the ones who watch you and know of you. But I saw you on the ship only by accident. It was fortunate; the police scum would not be gentle with you. It is useless to try to go away on these coastal ships. We can send friends away sometimes by smaller craft, but the foreign ship captains are afraid."

The lighter was nosing into the embankment, and the stevedores were scrambling up to disembark.

"You were not on the ship to work the cargo, then?" Fallon said.

"I was on the ship to work the cargo with the others. But I go on the ships also for other reasons. The work is useful, for by it I may meet people on the ships who are our friends."

"From your words, you have many friends."

"We have many friends, I-sheng, both here and in the world. Perhaps after tonight you will meet some of them, for I will tell them of you."

He was climbing onto the landing stage and reached down a hard hand. The others were already straggling away. The watch on Fallon's wrist stood at midnight.

"You have helped me and I am grateful," Fallon said.

"Gratitude can be shown in many ways," the foreman said, tapping the bottle under his jacket and displaying his teeth in a wide smile. "Foreign wine is good on such a night. Go now before the street patrols come yapping at us."

He turned quickly and went after the other stevedores. Fallon walked down the Bund, the only man on its broad avenue in that hour and weather, and came to the creek and went up the road, and found himself before his door again without having met anyone. The house slept. He ascended to his room and without turning on the light looked out of his window. Far down the river there was only blackness. The lights of the ship were gone from the mooring place.

8

In the morning it was just another day, like all the rest had been for so long, and Fallon, standing before his shaving mirror, paused in the operation to reflect that it might have all been a hectic dream. But it had been no delusion; his damp raincoat and the hat were there on the chair and he still had the taste of bad gin in his mouth. And yet it was hard to believe that his request for sanctuary had been denied by a British captain on a British ship, out there in the glittering harbor. The fellow had had the wind up, it was clear. And it was clear that he had been dutifully careful of his company's property and interests. One could hardly blame him, seeing it in the sharp light of day. Fallon had no claim on a man merely because they had the same color of skin. The bid had been rejected for sound reasons, though they may not have seemed so at the moment.

He drank his tea and smoked his cigarette. He didn't know what he was going to do now, but like the captain, he would have to "think of something." The captain hadn't thought of anything but to ask pointless questions. And in the end he should probably have called for the river patrol after all, if it hadn't been for that stevedore foreman.

The foreman with the friends, the ones who thought Fallon was a "good person," the ones who watched and knew about him. He had no idea what the fellow was talking about; no one was watching him that he knew of except his not-so-paternal wardens, and they no longer watched him very closely, else he'd never have got as far as he'd gone. Certainly these reputed friends were not friendly with the Security people or they'd have turned him in. Therefore they were against the Security people, and correspondingly against the police, the authorities, the regime. The friendly opposition, the critical minority. The underground. . . .

Fallon snorted and set down his empty cup. That was a stirring word, underground, except that so far as Fallon was aware it meant nothing. Oh, there was opposition, and plenty of it, but unorganized opposition. There was nothing like there had been, for instance, on Samar. At least, everyone said so except professional cynics and trouble shooters like Captain Kuo. Kuo read mass sabotage in a routine rise in typhoid. Kuo saw civil revolt in a bandit raid down-country. Kuo suspected disloyalty in Efremov and Albany and even the colonel. Kuo was a fatuous dunce, hence very dangerous.

Li's orderly put his head in the door and said that the colonel wished to see the doctor. It was just like yesterday; what accusations were to be made today? Fallon stamped down the stairs.

But the colonel's mood was light, and Captain Kuo was not present. "You are feeling better today?" he said when Fallon had accepted the inevitable tea. "Good. I can see it. You brood too much. Not enough to do, of course. I understand it, a soldier such as myself, bound here to a desk. Where were you last night?"

"What?"

"I say, where were you last night? We were all playing mahjong and I sent Huang to ask you to play and you were out."

"Oh, yes. I went to the hospital to see one of the patients."

"It isn't necessary in such weather, is it, unless an emergency?"

"I like to walk in bad weather."

"Yes. Well, I understand that also. Now, Fah On, perhaps I have a diversion for you. I have a special patient I wish you to see, one in whom I have a particular interest. A personal friend."

Fallon heard the midmorning stirrings of Judith Markham in the inner apartment; it was early for her and her voice was petulant as she gave orders to the cook. But it was not of Mrs. Markham that the colonel spoke.

"He is an old man whom I used to know—a missionary from a small parish in the north. He is quite ill; I suppose it is his age, but perhaps it is more."

"A priest?" Fallon smiled. "You once embraced the Church, and have kept it secret?"

"You know well enough I am not a Christian. I am probably only sentimental. But this old man—his name is Vauzous—he arrived here unexpectedly last night. While we were playing. I was very surprised. Somehow he had made all that long journey south, from a little market town above the Yellow River, up in Shensi. It is astonishing what sick old men can do; it gives me hope and courage. He seemed to have discovered that I was here, and found the house with the aid of a ricsha puller. It was shocking, his condition. He asked me for assistance."

"Where is he?"

"I sent him to the hospital. It's strange you didn't know, if you were there. Dr. Chu has strict orders to do what he can and to regard you as Father Julien's physician. You'll have no trouble there, I assure you."

Fallon waited. If Li continued to take stray aliens under his wing he'd soon have a mongrel foreign legion that might justify Captain Kuo's job.

"He is over seventy years old," Li said thoughtfully. "He has been in this country for fifty years—which is as long as I myself have lived here. By accident of birth he is a Frenchman. But by habits of mind and customs of the body he is a Chinese. By occupation he is a missionary. But he is more a Taoist than a Roman Catholic, though he probably doesn't know it. Once he sheltered me in his poor mission. He had few converts but many friends in that place. The abbot of a Buddhist monastery there was perhaps his best friend. He had not seen a man of his own race for many years."

The colonel smiled, privately remembering a frail man who made children laugh and soldiers speak softly.

"I was cut off from our main body in a skirmish and needed a refuge in the town with a dozen of my men. Kuomintang troops had isolated us and were hunting systematically. The monastery was no good—they would search it with thoroughness. The abbot sent me to this priest and he hid us. He fed us for a week. We told him we were going to our head-quarters at Yenan. It was wartime and we were fighting the Japanese, but the Kuomintang troops were so busy fighting us that they had no time to bother the Japanese. The priest asked if he could go with us and we humored him. Perhaps he saw in us a fertile field for his endeavors. He was with us for three years, until the Japanese were defeated. Then he went back to his mission."

"Did he find any converts among you?" Fallon asked.

"I don't think so." Li grinned.

"Did you convert him?"

"No more than I have converted you. Neither of us tried very hard. I am sorry for him. How he has ever made his way all this distance here I can't imagine. He says it is faith. It must be—he has no travel permits, no papers, no money, no health."

"Most priests are in prison."

"I don't know anything about that," Li said, suddenly angry. "That is work I don't understand. Wreckers and subversives should be in jail. But public trials for people like this old man are absurd. There used to be thousands of them, including their robed and hooded women, but now there are few. In three hundred years these priests have made only three million converts, so they can't be very dangerous. At that rate, it will be five hundred centuries before their Pope is spiritual ruler here."

He paused, reconsidering this reasoning, and smiled.

"Anyway," he added, "what do they do? Vauzous says they save souls for eternity. All right, I admire his persistence. In that poverty-stricken mission he ran a school, taught blind people to read and weave cloth, and kept a score of orphans. Have I ever done anything like that? Have you?"

Fallon went to the hospital. The assistant medical director was trucu-lent, but apparently the colonel had firmly impressed upon him the need for cooperation in this matter. He had even put Father Julien in a room by himself, and took Fallon in to see the patient. Vauzous was a fragile paper-thin ancient lying asleep on the white sheets of the bed; his ragged cassock was hung on a wall peg and a battered haversack lay in a corner beside a pair of broken walking boots. A bushy pepper-and-salt beard reached to his breast, a big hawk nose pointed toward heaven.

"What do you think?" Fallon asked.

"His heart is giving out," Dr. Chu muttered, not trying to be pleasant. "We've larded him with cardiotonics." He abruptly left Fallon to make his own examination.

The priest awakened, and when Fallon mentioned the colonel he became animated. His mind was still keen. He spoke fluent Chinese and some English but his native tongue was halting and broken. He talked feverishly and Fallon surmised that he had been deprived of human companionship for a long time. Although he did not say so, it seemed likely that he had known the inside of one or more prisons during his southward wandering. As Fallon did his work he encouraged the old man to unburden himself. The reedy singsong voice gained momentary strength.

He had not seen his bishop or even another cleric for a long while; he was cut off from his Order and his church in the north was now a village assembly hall. He spoke of this, and suddenly he was speaking of the time when, as a young man on his way to the East, he had visited the Vatican, kissed the ring and knelt in the street as the golden chair was borne past. He vividly remembered the splendor of that pageantry.

Fallon had completed the examination but he sat on beside the bed and heard Father Julien out. The priest had obviously led a chaste, obedient and disciplined life, though not a cloistered one. He had been a deeply devotional and ascetic man. He had often been assailed by doubt. In middle life he had scandalized his visiting bishop by declaring the opinion that a lost soul in Hell might some day, after centuries of torment, cease burning and sink into welcome oblivion. The bishop had told him that although he was imperfect, he might yet become a perfect conduit for divine grace. Vauzous looked up at Fallon as he related this, stopped, and chuckled mildly through the beard.

"What have you done since then?" Fallon urged.

"What does any man do, Doctor? I continued on in the market town." And Fallon thought of his lonely life, comforting the dying, advising the troubled, befriending the traveler, teaching the seekers of knowledge and living a moderately exemplary life. Vauzous was a man who accepted the Church's guidance, followed his routine with military severity and obeyed his instructions with precision.

Now his life and its meaning had fallen apart; he was adrift. Fallon did not think he would ever get out of bed again. Of one thing he was certain: there was no indication that Vauzous felt he had been contaminated by the new religion, or become spiritually derelict. There were ecclesiastical renegades, but he remained a plodding parish priest.

When Fallon went to arrange use of the operating room, he met Dr. Chu in the corridor.

"Don't keep the room long," Chu said. "We've a waiting list, you know. What do you think is wrong with that rotten old man?"

Fallon suppressed a retort. "I think I'll be dealing with an amoebic abscess of the liver in a moment," he said, "but I doubt if that'll do much good. I expect he has a fistula that's never closed. I'll want emetine injections and quinine irrigations." He looked directly at Chu. "I'm not asking him to give up his Church and join the party to get these things. I'm ordering them on the colonel's authority."

Chu didn't reply and went on. But just before Fallon's orderly wheeled Vauzous to the operating room, one of Chu's sycophants passed by and said, in a jocular tone, "Aha! There goes the old running-dog under the knife! The foreign monk whose Church supports that Fascist murderer Chiang."

Father Julien opened his eyes. "I support no Fascist," he said, slowly winking at Fallon. "The heretic is a damned Methodist!"

9

It had been a long day. But now Father Julien slept quietly and Fallon, sitting by the bed in a cane chair, felt a creeping content in his own weariness. He roused himself, listening to the priest's steady breathing, then went out into the silent corridor and past the single lemon light above the night nurse's desk. He took a ricsha for the short way home. Crossing the bridge he continued to think of Vauzous, the homeless man whose mission and whose work had been taken from him, and he could not shake off the thoughts. It had been a long day, one day more on Li's revolving wheel. Fallon no longer chalked them off on a calendar.

The house was astir, and in the upper reaches of it Fallon heard the blare of Albany's powerful shortwave receiver. Albany had a special license to use it because of the nature of his work. His radio brought friendly familiar intonations from across the sea and he regularly followed newscasts from the world he had renounced. But Fallon had hardly entered his own quarters when the mumblings and cracklings of the broadcast were replaced by a sudden stillness. He knew that Albany had snapped off the switch in the middle of a program.

Albany often did that. What he did afterward Fallon did not know— whether he cursed or wept or tore up paper or chain-smoked or lay rigid on his bed in the dark, Fallon did not know. He could only imagine, for Albany was not often confidential. What upwellings of bitter-sour regret, of nostalgia, of loneliness and futile anger, of resentment and hatred, Fallon did not know, nor was he curious.

Presently he heard Albany's faltering step in the hall. It paused before Fallon's door; the crack of light along the floor told Albany that the doctor had come in. The door was pushed open and it swung back, banging against the wall. Albany stood on the threshold, having difficulty adjusting his vision. His dark face was raddled, his uncertain gaze came into focus slowly on Fallon sitting in the chair.

"Thought I heard you," Albany grunted. "Li left a message for you. You're supposed to go back with me to this party at the hotel. The one I've been to. Gotta go back." His tongue was thick. "Jesus, I'm tired! They're having this damn banquet, see. I go for my department. Hundreds of people milling around, eating and swilling shaohsing. That stuff makes me sick, but I found some pretty good vodka. Down the hatch, comrade! *Kampei, tovarish! Do svidanya!*"

"I don't think I'm up to it," Fallon said. "Russians?"

"Visiting firemen on a tour. Technicians. Squareheads all. Local Russkies, visiting Russkies, local officials buttering 'em up, visiting officials from Peking, guides, big shots. Hell, I never did find out who they all were. Or care."

"Efremov there too?"

"Oh, sure. The infiltrator. Mud in his big blue eyes. Everybody's there —Li, Huang, Madame Markham. Efremov's plastered."

"He'll black-list you if you say bad things about him."

"Hell with him. Who's Efremov to put me on a black list? Just another squareheaded expert who's supposed to know all about our buddies in Southeast Asia. I'll bet he doesn't know Southeast Asia from northwest Omsk. This town is just like Washington, full of experts. I was an expert once in Washington—I should know. In Washington I was an expert on China, before I ever came here. In Shanghai I'm an expert on America. In Chungking I was an expert on Yenan. In Yenan I was an expert on Chungking. All you've got to do is specialize. You're an expert at rolling pills. Li's an expert at espionage. Kuo's an expert at saboteurs. I'll give you one guess what Judy Markham is expert at!"

"I'm going to bed," Fallon said. "You'd better too."

"Mustn't speak of Madame Markham—Papa Li will spank. Say, there's a Russian blonde with a big chest at the party. Hoisted a few with her. Secretary to the delegation, I think. Still there and going strong when I left."

He looked with speculative solemnity at Fallon. "That party'll be brawling all night. I had to come back here to okay some proofs and the damn things haven't been delivered from the printer yet. Not going to wait. I'm going back and be a comrade to Katya."

"You'll be a sad propagandist tomorrow."

"*Nichevo!* I'm always a sad propagandist. Tonight I'll be a mad propagandist, dancing to a lousy band with blond hair in my face. If she doesn't know how to dance anything but those squat-kicks we can always do something else. She's a little on the heavy side, but by God, she's white!"

He stepped back to his room and returned with a bottle in which some whisky remained, and lifted it. "Have a drink, Doc," he said. "Washes out the vodka taste. Why don't you come along? Don't be a stiff-necked recluse all your life."

"I'd not be welcome. Imperialist aggressor. Captive warmongering vulture."

"Maybe you're right," said Albany, beginning to grin. "Doc, you've got those semantic inanities down pat, haven't you? And how's that for saying semantic inanities—twice in a row?"

"It isn't hard to learn when you live with it. The diatribes come easy after a while. They grow on you, like witch's brew. All you have to do to make a speech or write a pamphlet is to have nothing much to say but get sore and repeat it over and over."

Albany's grin became cold. "Fallon, if I wasn't drunk I'd sock you. A quack trying to tell me my trade!" He laughed shortly and moved to the window and looked out at raindrops slanting against the pane. "You know, Fallon, I left the goddam banquet because I was sitting there drinking vodka and looking at those visiting Cossacks in their nice green uniforms with war decorations splashed all over their chests. They're a muscular lot, right up to their shaved scalps, insulting and scornful and swaggering around. I'm supposed to like them because they're our chums and brothers and they give us technical and political advice and make a united front with us. One of 'em got up and made a speech tonight and said his country was chosen by destiny to lead the earth's dispossessed into its inheritance. I think that's what he said. He had a lot of fine things to say about Mao and Nehru and Uncle Ho and Kim, and it sounded like he was calling for a kind of jihad for eight hundred million Asiatics. I guess he'd had as much vodka as I had and I don't savvy Russian very well, but he got Karl Radek all mixed up with Genghis Khan and Zinoviev with Tamerlane. Stalin had Zinoviev shot in a purge a long time ago, I think, so I suppose he was pretty muddled. About that time I had another drink and left."

"I'm glad you're not telling Captain Kuo all this," Fallon said.

"I'm not so drunk as that. But while I was sitting there I thought I kept hearing faint music. Funny . . . A reminiscent phrase from the Internationale, but very distorted. Discords, you know. But it was in the mood of that time—it seems far away now—when the hammer and sickle was some sort of symbol of liberty. The guys who carried it were going to represent a new world and a new race. . . ."

"When you start hearing music and describing it like that," Fallon said, "you must have got hold of some poppy juice instead of the vodka."

"Those moujiks at the party are a bunch of bastards!"

"Well, it's a little late for you to be finding that out, isn't it? Why go back, if you feel that way?"

Albany turned to the door. His flushed face stiffened, and he grinned again. "Katya isn't a moujik. Or if she is, she's a female moujik and I don't have to listen to her talk. Principles may be involved, but you can't be acting on principle all the time. I'll just do my duty by the department and cement relations."

He went out and stumped rapidly down the stairs, and Fallon heard the front door slam. He had left his bottle and Fallon set it away on the cabinet. He was depressed. Thorpe Albany, with whom he inevitably quarreled whenever they spent more than five minutes together, had seemed almost friendly for a moment. Albany was the only fellow countryman he knew or saw now, and they were diametrically opposed on virtually every issue in or out of the book of their daily lives. Or were they? Albany hadn't sounded himself tonight. But he would sound himself and more so tomorrow, without doubt.

Even after this enforced association Fallon knew little about Albany. He had said his father was a Chicago corporation attorney; "of good family," he had leered. There'd been a mention of Princeton. There had also been a mention once of a draft-beating berth in Washington. But Fallon knew that Albany had been one of the wartime State Department cubs at Chungking, caught in the bitter crossfire between Vinegar Joe and the Gissimo. Learning the difference between a Chinese general and a footslogging conscript, the gulf between strategy and administration, the arguments for air assault and land blockade, Albany had got a grandstand view of the graft and sabotage of an epic effort to fight a war and the hopeless attempts to buck a vast and riddled system of backward tyranny.

Somewhere he had run afoul of a great worm-eaten dictatorship, and had become absorbed in a mass of recriminations and military politics. Chungking had been full of bright young men who saw, as a solution, the need to bring the opposition into full partnership if the stalemate were to be broken. There had been a turning point, when he was dispatched as one of the observers into the blockaded Red areas. The observers sent back glowing reports and recommendations that were promptly buried under a mountain of smooth palaver and disapproving silence. The unorthodox were suddenly weeded out and ordered home, but Albany never returned. He had become an amateur among professionals, sucked into the postwar lunge for power, the final struggle to seize control of a nation. And he'd chosen the winning team, that was all. The reward was a sinecure with the powerful Information Bureau.

Fallon had no pat tag or explanation for Albany, any more than one for himself. No solution, either. The Chinese had an old saw to the effect that of the thirty-six alternatives, running away is best. But Albany had nowhere to run. None of them had—himself, Judith Markham, Father Julien. Nowhere but around and around inside Colonel Li's monstrous wheel. . . .

There were soft steps in the hall outside his closed door, and a faint rapping at Albany's room, and a waiting quiet. Fallon opened the door and looked out at two vague figures in the gloomy corridor.

"Albany has gone out for the evening," he said. One of the shadows moved into the light. A straight slight form, a girl.

"We thought so," she said, smiling. "We knocked just to make sure." She spoke almost unaccented English. Her blue cotton scarf and dark slicker gleamed with rain, her feet in cloth slippers stood in a spreading pool, and she looked altogether sodden. Drops sparkled from the tendrils of blue-black hair escaping from the scarf and from the long lashes of her faintly oblique eyes, and one hung comically from the tip of the small nose.

"He went to a function. I believe he was expecting a messenger to deliver some proofs. Is that you?"

She nodded, still smiling. "I work for the Information Bureau. I am Yin Kuei. We have the proofs, but we waited late until we were sure he wouldn't be here."

Fallon looked doubtfully over her shoulder at the figure looming behind. The man with her was equally wet. He nodded and his teeth flashed in a brief grin. He was the stevedore foreman.

The girl called Yin Kuei laughed aloud at Fallon's puzzled face.

"We thought it would be more pleasant to call upon a friend," she said.

10

Fallon smiled slowly.

"Please come in, then—friends," he said. He had not expected this so soon, if indeed he had expected it at all. Certainly not in this form.

She looked at her companion. "The doctor invites us to visit him." Then she added in English, "Tieh does not understand your language."

"I wasn't sure, though we have spoken together before," Fallon said. "Let us speak the common tongue. And welcome here."

They entered the room and stood in the center of it, looking about with interest though there was little enough to see. Yin Kuei removed the scarf and dripping slicker. Fallon took them and Tieh's ragged coat and hung them up. Tieh had no hat; his stiff hair defied the wet and stood up in bushy tufts above a broad strong face in which eyes, nose and mouth were all set just a little off center, as though he had been batted in the side of the head. Fallon had not seen him clearly the night before. He wore drab tunic and trousers, but they were not the rags of a river coolie. He was much larger than most and his rough hands were thick and powerful.

"You have met Tieh Lao-hu," the girl said.

"Informally. Lao-hu?"

Her laughter tinkled again. "You know? You have the ear for inflections, Dr. Fallon. Lao-hu—the Iron Tiger. It is a nickname." She turned solemnly to Tieh. "This is Fah On I-sheng."

Tieh continued to grin. "I knew him when I saw him on the ship. Some of our friends are employed at the hospital."

"I have here an inferior grade of tea and an inferior grade of wine," Fallon said to cover his confusion at this prompt and direct approach. For clearly they had used the excuse of running errands to enter the house and had chosen an appropriate time. "Which will you have?"

Yin Kuei preferred tea. "If the wine is the same you gave me last night," Tieh said, "I will have the wine."

Fallon brewed the tea, filled glasses with the whisky Albany had left, and gave Yin Kuei the teacup. He did not often play the host and the novelty of it was warming. He brought up two straight chairs and a serving table by the lamp, seated the girl in the plush lounge, and got a tin of biscuits and a tin of hard candy from his cupboard, feeling lordly.

He watched her as she sipped the tea, disturbed by something in her small oval face. He decided with some reservation that what seemed to set her apart from the run of women he encountered in his rounds was a certain quiet humor in her dark eyes and the faintly quirked corners of her full lips. The quality of humor, the basic zest for living, seemed somehow to have been lost to her race in recent years. They had always been a mellow, even roguish people, their humor born of tolerance and enjoyment at the farce of life. Once they had been realists, nonchalant and skeptical with mocking laughter or cheerful smiles at universal discomfort, poverty and even hunger. Perhaps it was still there but if so it was hidden and guarded.

"You are really with Albany's Information Bureau?" Fallon asked.

"Oh, yes," she said. "But I am only a courier there."

"With your English, they should have better use for you."

"They don't trust her," Tieh said in his hoarse voice. "Her father was an intellectual and a man of the upper classes. I knew him. He was my teacher in the north, when I was a student in Peking."

"I see." Fallon glanced at Tieh and the man shrugged.

"Yes, I have been a student, though I may not look it. I have also been a farmer in my native Hunan. I have also been a soldier—my division was one of those that deviated to the Communists. I worked in the Information Bureau briefly, as a coolie. Now I am a foreman of stevedores."

"Is that all? Apparently we are speaking frankly here, as friends." Fallon said this boldly, still inwardly cautious.

"Certainly as friends. No, that's not all. I am also a radio technician. I do a number of things. I run mimeographs, for instance, that turn out sheets to be posted on walls."

"And do you do anything besides work in the bureau?" Fallon said to the girl.

"Several things. Among them, I write the posters Tieh mimeographs. I gather information of a type not publicized by my bureau."

Tieh pulled a crumpled paper from his pocket and smoothed it so that Fallon could see the marching ideographs close-packed up and down the sheet.

"This is a poster that the police and Security patrols are tearing down from walls and poles almost as fast as we put them up," he said, grinning broadly. "It says that the People's Chairman does not have a mandate from heaven, as he seems to think, to found a new dynasty. It says the Chairman is not the true leader of the people as he insists, but is led about like a monkey by the Russians. It says that all these adventures in Indo-China and Korea are more imperialistic than any undertaken by our so-called enemies. That is the sum of it. People read it with interest before the angry police rush up and beat them away and rip down the posters."

Fallon nodded. "I see," he repeated. He turned to the girl again. "Is your father, who was a teacher, is he helping in this work?"

"No," Yin Kuei said, and he saw now that her fixed smile was mirthless. "My father is dead. He died in a prison in Peking."

"Her father was the inspiration for this work," Tieh said in his deep harsh voice. "He was even one of the early organizers of it. His philosophy deviated from government concepts and he didn't hide it. It is important to be realistic. He was unrealistic. He was also reactionary. He did not last long. His friends among the Soviets thought he might be useful but they found him dangerous."

Tieh spoke with a depth of irony and bitterness that startled Fallon. He looked like what he had been—a big, phlegmatic, pugnacious rice farmer of Hunan, and his voice was that of a riverfront laborer, but his blunt words were not.

"Her father was a fine teacher, but politically he was blind. He was a scholar but he lacked common sense in some things. He lacked an instinct for science and logic—and also, I think, an instinct for self-preservation. He ignored the dialectic. That is fatal. He talked about beauty and humanism and the doctrine of the golden mean. He said the sum of knowledge is to serve happiness, and he said the machine is made for man and man is not made for the machine. For that they put him in prison."

Fallon waited, silent.

"My father was concerned with life and earthly joys and human affairs," Yin Kuei said. "He was ethical and asked no one to sanction his conduct. He said that his greatest achievement had been to attain some harmony and happiness while still living—he didn't expect much else."

"Your father must have been a remarkable man."

"Dr. Chung was too remarkable," said Tieh, his voice rough. "He taught moderation and control through the middle way. That was indiscreet—it was in direct opposition to the tenets of the new faith. Which is that the individual exists only for the State, and the strength of the nation is more important than the welfare of the person. He was so bold as to declare that the soulless machine government would always fail among our people. So he was permitted by the So-wei-ai to die in a cell."

Fallon busied himself loading and lighting his pipe. Inwardly his amazement was increasing, and his excitement. In former times these people were full of frank talk, complaints, gossip and criticism. They were born talkers and their gatherings had always reminded him of the cracker-barrel discussions in the general store near his own father's Maine farm; he had admired their oratorical ability to put a finger on the most sensitive spot. Nowadays nobody talked. The voice of China, shrill and insistent and eternal in the streets, was silent, and the face was sullen, the eyes downcast

"Did your father teach you your English?" he asked Yin Kuei.

She brightened again. "Oh, no. We lived in America for ten years when I was a young girl. My father was an exchange professor of philosophy from a Peking university and he taught in many of your schools. We didn't come back home until after the last war. So you see, I am not now completely trusted here, because I have been exposed for so long to degenerate influences overseas." Her narrow brows arched.

Fallon's excitement could not be retained. "Why do you two come here to me like this, a stranger, and expose yourselves to me?"

"Because you *are* a stranger," Yin Kuei said candidly. "We know all about you. We have been told how you came to this country to live and try to do good work—not like a missionary but like what you are—and now you are a prisoner who can do nothing."

"Last night you tried to escape because there was no more work for you here," Tieh added. "You failed. But perhaps you were mistaken. There is much work here. Medical work, of course, but other things too. Very important things."

Fallon grimaced. "There's little enough a marked foreigner can do. You are suggesting that I might give some sort of aid to your—your friends?"

"Yes. You're in an excellent position, here in the Southeast Asia Bureau, to help us. We are particularly interested in its affairs."

"Your frankness is refreshing, though very flattering."

"One must say what he thinks sometimes," Tieh muttered. "Or strangle. There is little enough friendship and understanding now, only cruelty and callousness."

"True. Now I will be frank also. I sincerely doubt that there is enough organized opposition to make these small efforts effective. It may be there but it is scattered and weak. One cannot think of it truly as an underground force."

Tieh stood up. "You are wrong, I-sheng. There are many efforts, and they are being welded into one, with the help of powerful and influential friends outside this country. Not aliens, but people of our own race. Not those rat-nibbled Nationalists, either. I can't tell you more now, but believe me."

"What are they trying to do?"

"Bring about conditions so that the people can finally attain what they really want some day. It isn't this perverted thing; Marxism is worse than dung when it's taken as dogma. It isn't what we had before, either; that's finished forever. It's something new. And there's enough money and power and force among the free people of our own race to bring it about if we work for it. Work is all most of us have to give."

"The government is very strong, and deeply entrenched," Fallon said.

"The government is like the wind bending the grass," Yin Kuei said. "My father taught that. The grass isn't uprooted and destroyed. The wind always passes and the flattened grass rises straight to the sun again, stronger than any wind that ever blew."

After a time Fallon knocked out his pipe. "I don't know what I could do, but I'd like to meet your friends."

"There are plenty of them to meet but you shan't know many. We were sent to see you, Tieh and I. Soon we will see you again. So please, I-sheng, don't give up hope and don't try to go away again."

He flushed. "Then don't give me that title. My name is Paul."

"We hear that you have a new patient," the girl said casually. "An old man—a priest. Will he recover?"

Fallon looked at her doubtfully. "I think partially. What's your interest in him?"

"Nothing in particular. I only inquired. We have been informed of your work at the hospital—"

"There is something we want in this house," Tieh interrupted in his direct manner. "I will come back and tell you when we know more."

"Come when Captain Kuo is not visiting the premises, then." Fallon grinned.

"I defecate on Captain Kuo!" said Tieh.

"Please excuse Lao-hu," Yin Kuei said. "He is only a coarse provincial."

"The Hunanese are coarse and dirty, fight-loving and honest," said Tieh. He took his coat and the girl's slicker over his arm as Fallon held open the door. Then he looked into Fallon's face and added, "If you want work to do, Fah On, we will find more of it than will please you."

"Good night, Paul," Yin Kuei said in English, still smiling.

II

The Knot

Gregor Efremov was nominally the bureau's consultant on Southeast Asia, but for the past month he had been far from that theater, in the wastes of Sinkiang, in the market places of Hami, Tihwa and Urumtchi beyond the Altyn Tagh, conferring with colleagues from across the long Central Asian frontiers, talking with knowledgeable men like himself in Kashgar and Tashkent, flying over the wind-scoured emptiness of the barren Taklamakan and above enormous knots of tangled mountains at the roof of the world. He had had urgent business at those high bases for conquest, had departed the day after the party for his visiting compatriots, and now he was back in his room in the house on the creek again, beside the turbid eastern sea. And, as he complained to Fallon, he had the bellyache.

He lay in his bed and groaned listlessly, weak and exhausted while his bowels turned to water, and he said that he was dying. Fallon had his doubts. Men with Efremov's great physical strength and driving energy did not often die of this form of catarrhal dysentery. The tests were emphatic and the treatment plain, but Efremov disputed the diagnosis.

"You ate something you shouldn't have, up there," Fallon said. "Those transport pilots at the airfields gave you bad liquor. What did the Kazakhstani cooks feed you? Half-raw mutton, too many apricots, that barley slop?"

Efremov's large lipless mouth coiled back like a snake and his pale blue eyes became milky. "It was the Kirghiz girl in the Qara Shahr bazaar," he glowered. "She takes me too seriously."

"Nonsense. Girls don't give you colitis. You're a great egotist. Why do you think she poisoned you?"

"She is a dancer who came to me in the caravanserai, and she swore I would never leave her. You have no idea of the emotion—the passion, the breast-beating and jealousy. She fed me a secret potion!"

Fallon injected the needle's contents in Efremov's hard arm. "You should be in Moscow writing tragedies. You'd be another Dostoievsky. What depths! Only in America, you'd be cast in a Hollywood comedy."

"In America, ptui! You think medical science has all answers. Let me tell you something, friend. I have seen strange things. There are drugs your laboratory cannot detect, known to such women. They give it to you together with the antidote. The toxin accumulates in the blood and nerves, but it is checked by the antidote. But if you leave the woman, you no longer receive the antidote—then the poison strikes, you soon become ill, you die. You can avoid it only by returning to that woman, who holds you captive. You are doomed."

"I'll lay you twenty copecks you aren't," Fallon said. "Swallow this, and tell me more about this perfumed bazaar dancer. Do you spin such Fu-Manchu yarns to your Slavic friends in Tihwa about the purlieus of Shanghai?"

"Bah!" Efremov ground the pills between his strong white teeth. "You have no imagination." He lay quietly, a middle-aged man with big shoulders and powerful arms. His face was broad, his eyes were small and set wide apart, his hair was a dirty blond, cropped short. Fallon saw that the dark Russian blouse he wore as a pajama jacket was shaking; he was laughing and the humor lay far back in his pale eyes.

"It is wise to question my stories, Doctor," Efremov said. "I tell them because I love to exaggerate, and for relief from the dialectic. You have no idea how tired I get from my work. It is endless. So I tell stories, and those people in Tashkent look at me and say, 'That Gregor, that lying son of bitch!' Ho, ho!"

"Was there any girl at all in Qara Shahr, then?"

"Sure, plenty girls there. Also every place. Fat ones, skinny ones, light and dark, smooth and greasy. Iranians, Afghans, Mongols, Jewesses, Caucasians—take your pick. Girls with old Greek coins for earrings. Girls from vermin pits that were sacked by Kublai. Give me a cigarette, friend."

He rejected Fallon's packet and took his own long *papyrossi* and lay smoking. In this ménage he was an independent operator, coming and going as he pleased. He was absent much of the time on extended journeys such as the one from which he had just returned. He worked closely with Colonel Li, and Fallon surmised that he was an attaché rather than a subordinate. He had spent many years of his youth in Central Asia and returned periodically to contact points there, presumably for detailed reports and further instructions, but his work lay in centers far to the south. He spoke six languages with fluency—his native tongue, French and English, Hindi, Malay and mandarin Chinese—and another half a dozen obscure dialects of the inland nomads. He had to have these languages, he explained to Fallon; he used them to advantage on frequent anonymous visits to Calcutta, Singapore, Jakarta and Saigon.

"You think all revolutionaries are agents of Moscow," he said once to Fallon, smiling. "That is the naïve, melodramatic and popular view in the West. They are not, of course; they are nationalists of many races. But they often need advice and help and direction from experts. A few direct agents of experience are necessary. I am a traveling salesman. What you call a trouble shooter."

Now he smoked musingly, looking out at the high yellow sky of autumn above the city, while Fallon cleaned the hypodermic.

"I wish I might have gone with you and got out of this sewer for a while," Fallon said. "I went up as far as railhead in the Mongol country once, but I suppose it isn't the same."

"No," Efremov said, shaking his head. "Not the same at all. That Ordos region where you went is howling desert. Sinkiang is a garden."

"A Soviet garden, perhaps."

"We cultivate beautiful and useful gardens," said Efremov. "It is greatly changed from the first time I went there as a young surveyor. Very industrial now, very rich. Air bases below the high Pamir passes, army bases in the desert, canals to carry the Tien Shan snows to the cotton fields. They are building a railroad where the old Silk Road ran. No, not like when I was a young man. I miss the orchards of Aksu and the yurts of the Kirghiz. But in such an ageless land many things cannot change. Last week I flew to the oasis of Kashgar, right over that ocean of red sand and the sterile mountains, in two hours. I looked down on the dunes and clay plains and I remembered crossing there once in the burning sun in a caravan. But one still sees the great white Mustagh-ata, father of the ice peaks. It doesn't change. You know, Moslems say that Moses is buried on the top."

"Then he wandered far from the Promised Land," said Fallon, idly straightening the disorder of Efremov's room. The Russian did most of his work in this badly lit cubicle, and one wall was lined with wooden filing cabinets. Fallon went slowly along them, pushing drawers into place.

"It was the Promised Land for me, when first I crossed the Turugart into the yellow basin. We were surveying new roads then to India and China and Tibet. New ways to Lhasa. We were the advance guard. Where there are minerals, you know, the days of hermit monks are numbered."

Fallon picked up the medical case he had brought across the hall from his own quarters.

"You'd probably be happier," he said, "if you'd stuck to surveying. You could be living in Qara Shahr now with your woman and her black magic instead of wasting your time on revolutions."

"Do not chide me, friend," Efremov said sadly. "I am dying. So please, now I eat a little, sleep a little, drink a little wine—"

"Eat and drink nothing I don't prescribe. You and your bazaar poisons and mysterious antidotes!"

"No pastry? A small glass vodka? For poison, I always take double vodkas with lemon peel."

"Good-by until this evening."

"I am abandoned. I shall tell the colonel the reactionary Amerikanetz doctor is trying to kill me, to block the progress of Soviet culture."

"Okay."

Efremov lifted his glass of weak tea in a sardonic toast. *"Vashe zdaravye!"*

Fallon departed on his afternoon calls. But as he passed the landing the colonel came out of his door, hurrying to his waiting car.

"How are my patients?" he demanded cheerfully. "My Russian and my Frenchman?"

"Both improving," Fallon said. "Father Julien has done remarkably well in the last month."

"Good, good!" Li clattered on down the stairs. Fallon was following more slowly when his name was spoken and he glanced back. Judith Markham stood on the landing, a slim and elegant figure in a bright flowered frock, smiling at him tentatively. They rarely met, Fallon was hardly aware of her in the house, they were still on fairly formal terms after so long.

"You are going out, Doctor?" she asked. "I am going shopping. Shall we walk to the corner together?"

He was impatient to be gone for he had an urgent appointment, but it wouldn't do to reveal its nature to Mrs. Markham. They strolled in the sunshine.

A year before she had been what he regarded as a pretty woman, with high pink and cream and gold coloring. Those shades had now faded in Judith. Her hair was more like hay than wheat, her restless eyes were flat gray agates, her skin had lost its luster. But she was still attractive; she had cosmetics from the colonel that were becoming rare in the city, and when she applied these and abandoned the customary negligee she wore in the suite for one of her artful frocks she became more than plain. Her figure was unaccountably excellent, and a Hungarian dressmaker's sleek designs transformed her into an un-English copy of the chic Slav girls who had formerly promenaded on Avenue Joffre. There was a kind of feverish animation about her today, Fallon noticed absently. She had set her hair and done her nails, and he suspected that this vivacity resulted from a breakfast at the colonel's liquor cabinet.

"That obnoxious Captain Kuo came in this morning," Judith said.

"Yes, I noticed him."

"He had a row with Thorpe Albany. Something about Thorpe not showing up for work. Then Thorpe's girl friend arrived and interrupted them and Kuo left."

"His girl friend?"

"Oh, you know. That little Chinese trollop from his office who's always coming to see him."

He frowned. "That's an Information Bureau messenger, if you mean Yin Kuei. I've met her. She runs errands, brings Albany directives and whatnot. Part of her job."

Judith lifted a carefully penciled brow. "You men!" she said. "You stick together. What can you see in those slant-eyed yellow girls?"

He stared at her in amazement and with difficulty suppressed a shout of laughter. Judith Markham had become the companion of Colonel Li nearly two years ago, and since then had lived a secluded life of ease and comparative luxury. She saw his amused face and tossed her head defiantly.

"I can't understand it," she said. "I used to know a gentleman here in the old days—he was in export-import—and he supported half a dozen girls of as many colors in his time. Openly boasted none of them was entirely white. Imagine! I doubt if one of them was entirely faithful, either."

Fallon said nothing, being unable to think of anything adequate. She looked at him covertly, the high heels of her shoes tapping the pavement.

"Tell me, Doctor," she said, "do you think I'm unattractive?"

"Not at all," Fallon said, his face expressionless. A thousand physicians, ten thousand arch patients had played uncounted games of catch with these neuroses, and would again.

"But you don't seem to like me very much. When you come to give the colonel his treatments you're barely civil."

"I'm too busy these days to be civil to anybody very much," he said.

"Everyone seems so cold and unfeeling."

"Everybody's pretty absorbed with personal problems. The times are out of joint, you know."

She lit a cigarette. They had reached a corner where their ways parted.

"There's something I want to tell you," she said. Her manner was unnaturally gay and Fallon was uncomfortable. There was an explosive force in her hurrying words.

"I know what people say about me. They don't believe I was really married to a utilities engineer here, before the collapse, and that we were divorced. They all think I was in one of those houses. You know. I don't care, the opinion of these filthy native Reds is nothing to me. But I do care what you think."

"I don't think," Fallon said, feeling the perspiration on his face. "It's outside my line to think." Judith Markham's carefully reiterated account ran to the effect that she was the daughter of a Singapore bank official and for a decade before the Takeover had been a China Coast executive's wife. When Fallon occasionally dined in Colonel Li's apartment he was treated to Judith's scintillating reminiscences of Malaya. He did not know why he now stood here on a sun-blasted corner listening again to her queer confidences. She rattled on and he tried to cover his irritation. It was his private belief that this fellow Markham was a desperate phantasm. She had probably created him out of an ill-defined fear of drowning beneath the yellow flood that had overwhelmed her. She told a good story, full of detail, entertaining and amusing, not entirely convincing but designed to shock.

"I've got to go," he said, staring at his wrist watch.

"Yes, of course." She laughed, the sound shrill in the street. "Please forgive me for keeping you from your rounds with this silly chatter. But thanks so much for walking with me." She smoothed the fabric of her dress over her hips.

"D'you know, Doctor, what I really wanted you to understand is, until I met the colonel I'd never had anything to do with a Chinaman."

He glanced at her with rising exasperation. Did she expect congratulations or commiserations?

"Except," she added thoughtfully, "for a houseboy my father had in Singapore when I first came home from school in England. Just before I married, you know. I haven't thought of it in years."

She tapped away rapidly down the street. And Fallon, wiping the damp from his face, resumed his course.

2

It was nearly the end of the afternoon when he reached the busy corner where Nanking Road debouched upon the Bund. He stood against a wall opposite the big hotel in which the Information Bureau had its offices. The crowds swirled around him and he was obscure and alone in them, as solitary and rejected as the most leprous beggar, with only an occasional sharp or hostile glance cast at him.

The taipans and most all of the others, for one thing, were gone from the streets and the clubs, along with the fortunes they had made on the fluctuations in exchange in the easy days of credit, race meetings, houseboats on the canals and all the rest of it. Gone with the foreign troops and foreign warships, the adventurers, oil and tobacco men, merchants and shippers, missionaries and confidence men, bankers and gamblers, policemen and beachcombers. They were scattered across the earth and the lives of those few who remained grew steadily more intolerable. A new and terrifying environment yawned behind the Western rear guard, where before they had been protected from its sordid ugliness, its cruelties and poverty and misery and dirt and its inflowing masses of human beings.

Fallon's life had not been set in the rigid caste lines and had not been compartmentalized and cut off from the millions that surrounded him. He had never known this city or thought of it as an island of neutrality and remote Western order in the midst of thunderous crowds and agitation. He walked the streets alone and saw the city as it was: cluttered, drab, a shifting wilderness.

He roused from his contemplation of the crowd and turned to the hotel doorway. Yin Kuei stood there on the steps, searching for him with her eyes. Her working uniform was slacks and blouse, but today she wore a dress. It would have been fashionable in decadent bourgeois Hongkong, but was unfashionable on the steps of this great rundown hotel in proletarian Shanghai. The dress was of turquoise linen, cut simply in the style of the West, and one saw such clothing on the streets only rarely now. With it she wore heels and earrings. Passers-by turned to stare at her, some in heavy disapproval, most in open admiration for both her beauty and her unconventional boldness. She saw Fallon and raised a slim tanned arm, and something deep inside him was disturbed and moved in its slumber to the sudden hard stroke of his heart, and having stirred it lay awake, quiet and waiting.

It was the third time he had come to meet her here like this since the night she had stood, rain-drenched, at his door. The first occasion had been the result of a message sent to the hospital by Tieh. The others had followed in their natural course. He came at the end of the working day and waited here on the street. It was far from wise. There were so few foreigners and all were suspect, and she was automatically compromised by a public meeting. But after that first encounter she had insisted on it, indifferent to the crowds, the suspicious or wondering faces, the chance acquaintances they might pass. It was her risk, she said; no ordinance or edict that she knew of was being violated, and she was careless of reprimand. Until the Big Changeover, there had certainly been nothing unusual about the sight of a foreigner strolling with an attractive Chinese girl. This city was a meeting place and a celebrated melting pot; the opportunities for meeting and melting were less now, but they still existed. One occasionally saw Russians or Britons with girls of the country, together in the sad surviving night spots and cafés. What had once been commonplace was now unusual enough to draw comment, mostly unfavorable and directed toward the lady. But Yin Kuei did not mind.

She came up to him, smiling and serene, and laid a hand like curving willow on his arm. Her hands had fascinated him since the first time he had seen her, for when she talked they sometimes swayed in gesturing accompaniment like those of some dainty Siamese dancer.

"I am glad you could come today," she said. "I thought you might. Where should we go?"

That was it. There was nowhere they could simply go, to be together, without attracting attention. The restaurants at that hour were as jammed as the streets. There was the faint stirring of an evening breeze that came across the river, rippling the oily surface, and it brought coolness and a sense of ease and relief. Then he thought of a small tea shop on a narrow street nearby, back from the foreshore and probably still hot with the lingering closeness of the day but perhaps for that reason a retreat from the ever-present hordes.

The shop was dim and almost empty, the wizened proprietor incurious. She sat opposite Fallon, facing the light from the street window, with the tea glass between her hands. Her skin was like warm honey and he was silent, studying the small bones and fine features. Her eyes, under long and gently tapered brows, were large and dark and their whites were clear as fine china; her nose was delicate and slightly aquiline, her lips full and with that tilt of humor, and her hair sprang from a smooth forehead like ebony wings, repeated beneath by shadowed hollows under the cheekbones. Today Yin Kuei wore her long hair in plaited coils around her head, held in place by small green combs.

"Why do you stare at me?" she asked, unperturbed by his steady gaze.

"I'm sorry," he said. "I was only thinking that you are beautiful."

"The world is full of beautiful people. I have seen many lovely women in America, for instance. So that is nothing extraordinary."

"You are extraordinary."

"Paul, you are absurd." The intimate sound of his name still was strange to him, for he was on familiar terms with so few. They called him Fallon, or Doctor, but she called him Paul.

"In America they called me Margaret," she had said. "Margaret Chung. But here I am Yin Kuei again—it is better."

Now he asked, "How old are you, Yin Kuei?"

"How rude! I'm twenty-three by your count, twenty-four by ours. Why?"

"I was nearly ready for medical school when you were born."

"So? One would never know. Men remain adolescent so long, their minds develop so slowly. You see? Some say a woman should be half a man's age plus seven years."

He grinned. "You're not quite there yet, in that case. What I meant was, you're very young to be sticking your lovely neck out like this. Someone may make it difficult for you."

"You mean, for being seen with you? That's absurd."

"No. I mean the sort of thing you and your friend Tieh are doing. It's dangerous."

"Ah. Tieh Lao-hu isn't worried. He's been well trained for his job. He has trained me, in turn. Besides, what dangerous thing are you talking about?"

"Look here," Fallon said uncomfortably. "I think I know perfectly well what you're up to. I won't dramatize it by discussing it, but you haven't tried to conceal it from me, either. I don't think of you in any such nonsensical role as a beauteous female spy. You're a reckless kid headed for trouble. These people—the ones you work with and also the ones like Captain Kuo—they're playing for keeps and don't take crazy chances. It's a serious adult game. They have no patience with inexperienced Mata Haris."

"Paul," she said, her voice low and cool, "I know what I'm doing. I've been working with Tieh and his group for several months and I went into it with my eyes open. We believe our work is valuable."

"A mountain isn't easily moved with chopsticks, I've heard, especially when you have to operate secretly in the dark, and without outside help."

Yin Kuei's eyes flashed. "Is that what you told those Filipino guerrillas you doctored when they were fighting Japanese odds?"

"That was different," he said, beginning to feel warm. "We had a chance then. This is—well, Tieh talked optimistically, but it's a few well-meaning fanatics arrayed against a nation!"

She had stiffened, but now she relaxed slowly and smiled again. "A few well-meaning fanatics? You must have been listening to your colonel, or that Captain Kuo. Paul, I can't explain in a place like this, even if I had the right to do so. But believe me, this isn't a children's crusade or a paper resistance. Tieh and his friends aren't a lot of young and zealous firebrands. They don't go around sabotaging the waterworks, as your Dr. Chu hinted, or throwing homemade bombs. They know what they're doing. Right now they're coordinating groups and collecting intelligence. That's all I can tell you. Except that they have tremendous support overseas. Not officially, I don't mean Formosa or the UN or anything. That's ridiculous. I mean international wealth and assistance from our own people. In Southeast Asia, and in America, and everywhere—people who don't want this to spread any further and want to stop it and roll it back here. Do you see?"

Fallon looked at his cigarette. He had learned to keep a short rein on his enthusiasms, he had cultivated patience, and he avoided the semblance of nobility. But he felt his skepticism shaken, a belief that nothing short of global cataclysm could possibly make any change in what had already taken place. The habit of fatalism was easy to acquire, difficult to break.

"All right," he said at last. "If you say it, I'll take your word for it. But that doesn't change the fact that I'm chiefly concerned right now about your personal safety. What Tieh and the rest of them may do is something else."

She tapped his hand complacently. "In that case, Paul, did you do what Tieh asked?"

Fallon hesitated. "You mean the job you passed on to me last time I saw you," he said. "Yes. Yes, I did. I thought it was unwise, but it was Tieh's affair. And not yours, do you understand?"

He drew a small wad of newspaper from his pocket and unrolled it, revealing two shining new keys. She took them with unconcealed delight.

"This larger one," he said dourly, "is to Efremov's door. The smaller opens the files. I took both the other day while he was sleeping under a sedative and had copies made in a few minutes at a shop down in

Szechwan Road, and then returned the originals. I think the whole plan is dubious."

"Lao-hu doesn't think so, and neither does our chief," she said, putting the keys in her purse. "If he can have a few hours with certain of Efremov's reports, he'll make photostats of them and put them back and they'll never have been missed."

"Efremov's on his feet again and he's in and out," Fallon warned. "Mostly out after dinner. Tieh should come in the evening, and return them not later than the next evening."

She looked at him calmly. "I may be inexperienced, as you say, but Lao-hu isn't. He knows exactly what material he wants and how to handle it. He already knows his way around the house from our first visit, and how to leave without being noticed. You needn't worry."

"I don't worry about Tieh. I worry about you, Yin Kuei. You've promised to keep clear of it, remember? Anyway, I think Tieh's friends exaggerate the importance of this stuff Efremov has. It's routine paper work so far as I know, and I don't see what can be accomplished."

"Maybe nothing. Maybe a great deal. Our friends say Efremov's section makes what they call blueprints for conquest."

"Very glamorous, if true," said Fallon. He regarded his tea glass wryly. Yet the colorful phrase stirred him, which was surprising enough in itself.

Yin Kuei was ready to leave; he knew she wished to hurry away and give Tieh these bright yellow keys Fallon had provided after much debate with himself. They would be grateful, they would go ahead with their work. At least they were not apathetic, those friends of Yin Kuei's. They refused to accept tyranny and misrule, whether from a Fascist or a Communist dictatorship. They had as colorful rogues'-gallery labels for their enemies as their enemies had for them. But they were not content with general utility cuss words. They weren't satisfied to gather cozily in secret and talk, to play it safe and avoid being hurt. They demanded action. These keys would help provide it.

Fallon experienced a curious breath-catching stimulation, such as he had not felt since the days of Samar. Tieh was right; there *was* something that could be done. But he kept his face impassive.

"I've got evening calls to make," he said, pushing back his chair. "Remember your promise."

"Yes, Paul," she said, and touched his cheek quickly with her fingertips. Her eyes sparkled with anticipation as she rose, long-limbed and direct and vigorous for a woman of her race, and accompanied him to the door.

3

Gregor Efremov was lethargic, and wanted to be persuaded. He sat grumpily in Fallon's room, a silk muffler tied about his thick throat, and looked out at the dusk, waiting while the doctor sterilized instruments over his alcohol burner. Swallows darted out from the eaves above the window, swooping among the upper branches of the garden trees, skimming the wall and dipping across the road to bank over the creek on twilight flights. Across the waterway lights began to flash on in the hospital and the apartments. Lights gleamed on the standards marking the bridges and on the water below where dark boats quietly glided. Lights speckled the towering residence-hotel where high officialdom occupied lavish quarters that had once been the homes of Western executives and corporation taipans. Lights glittered in the squat square fortress of the big post office with its clock tower. Evening muted sound and autumn was astringent in the nostrils.

"I am sick," Efremov said, sniffing. "I should be in bed."

"You've been in bed a week," Fallon said, pulling on a tweed jacket. "You need air and exercise. Your bazaar dancer's poison has met its Waterloo in me. Come along now."

"Where must I go?" Efremov growled. "Forever walking! As if I have not walked enough in my life. I have walked half across Asia. I have climbed the Kunluns and the Himalayas. I have walked the length of every city in the East, to pass dull time, from Karachi to Surabaya. I have flat feet."

"To the chemist's," said Fallon cheerfully. "Your guts are too primitive to respond properly to civilized Western medicine, so I'm going to buy something like bear's gall bladder and experiment on you. I'm safe enough—nothing known to Oriental or Occidental medicine can kill you."

"Perhaps," Efremov said with a note of hope, "we will pass a bar. A café of an expatriate. Vodka is excellent for the liver."

"It's possible," Fallon said, glancing at him thoughtfully. They went down the hall past Efremov's locked door, down the stairs and out into the garden. At the street gate they turned toward the city's center and as they did so Fallon saw from the tail of his eye the stocky figure of the Iron Tiger, lounging on the embankment rail in the gloom.

You're committed now, Doctor, he said to himself. What would you prefer? The firing squad or the headsman's axe? Or maybe the death of a thousand cuts?

They walked together up the creek and swung into the jangling glittering canyon of Fukien Road, moving deeper in the light and noise and smells and eternal good-natured confusion of a great shopping and pleasure district, a district unchanged by any political or economic eruptions. Above the overhanging balconies and the swinging signboards the night closed down as far as the rooftops, but no night ever penetrated that region of brilliant clashing sound and color and flowing streams of people. The movement, the hum and clatter and cry of uncounted thousands never ceased here from dusk to dawn; the restaurants, tea shops, theaters and pleasure palaces persisted despite the steady pressure of austerity; a race of instinctive merchants and hedonists pursued its practical and individualistic way in these winding streets and alleys. Pandemonium and riot seemed the normal tenor here, a cacophony of ricsha bells, horn toots, hawker's cries, the high shrill voices of women, discordant music with the theme carried by wooden clapper beat, drum pound and whining flute. The most tolerant social system, Fallon reflected, that anyone could desire.

He found his way unerringly among the shops for furs, food and fantasia to the druggist's stall, and drew Efremov into the quiet recess. The elderly man who owned the Hall of Herbs of Immortality knew Dr. Fallon, from previous visits, as one of those extremely rare men of the outer world who came in courtesy and respect to examine this exotic merchandise and make an occasional modest purchase. Here behind the counters were large drawers of powders, roots and barks; on the shelves stood blue and white jars of tonics and syrups to ward off the feebleness of age and to insure easy delivery; below in smaller jars were seeds and expensive vegetable substances. In an alcove at the rear was a small altar to the God of Medicine, flanked by tribute panels glorifying the ancient herbalists.

"I think in your case," Fallon said to Efremov after a leisurely examination of the stock, "that we'll skip the dried tiger stomach, otter liver and rhino horn, and buy a belly plaster." He did so, and the pleased proprietor watched with interest as Fallon ordered his huge companion to push down his belt and open his shirt for its application then and there. Efremov swore bitterly in Russian but made polite and complimentary sounds in Chinese.

They left and strolled on, Efremov muttering.

"You think this is a joke," he said. "Let me tell you, my friend, it is not such a joke. I know something of this matter, for I have been sick more than once in places where I had no one but a dirty shaman or a village healer to attend me. In Russia we have the most advanced medical science in the world today, but I am not above witch doctors."

Fallon guided them out of the close-packed streets into wider thoroughfares. It was necessary now to keep Efremov interested and occupied for an hour or so more. In Yunnan Road there was a little bistro that had survived the upheaval; it was run by a rheumy-eyed Pole with whom Efremov had an acquaintance and he made for it. Fallon did not protest. The strong raw vodka was distilled from local maize, but Efremov didn't mind. He had a gnawing thirst.

"I doubt," Fallon said, "that this stuff will do your stomach any good, but one never knows. I've seen some odd cure-alls in my journeyings and I'm always willing to learn something new. In your case, the combination of that plaster over your navel and this firewater may be just what the doctor ordered."

The diversion entertained Efremov and they lingered at the Pole's bar, Fallon appearing to grow more voluble over the rising stack of counters. He spoke at length of the melding of Eastern and Western medicine. Then he shrugged. "As a guinea pig, of course, you're not a typical subject."

Efremov was eating slices of garlic sausage and cucumber provided by the Pole. He laughed. "No, I am not typical. If I were typical, I would not be standing in this rat hole drinking with you. I would not tolerate you, I would not trust this man behind the bar. I would be at the Metropole, talking to the trade commission people and the technicians from my own country. We would be talking about things that are important, not about medicine and magic. Important to them, at any rate. But boring to me. I have spent my life going about, doing my work in queer corners, and what they have to say no longer interests me. Between you and me, it is dull, this infantile parroting that goes on everywhere. I became tired of it years ago."

He banged his glass on the counter and the Pole jumped, and filled it from a gray bottle. If the proprietor understood English, it didn't matter. Efremov was a hard-headed, enlightened and sardonic man, a man beyond gestures and sycophancy and ideological taboos. He could talk freely of heresies without the fear of being overheard. He was neither a peasant nor a bureaucrat.

"You must be very tired of it, then," Fallon said. "It's your job."

"Ha! My job is like your job. You fight parasites and germs. I fight the loathsome social diseases that breed them. You give men a dose of salts for their aches and pains. I give them weapons to purge corruption."

He turned the full pale lamps of his eyes upon Fallon. "Asia is my patient, but the cure is more complex, it takes longer. I give them the medicine and the advice, but they must do the doctoring themselves.

India, for instance. I go to our headquarters in Khetwadi Main Road in Bombay; all the cautious little Anglo-Brahmans and illiterate village delegates are arguing and getting nowhere. They are arguing about that half-Marxist Nehru, or a rising in the rear in case of a Pakistan war, and the party goes to hell while they fight, repudiated by the Cominform, bled by the Socialists, split in the unions and in Congress. So they are still demoralized serfs, afraid of strong action, sick in their bonds of caste. In Delhi and Calcutta I also despair. The revolts are like a cache of dynamite dug deep in the ground—it explodes and bursts upward, makes a big noise but does little damage and leaves a small hole in the dirt!"

Efremov lifted his glass, drank, and his lips spread in a bleak smile. "But that, Doctor, is only one of my many patients. I have not told you about the ones I have in Rangoon, Singapore, Jakarta, Saigon and Manila. Tragic places. Also comic. Buddhist scholars running Burma who would rather be beggar monks. Grotesque rebellions like fairy tales. The Oriental mind is supposedly acute, yet it finds Marxism inscrutable. A Malayan party executive came to me and said, 'I am sorry, sir, but I do not understand what on earth the *Communist Manifesto* is all about!' Well, perhaps it is complex to an anarchist thug without root in the country. All he knows is ambush and there is no true belief in victory, neither among the Vietminh in Annam nor the Huks in Luzon."

He turned abruptly to the bar. "Give me an uncorked bottle of that," he said to the Pole. "I will take it with me." He slapped down the money, pushing Fallon's wallet back. "I must go home. I have work to do, and I stand here getting drunk. It is a pleasure to exchange diagnosis with another scientific man, an observer of sick bodies. He has cured me of colitis, and I have described some peculiar ills with which he is not so familiar."

He laughed loudly and clapped his big hand around Fallon's shoulder. "March, Comrade! Back to our labors among the sick and wounded!"

4

His labors among the sick, if not the wounded, kept Fallon engaged for the better part of the following day. He left the house in midmorning and paused at Efremov's door, hearing the room's occupant moving about inside. Efremov answered his knock immediately, appearing jovial, unshaken and in shirt sleeves, and from the sheaf of papers in his hand

and the littered condition of his desk Fallon judged that he had been at work.

"Aha!" Efremov exclaimed. "The doctor comes to the patient for a remedy. What is it those English say—the hair of the dog . . . ? Come in."

"No, thanks. I just stopped to see how you're feeling."

"I am good. The plaster worked—or was it the Pole's compound? I am revived."

Fallon went on down the stairs. If there had been any disturbance of his files the previous evening, the agent did not seem aware of it. The house was quiet. He rapped again at Colonel Li's suite and was admitted by an orderly, who said that the colonel had gone out. Through the door to the inner room he saw Judith sitting by an open window, mending a seam in one of her treasured frocks. She was stripped to a minimum because of the still sultry weather. She looked up and nodded calmly. There was little formality in their existence in the house, only a dull monotony of passing hours and days, and Judith frequently strolled about her quarters in a gaudy green negligee flamboyant with red and yellow flowers, voluptuous and defiantly shoddy. But Fallon had never before encountered her in the briefest of lingerie, her feet thrust into frivolous mules.

"Hallo, Doctor," she said, smiling and casual. The orderly made a frantic gesture and was ignored, and he retired. Fallon looked at her with reluctant admiration. She was still slim and piquant, and her faded ash-blond mass of hair was pulled down tightly into a long twisted braid behind her ears. Her eyes were flat and tired but they held his with a determined merriment, and her full red lips pouted above a pointed chin.

"Excuse me," Fallon said, turning away. "I stopped to check on the colonel."

"He's okay for the shape he's in," Judith said. She worked assiduously at Americanisms as she understood them. She had had lessons from an air force officer after the liberation and for a time had tried to be taken for a product of his native place. This was manifestly difficult, since he had come out of Galveston, which did not sound much like Singapore. But she had made progress.

She leisurely picked the green garment from the back of her chair and pulled it on. "Will you have coffee with me?" she asked. A husky undertone crept into her voice in lazy imitation of a cinema beauty who had once been her model before movies went out of their lives. Judith missed the movies dreadfully; they told her all she wished to know about America.

"I'm overdue at the hospital," Fallon said, and as he spoke he heard a step in the hall behind him and saw that Thorpe Albany had come quietly up from street level. "Here's somebody who probably could use coffee."

Judith came to the door, looking perplexed, and her breasts pressed against Fallon's arm as she peered out. Then she laughed.

"Thorpe!"

Albany nodded guardedly. He had always kept to himself, aloof and contemptuous, uneasily brooding, infinitely alone. He could not often relax with the others, join them in their conversations. He rarely passed more than the most perfunctory remarks with any of them. He stood watching Judith, his mouth compressed. Everything about Albany sometimes moved with his inner restlessness: his lips, his eyes, his hands, and if he stood still his toe beat a rapid light tattoo. It was very likely, Fallon thought, that he twitched throughout the night in his sleep.

But now he nodded again; yes, he would have coffee; he had gone out early without breakfast. Fallon started to leave. He caught Albany's hostile glance on him and grinned. There was a movement in the entry hall below and he looked over the railing.

"Here's the *En-kay-vay-day*," he said. "Traffic's heavy today."

"Kuo?" Albany asked, and at the doctor's widening smile he went hastily on up the stairs toward his room, and Judith's door clicked shut. Fallon descended. No one wished to meet the Security officer, including himself, and he was relieved when he saw the captain go into Major Huang's office. The arrival was not unexpected since Kuo called at the house nearly every day. Avoiding him, Fallon went out into the street.

He decided that he was too apprehensive. Captain Kuo was a common visitor; Li and Albany frequently rose early and went to their work. And Efremov could not deceive him. But he had slept badly, and the narrow dark-eyed face of Yin Kuei had come repeatedly to waken him.

There was his own work to do to keep him busy and he spent most of the day at the hospital. Father Julien was slightly improved, though still very weak. As the hours passed, he felt an increasing and unreasonable concern for Yin Kuei. He left the hospital at last and walked home, trying to repress his uneasiness. But he was no longer in doubt about his future course.

He had arrived at his conclusion by no logical or conscious route. He was still determined to go, to run, but it would be here, not away. It would be with this vague nameless society that struggled for freedom and cried for direction, that stood against a foreign tradition and an alien doctrine. Whatever they were, they were drawing together and giving meaning to the rebellious dissidents who filled the woods, the ones without a code, the opportunists who were dissatisfied and the angry men who jockeyed for position in the second phase of the revolt against an old order. Independent forces were still active in regions where the machinery of new law had already broken down in minor explosions of riot and massacre.

He stopped in the gloom of the street to light a cigarette and the glow shone on his hands. His métier, he thought, was not moralizing or plotting; his special genius reposed in the strong fingers that performed surgical legerdemain. But they could do other jobs too, for they had in the past. They had swung a potato hoe and guided a team, they had hauled on lines and washed restaurant dishes, they had lifted bloody litters and driven ambulances and swabbed down makeshift wards. They had also held and effectively used rifle and grenade in green ambushes, and they could again, or do anything else that was required. The indecision, anyway, was past.

Now, in the spreading darkness of the river, Fallon was about to turn in at Number 68. There were lights in the upper windows over the garden wall, and a car before the door. As he started across the road, his step quickening, he felt a hand on his elbow. Tieh Lao-hu stood beside him, pulling him back into the murk beside the embankment rail.

5

The night and the passing crush of pedestrians enfolded them and held them together, their backs to the stream. There was only the constant shuffle of cloth-soled shoes and the subdued hum of voices, the creak of axles and the slap of water against the stones below them, the impatient warning shout as a high-piled cart rolled by and the uneven clatter of a launch engine echoing in the low canyon of the waterway. Fallon's senses tightened; sounds that a moment before had been muffled by river mist and his ear's indifference now rapped at his brain, each with its own significance. Everyday odors rose sharply into his nostrils: the scent of unwashed humanity surrounding them, the stink of creek mud and ammonic pungency in the gutter at their feet, the penetrating smell of peanut oil from a food hawker's street kitchen.

Tieh's waiting silence irritated him. "What's the matter?" he demanded, speaking the dialect roughly but keeping his voice low.

"Nothing," Tieh said. "I have watched for you. It is better I tell you what is happening before you enter the house."

Fallon looked again at the gateway opposite. "Is there trouble?"

"I don't know. Yin Kuei is in there. She insisted that she could replace Efremov's folders in the file more easily than I, although it was I who took them last night while you and the Russian were away."

When Tieh spoke, his breath came into Fallon's face, strong with harsh tobacco and the accent of Hunan. These central plains people, Fallon thought, morose and traditionally hostile to all foreigners and to the foreign customs and fashions of the coast and the world beyond it. Transplanted, Tieh would make a good solid isolationist Midwestern dirt farmer. He was a rugged and loyal giant of his race with a contempt for the retrograde sophistications of coastal people and at the same time with an oddly cultured manner and deep sensitivity. What danger had his rash enterprise got Yin Kuei into?

Fallon flung out a vague epithet at Tieh in his sudden anger at this foolishness. "What do you fear, then?"

"I don't know," Tieh repeated. "She has been a long time—too long. Efremov is out, and it isn't that. There is Captain Kuo's car, and he is having dinner with the adjutant in his office. Nothing has happened, but she does not return."

There was a light on the top floor in the window of Albany's room. "Perhaps she met Albany," Fallon said, "and is talking to him, making some excuse for her visit. You should have put the folders back yourself —it is your plan and your risk, not hers! I would not have helped you at all if I had known you would put her in this position."

"She is not easily persuaded," Tieh grumbled, still smarting under the sting of the reflection Fallon had cast on his ancestral virtues. "She wishes to have a part in this work, and she has more reason to be inside the house than I do."

"Then I'd better go in and see why she's delayed."

"Wait a few moments more," said Tieh, touching his arm again. "There's time to spare before alarm."

The doctor stood at the railing, fidgeting in spite of himself and watching the gate. "Look here," he said, "before I go along any further with you, you'd better tell me what possible use you can make of Efremov's reports."

Tieh shrugged. "I see you underestimate that man's work. His documents are highly confidential. Recently a regional conference was held of party delegates at Rangoon, and plans were made and orders issued there for simultaneous harassing strikes and riots in all major centers of the Southeast. The outbreaks came on schedule. Efremov has details concerning them in his files, with the identity and future assignments of the organizers. That information is of great value abroad, to the leaders of counterrevolt."

His voice was pitched low but it was matter-of-fact and not conspiratorial; Fallon detected a sarcastic note, as though Tieh were lecturing a more than ordinarily obtuse freshman in the simple elements of political science.

"All right," he said. "I don't pretend to know anything about Efremov's business. Perhaps it's of interest to those fighting the spread of his type of cancer. It's a job for organized forces, special intelligence groups. Not for amateur desperadoes working like housebreakers!"

"We are not amateurs," Tieh retorted. "And we are organized better than you think. We have veterans of experience and knowledge in command. They have been soldiers and executives, and many have spent more time than their share in prison. I have, myself."

"Professional troublemakers, making nothing but more trouble for a people that has troubles enough," said Fallon, but without conviction.

"You speak," Tieh said with bitterness, "like a friend of your jailers. Do you think it is important to me who oppresses and beats me? Do you think I prefer to have the Communist secret police kick me in the belly until they break my insides, and love them for it? Would I rather have it done by benevolent Kuomintang police? Whose kicks are most brutal, whose hurt the most? Maybe Russian police are more gentle when they swing their truncheons, eh? Maybe British police in Singapore, or French police in Saigon, or Amboinese warders in Macassar?"

Fallon was silent for a moment. Then he said, "You don't make it any clearer. What do you want with this information you've got from Efremov? What do you do with it? Where does it go? Apparently not to the most obvious enemies of the regime."

"If you mean," said Tieh, a note of amusement creeping into his voice, "to the reactionary Chiangs and Rhees and Bao Dais supported by your own country, no. We have had more than enough of their kind, too. Not to the Kremlin bootlickers like Ho Chi Minh and Taruc, either. We work with private citizens and groups who are true patriots, not officials."

He hesitated, glancing across at the house. "This is no place or time to tell you of things you should know, Doctor. You have helped us because your heart is good, but you have been buried in your captivity and your work and you don't know what is going on all around you. You have straggled. Sometime I will try to explain it, but now I think there is Yin Kuei to consider."

The practical reference to the problem of the moment brought Fallon around with a start.

"I'll go," he said. "Wait here." And he crossed the road again, detecting a tightening of his own determination, a rising of anger that had noth-

ing to do with his distaste for being bogged in espionage and counteres-
pionage.

The lower hall was deserted, but there were murmuring voices and a
dim illumination from Major Huang's office under the stairs. Two men
talking casually; that would be Huang and Captain Kuo.

He climbed to the upper floor and stood in the hallway. The door of
Albany's room stood ajar and a bar of yellow light fell across the floor.
Fallon went directly to the door and pushed it open.

Albany was sprawled in an armchair with a glass in his hand, and
looked up in quick surprise and annoyance. Yin Kuei sat opposite him,
poised on the edge of a padded stool, and Fallon saw the expression of
quiet desperation in her face, one that changed quickly to joyful relief.
The tableau was so pat and obvious that Fallon felt both a violent up-
surge of fury and a distinct desire to laugh.

"You're butting in," Albany said flatly, staring at him with intense irritation.

But Yin Kuei had risen from the stool. "Oh, no," she said. "We were
just discussing a project script I brought from the office. I must go."

"We were discussing nothing of the sort," said Albany. "Take off,
Doc!"

"Please!" the girl said, looking at Fallon. "I've stayed much longer than
I intended."

Fallon decided to force the issue. "I'm not sorry I intruded," he said.
"This has all the earmarks of an old-fashioned seduction scene, complete
with helpless cornered heroine and the half-soused cad. You'd better run
along, Yin Kuei."

Albany set down his glass and got to his feet. "Fallon," he said, "I
don't want trouble up here. Kuo's downstairs and everything's peaceful.
But you're damned obnoxious and insulting. Get out of here."

"I don't usually jump to conclusions," Fallon said. "Still, the setup's a
little raw." He felt extremely absurd and pushed on regardless. The thing
was to get Yin Kuei out of the house, and if mock heroics and even a
fight were required for that purpose, he would provide them. "If your
messenger wants to leave, I think she's wise to do so." He saw Albany's
hands knotting into fists and added, "I don't think you'd like Colonel
Li and the rest of them coming up. Judith too."

Albany controlled his outrage but he was trembling and his face was
white and damp.

"I never heard anything so goddam stupid in my life!" he declared,
his voice rasping. "Who the hell are you to barge in here telling me how
to behave? What's Judith got to do with it? What do you think you are
around here—the defender of public and private morals or something?

What's this little chippy to you, when I catch her sneaking out of Efremov's quarters?"

Fallon had moved forward, tensing to end the outburst with a blow, but he checked himself. The three stood poised in stillness, and then Albany let out his breath in a burst of angry disgust and sat down in his chair. His eyes were narrow and taunting.

"What's the matter?" Albany said. "Virtuous Chinee maiden not so virtuous, huh? Little different light on the picture?"

Fallon relaxed gradually. Good, he thought. If that's what Albany imagines, don't overdo it. Let it ride. Now she could go, and he summoned up indignation.

"What do you mean—coming out?"

"What I said! She even has his key." Albany's tone was suddenly so reproachful that Fallon almost grinned. "I thought I heard a noise down there, and looked out and saw her leaving. So I just hauled her in here for a little talk."

"Well," Fallon said, cocking his brow at Yin Kuei, "in that case it seems to me that both of us are a bit overwarm about this. None of our business, eh? Best if she just slips off, it seems to me."

Albany glared at him. "It isn't quite as simple as that. What's she doing, prowling around in Efremov's room, that's what I've been trying to find out. He isn't home."

"If Efremov gave her a key, that'd be his affair. Maybe she was waiting for him. It looks to me as though you're trying to take advantage of the situation—and if Efremov finds out about it, he'll be in here speaking to you. If I were you I'd forget it. These tough Slavs are a jealous lot, and he's not only got a lot of muscles, he throws a lot of weight."

For a minute Albany drummed his fingers on the chair arm. "This girl works in my office," he said querulously. "She's a damn sight sharper than she looks. Speaks good English—not the kind they teach 'em in mission schools." He stared at Yin Kuei with curiosity. She had edged toward the door with eyes downcast and the impishly innocent air of a child caught stealing jam, and she maintained her discreet silence.

He made an abrupt motion of dismissal at her, fished on the floor beside his chair and retrieved a bottle standing there. "Go on, kid. Beat it!"

Yin Kuei slipped out of the door, giving Fallon only the briefest glance, and they heard her slippers patter softly away down the hall. Albany chuckled ruefully, his animosity and suspicions seemingly forgotten.

"Hell, have a drink, Doc," he said. "I don't like you and you don't like me but we're stuck with it, in this stinking house in this fouled-up town, and no use getting into a fight over a tart. There's millions of 'em like her, though she's a better dish than most."

It was just as well, Fallon thought, to let Albany consolidate his views along those lines for the time being. He sat down and filled his pipe, but declined the offer of the bottle.

"You should keep your hands off the women of Russians and Commie intelligence colonels, Thorpe," he said agreeably. "I'd hate to see a fellow countryman get put on the griddle."

"Even a fellow-traveling countryman?" Albany jeered.

"You may have been a sympathizer once," Fallon said. "But the racket has turned sour on you."

Albany stared at him, gulped down the contents of his glass, and his eyes grew vacant and moist behind the thick lenses. "I'm in it ten feet over my head," he said shakily. "Some day if you ever get out of this mess, you can go home. But me, I can't, ever!"

6

There were more things in the Asian heaven and on the Asian earth than Thorpe Albany had ever dreamed of. Nor did he want to dream of them, for what he already had seen and sensed gave him nightmares.

He sat hunched in his chair, indulging his misery, an uneven blending of remorse and self-pity welling in him. Yet Fallon, watching thoughtfully, did not feel scorn or even strong dislike. No one, he believed, sunk in a gall-wallow not entirely of his own making should merit opprobrium, and Paul Fallon was far from personally satisfied with his own conduct up to this point. From now on matters might be different in his own case, but they had both reached this same desolate bit of purgatory. The motives and drives and misadventures that had propelled them here to share adjoining cells were far more complex, at least as far as Albany was concerned, than he was prepared to analyze. His own labyrinth had been intricate enough to keep him bemused; he disqualified himself for venturing far into Albany's private maze.

Fallon had no desire to be the younger man's confessor. He said so bluntly now, though Albany alternately flagellated himself and berated the fates that had brought him to this impasse. His scapegoats were varied; they included a quondam professor of economics who, Fallon surmised, would be mildly astonished now if he found himself in the motley company of Albany's whipping boys. There was a former fellow student, apparently a sort of bellwether who had led many an intellectual admirer up strange paths and now basked in the security of an unassailable Foreign Aid post in Washington. A military attaché at Chungking who had seemingly gone over the hill with loud rallying cries of protest. A correspondent with a glib facility for writing appalling half-truths. A host of dull and brilliant friends, acquaintances, chance advisers, evangelists of the crimson dawn, angry and vindictive crusaders, confusing voices expounding the elegy of Albany's youthful world. Birds of passage. Fallon had no sure conception of the gantlet Albany had run, but now the publicist sat and called down malediction on that dim host that had guided him to this point from which he saw—or so he imagined—no return.

It was a long time since those inspired days of his decision, far back in the years of an old war, and it was hard now for him to think of himself as the outraged young secretary in the deep inland capital on the river bluffs. But he ran down the list of men and women he had known then, and wondered what had become of them. Many had talked bravely, but he had seen nothing of them since. Perhaps they were in other capitals in other lands around the earth, still talking bravely, and to them he was dead. He had long ago lost interest in them, anyway. Except that in this past year he had endured the leisure in which to consider himself and his present associates more critically. The unpleasantness of this experience distressed him. He was, as Fallon charitably tried to put it, becoming more than a little morbid.

The quarters themselves, Fallon believed, reflected Albany's untidy existence at this stage, and now as he sat half-listening to the plaintive harangue, content that this distraction should be sufficient for Yin Kuei's safe departure, he looked around the room again with curious eyes. The room always offered some new and usually grotesque facet over which he could puzzle. It was filled with worn plush and heavy gilt objects left by the previous occupants, the sad debris of the serail, and cluttered with an amazing collection of native antique bric-a-brac ranging from heavy camphor chests to Sung nature scrolls, camel bells and incrusted lacquer pieces. All this careless litter represented a considerable investment, for Albany still had a comparatively imposing income.

In the midst of the museum on a desk stood a large radio and a typewriter, and grouped on a shelf behind stood several framed photographs. These were portraits of a gray and lean-faced man who was his father and whom Albany resembled in no particular, and of his brothers—the West Point major who had fallen at Kwajalein and the younger one who was a Michigan schoolmaster. And Fallon, glancing with wonder about this retreat, saw at last the additional adornment he had expected:

a gay Princeton pennant resurrected from a travel kit and tacked above the door.

Presently Albany subsided into a sulky silence and sat glass in hand, staring at the scuffed toes of his shoes.

"Don't you think you rather exaggerate your position?" Fallon asked. "Your former friends and associates probably regard you as just one of the unfortunates who happened to get caught, and maybe they're still trying to spring you from some imagined dungeon."

Albany shifted irritably. "They know what I'm doing, all right. Radio stuff, pamphlets, the news magazine—hell, the word leaks out. They're probably hollering about treason."

"Nonsense. Nobody at home knows or cares about this Bureau of Proletarian Prevarications and Distortions. Nobody's got you up on a pedestal yet with Benedict Arnold and Lord Haw Haw. At worse they may think of you as another eccentric crackpot who got taken in, and good riddance. But they aren't getting a warrant out for you."

Albany's face became suffused. "What about those guys who did propaganda work for the Japs and Germans? What happened to them?"

"That was war," Fallon said wearily. "This is too, I guess, but somehow it's different. Any time you can sneak out and go home I don't think they'll bother about you."

He saw that this deprecation further outraged Albany, and smiled. "You know," he said, "you came out here from a soft life of gadgets and movies, good schools and mass-produced luxuries, nourishing food and new cars and jukeboxes and a modern drugstore on the corner. Then the government set you down in the middle of the most primitive misery you ever imagined. It wasn't lush or fascinating or mysterious—it was just squalor and poverty and degradation and it seemed incredible. It made you mad, I'll bet, didn't it? All these disease-ridden Chinamen looked like a sort of subhuman species, eh?"

Albany jumped to his feet, his face becoming more flushed. "I suppose," he shouted, "you were a sort of cosmopolitan superman who knew all about this before you ever left your Maine farm and your dissecting lab!"

"It was dished out to me like to everybody else," Fallon said, "but spread over a longer time. When I first left the ships and settled in the islands I thought this part of the world was God's backside. I stuck to the port towns where I could find other people like myself and their transplanted way of living. I was disgusted with the plain dirt and human toil everywhere I looked."

Albany grunted. "You were a boomer. I was briefed and studied special prep stuff in Washington. What in hell are you talking about?"

"It didn't do you much good, though. You got out to Chungking and saw arrogant troops and dishonest officials and got mixed up in wartime aggravations and you got sore. Don't blame you. I saw the corrupt bureaucrats and black marketeers and fouled-up army commanders too."

"Sure," Albany said. "A nation of hopeless sloppy sons of bitches squeezing and grafting and bungling, filthy and crooked and greedy. This government is trying to change things, maybe, but you can't change a race overnight. I'm sick of it!"

"You're right," Fallon said, rising. "There's still medieval law and the people are just as ragged and starving and miserable and groveling as ever. Still maltreated by officials, still beasts of burden, still hordes of conscripted paupers in the armies, still venality and ugliness and viciousness. I don't think this government is going to do much to change it. But somebody's got to start somewhere. I think maybe a start's already been made, somewhere. Things may get worse before they get better."

Albany watched him as he went to the door, a lump of muscle working in his jaw. Then he laughed shortly and reached for the bottle.

"You ought to work for the bureau, Doc," he said. "Maybe you could start changing things and curing the ills. But you'd have to work fast— they crucify wise guys like you."

"Well," Fallon said, "one way to cure ills is to take drastic measures to hasten the crisis."

7

When Fallon had closed the door, Albany walked to the open window. He could smell the alleys and the creek and could hear the sounds of the night city. And with the wind from the east across the delta, he imagined he could sniff the salt sea some twenty miles off there beyond the rice and mulberry fields and gravy-thick truck farms, the sea that stretched wide and empty and gleaming beneath the moon over the great smooth curve of the world to a remotely distant shore that had once been his homeland.

And he thought of what Fallon had said. The land lay out there westward, a writhing snakepit of malevolent terror and grinding hardship, as it was now and ever should be. Upon it stood the artisans of violence with their archaic systems of slow and sudden death, the brutal and able brigands who had succeeded a bastard monster ruling class.

Down on the creek shadowy boats drifted by. Old Bonaparte, wasn't it, who'd cracked that China was a sleeping giant, so let her sleep? Five thousand years of poppy-dreams, and now she stirred and stunk to heaven. What was needed here was not a savior but a Hercules to clean out this Augean stable, some fabulous giant to shovel out all the filth from over the buried cities and scoop away the decaying mass of misery-soaked and hopeless humanity, steam-shovel it all out, deep down to bedrock. Maybe then they could start fresh and raw. Say with a man, a woman and a water buffalo to pull the wooden plow. Then, if the world was wise, it'd leave the whole thing strictly alone for another five thousand bloody years!

He threw his glass out of the window and it tinkled on the paving below, and he heard a faint startled yelp from an unseen passer-by. He laughed aloud, the laughter reverberating in the room and making him jump. He turned back, snapped on his light, looked at his radio and reached for the dials but withdrew his hand, looked at the framed photos on the shelf and averted his face. And stood in the midst of his treasures, his glasses askew, his strong body sagging, a witness to the decline and fall, the patrician in chains at the oxcart wheel, dragged on by his barbaric captors. The man on whom a door had closed, the despised servant of a rabble, the propagandist without peer, the Voice of Asia, the Disseminator of Dung.

And a step on the stair and through the hall, the rasp of a key in a lock, the creak of a hinge, sounds he had heard earlier this evening. He reached his door and flung it open and stared, seeing the big powerful figure of Gregor Efremov, the night-prowler, returning home from his labors and pleasures.

For only a moment Albany waited, but he was charged with the need for diversion, some violence or speech or anything that would draw his spinning thoughts from his bursting skull, and he went quickly along the hall and came up as Efremov's door was shutting. It was opened immediately at his peremptory rap, and the Russian peered out in questioning surprise.

"I caught a young lady in your room tonight," said Albany in a strained voice.

"Eh?"

"Anyway, she was coming out, and had a key she said you gave her."

Efremov looked in Albany's face and smelled the odor of his breath. "Nu, nichevo," he said. "It is late, I am tired, and tell me tomorrow, yes?"

"Listen, you squareheaded dummy, somebody had a key to your room! Do you have anything valuable in there that could be stolen?"

"Ekh, friend, don't talk foolishness. I am not rich."

"No, but you have top secret stuff in those files of yours, don't you?"

Efremov looked at him again, closely, and opened the door a little wider. "Nobody has a key to this room but me," he said. "Who is this you see?"

"A girl, I said. A Chinese girl, she's a messenger, works in my department and comes up here to see me sometimes. I guess you know her. If you gave her a key, okay, and it's none of my business. But I took it away from her—took two keys away, in fact. Here they are."

Efremov accepted the yellow keys and studied them. "I gave no one a key. But—"

"Then," Albany said, brightening, "you'd better look in your files and see if anything's missing or been disturbed."

The agent considered. "Yes," he said finally. "Maybe so. Come in, dear." It was his habit; he called those whom he did not like by that affectionate term.

Albany stepped inside and shut the door while Efremov went to his cabinets, took the keys and opened them. He stood glowering over them, riffling through the folders with thick fingers, and his shadow bulged and swung against the wall from the still swaying light globe behind him. Presently he closed the drawers.

"Well?" Albany asked impatiently.

Efremov walked to his own desk and stood knuckling it for a moment, frowning. Then he nodded.

"I do not think anything has been taken," he said. "But it has been changed. I know my work like I know my hand. I am methodical. The order of the folders is changed."

"I was right, then!" Albany said in triumph.

Efremov glanced at him thoughtfully. "Yes, I think maybe. It takes two keys to reach them, but I still have my own. See, these two you have given me are the same, but newer. Now, who is this woman you speak of?"

"They call her Yin Kuei, but I suppose she's got a family name. Chung or something, I think. She's in my bureau."

"Yes." The Russian nodded, still frowning. "The devil take it! If someone has read my reports who is not authorized—"

"I take it you didn't invite her here after all," Albany said, and at the Russian's quick amused glance he added, "Well, she's only a runner but she's clever. Shall I ring up my bureau and find out what they know about her? Someone's on duty there."

"Not yet. First, does anyone else know she was here?"

"Just the doctor."

"Eh, the doctor? Oh well, he has nothing to do with this. But it might be serious. There are elements— We will go down and talk to the colonel now. If he thinks as I do, he will report it to the angels."

"What?"

Efremov smiled without mirth. "You do not know of angels, Comrade? But then, you are from a country where everyone is trusting and good. The security police. That Captain Kuo."

"Well, now," Albany said, feeling a first prod of doubt, "I don't know as I'd suspect Yin Kuei of anything like prying into your confidential stuff. After all—"

"After all," said Efremov, lifting his heavy fair brow and baring white teeth in a malicious grin, "a little Chinese lady, eh? Too bad. Do you know what the Mongols say? A hero may be willing to lose the world, but he will not be willing to lose his concubine or his horse. Let us go, hmm?"

8

Fallon slept badly and woke with a start. He lay for a time in the dawn half-light, smoking and listening to the sounds that heralded the day: the hoot of steam tugs on the stream, the slap of myriad feet of passing early workers, the tocking of a beancurd huckster advertising his portable breakfasts on the embankment, the rumble of the two-wheeled honey-carts moving like odorous and filthy cockroaches among the byways and alleys where the night-soil coolies were at work, gathering up the city's waste to trundle out into the fields and sell to farmers as fertilizer for the city's food. But his mind was not on these commonplaces; it was remembering the echo of voices and the creak of steps heard in his troubled dreams, and he knew people had been walking and talking in the hall outside his door not long before.

He rose and looked from his window at the street, and immediately noticed the bulk of a car parked before the gate. Only one car of that type came to the house, and that was the vehicle used by Captain Kuo. Fallon went to the door and opened it cautiously. There was no one about, no cracks of light showed, but from the stair well he heard noises indicating activity below on the second floor. He sat on the edge of his bed for a time, finishing his cigarette. He was alarmed, and needed no analysis to tell him why.

He dressed, then caught up his emergency medical kit and went down the stairs. On the landing he encountered a waiting constable, and saw another down in the entryway on the ground floor. There was a murmur of voices in the commandant's suite. Fallon boldly knocked.

He was admitted and found the office quarters crowded. As on a previous morning, Colonel Li was at his desk, and sitting opposite was Kuo. Both Albany and Efremov were in the room, still dressed, but Major Huang was in incongruous dishabille. Two uniformed men of Kuo's department stood at the rear. Judith only was absent.

They all stopped talking when Fallon entered and turned to look at him. He offered the explanation he had prepared: he had awakened and heard a disturbance in the sleeping house, and if the colonel's health—

Li shook his head; it was an emergency of another sort, he said. His mouth was grim. Efremov was nonchalant, Albany fidgeted nervously. Captain Kuo's strangely brilliant eyes never swerved from Fallon. The colonel's words were Fallon's dismissal, for he was the outsider here, no member of this council. He turned to leave but Kuo's flat voice halted him.

"Perhaps," said Kuo, "your physician can confirm that there was a visitor."

The suggestion was a command, and Li's face was unhappy, but not as unhappy as Albany's. Fallon waited at the door.

"You saw a person on your floor last night who does not reside in this establishment?" Kuo asked Fallon. His tone was low and unexcited.

"I told you all that," Albany said angrily before Fallon could reply. "I told you the doctor came in and saw her while I was questioning her. That's all there was to it."

When Kuo continued to look at Fallon, it was necessary to answer.

"If you mean the girl who is a frequent visitor here, a messenger from the Information Bureau, I saw her in Albany's room last night," Fallon said noncommittally.

"Was it your impression that she was here on bureau affairs, or for some other reason?"

"I know nothing about why she was here. I suggested it was late and she should leave."

"You did not see her entering or leaving Efremov's room?"

"Albany said he had noticed her leaving that room. I saw nothing."

"But," Kuo persisted blandly, "what was your impression of her visit?"

There was a sudden stir in the room behind the colonel's office and Judith came into the doorway, her hair disarrayed, her night robe hastily gathered about her. It was evident she had been listening; Judith had learned enough of the language through her association with Li to follow a conversation. She stared at Fallon and her face was flushed and her eyes were bitter.

"Why don't you tell them?" she demanded, her voice pitched high and the vernacular tumbling out broken but intelligible. "Why don't you say the wretched little slut comes here at Thorpe Albany's suggestion because he has no better taste? She comes and goes freely as a messenger, perhaps, but that isn't what he uses her for. It's disgusting!"

Colonel Li swiveled in his chair and spoke to her sharply. She hesitated, trembling with suppressed fury, and then wilted and retired into her own apartment. Li's face showed no emotion but Fallon knew he was angry, both at the interruption and at the revelation of Judith's obvious resentment. For the implication was clear to them all: she resented competition, particularly for Albany's interest.

There had always been an unspoken meeting of minds between Fallon and Li concerning Judith Markham, marked by sympathy on one side and embarrassment over a bad bargain on the other. Now Li had lost face again because of her.

"My impression," Fallon said, instinctively covering for him and answering Captain Kuo, "was that the messenger was here on business but at an indiscreet hour."

Kuo examined his own long narrow hands and said, "Well, we will soon know, when the fingerprint checks are completed." His glance was Fallon's second dismissal and the doctor went out. He took his kit back up to his room and smoked another cigarette, watching the gray day filtering across the town.

His apprehension was growing, but with it came a stubborn urge to lash out, to take some positive action. He felt no guilt but a strong responsibility. He had gone along with Yin Kuei's and Tieh's scheme and supplied them with the keys they required; his cooperation could not end there. Already, he realized, he was implicated somehow in Kuo's manhunting brain. And Fallon also realized that his faith had stiffened overnight in that ephemeral underground resistance; in his mind it had taken on strength, depth and effectiveness. There must be something to it because there was deliberate official talk about it. The talk, of course, was to stir up civic fears and wraths and keep the public on guard and disciplined. Whatever it was, it had better be alert; an underground would have rough sledding in a nation whose leadership was composed of ruthless men who had spent their own lives in underground endeavors until lately. They knew from hard experience how to deal with recalcitrants.

Presently Fallon put on his hat, took up his visiting bag again, and went down the stairs. It was early light, and in the entry he met Major Huang, now dressed. The major looked at him in surprise and Fallon explained that Father Julien was in a critical condition and he intended to visit the hospital.

"Aaah," the adjutant nodded absently, "the old running-dog! Why the colonel protects such a parasite I do not know. And for that matter, why the colonel protects such another parasite as he keeps in his rooms I do not know either. It is disgraceful to be the slave of such a creature!"

Fallon grinned; these were strong words for Major Huang, and the man realized it as they were spoken and glanced quickly about to see that the constables were not in earshot.

"Never mind. I'm talking to myself, going balmy! I suppose I must sit up on guard all night to keep streetwalkers from sneaking in and out of the premises! I get the blame for this business, whatever it turns out to be—theft or lust. But you can be sure Kuo will take that little messenger girl by the heels soon enough, and then we'll see. I wish the colonel would throw both his silly woman and his drunken propagandist in the river and get down to some work."

"And his doctor also," Fallon murmured.

"No, no, the colonel needs you, I-sheng," Huang protested nervously. "I don't know why, but there's always something wrong with him, and none of these other quacks know their jobs. You are a good man, and it's only too bad you are so deliberately blind to the truths and facts of this life, and don't freely join us."

"I'm like the old priest—just a foreign dog's hips," Fallon said, and went out. In the street he melted into the morning throngs and walked toward the river. But at the Garden Bridge, instead of crossing it he turned the other way up the wide Bund and went purposefully along the paving until he approached the Nanking Road corner where the great hotel reared into early autumn mists.

The big clock in the tower of the Customs House told him that it was nearly the hour when government offices opened, and the crowds about him here were clerks and minor officials. As he drew near the hotel entrance he slowed his pace, then stopped. He did not know the half a dozen men lounging about the door, but he knew their attitudes and the set of their faces. They were Kuo's plain-clothes men, as obvious as such types are anywhere in the great cities of the world, and their purpose was evident to him, if not to the unmindful workers hurrying by.

Fallon was always conscious of his height and color; in the swollen city of nearly six million there were few enough left of his sort, and he stepped into an alley running along the rear of the hotel, and went through it among the slops and refuse until he had bypassed the entrance and came out into Nanking Road. He had learned where Yin Kuei lived; she had told him that no one but Tieh knew of her actual residence though she was registered elsewhere and her papers gave another address. It was a poor and rundown district not far from here and he knew she walked to and from her work. Near the Szechwan Road intersection he lingered in the arcade of a building that had once housed a famous British department store with a proud century of profitable trade on its ledgers; it was now occupied by an agency dedicated to the control of the regional rice supply and price. It was too close to the hotel, but here he could best waylay the girl.

His luck was with him and his patience rewarded: he saw her coming, after a time, and as she was passing he spoke her name. She paused, startled, staring at him in the dim shelter, and then stepped up beside him where he stood in the empty backwater of the current.

"Paul!" she said. "What are you doing here?"

"Waiting for you," he said, looking down at her gentle beauty, his gaze touching the skin like old ivory, the large dark eyes and delicate nose, the soft curve of her throat and breast. He felt a new surge of tenderness for her; his hand gripped her arm as though he would draw her close.

She understood immediately. "Albany?" she asked, her voice calm. "He reported me?"

Fallon nodded. "They're watching for you at your office. Kuo's people. I came to tell you you mustn't go near there now. Kuo has your fingerprints—I suppose you left them all over Efremov's place. Doesn't your tong even teach you modern methods of burglary? Tieh at least should have taken the risk!"

"You came like a dashing prince to my rescue last night," she smiled. "Albany was making me a most immoral proposition, really. I suppose the Russian found something wrong?" When he nodded, she said, "Well, it doesn't matter. I was ready to leave the bureau anyway—there are too many other things to do that are important. But I must warn Lao-hu, as you have warned me."

"Let Tieh fend for himself," Fallon said almost angrily. "He got you into this—now you've got the police after you."

"He'll be coming along here very soon," she said, her brow wrinkled with concentration. "I'll go back up the street and intercept him on his way."

"What will you do then?"

"I told you—the work that is more important. Lao-hu and the others will find more than enough for me. I can go to live with his wife and him."

Fallon had not been aware that Tieh was married. Somehow it made the man more human and considerably more acceptable to the doctor.

"You must let me know," he said. "Tieh must keep in touch with me. He can do it best at the hospital; I'll try to be there most every evening when not many people are about. But I must keep track of you, Yin Kuei."

She met his eyes. "Yes, of course, Paul," she said, her lips parting in a quick smile. "Just as I must keep track of you too. We're all in this together."

"Exactly," Fallon said dryly. "Let's keep together—I don't want to lose you."

"That's what I meant," she said. "I know you're concerned about me. And I for you."

"You miss the point."

"No, I don't think so. Do you think I'm a little girl? Do you think I lived the sheltered life of a dutiful daughter all the while we were in America? I've gone to your schools and talked to other girls and boys. I've read your books and seen your plays. I've been around!"

She was laughing at him and he was confused. "Then act your age, Yin Kuei!"

"Which is only fourteen years less than yours," she retorted. She leaned out of the arcade, casting swift glances in both directions. "I must go," she said. "Lao-hu will come to see you very soon."

"I don't want to see Tieh, I want to see you."

"He'll bring you to me, Paul." She stood on tiptoe and quickly kissed him, and was gone. Leaving him alone in the arcade with the full morning shining on the streets and the people walking past, casting curious or indifferent glances toward him. He stood for a moment, feeling his lips still warm with the swift touch, no longer entirely alone among a people that had turned inexplicably against his kind.

Then he tramped back toward the hospital, avoiding the route past the hotel and the waiting police, who would wait impatiently for a long time. Captain Kuo would be extremely annoyed.

9

Now neither Captain Kuo's impatience nor that of his minions was comparable to the impatience of Paul Fallon. But while Kuo might vent his irritation on everyone who crossed his path, including the unfortunates of the Information Bureau and all the occupants of Number 68, Fallon must conceal his feelings and go about his daily routine as usual, though more quietly if possible to avoid the captain's shrewd attention.

Kuo instituted another round of interrrogations and no one was neglected, from the infuriated Colonel Li Han-tsen and his razor-tongued blond mistress down through the harassed adjutant and his staff to the last kitchen coolie. But the security officer reserved his special sessions for Efremov, who was as cooperative as his arrogant nature permitted,

Albany, who was reduced to quivering impotence by a forced but complete confession of his basic intentions toward Yin Kuei, and Fallon himself, who was laconic and unfriendly after his ordinary pattern.

The degree of importance of the raid on Efremov's files was measured in detail by the agent and the captain and was judged to be high, for Efremov's completed reports were of an international significance. Just what they implied might be obscure to Kuo, who was not a planner or provocateur but an efficient policeman. He was not so concerned about that as about the vulnerability of Colonel Li's headquarters and the inability of his own formidable organization to turn up, from the city's bubbling scum, so simple a bit of flotsam as Chung Yin-kuei, a hitherto insignificant girl in a petty post with a government bureau.

Her dossier was relatively complete; it disclosed many ominous items to Kuo that had been overlooked by her superiors, and he took them severely to task for their carelessness. Albany protested that he had had no idea whatever that Yin Kuei was a returned student; she had never said a word to him of nearly a decade's residence in America, and he had only supposed that her fluent English, even to the casual slang, was due to mission schooling and perhaps close association with American soldiers and sailors of the postwar liberation period. Kuo regarded Albany's obtuseness with suspicion, but let it go at that.

Fallon simply denied any knowledge whatever of Yin Kuei, and there was nothing to indicate to Kuo that he was lying. The doctor had no relationship with the bureau where she had been assigned.

Kuo pondered over the dossier for many hours, drawing numbers of peculiar conclusions from it. She was of the upper and intellectual classes, her father being a teacher who had lived long abroad and had been tolerated briefly by the regime on his return until his reactionary philosophy was disclosed, after which he had vanished into a northern prison. The girl's address listed at the bureau was found to be fictitious. Why she had ever been trusted in any government office, even with serving the tea or cleaning the earthenware spittoons, Kuo could not imagine. It revealed again the same old chinks in the armor, through which the enemy bored into the sensitive body of a struggling new nation.

Captain Kuo Liang was an assiduous and single-minded man. He normally spent a working day of sixteen to twenty hours, slept on a bunk in an alcove in his office at the Central Police Station—an office that had once been occupied by the British assistant commissioner of Settlement Police—and he was always tired, but never too tired to do his complex job with thoroughness. He had, actually, great strength and endurance, a heritage of generations of Shantung farmers who had wrested a meager living from sterile hill-patches. He was highly literate, a self-educated person who had spent much time in the political police sections of the Red Army, and he fancied himself a master of psychology, which was not too far from the mark. He was an agnostic and unmarried, despising women because they distracted men from their work for the State. His techniques were deft. He could be cruel but he was not normally sadistic. A fifty-hour-long inquisition of a prisoner or suspect he did not regard as extraordinary if it got results. He was usually mild in manner and cultivated in speech, and he spoke some Russian and English. His past had been adventurous, hazardous and hard, and it had taught him how to combat a network of counterrevolutionaries and how to trap and exterminate traitors. He headed a remarkable apparatus with an alertness that was almost neurotic. In this Yin Kuei case, as in most similar cases, he considered the situation very harmful.

The problem obsessed him. And he had made an extremely astute discovery. He had learned something about one Tieh Lao-hu. The fellow was a stevedore foreman who had been under suspicion for some time because of reportedly irregular activities aboard ships in the port. The river police had had their eye on him. He was now missing from his job and his usual haunts. Kuo linked him to this case for the simple reason that at one time in the past Tieh had been employed in a menial capacity in the Information Bureau and was known there to have been friendly with Miss Chung. Why should they vanish at the same moment unless they were accomplices in this business? Tieh's incomplete dossier lay with Yin Kuei's on the desk in the below-stairs office Kuo had requisitioned from the adjutant. But Tieh's brief personal history was, while spotty, nothing to arouse special interest aside from this coincidence of disappearing. Kuo thumbed through it while Fallon, who had been brought in for another talk, waited with resignation.

"But you say you never knew this Tieh?" Kuo asked, turning his sphynxlike colorless face toward the doctor.

"Why should I?"

"That is no answer. Never mind. Now coming back to this time when you say you met the girl. She was looking for Albany, and brought some proofs for him. What about that?"

"I let her dry out in my room while she waited. He didn't return, so she left."

"What did you talk about, then?"

"Nothing important that I recall. She didn't stay long and I was uninterested in her."

"Just as you are uninterested in whether I succeed in finding this woman. As you are uninterested in anything that we are doing here in this city, and in this country, and are only interested in getting out if you can manage it. I suppose you realize that you are a very lucky person not to be under arrest, instead of enjoying the patronage of Colonel Li? Many of your countrymen are not so fortunate, you know."

"I'm aware of that."

"We have a few of these wreckers and foreign spies behind bars where they belong, and others under house detention. You should demonstrate your gratitude for your freedom by helping us. How could you spend an evening with a young woman who had lived for years in your country and not talk about it, or question her, or learn something about her views and activities and friends?"

"She didn't mention my country. She was just another office messenger to me."

Kuo did not lose his icy self-possession. He lit a cigarette and then, as an afterthought, offered Fallon the pack. Fallon declined and filled his pipe.

"I suppose you know," said Kuo, "that these reports that were tampered with concern a part of the world with which you are especially familiar. The Philippines, you know, where you lived for some time."

"Where I fought the Japanese, just as you were fighting them here at that period."

"Yes. Well, we fought a common enemy then and we have another common enemy now, but you don't realize it, or won't admit it. Down there, those ragged Huks are struggling just as we did against the oppressive big landlords and a decaying government whose policies are bankrupt. They fight, as we fought, for reforms that are urgently needed. A peasants' revolution is coming there, led by men with a tradition of half a century of revolt behind them, ever since your American imperialism began in those islands. You were with them when they spread guerrilla terror against the Japanese, but you didn't stay with them. Why you came here, I don't know, for your sympathies are not with us."

"My sympathies are with the people who are sick and wounded and need help, regardless of their politics. The need seemed greater here than in the islands. More practically, I got a job with a relief organization."

"Well, it is nice if one can afford such humanitarian pursuits. The need is also great in other places with which those same reports of Efremov's deal." Kuo flipped over Fallon's own dossier. "Indo-China, for instance. You had specialized in tropical medicine, and if you wished to come to the mainland to practice after the war you might have gone there and not become entangled with us here, whom you apparently despise. But you may have had some secret motive in coming here, eh?"

The trend seemed aimless to Fallon; Kuo frequently led him into oblique discussions. He shrugged and said nothing.

"You might have gone to Saigon or Hanoi and helped the French imperialists in their brutal efforts to reimpose colonial rule upon a strongly nationalistic race. Or if you love the people so much, you might even have gone to doctor our sick and wounded in the jungle who fight as guerrillas under Ho against foreigners who would destroy their proud traditions and who deny them any social or economic benefits. These reports by Efremov show that the French are now in a catastrophic position, as well they may be in their futile attempts to put out the raging fire. Their efforts are too late, they fail despite aid from your country with heavy weapons for the campaigns of mercenaries. It is proving a costly war in men and money for the colonials."

"I know nothing about the situation in Annam," Fallon murmured.

"I know. But I am giving you a little lesson. You might need the information if Colonel Li should take you there, or if he could be persuaded to part with your services. You might be sent to doctor the free fighters, you know." Kuo smiled enigmatically. "It would do you no harm to see our volunteers throwing the stubborn French into the sea, along with their despicable puppet rulers. They're besieged in all their ports, their big redoubts are crumbling along the frontiers, and the flames are spreading."

Kuo traced a long smooth finger across his desk in a sweeping gesture. "We push aggressors and enemies out on both our flanks—from Korea in the north to Cambodia in the south. Presently, in our center, we will hurl them from their precarious little footholds on Hongkong and Taiwan. And then, my friend, from where will the support come for these termites here among us who spy and sabotage and work against us in miserable little groups? Who will this girl Yin Kuei turn to then, with her stolen campaign plans? To whom can she fly for protection when our wrath descends? No one will be left to aid her or her friends, probably this fellow Tieh among them. She is lost!"

He kept his watchful eyes fixed on Fallon. The doctor stirred and knocked the ashes from his pipe into his hand. "How true," said Fallon. "She is indeed lost, apparently, to you."

Kuo's face stiffened; he did not understand levity, and nonchalance pricked his skin.

"She will be found," he said. "We will find these people, whoever they are, wherever they are, and one by one tear off their hides."

"An effective way to eliminate opposition," Fallon said unperturbedly. "Rather unscientific, from a surgeon's viewpoint. Crude and bloody."

"The crude and bloody method has its advantages in my own branch of science," said Kuo. "If you happen to be concealing any knowledge from me, you will very likely learn that. You may leave. It is time for the noon meal."

10

On an evening of soft fog Fallon, relieved of further questioning, strolled on the Bund and sought that small bit of bypassed solitude afforded there in the immense loom of the bridge, the little park on the foreshore overlooking the broad curve of the river and the mouth of the creek. He sat on a bench beneath a tree near the spot where he had once launched a futile attempt to shake the dust of this frenzied city from his feet. From the bench he could watch the slinking water in the twilight, and the stark outline of the bridge above was made almost graceful by a gentle lifting of mist. Its reflection, and those of passing river craft, were artfully distorted in the murk of the converging streams. The boats went slowly by—the great ungainly barges, the cargo lighters with their straw-stack housings, the disreputable Wenchow junks working downstream on their way to the vast Yangtze estuary and the sea beyond. The traffic, as ever, was dense, but all was in wavering focus.

He had heard nothing from Tieh, though a week had passed and Captain Kuo appeared to be exhausting his resources. Fallon pursued his labors among the wards and surgeries, independent and detached. Others swaggered the hospital corridors in the uniforms of the Army and the party, but his uniform was a cotton gown, and the badge of his magic office was the revered *ting-ting kason*, the stethoscope. He had no illusions about what was being accomplished there. Nothing yet devised could stem pestilence and disease, mankind united could not halt the wars that fostered them, and only the gods themselves might take a hand in the great periodic famines, floods and droughts that swept the land in a recurring series of catastrophes so vast as to be beyond comprehension.

Once, very recently it seemed, Fallon had been tempted to flee the whole festering and tumultuous East, as from the plague, breaking out of a situation that had been growing intolerable. Now he had somehow become entangled with something that persistently intruded into and was starting to fill his personal life. Strange as it might sound to the echoing walls of his more austere mind, he had to speak it to himself: he loved her.

He tried to recall his first impression of her, that she was a lovely and sweet-faced, almost doll-like child, with all the attributes of attractive Chinese children. But ultimately he knew that Yin Kuei was no child, either in body or mind, although he was not so strongly convinced about her spirit. He thought of her: a girl a little taller than average, more robust, her individuality not pressed into a pattern. She was not the national ideal: women for centuries had been subjugated, secluded and sacrificing, their virtues centered in obedience and inequality. They had not known or wanted freedom, though they had ruled the homes and tilled the fields. Now such women were ridiculed. The model of the good wife and wise mother was old-fashioned. A young woman was expected to read the chosen books and do the assigned work of the State, relegating romance to the past along with concubinage and foot-binding, and break the restraints of her bondage. The net result, Fallon pondered, had not been entirely happy.

Wisdom and dignity had been abdicated by a people rushing to embrace a solemn adolescent anger. They had become boring and boastful exhibitionists, wallowing in a vast ideological bath and thoroughly enjoying it. Clever brains now memorized slogans and parroted empty phrases. Cherished values meant nothing any more. The first spontaneous enthusiasms were dying. Fallon could anticipate their exact language, behaviour and reaction; the idiom of their patter never varied. Nimble minds had withered in an arid intellectual climate. The new mental furtiveness was degrading to him.

But Yin Kuei was not like that. He had never known anyone like her before.

Fallon's experience of women was not exceptional one way or another. It was perhaps more varied than that, say, of former classmates who had settled down long before to community practices and homemaking wives. On the other hand, it was much less extensive than more recent friends and colleagues might imagine unless they were intimate with him, and few ever became that. Not because Fallon was a frigid man, either in admitting friends or temporary lady companions to his inner counsels, but because he was highly selective, a trait he himself regarded as a vice rather than a virtue. It would have made a wandering life much easier for him to have modified his qualifications for companionship, and he occasionally studied the puzzle of his heritage, for the Irish are not an exclusive or overly discriminating lot, nor celebrated for their discipline or emotional reserve. But he concluded that the Irish strain had been considerably diminished by the toll in sweat of three generations, poured into New England's flinty soils. He did not care to explore beyond that point, skirting the pitfalls of self-analysis.

For a man who had been exposed to many lonely and vulnerable women on long voyages, alleviating their sea-qualms and more complicated ills in the soothing atmosphere of ship dispensaries, Fallon considered that he had acquitted himself with remarkable though not inhuman restraint. And the plantation villages of Samar, the relaxing byways of Manila, even the forbidding hinterland of loess plains and barren hills behind the marching armies of the north, had not been devoid of women. There were women everywhere for those who sought them, even for those who did not search. And Fallon was bound to confess that he had known a few even as entrancing as Yin Kuei. Superficially, he amended.

He had, in fact, at one time been legally married, and this was a thing that astonished him whenever his thoughts dwelt on it, which was becoming increasingly rare. For that had been for a period of a year in the dim and thoroughly dead past of his internship, and he could not now conjure even a clear recollection of her features. He remembered only an absurdly pretty pile of tight auburn curls and a dulcet voice that could grow strident on short notice when matters of opportunities and economic security were introduced into the conversation. She had been a nurse in a Boston hospital, and she had gone on to better things, he supposed, while he'd gone on to sea. At least, he hoped she had. One deserved whatever one fought for so valiantly. Only for him it had been useless. The sea had offered a living not to be rejected, a chance not too common in those hard years for a young doctor deep in debt for his education. And the sea had eventually brought him to this place; he could thank it for Yin Kuei.

In the darkness just before Fallon's withdrawn gaze a soft glow flickered. Becoming gradually aware of it he slipped forward on the bench, leaning over the low rail of the embankment, and looked down. A flight of short stone steps led to the water and a long sampan was moored there to an iron ring. The boat rose and fell gently under the swift slide of the tidal ebb, its flat bow rhythmically slapping the surface, and back under the open mat shelter he saw that the illumination came from a charcoal brazier about which the boat family squatted, filling its rice bowls from the common iron pot above the heat. And over their heads on a bamboo crossbeam swung a single oiled-paper lantern containing a candle. It was a common cargo boat, used for transporting produce into the city, and the people were one of the countless river families—the boatman, his woman, their children, and the usual graybeard ancient mumbling through his chopsticks.

It was the swaying lantern that caught Fallon's bemused eyes. It was an ordinary lamp such as was sold for a few coppers in the waterside markets, but as with so many common utility articles it was shaped and painted with a delicate artistry. The lantern revolved slowly from its string, bringing its several sides into perspective, and Fallon saw that on the red paper had been illustrated in green and gold a number of symbols. He had seen them often before, they being ordinary standardized decorations, and recognized them for the Buddhist emblems: the Wheel of the Law, the Conch-shell of royalty, the Umbrella of rank, the auspicious Canopy, the Lotus of purity, the Jar and the Fish of abundance. There was an eighth face to the lamp and the symbol there was one he knew only as the Mystic Knot, but its significance was lost to him.

He must have made a small noise or his face caught a gleam of light, for they all became aware of him at once and squatted motionless, looking up at the queer outlander's head and shoulders thrust over the embankment edge, watching them. Their chopsticks were still, the mouths of the children gaped and the *laodah's* narrow eyes widened.

Fallon smiled. He pointed at the lantern. "Lao-yeh, I only sit and admire your beautiful lamp," he said. "Please pardon my bad manners."

They took his intrusion in stride, the children laughed, the boatman nodded. And the grandfather, displaying his gums, agreed that the lamp was indeed a good one, though old and somewhat torn.

"I understand the markings on it," Fallon said, "all except the Knot. I am an ignorant foreigner; will you tell me what it means?"

"Eh, eh, the Knot?" The elder looked at the lantern solemnly. "Why that, as everybody knows, is—well, it is the Knot." He paused, wrinkling up his brown face in reflection, and the children laughed again, and their mother hushed them. "Well, that is, it is the Knot of longevity, as any man can see! It is a part of the whole, it has always been—"

He abandoned his attempt to explain this abstraction for he had never been called upon before, out of a clear night sky by a foreign devil, to tell just what it signified. He got up, his bare knees creaking, reached into the shadowy recesses of the mat roof, and brought out a length of worn silk cord, something torn and discarded from some larger and highly decorative piece, perhaps a tassel from a great temple hanging. He held it up in his claw.

"This is the same Knot," he said, now on firmer ground. "You see? It is woven into a ball of twisting cords that never end. It brings long life. Look at me! I have seventy and three years, myself." He thumped his lean chest and grinned and they all laughed again, and Fallon joined the laughter, thanking him.

But the *laodah's* wife spoke quickly and at some length and they listened; Fallon did not know her dialect and they saw he was not following her words. She shyly lowered her eyes in the smooth, still-young face, and sat smiling as the old man muttered and grumbled a bit over her foolishness. Then he looked up again, shrugging at a woman's nonsense, and said, "My worthless daughter says that the Knot is not only for long life, but also for constant and never-ending love!" He spat out the phrase, adding, "Whatever she means by that!"

Fallon looked at the Knot and the grandfather mistook his stare for one of admiration for the tassel's color and soft beauty.

"Here," said the elder, reaching up. "It is yours. Take it; no, no—take it, I say! It is nothing, a poor thing I found floating in the river and put away and forgot. I give it to you."

Fallon took the cord. He thanked the old man and all of them, and they bobbed their heads with glee and the children laughed and everyone was happy, and the rice steamed in the pot and the water lapped at the boat. Fallon accepted the gift as it was offered and sat back again on the bench, holding it in his hand. The Knot of old men, or the Knot of lovers, it was the same, an endless weaving and forming of a pattern.

Presently, with the meal finished, the boat family bustled around below, untied the sampan and poled off downstream into the gloom, where ships' mooring lights threw spangles across the water and the sampan splintered them into thousands of fragments of silver and velvet. Fallon watched it vanishing, leaving only the bobbing coins of reflection, and the knotted tassel lay warm in his palm.

The Drum Tower

III

The day was unseasonably brisk for so early in the fall. A benign sun deposited golden pools of warmth in the sheltered streets. But a breeze popped and cracked the five-star flag of the People's Republic from a thousand poles above the roofs. It was an exhilarating day, after the long summer's damp heat, and Colonel Li decided to walk home through the city. It was an unusual course, for the colonel shared with most of his countrymen an abhorrence of anything smacking of unnecessary exertion, and when he dismissed his driver the man looked at him doubtfully and had to have the order repeated.

But the colonel, who was in his middle years, had always lived actively and the sedentary nature of his present work demanded periods of exercise, whether he liked it or not. He was proud of his lean hard body and deplored the lassitudes that sometimes seized him, and hated the first layer of forming fat, particularly about the waist and neck. The deep bronze of his skin had faded in these past four years indoors, the snapping clarity was missing from his eyes under which he detected dark pouches. He spent a good deal of time pessimistically examining himself, naked in his bathroom beside the big round Soochow tub or before a long mirror; his shelves and bedside stand were stocked with elixirs and balms he purchased from apothecaries in defiance of Dr. Fallon's disapproval. Beside the two major burdens of the flesh he bore—diabetes and ulcers—he seemed heir to nearly all the ills that overstocked the country, and in his anxiety to triumph over them he often suffered ailments his physician could not detect.

But today the colonel felt relatively well and he strode along in a smart military manner through the crowds, drawing attention only by his height and vigorous bearing because he had chosen to wear civilian dress, reverting to a black silk robe of the old style and a commonplace fedora. This gave him a pleasant sense of anonymity. He did not relish the spotlight, and while the nature of his confidential work spared him much of the glare, he could not entirely avoid it. For he stood high in the councils and was forever being called upon to attend functions, reviews and displays, speak at mass meetings and demonstrations, and make other uniformed appearances with the local dignitaries for the instruction of the public.

He had been on a routine duty call across the city in the former French Concession and now he walked back toward his intentionally obscure headquarters in the old Settlement, following a route with which he was familiar from former days, down through Avenue Joffre and along Boulevard de Montigny and swinging across the busy square past the Great World amusement center into Tibet Road bordering the Race Course. The Race Course, that is, of prewar extrality times, the great open recreation ground in the heart of the crowded community where the British and other European businessmen and the Americans had once raced their Mongolian ponies under gentlemen jockeys and played their games of cricket and rugger and baseball. It was now filled with flimsy mat barracks and other unsightly structures that offended the colonel's aesthetic eye, but of course he would have told no one that, nor would he have said that he had rather enjoyed Race Week in the bad old years and preferred the obsolete names of streets to the new ones arbitrarily chosen by the Republic since the Takeover.

The fact that the colonel had once made Shanghai his home was known to many, but it was generally supposed that he had been one of the militant and police-hounded Soviet Opposition at that time, working from a hideout in the era of the Kuomintang terror. Only a few knew that the colonel had actually occupied a considerably higher and more tranquil position in life during that distant period, having been a Kuomintang army officer stationed at the arsenal. By mutual agreement of his superiors this was glossed over in his party dossier. The concealment of his defection to the Reds at the head of a company on the Kiangsi front during the early anti-Communist campaigns twenty years previously had been part of the terms of his transfer. Expediency and the colonel's mastery of his profession had helped to bury the past.

Nevertheless, in walking alone through the city he was not required to view it with the critical and supercilious eye of the New Order, and could indulge his private recollections and thin nostalgia. He had little expectation of bumping into former comrades; most of them were now dead and the survivors were probably across on Formosa, savoring the bitter gall of rout, defeat and exile. Nor was he likely to meet his first wife or any of her family, who were refugees somewhere in the south whither his father-in-law, a nationalist banker, had carried them.

He dawdled a little in the sunshine on Tibet Road, for it had once been his favorite district for relaxation. Only the surface had changed— the flags and the signs, reflecting the present and the ambitious hope for the future. The past remained in full view: the second-class theatrical hotels where the lacquered girls swarmed like butterflies, the old men leisurely strolling with caged songbirds and crickets on their arms, the tiny jewelry and silk shops, the dealers transacting business in the little tea stalls. It was as if there had been no change at all, and the street openly flaunted its unconcern with decrees.

Colonel Li was not entirely disconcerted by all this. It was universal in a city that seemed to speak aloud, in its jeering clamor and raucous disregard for new convention, of a deep-grained aloofness toward upstarts, a coarse-nerved and grim-humored cynicism about the superficialities of the passing scene. Li would have been faintly disappointed if the populace had displayed any other attitude. He himself, a normally volatile and progressive Szechwan product, had acquired more cautious habits of mind in recent years beyond the usual fund of mellowness, patience and indifference of middle life. He repressed the sudden ardors, he played it safe when he could without drawing attention of his superiors, and he had developed skepticisms he kept under wraps. Being a realist, he knew that all problems boil down to that of the rice bowl and that in the long run all law, government and public institutions must fail in some degree. Li had no special philosophy and expected to see no utopia, and he knew very well that his fellow men were slow to change their habits and customs. There were a few hotheads among them, but so far as Li was concerned he had seen evidence that the good men, the natural leaders, always avoided leadership and stayed out of it in some disguise, if possible. A measure of leadership had been thrust upon him by destiny but he did not want it, for the wheel of the system ground leaders small.

Now sauntering along the street he observed the old men with their birds and the painted girls posing negligently in the doorways and the ogling apprentices and the runners and idlers and gawping soldiery and marketing women, and he came to a huddle of people blocking the way and paused in curiosity. In their center, seated against a wall, was a blind man, a wandering beggar whose stock in trade was entertainment. He was a storyteller, squatting among his dusty rags and tatters, and he was relating with great verve and animation one of the old tales of Lau Shu, the legendary outlaw hero of whom everyone has heard.

"And so while traveling among these wild mountains," the beggar was saying as Colonel Li bent an ear, "Lau Shu was suddenly attacked by a huge fierce tiger. The beast, slavering with hunger, leaped upon him. But the valiant Lau Shu seized the tiger by the leg and dashed its head against a big rock, and slew it!"

The storyteller halted, the crowd shuffled in anticipation of the expected moral, and a few coppers showered down at the man's feet on the paving. He raised his head.

"That mountain cat was tough," he said, his wide mouth curling back in a toothless grin, "but he was no match for that rock!"

His audience was startled and gratified and the people raised hands to hide sly smiles, and nudged with elbows and glanced hastily around, and a few frowned, and many walked quickly away, Colonel Li among them. As he went, he heard more coins dropped for the storyteller.

He pushed on more rapidly toward home, for work was waiting there. But as he walked he thought about the story of Lau Shu, and a faint smile touched his own mouth. The brazen beggar had a nerve, he reflected, for there might have been plain-clothes men in the crowd. But the people were becoming bolder. Li wondered if it would be amusing to repeat this story at dinner to Major Huang and decided against it. The adjutant was too nervous for such lightness. The word for "cat," of course, was all right, being *mao*. But the narrator had used the colloquial term *shek* for the word "rock."

Well, Li thought, making his way down Nanking Road, perhaps Dr. Fallon might enjoy it—if the joke didn't have to be explained to him, for Fallon's knowledge of vernacular had its limitations, even if his appreciation of subversion did not. Fallon would probably pass it on to old Father Julien at the hospital, but otherwise it would not be repeated. Certainly not to Albany, whom Li regarded with restrained irritation. He did not quite realize it though the hint was sometimes close to the surface, but the fact that Li himself had defected in the past set his teeth on edge in another turncoat's presence. He told himself that he simply did not like foreigners, Americans in particular—with the exception of the doctor, naturally. He did not even care for Efremov, though he had to put up with the fellow.

Li's stable of foreign protégés was sometimes embarrassing to him, when dignitaries chided him about it over the wine cups. They all knew of Li's eccentricities, his morbid hypochondria, and they were tolerant. He was not only respected but he wielded an influence most of his associates in other bureaus and departments did not possess, and the nature of his special work they only vaguely understood. That he should be entrusted with this branch of the Southeast Asia Bureau baffled them, since so far as they were aware he was purely a soldier and had never been any nearer the exotic regions of Nan Yang than Canton. But a personal knowledge of Indonesia and all those mysterious southern lands was obviously not a requisite for the post; Colonel Li was an efficient organizer and director, and it was queer people like the overseas fellows he had on his staff and outlanders like Efremov who did the specialty jobs.

At any rate, it explained to them the presence in his ménage of Efremov and, to a certain extent, of Albany. And his personal anxieties, which mildly amused them, were excuse enough for the doctor he had taken under his wing. For Li's championship of Fallon was fierce and loyal, despite the man's stubborn refusal to compromise or cooperate in any way beyond jabbing Li and his suffering subordinates with the hollow needle, and for this he got only an extended reprieve from the Ward Road Prison. Li occasionally insisted that some day he would free the doctor, but all knew that any such release depended on the fluctuations in Li's health.

So far as the colonel's lady was concerned, his colleagues had nothing to say at all—to him. A man had the right to choose his own poison, but why he should have saddled himself with such a foreign hussy they could not imagine. If she had been an expatriate Russian it might have been clearer: many men had a perverted taste for white flesh, and it had been common enough in the old times among those who could afford it—warlords, wealthy merchants, even emperors. But she was a stinking Britisher, and as such was outside the pale. They knew her story, or the story Li had caused to be spread, but they did not believe it for a moment. They said she was undoubtedly straight out of a Kiangsi Road brothel. She did not like Li's friends and they did not like her; they thought her boorish and ill-tempered and a thorn in his bosom, yet he nurtured her. It was beyond reason.

And he nurtured also that old man in the hospital, the French priest, the representative of a state within the State and even of a state above the State. He was a puppet controlled by a Church in Rome, subject to his own religious commonwealth, loyal to an authoritarian structure far away. They should not have tolerated or protected the old running-dog for a minute. But Li, as they repeated, had his peculiarities.

The colonel came into the house a little breathless in the late afternoon, knowing he should not have delayed so long on his walk. His body cried for insulin, and he hoped the doctor was there, otherwise he would have to give it to himself since Judith would not touch the needle, declaring it made her ill. He was about to mount the stairs to his rooms when Major Huang put his head out of the office door to see who had entered. His harassed expression eased at sight of the colonel.

"Sir, I have waited for you since your driver returned and said you were walking. We have an urgent communication from the Secretariat. Captain Kuo has already been notified." He held out a dispatch.

Li glanced at it impatiently, one foot on the step, then read it carefully, wrinkling his brow.

"But who is this fellow, that we should roll out the crimson carpet for him?" he demanded. "He is not identified here."

"No sir," said Huang. "He is obviously too important to identify until he arrives by the plane tonight. You only have time to dress and drive to the airport to welcome him, and I will have to call in the staff if he is to be shown the work of the bureau tomorrow. His suite at the hotel is already set aside."

Li frowned. "Damn these junketing Russians!" he said loudly. "Damn their arrogant eyes, with their swank and rudeness and ignorant barbarian manners! I spend half my time lately playing host to them and taking them on guided tours and giving them polite lectures, and they expect me to lick their big dirty boots for it. I've never had a word of thanks from one of them for our hospitality—to them, everything is a matter of course, as if we were just another of their sniveling satellites. They sneer and want the best and make coarse jibes about it and swill good food and wine and demand women, and we put them to bed drunk in silk robes. And they go back to Peking and make complaints, and make more when they get home. Who in hell is this so-important traveler and his retinue that we must turn out a special guard corps and not even know his name? Eh?"

Major Huang had listened to this outburst with resignation. "Sir, I don't know," he said sadly. "Somebody very special, apparently. But I must remind you of the time."

"Blast the time! I've got to have a shot in the leg. Is the doctor in?" He stumbled hurriedly up the stairway, unbuttoning his gown. "Damn the unmentionable obscenities from Russia!"

2

The doctor was not in; Colonel Li had to administer his own medication. At that moment Fallon was a mile away, idling on a street corner in the heart of the district called Nantao, the Old City around which a great stone wall had once stood to protect honest merchants from piratical sea raiders. The wall was gone, the fourteenth-century buccaneers with their high-pooped junks and brass cannon were only legend, but the maze of cobblestoned alleys that had wound inside the battlements remained. In former years, Shanghailanders of the Settlement and Concession had, with flippant disregard for geographical or political precision, called this medieval slum Chinatown; in tropical Asia it would have been termed the native quarter, or the kampong. Now it was simply an extension of the larger city, distinguished by overcrowding in the most overcrowded community on the seaboard.

Fallon stood before a small open-front shop in the center of the bazaar and tried to make himself inconspicuous, an impossibility. Foreigners had never penetrated Nantao in large numbers except as guided tourist parties from cruise liners, and now a Westerner was something at which the shopkeepers and blue-gowned crowds might stop and gape. He shifted irresolutely, not knowing whether to wait longer or to return home. But his hand in his trouser pocket felt the slip of directions that had been pressed upon him by a passing pedicab coolie near the hospital gate that morning, and he determined to give Tieh another quarter-hour.

The air was thick but fairly cool under the bamboo *pengs* that arched over the narrow Street of Jade where he loitered; sunlight filtered through the matting to scatter yellow patches on the ancient stones like fallen autumn leaves. High above rose the rickety wooden tenements with curved eaves and ridges to form a sea of sway-backed and weather-beaten roofs, occasionally broken by a low pagoda-like tower or the spire of a guild house. Fallon had strolled to this designated point by slow stages, not wishing to show that he had a goal. He had lingered before the shops with their counters and cases, observed by curious dealers. The streets were filled with a soft babble of voices, lulled by the late afternoon warmth to a lazy hum. Trade was listless, shoppers moved languidly from door to door, gazing at the displayed wares and murmuring with disinterested apprentices and assistants. There was no hurry.

Fallon stopped now and then to inquire about a brilliant stone or bit of embroidery. The dealers sat quietly aloof in the dim caves, smoke curling from cigarettes or water pipes. It was never a day for business in

Nantao, even under the new regime; it was always a time to haggle and dream. For a time he moved through the bird market with its myriad lacquered cages and its bedlam of shrill cries and trills and crackling bird-talk. But he did not make any purchases. The bazaar was soothing after the roar and bustle of the modern city, and it buzzed quietly like a beehive where porcelain, silk and gems were stored rather than golden honey.

The quarter-hour passed and he turned reluctantly to leave. As he did so a voice spoke behind him.

"Fah On I-sheng?"

He glanced back. In the vague blue recess of the little shop before which he had been standing he saw, seated motionless on a stool, the proprietor, a man who apparently sold a variety of teas and herbs. He was a huge and hairless fellow, his great paunch flowing out over spread thighs and his hands resting on chubby knees. Naked from navel up, he had been sitting silent and serene, a cigarette drooping from thick lips, his eyes half-closed against the smoke, his body gleaming.

"That is my name," Fallon said.

"Do not go, then. Please enter my humble shop."

Fallon obeyed, experiencing irritation. But he said, "I have not come to buy."

"I know," the fat man said laconically. "You have come to meet a friend."

"Yes. Would it not have been better to speak sooner than to have kept me standing in the street, drawing attention?"

"No, it would not. We wished first to ascertain if you were followed."

Fallon's irritability did not decrease. He had never been attracted or entertained by the atmosphere of mystery and intrigue with which Asiatics and their affairs were popularly endowed, nor had he seen much of it, and chase-'em-in-the-dark tales left him cold.

"And was I followed?"

"The guardians of the people are growing careless," the man said blandly. "Please pass through the door at the rear."

Fallon did so, and closed the door behind him. He found himself in no den or dive, nor had he expected one. It was a plainly furnished living room permeated by the faint odor of cooked cabbage rather than incense, on the wall were a framed portrait of Sun Yat-sen and a torn calendar depicting a bulge-domed sage at his meditations, and on a table was a tray bearing a steaming teapot and a cracked cup. He sat down and helped himself to the tea.

Presently an inner door opened and Tieh Lao-hu entered, smiling broadly.

"Well, Dr. Fallon," he said, "welcome to the padded cell in our asylum."

Fallon worked this over in his mind a moment until he had the free translation, and said, "More like the air-conditioned room in hell." But his face creased in a grin to match Tieh's and they both laughed. "I take it I'm not important enough to be trailed."

"You are still important," said Tieh. "But all Captain Kuo's ferrets are needed elsewhere this evening for an emergency."

"Don't tell me the counterrevolution has broken out! Why aren't you leading your battalion?"

"A lake cannot be emptied in a day, but nevertheless it can be emptied. Our front man in the shop can testify that even you have a small portion of patience. Come with me, Doctor. I wish to show you something."

"Yin Kuei?"

"That portion of your patience is still very small indeed." Tieh led Fallon out of the rear door into a long corridor that penetrated the rabbit warren lying back of the Street of Jade. At its end, beyond still a third door, was a large, almost bare cubicle without windows. Three men who sat beside a big table rose as they entered. On the table was an object that Fallon recognized because he had seen similar instruments operated by guerrilla field units on Samar. It was a transmitter of a shape and size that might conceivably be packed into a large suitcase.

The trio of operators were introduced to him, not by names but by titles: the Snake, the Carp and the Buffalo. "They are a few of our cell," Tieh said, and added cryptically, "They are White Chinese." It seemed that Fallon did not require an introduction.

Tieh proceeded to demonstrate the transmitter, talking rapidly while the others stood by, nodding from time to time with pride of achievement. Fallon followed with difficulty for the subject was technical and one to which the abstractions of the language did not readily lend themselves. The machine looked to him like a repairman's nightmare, rebuilt from an old standard model probably liberated from some abandoned city apartment. A great deal of improvisation and invention had gone into it and to Fallon it looked strictly hambone, but Tieh assured him that it was efficient and with it one could both send and receive. The antenna, one of the operators volunteered, was cut according to the formula of their frequency and could be raised or lowered on the rooftop when needed. They rattled on with enthusiasm about volts and watts, of earlier struggles with fused transformers and frequent condenser breakdowns and of forays to obtain spare parts, and of how old cylindrical encoding devices left by British garrison forces had been adapted. But there was electric power in this district and while the block of houses was not wired, it had been tapped. Now, Tieh said, they were on the air at scheduled intervals with similar stations in Peking, Canton, Hongkong and on Taiwan. He rattled the key in triumph, flipping switches, and the machine hummed loudly and gave out a dutiful *gak-gak-gak-gak-gaaak*.

Fallon felt beads of perspiration on his forehead. "But look here," he said, "can't this be located with direction finders by triangulation and that sort of thing?"

"Certainly," Tieh said. "Fairly easily. Our signals are clear and powerful. But this is a compact instrument, and with such a mobile station we can move about from one part of the city to another and thus elude the monitors. In a few minutes this room can be stripped and become the bedroom of a workingman's family, while we are in another room not far away, or even on the other side of the river."

"What about the noise?"

"This is a noisy district," Tieh shrugged. "If necessary, we bring in the big Shanghai station on a receiver and that drowns out our set."

"Well," Fallon said, feeling admiration for perseverance and boldness if for nothing else. "I don't pretend to know what sort of messages you send and receive on this, or whom you're contacting, but you seem to be a going concern."

"This is for distance," the operator called the Buffalo said. "We have constructed several smaller mobile sets for local communication." From the corner he picked up what looked to Fallon like a portable typewriter, and opened it. Fallon could only see that it was a very complex and delicately made machine filled with wires and small tubes and a great length of fine copper wire wrapped in a coil. The Buffalo flicked a switch and the tubes glowed as the batteries warmed; he lifted a single tiny earphone; he snapped another switch and mumbled a phrase into a minuscule microphone. He turned the switch to the "off" position again and stood grinning from ear to ear.

Fallon looked at Tieh. "I'm prepared to admit," he said, "that you're well organized. I suppose you got supplies like this off the ships you met."

"I still meet them, but not as a stevedore," said Tieh. "Our friends overseas keep in close touch. Doctor, I mentioned that Kuo's police are very busy tonight. I said so because we received information here about it just before you came. Had you heard of an important visitor arriving in the city from the north? A Soviet emissary on tour with his staff?"

"How should I hear anything like that?" Fallon said. "I'm not entrusted with secrets, if it's anything really confidential."

"This is highly confidential, but it mainly concerns your Colonel Li because they are studying the work of the Southeast Asia Bureau. The colonel is therefore responsible for them during their visit here and they are under special protection of the Security Police. Entertainment and demonstrations are being arranged."

"I'm happy you're so well informed about it," Fallon said, amusement glinting in his eyes. "You clearly obtain much more information on this machine than I should ever hear by accident. I suppose your Peking friends put it on the air?"

"Yes, of course. The delegation is going on south later and we have transmitted the word to Canton. I thought you might know who this emissary is."

"Don't you even know the great man's name?"

"They're very cautious about him," Tieh admitted. "So cautious that I suppose we shall have to go and look at him at the hotel and follow him around."

"Do, by all means, if you must," Fallon said. The emissary and Colonel Li's responsibilities were of no interest to him. "I shouldn't take a pot shot at him though, if I were you. Captain Kuo might be angry."

"We're not nihilists!" Tieh said shortly. "We're only an intelligence group."

The doctor was restless. "It's getting rather late," he said, "and I should make some calls tonight. Is Yin Kuei here?"

Tieh's face cleared and he resumed his good-humored smile. "Of course! A thousand pardons—your portion of patience is greater than I realize. Please come."

3

Tieh led the way back along the deserted corridor and opened a door midway to the shop. "A visitor!" he called, and left Fallon alone in semi-darkness. When his eyes had become adjusted to it, he saw that he was in a living apartment, comfortably furnished in a manner which he judged was several cuts above the standards of the neighborhood. It was small but lacked the austerity Fallon had become accustomed to; it was distinctly a feminine room in which he stood, but he had no time to examine it before Yin Kuei hurried from an inner compartment, brushing aside the cream-colored hanging at the connecting doorway with a sweep of an arm in her haste.

She was wearing Chinese dress; the first time, Fallon realized, that he had seen her in such clothing. The narrow close-fitting gown of pale green made her seem much taller, and her unpinned hair fell in a black silk wave down her back. She came to him eagerly, seizing both his hands in her small ones.

"Paul!" she cried. "I heard Lao-hu say visitor, but I didn't realize at all . . . He didn't tell me you were coming here." She turned her intent gaze upward to his face. "It has been days!"

"I suppose he didn't know if I'd make it," Fallon said, feeling dry in the throat and more awkward than he had felt in any circumstance in a very long time. "But he sent a message telling where I was to come and wait, and he's just finished showing me his transmitter. I've been anxious about you."

"There's nothing to be anxious about," she said with open surprise. "This is a very nice and safe place to live—and to work, too. In the morning, the shadow of the Nantao Temple falls right across the roof, and down the lane is the bird market. What more could I need?"

She drew him down on a k'ang covered with finely woven mats. Her hair, a long sleek cascade, lay smooth and close as a blackbird's wing, and silver bracelets jingled gaily on her arm. "Are they looking for me very hard?"

"They were, but they're getting tired of it. Kuo's a bit piqued."

"He takes his work so seriously," she said, and giggled. "But I hope he didn't make a difficult time for you."

"Why should he? I don't know anything about you."

"Don't you? I thought I told you quite a lot about myself."

"A little, here and there, in the few times I've seen you," he admitted. "You've never told me, for instance, why you're exposing yourself like this, running this risk."

"I think I made that plain, Paul. And Lao-hu has told you what sort of man my father was. And if you want to confirm it, the stout man in the herb shop out front was my family's butler in Peking, in the old days before we went to America." She smiled fleetingly. "Of course, I was very small then, but he and his wife have been good to me since I came here."

"You've not told me much of your life in America, either."

"What can you tell about the life of a Chinese family in America? A father teaching Oriental ethics to university students, and faculty wives making a fuss over his daughter because she is foreign and has no mother? Public schools and private tutors to instruct a small heathen in American language and deportment? American college girls—and men too—making a bigger fuss than the faculty wives over a classmate because she's an Asian? When I was in school, you know, Americans were fighting the Japanese and discovering that the Chinese were their allies and consequently making a cult of things Chinese. That was fun, except when they took me for a Japanese. Some thought my father had a laundry, others asked me for recipes for chop suey, a few wondered if Chinese girls are different. Now, I suppose, Chinese aren't so popular. But oh, Paul, it was a giddy whirl! I was sensational!"

She was laughing, but he saw that there were tears too close to the laughter.

"I hope," he said lightly, "that you were a good representative of your country abroad and a model of well-bred decorum, befitting the daughter of a celebrated doctor of philosophy."

"Oh, I was decorous . . . But once just before we came back home a Stanford boy decided he wanted to marry me and his father came to see my father and there was a fearful row. His father was an insurance executive in Los Angeles and he quoted Kipling to my father."

"Never the twain," Fallon murmured. "What did your father say?"

"Well, of course there are half a hundred applicable proverbs and he quoted a few of them, generally to the effect that oil and water don't mix, and he discoursed very learnedly on the advantages and disadvantages of Eurasian offspring, and made some remarks about filial piety. And he emphasized the clan's regression and loss of face if a highborn daughter were to wed a coarse and ignorant foreigner. He greatly enjoyed himself and the other man was furious. But finally my father said that because he was a liberal and believed in the emancipation of women, he would be forced to leave the decision up to me. It was the price he would have to pay for exposing me to Western culture."

"And what did you say to that?"

"Why, I said I had never taken the boy seriously, and didn't want to marry him. I was much too young—hardly seventeen. I thought his red face and blue eyes were repulsive. I think the man sent his son to their New York office the next day."

Fallon grinned. "Do you still find those features repulsive?"

"No," Yin Kuei said judicially. "I'm broader-minded now. I can stand blue eyes if I don't look into them too closely."

"You're not looking into them closely at all. Your own are closed. Is it that you can't bear the sight, Yin Kuei?"

She swayed nearer, tilting up her face. "My decadent Western education," she said quietly, "taught me that this is the proper attitude to assume in the circumstance."

He did not hesitate now, where he might have done before. His mouth was strong on hers, he drew her close and his hands flattered her. She clung to him with a fierce demand that could not be denied, and with a need that belied all lightness that had gone before and that had been the basis of their meeting until now. The lightness melted between their lips, but not in eagerness or despair, rather in full recognition that the thing stirring in them at their first brushing glance was wakened by this touch and trembling pressure, and in unspoken avowal. For while they drew away a little then, it was not for words, since words and broken phrases were unworthy, passing things. It was for confirmation, perhaps, but there was no further need of it. Because she was assisting him in his gentle fumbling, aiding their pleasure and urgency and knowing his awkwardness better than himself, whose instinct in this turmoil of brain and body was not as sure as her own. Where he had known others to her knowledge of none, she brought up without effort the balance of feminine certainty, by the strength of longing and the heritage of arts all but lost to his tribe.

Later she lay, smooth and firm and ivory-gold, in the cradle of his harsh caress, and when his softened face finally sank against the full blue-veined breast she put her mouth beside his ear.

"What barbarism," she whispered with a small return of gaiety.

His gaze was curtained by the black sheen of hair across a curved shoulder. "And decadence?"

"No, no. It is impossible for us to be decadent barbarians, Paul."

"Naturally. They are repulsive."

"Oh, yes. See? I can detect the pulse."

"The pulses. There are several of them."

"Of course you should know. You are a specialist."

"No, you are the specialist here. I am the patient whom you've healed."

"You have been ill?"

"Obviously," he said. "But I am well now."

"Do you feel, then, any gratitude toward your healer?"

"The emotion isn't one of gratitude, Yin Kuei."

"I had forgotten. In the West it must by convention be called love."

"Not necessarily. But in this case I think the word might be good."

"I think so also. Would you like to use it in the conventional way?"

"Yes, but not because of convention. Because I love you."

Her breath caught in her throat and was expelled against his cheek. "That's strange, Paul," she murmured, but there was no banter in it. "For I love you also. Is it a coincidence?"

"By any other name," Fallon said as though to himself, "it could not be so sweet."

Presently, as she buttoned the green robe and tossed back the black hair, she said, "Now I will make tea. I am a poor hostess. When I came to your house you offered me wine and tea. There is no wine, but I can send for some."

"I have had the wine," Fallon said.

She had started toward the inner room but he halted her. "I was late when Tieh brought me here," he said. "I'm very late now. The colonel will be asking me what I've been doing."

She turned in the doorway, smiling. "And you will betray me?"

"I can't. I've already done so."

She came quickly back and put her arms around his neck. "I think you told me once that you were from Maine. I lived in New York and heard about Maine. It is like Lao-hu being from Hunan. They are both places where the people are very upright and moral and cold, no?"

"I've come a long way," Fallon said, slipping on his jacket. He reached in his pocket for a cigarette and his fingers touched the sampan tassel. He drew it out and put it in her hand. "D'you know what that is?"

She studied the curiously twisted cord. "Yes. It is the Mystic Knot. For the old and for lovers."

"Let's forget the old and concentrate on the lovers. I've never given you anything, so we'll start with that. Perhaps when I'm head of the People's Hospital I can afford something a little nicer. Like a pearl necklace."

"A necklace would not be nicer, and I don't want a lover who is head of the People's Hospital." She kissed him.

"I'll be the janitor of the People's Hospital if I don't show up pretty soon," he said, his face buried in the black silk wing.

4

For three days the colonel was absent from his headquarters, though Fallon was informed that he came home in the night to snatch a few hours of sleep. Absent with him were most of his top officers and advisers, including Gregor Efremov, and Major Huang intimated that the demands on the bureau's staff for time and attention devoted to the visiting Soviet mission were unprecedented. The colonel, on whom lay the burden of instruction, briefing, demonstrations and entertainment, was tired and irritable, he said, but bearing up. Fallon anticipated a relapse after the mission's departure for the south.

Meanwhile he was relieved of a weight of petty ailments and soothing sessions and could concentrate on his hospital patients, notably Father Julien, who continued to improve, though too slowly. Judith sulked in the suite, left out of the round of official parties. Albany evidently felt that the Efremov episode put him in a questionable position in his own department and he spent most of his time at work, mending fences. Captain Kuo dropped the investigation to direct the reinforced security net placed around the foreign visitors. And Fallon did not dare pay a call too soon again to Nantao.

But on the third night, as Fallon was about to retire, Li's orderly put his round head and doughy face into the doctor's room about midnight and said that the colonel requested his immediate presence. Fallon sighed and presented himself in the commandant's office. He found Li in full dress uniform, anxiously pacing.

"I-sheng," he exclaimed before the door had closed, "I am in an extreme position!"

Fallon waited. The colonel offered cigarettes and declared, in the idiom, that there was hell to pay in his shop. The head of the Russian mission, The Man Himself, was seriously ill. He looked at Fallon expectantly.

"What's the matter with him?" Fallon asked.

Li waved an agitated hand. "That is why I've called you in. This is a very grave matter, I cannot overemphasize its gravity. To have him fall suddenly sick, right here on my doorstep . . . It is terrible! I am entirely responsible for his health, welfare and safety, you understand. It is an impossible situation!"

"I thought his safety was Kuo's affair. Don't tell me he's been shot."

"No, no, of course not! He has collapsed of an ailment. Tonight, in the midst of a dinner party at the headquarters of the Regional Defense Command, right at table. It was awful. I am at my wit's end!"

Fallon was becoming annoyed, but held himself in check. The colonel was horrified, and his nervous gestures reflected something of the magnitude of the disaster. The doctor had not seen or spoken to the colonel since the arrival of the mission, and Major Huang had been reticent, but the party's presence in the city was generally known. They spoke of it obliquely at the hospital, and the populace was informed by the tripling of People's Police patrols along the thoroughfares whenever the mission's escorted motor cavalcades moved, and by the massing of guards about its hotel. Such protective measures were not uncommon when high dignitaries arrived from Peking, but they had never been as strict or extensive as now. There were, of course, a thousand whispers and rumors, but no public announcements or appearances, no mention in the press or on the air.

"You must help me," Li said. "I trust you implicitly, Fah On."

"You've got a corps of specialists among the top medicos in the city," Fallon said. "Good party members all, I expect, and all natives of the country. What are they doing?"

"They've already been called, naturally. Dr. Chu was among the first to arrive. They have made a preliminary examination on the spot—we removed him from the banquet hall to General Yang's suite—and then they had an ambulance transfer him an hour ago to the east wing of the hospital. The top floor there has been cleared for the emergency."

"And what does Dr. Chu say?"

Colonel Li looked at his knuckles. "Dr. Chu and the others have been in consultation, but do not appear to be in agreement on the nature of his attack or on how to proceed. I just left the hospital and came here to talk to you about it."

"Frankly," Fallon said, "I'd greatly prefer not to be involved in any way. The reasons are apparent. Dr. Chu doesn't trust me and we don't get on well. I'm an outsider and he only allows me in the hospital because of your orders. Certainly if this fellow is as important as he seems to be, I shouldn't be permitted within a mile of him."

"Nonsense! If I wish to call you in on this no one can question it, including Dr. Chu. He has only medical authority, and in this case my authority supersedes that of everyone, including the general and the Security people, for the mission is my sole responsibility while it's here. It extends over the individual members of the mission itself—some dozen or so Russians and a number of special aides sent by Peking. And if I desire you to examine him, you will do so."

"You place an unwarranted weight on a man in my peculiar position," Fallon said. "If you don't mind, just who is this person?"

Li cleared his throat and lit another cigarette off the butt of the last. "His name is Pregnesky," he said casually. "An influential and highly placed person sent here on a special mission. It is significant, and we are ordered to avoid all publicity about the tour. That is all I can tell you, but you can be sure that Peking will be concerned about him, including the Soviet Embassy."

Fallon had never heard the name. The Chinese press and radio were full of Russian official news, Fallon had been taking cursory language lessons from Efremov to pass time and reading Gregor's copies of *Pravda* for practice, but although he thought he was well informed, he had no recollection of a Pregnesky. He glanced at Li and decided this was the pseudonym the government had chosen.

"All right," he said. "What seems to be wrong with Comrade Pregnesky?"

"He's only been in this country two weeks. When he left Moscow by air he was in good health. He is a strong robust man in his middle years. His secretary tells us he has had a chronic ear condition, but nothing bad. Since he began his tour he has been suffering from severe headaches and recurrent fever, and a sense of depression. That is all I know. When he arrived here, however, he seemed excellent."

"Well, what happened tonight?"

"His illness was very abrupt, at dinner. He lacked appetite but ate a little, and was to speak. Then he vomited and fell over. Since he arrived at the hospital he has had several convulsions. They have given him sedatives, I think, and are all arguing about it, but he is very bad. I am alarmed."

Li might well be alarmed, Fallon reflected. It didn't sound like an ordinary thing such as a stroke, but of course one couldn't tell at long range. If this Pregnesky didn't rally, Li stood in a good way to being not only stripped of his command but if the importance required it he could be placed against a wall for permitting such a catastrophe to occur.

"What do you want me to do?"

"Go with me to the hospital at once," Li said, buttoning his tunic. Fallon nodded, said nothing more and went to his room for his jacket and bag.

The reception lobby of the hospital seemed congested when they entered, though it was after one o'clock. There was a subdued buzz and a nervous scurrying. Fallon recognized several of the staff physicians who were normally off duty at night, and they looked at him quizzically as he passed in Colonel Li's hurried wake. He saw a number of Li's colleagues, the heads of associated departments and their assistants, and a few of Li's own staff. The place was alive with Security men who had stationed themselves about the entrance and along the corridors, and Captain Kuo was in command. They went immediately to the second floor and the far wing, where the press was not so great, except for the police. But here there were three members of the mission, stonily silent white men wearing worried expressions; they had their aides and interpreters with them and stood apart from the Chinese officials and attendants, aloof and stiffly anxious. Dr. Chu and one of his staff were talking with them.

Chu saw the colonel approaching with Fallon and stopped in mid-sentence, frowning. Li wasted no words.

"How is he?"

"The same," Dr. Chu said. "Perhaps a little worse. Another convulsion, though the drugs have eased it. There seems to be a developing condition of optic neuritis; his sight is glazed."

"What have you decided?"

"Our diagnosis has not yet been completed," Chu muttered, eying Fallon. "This is very complex, you know."

"Then what have you done?"

"Well," the assistant director said, hunching a shoulder, "one can do very little until one has established all the symptoms and correlated them. There are many things to be considered. There is a retarded pulse and a slowed respiration, for instance. There is a deep apathy—also the onset of a slightly delirious condition." He hesitated. "There seems to be a localized paralysis—"

"I believe," Li said, "that Dr. Fallon had better make his own separate examination. Now, if you don't mind."

Dr. Chu's fleshy lips thinned and he cast an angry glance at Fallon. "I do mind, Colonel. This is not a routine or charity case. His Excellency's condition is critical. I do not have confidence in Dr. Fallon's abilities."

"I do," said Li. "I have more confidence in his abilities than I have in yours, or in anyone else's around here. That's why I put my own people under his care and not under yours."

Chu's face became purple and his eyes began to bulge. The three Russians standing by obviously did not understand the interchange, and stirred impatiently. Li looked at them.

"Tell His Excellency's aide," he said to the interpreter, "that this is the foreign physician of whom I spoke before I left. I place full faith in him and recommend that they do the same if they wish me to provide the best available attention." He paused. "Tell them that it may seem irregular to go over the head of the respected medical director of the People's Hospital, but this is my emergency and my privilege."

The interpreter hastily began to speak and Li glanced at Dr. Chu and added, "If you question this you can appeal to your superior, but I may say that I have obtained the permission of Major-General Yang of the Defense Command in this matter, as I anticipated your objections. His staff officers downstairs will verify it."

Chu won his struggle for dignity. "You have the arbitrary authority, naturally," he said. "If you prefer a suspect refugee picked up in some little field hospital—"

"Never mind that. I want the cooperation of yourself and your staff."

"This way, Dr. Fallon," said Chu coldly, indicating a closed door behind them. "I will accompany you, if you don't object."

"I don't object at all," Fallon grunted. "I only object to the whole affair." He entered the enclosed and guarded room, in which a dim blue light burned above a high bed. Three frightened nurses crouched nearby; he approached the patient.

Outside the door, the Russians walked and smoked in the corridor, talking in low voices among themselves. They had given Colonel Li their approval of anything he thought was best with hardly a glance at Fallon, and thereafter they ignored the officer. Li waited alone. The guards came and went. Captain Kuo checked them, stopped near Li's chair, started to speak and moved away again. The hands of the clock moved on in their circle on the white wall. The tomblike building, which European money, architects and medical experts had constructed with the aim of establishing the finest facilities of their kind in the East at the time, effectively eliminated all night sounds of the city. The inheritors of these facilities marked time, along with their allied guests and with Li.

Sometime after two, Fallon and Chu emerged into the corridor, and the pacing and smoking stopped. Li asked the first of his three stock questions.

"The delirium has subsided," said Dr. Chu. "He is in a coma. The paralysis is gradually spreading. For the moment, I have administered sulfanilamide orally."

Li was barely listening to him, but held his gaze on Fallon.

"What have you decided?"

"His Excellency," said Fallon without expression, "seems to have an extremely active and severe abscess in the right temporal lobe of the brain. The onset has been abrupt and acute. In my opinion, surgical treatment is called for, and he should be prepared for it. Alternative dosages will do little if any temporary good."

Dr. Chu's eyes were glistening, as if he were about to give way to tears. "I am much opposed to surgery," he declared with slow emphasis. "An operation of such a delicate nature is very complicated and dangerous. His Excellency—he might die. Colonel Li, consider my position, consider your own! We can give palliative treatment here and fly him back to Peking immediately. They have excellent surgeons and facilities there. It is even possible that such treatment could continue until he has been flown to Moscow. Sir, I am strongly—"

"Do you agree in principle with Dr. Fallon's diagnosis?" Li demanded, interrupting this rapid flow.

"Well, in principle, yes. Yes, it is probably an abscess. But—"

"The facilities here are equal if not superior to those in Peking, aren't they?"

"Of course, as a director of this hospital, I—"

"He might die anyway if the operation is not performed?" Li asked this of Fallon.

"I said it was acute," Fallon muttered. "Who knows? You asked me, and I told you. If he were my patient, anywhere else, I would operate in the morning. He must be prepared and observed first."

The interpreter's murmur had been a steady undertone behind them and Li glanced around at the Russians. The aide was speaking to them in hoarse whispers, but there seemed to be no disagreement. He looked at Li and nodded.

"He *is* your patient," Li said to Fallon. "You think prolonged delay might be dangerous?"

"I believe personally that it would be fatal. The condition may move at any time into a rupture, resulting in encephalitis or even meningitis. The abscess is doubtless encapsulated, and it should be opened and the pus withdrawn as soon as possible."

"You will order the preparations, then," Li said. "For the morning. The staff here will give you all assistance. You had better go home and rest, while they carry on. Good night, Dr. Chu and Comrades."

5

The colonel's car halted with a squeal of brakes before Number 68 and Li stepped down into the gateway, with Fallon behind him. Even at three in the morning there were a few shadowy figures moving in Soochow Road; at no hour were these streets ever entirely deserted. As the driver pulled away from the curb his headlights picked up one of the pedestrians standing deliberately in its glare and Fallon had a brief but sharp view of him. Then the car was gone and the stroller was in thick gloom again beside the wall.

They went through the gate, but in the entryway Fallon paused. "I would like a few moments of quiet to think about this," he said to Li, "and to plan what is to be done. I need the air. There is a bench here in the garden."

"Do as you like," said Li. "I am exhausted." He went up the steps and disappeared.

Fallon stood on the walk under the trees. The Security people had put a guard on the door of the house since the Efremov affair, but it was only a precaution and tonight the sentry was inside, out of the chill. Directly across the creek, the lights of the hospital had been extinguished except in the lobby and on the second floor wing. A few official cars were still parked there in the drive. Fallon moved to the bench, over which hung a lush and aromatic tree-peony, and sat down. He had to wait only a moment.

Tieh came into the garden from the gate, followed by two others. Fallon scraped shoe leather on gravel and they found the bench. In the heavy blackness before the first faint light, he could see virtually nothing of them except for the dimmest of silhouettes, but he had recognized

Tieh in the car lights. And now he felt a small groping hand fumbling for his, and he knew that Yin Kuei was here also. His scalp prickled; this was a reckless thing for her to do. Her face pressed close to his.

"Come with us across to the embankment," Tieh said in a low voice. "Police may visit the house at any moment."

They left the garden, crossed the road to the railing along the creek, and descended one of the many stone ladders to the water's edge. Here a small sampan, a water taxi with a curved mat roof, bobbed at its tether against the current. It was barely large enough for the four of them and tilted precariously under their weight. Tieh snapped on an electric torch with a blue shield, and their disembodied faces were etched in unearthly distortions around it.

"It is safer to talk here," Tieh said with his twisted grin. "Though not so pleasant as your garden. We crossed the creek from the hospital in this boat while you and the colonel were driving around, over the bridge."

Fallon could hardly see Yin Kuei's features, for she wore a robe with a hood that could be pulled forward for concealment. But she folded this partially back and smiled at him, and their hands touched again. Tieh saw it.

"I am sorry, there is no time for that," he said. Fallon recognized the fourth person as one of the radio technicians, the Buffalo. The man had a deeply pocked face and a queer cast to one eye; he was altogether villainous, and Fallon repressed an urge to laugh aloud at the absurdity of this conspiratorial scene.

"You choose odd hours to call on me," he said. "I should be resting."

"We know," Yin Kuei said, leaning forward. "You are to operate in a few hours. We have friends among those who work in the hospital."

Fallon savored this. "I suppose," he suggested, "that you even know the nature of the case, what I shall do, and how I shall do it?"

"We know enough," said Tieh, unabashed. "Fah On, this is not a social visit. It is an urgent one or we would not have risked it. But we had to see you immediately." He gave Fallon a steady and penetrating look. "When you saw your patient, did you recognize him?"

Fallon hesitated. "I have seen him in photographs several times," he said finally. "In newspapers. But I confess, I don't remember in what connection, except that he appears in groups, wears a uniform and medals, and usually looks much more stern and uncompromising than he does tonight. He is called Pregnesky here."

"Yes. Well, identifying such people is not your business, it is ours. His name is Malov. Andre Povich Malov. He is a general and a hero. He is the Defender of Voronezh. He enjoys the prestige of the Leader's confidence. Does this mean anything to you?"

"Not much. When the general was defending—Voronezh, is it?—I was helping defend Catbalogan on Samar, and our paths didn't exactly cross."

"They cross now. Malov is a powerful and influential man in the councils of the Soviet Union. He is an activist in the Cominform and a member of the Military Council. He has a distinguished record, but that's all you need to know. Except that this trip he is making is no idle goodwill tour. It has direct bearing on the support that will be given in arms and matériel in event of a large-scale southward expansion, in the future. Does that make it clearer?"

"A little," said Fallon. "I'm not interested in Malov's political or military prominence, or his job. I'm only interested in what's inside his head."

Tieh lifted an eloquent hand. "So are we. Both in the part of it that knows and plans and makes decisions, and in the part that is diseased." He bunched the hand into a fist. "Do you know what would probably happen if Malov died?"

"I suspect there'd be rather a fuss."

"There would be more than a fuss. There would be an explosion of the first magnitude. If the Soviet Ambassador in Peking were assassinated tonight, that would be a fuss. But it would not be important; he would be replaced, and relations would continue as usual. But if Malov died on the operating table . . . *Fan liao!* Heaven would be overturned, the world would end, as we say."

Fallon smiled. "I'm not concerned with *fan liao*. You aren't suggesting anything, are you? If you are, it will have been the first time in my undistinguished career that I've received such a suggestion."

"There is a first time for everything," said Tieh.

Fallon studied his strong ugly face in the blue light. Tieh's eyes were steady, the twisted mouth was grim. He glanced at Yin Kuei. She had pulled the hood forward again and sat motionless on the sampan seat, her head bowed. The Buffalo was rolling a cigarette and did not look up.

"As long as I'm here, would you be more explicit?" Fallon said.

Tieh shrugged. "I am no doctor, but I know what you will do tomorrow—or today. I know Dr. Chu will be present, but only assisting. Your hand holds the instruments, and the best man's hand might slip."

"And the result would be *fan liao*? What would be accomplished by that?"

"Who knows, Fah On? But quite likely a serious disruption of relations. A delay in providing full cooperation, lengthy bickering, mutual recriminations and mistrust, a political strain, a great embarrassment to the regime and a corresponding advantage to the forces of liberation. A chain reaction, I think."

Fallon appeared to consider deeply, but he was conscious of a clammy chill down his back, doubtless from the river mists before dawn. He put out a hand and lifted Yin Kuei's chin. "What do you think?" he asked.

She stared at him, and then with defiance at Tieh. "I think it is a mad idea, conceived on the spur of the moment by a madman who does not consider the consequences, either to his cause or to you. I told him I opposed it, but we have not even had time to talk, he was so anxious to catch you. Tieh has no authority to even suggest this, he has consulted with no one but himself. It would mean certain death for you, Paul. And I have no faith in Tieh's chain reactions."

Fallon moved heavily, so that the sampan rocked. He stepped back onto the landing and stood on the embankment stair.

"I'll sleep on it," he said, "what little time for sleep I have. I'll say this, Lao-hu. I'm not what you or anyone would call an idealist, either in this country or my own. I'm not actively concerned with chain reactions or international repercussions, even if I thought I could have a hand in them. You may have heard of what Westerners call the Hippocratic oath. It's just an oath taken to a code of medical ethics. I'm not even a strictly ethical man. But I think that if you hear bad, or good, news from the hospital, depending on how you interpret it, you can't take credit for the slip. A slip, as you imply, is always possible. But it isn't probable. If I can I'll see you in Nantao in a few days."

He climbed the steps. The blackness had faded, the traffic had gradually increased on the road above, the house stood against the lightening sky. He crossed and entered and went up to his cell to bed.

6

The second floor corridor had at last been cleared of curious officials, glowering members of the visiting mission, excess attendants and even a few ambulatory patients who had wandered in, and Captain Kuo had doubled his guards on the wing. It made less confusion and noise, at least. Fallon stood in an anteroom of the main operating theater, donning a white coat and cap, and Dr. Chu and the assistant he had deputized were doing the same. The assistant was a young man with a tic, but he seemed steady and Fallon winked at him. The dresser and the chief nurse, on whom Fallon had passed, were ready. Fallon had not slept but he was not tired, and was astonished at how fresh he felt.

"I trust," he said maliciously, "the room has at last been cleaned and disinfected." They were standing side by side at the scrub-up basins. Chu shot a venomous look at him and said nothing, but finally nodded.

"And," Fallon added, "I hope the procaine hasn't been boiled." Chu disregarded this entirely.

They went into the larger room where the patient lay. He was a tall heavy man with a square rough-hewn face like a chipped rock. Fallon went up to him and stared down at his features. Pregnesky met his eye and muttered, *"Odin mir."* His shaved head had been washed with alcohol and Fallon began at once to administer the local anesthetic, which he had personally arranged. Pregnesky appeared to doze, and Fallon made a knife scratch to indicate position for the cut. The assistants placed a frame over the emissary's head and the nurse set up the blood pressure apparatus. Dr. Chu turned on the diathermy electrodes, equipment left over by his predecessors of which he was extremely proud as it provided a continuous warm drop injection.

Fallon glanced up and saw that the only spectators were Pregnesky's aide, an interpreter, Colonel Li and Captain Kuo. They looked at him and Li cocked an eyebrow. Fallon paid them no further attention, but went to make the incision and final swabbing while Chu's assistant, his tic diminishing now that he was doing an impersonal job he enjoyed, fixed and tied sealing bandages about the area. Chu turned to his second love, the electric cutting apparatus, and Fallon arranged several light clips to prevent hemorrhage after his incision and took up the pistol-like trepanning instrument.

He began to work with deliberation, thankful that he had Dr. Chu and this young man to help, for they knew their business, and he forgot Chu's animosity. Rapidly he bored the four holes in the skull, took the saw to make the connections, and the assistant passed wax into the fissures, carrying out the ligatures with fine silk and arranging the membranes. Fallon was pleased; there was virtually no bleeding. The hospital equipment for this case was adequate enough, and Chu had made his preparations with efficiency: this was no humanitarian matter, but a crisis involving the interests of the State, and he had given the best he had to it. For once the room, its occupants, the instruments, all were completely sterile.

Fallon, laying open the convolutions of the brain, did not look up to catch Dr. Chu's watchful eyes, but he knew they were fixed upon his hands. He felt at ease, relaxed and rested. The facilities were, from one viewpoint, a little old-fashioned, but they were the finest available here and Fallon could ask for nothing better. It had been a very long time since he had performed such a job with these amenities, though he had done it several times in recent years in circumstances less than satisfactory, indeed under primitive and almost hideous conditions the recollection of which still caused shudders.

The great abscess lay under his fingers. He inserted the cannula and made the puncture and the draining began of the mass of fluid matter. Using the pneumatic syringe and the electric knife, he proceeded smoothly, cutting and rinsing, until he was into the depths of it. Presently the capsular material had been cleared. Dr. Chu appeared fascinated, whether by the size of the hollow space revealed or by the speed with which the surrounding area was gradually swelling to fill it, Fallon did not know. Perhaps, he thought, Chu was petrified by fear. He glanced up at the assistant, who was mildly perspiring but whose hands were quick and sure with the clips and the instrument table. Once Fallon's frontal lamp, glowing down from his forehead to prevent the brain from chilling, slipped; the assistant reached across and straightened it, wiped perspiration from Fallon's skin with a bit of gauze, and belatedly returned the wink he had received before the work began.

The slow and gentle manipulation of the fingers went on in the depression until, at length, no depression remained. Chu stepped forward to cover the surrounding areas with small wads of cotton wool and to renew sodden ones, the only activity in which he had engaged for some time. Fallon had no idea of the hour; he had started at ten, but there was no clock in the room. He began to arrange the temporosphenoidal lobe in the position he desired.

The explosion was incredibly sharp. It shattered the stillness, destroyed the calm, crashed through the deadened atmosphere to tear at nerves and jerk muscles. Glass tinkled and spears of it whined; plaster and plaster-dust fell in a rain from the high ceiling, clattering on the metal of the overhead operating lights. A strong acrid wind blew through the room, the dust swirling in it, followed by vagrant puffs of smoke.

Fallon bent forward over the exposed head of his patient, shielding the open brain with his own shoulders and chest, and felt a light patter of rubble striking his back and trickling off. His fingers were motionless, one hand holding a bit of wool to stanch the last small bleeding spot, and he drew in his breath but made no other movement. The blast was followed by reverberating echoes and then silence, and there were no more like it. But there were faint shouts and cries from outside in the corridor. Dr. Chu shrank back from the table, the visible parts of his face above the mask ivory-pale, and he made an unintelligible exclamation. His assistant stood frozen; the nurse and dresser remained in their places.

"It is nothing serious," Fallon said conversationally, enunciating clearly to be understood through his own mask. "Let's finish this, for it's almost done."

He straightened as the dust settled and went on with the job. He was correct, and it had already neared completion. There were only a few more minutes of work to do. The assistant continued as before, but Chu hung back as though hands held him away from the table. The dresser took his place, since it was his turn anyhow. There was nothing left for Fallon. Presently he stepped away and looked around for the first time.

The Soviet aide and the interpreter remained where they had been from the start. The colonel and Captain Kuo had disappeared. Fallon bent over his patient once more, saw that he was quite satisfactory, and turned away again, stripping off his gloves and removing his mask and cap. He tossed them aside, glanced at the others who were engaged with final duties, and went into the anteroom and out into the corridor.

The hall was filled with a haze of dust, and plaster littered the floor, along with splinters of glass from several broken windows. It was extraordinarily quiet there. The bright noon sunlight glared down outside, filling the corridor with light. Guards stood at either end, fingering their rifles. Captain Kuo was shouting something up a staircase, making the only commotion, and held a pistol in his hand. Colonel Li sat at an orderly's table, smoking a cigarette. He saw Fallon emerge and held up a hand.

"Did it go all right?" he asked. He was overly casual, but Fallon knew him well enough to see that he was very excited.

"It went well," Fallon said, starting to take off his gown. "It is finished."

"You think he will recover?"

"I can't say. The operation was not complicated by anything, and he should recover."

"Not complicated by anything!" Li sniffed.

"Well, as for that, you've been in operating field dugouts with me under heavy artillery fire," Fallon smiled. "How did it compare?"

"Oh, I wasn't too alarmed. Kuo is, of course. I saw that you had it under control so I joined him. It was a grenade, or a home-manufactured bomb. It exploded on a skylight just over the inner corridor, next to the operating room. They have found the pieces, now they are hunting the thrower."

"What do you think about it?" Fallon asked. He accepted one of Li's cigarettes, and inhaled gratefully.

"I think someone threw it from the roof and has already escaped down a fire exit. They won't find him lurking here." Li tapped his long fingers on the table in thought. "I think the thrower knew that the skylight was not directly over the operating room. He intended to disrupt the operation, cause confusion at a critical moment. It is likely that he had a confederate inside somewhere who could signal to him to throw it just at a time when, perhaps, your fingers or your knife might do damage. His timing was bad, and he did not achieve the objective anyway."

"Why should anyone do that?"

"Why indeed?" said Colonel Li. "To kill the patient, naturally. Comrade Pregnesky's life would be a great feather in the cap of the enemies of the State."

"Comrade General Malov," Fallon said.

Li looked at him keenly. "So?"

"His picture is in all the papers from Russia quite regularly. They are even published in papers here. I have been looking into his face now for—let's see, it's about two hours, isn't it? How can one fail to know the Hero of Voronezh?"

The colonel covered his confusion by lighting another cigarette. "I had forgotten how observant you are. Nevertheless, I am happy that you assure me Comrade Pregnesky did not suffer from the incident and will probably recover. It is better, we say, to save one man's life than to build a seven-story pagoda."

"Depending on who the man is, I suppose," Fallon said. He went into the anteroom and got his jacket. They were moving the patient through to his own room, his head swathed in preliminary bandages. He was conscious, and as his table was trundled by he saw Fallon's face. Seeming to realize where he was and that this was a doctor who had done something for him, he lifted his hand a little, and again their eyes met.

His interpreter and the aide were trailing behind. "What does *odin mir* mean?" Fallon asked.

"It's a toast," the interpreter muttered, puzzled. " 'One peace.' I do not know the significance of it precisely."

"Father Julien would call it a prayer."

7

September faded. The heat was gone, the mists dispersed over the coastal plain and the skies were a cloudless pale amethyst. The scraggly trees in the park on the Bund began to shed brown leaves; at evening there was a stillness even in the heart of the city, a suspension of sound and movement when one smelled the placid river and the charcoal cooking fires and the rich country fields of early autumn. It was too soon for the bitter Siberian winds, too late for the lethargy of summer.

At such a season Fallon felt his captivity with a poignancy hard to bear. He was restless and hated the confinement of the town, thinking of the blue windy hills of the north where he had spent three satisfying years, and waking from dreams in which he was again aboard a free-roving ship bound down through the islands. He never dreamed of home; he sometimes pondered that, and decided it was simply that he had been too long away. The thread was severed.

Fortunately he had plenty to keep him occupied. His regular patients were routed to Dr. Chu's assistant at his own request, with the exception of Father Julien, so that he might give as much time as necessary to the recovery of Comrade Pregnesky. The man had great vitality, convalescing rapidly and taking the secondary surgery with no falter in his stride. He had no Chinese or English and Fallon's Russian was rudimentary, but the two got on well enough together.

Colonel Li told Fallon that the entire matter was one of utmost secrecy, so far as the public was concerned, and it was given out that the mission had departed for the south. A series of communications between Moscow, Peking and Shanghai had determined this course; it amused Fallon, since the press had been prohibited from any mention of the emissary in the first place so that technically he had not been present at all. Everyone had seen the earlier processions and the activity around the hotel; everyone saw the members of the mission dawdling away the days while their leader lay in a guarded suite, and the name of Pregnesky, if not Malov, was on all lips. But officially there had been no tour, nor any hitch in it. Presently, when Fallon believed his star patient would be strong enough, he would be whisked into a transport and flown north to Peking again, and after a brief rest and checkover there at the Institute he would return by air to his homeland. The balance of his tour was canceled, and the anticipated results of it were left in abeyance. Everyone was simply relieved that Pregnesky had survived the disaster and hoped to get him out of the country and off its hands as quickly as feasible. Meanwhile, the whole thing was buried in a tomb of reticence and hadn't happened.

Fallon had only one opportunity in the subsequent week to visit Nantao, and then only for a hurried hour. The fat herb merchant admitted him, Yin Kuei drew him into her apartment, but he had only a few minutes alone with her. There were other and more intimate things to be said to waste words on Comrade Pregnesky. But before they had hardly been spoken, Tieh was at the door, insistent on his interruption. He had questions which Fallon answered with reluctance and in the shortest manner, eying Tieh with resentment. The patient was recovering, he would go away soon, and that was all.

"The diversion during the operation," Fallon added, "did not succeed. The bomb burst off center, was delayed past the most delicate point, and would not have done any harm even if these errors had not been made. The bomber was a fumbling amateur."

"We heard a rumor of it," Tieh said with equanimity. "Very bold maneuver, we thought. But of course, there have been many rumors lately. It was widely circulated that an attempt had been made to assassinate Malov."

"Fairly close to the truth, these rumors," said Fallon. "Bomb-throwing amateurs are usually poor marksmen. I suggest you go out in the country and practice a little. You're rusty since the old days of the Communist underground."

"He is a fool!" Yin Kuei said, sitting beside Fallon on the k'ang and pressing her shoulder against his. "His superior is very angry."

"His anger has been dissipated," Tieh grinned. "These rumors deserve wider circulation. Wait until tomorrow."

He left them then. But Fallon had to return to his duties. The interval was brief, Tieh's wife entered inadvertently, there was a false alarm in the establishment because an unexpected police patrol passed too close for comfort in the neighborhood, and the tea grew cold. Yin Kuei clung to him.

"I wish you would leave this place," Fallon said. "Tieh's too energetic for my peace of mind. You'll be in bad trouble. You know why I say this—because I love you."

"Your love for me is no greater than mine for you," she declared. "I have my work to do, and you have yours. Perhaps later."

Fallon departed. The following evening as he sat reading in his room, Albany knocked and entered, an odd smile on his face.

"Have you had your radio on?" he asked. When Fallon said he had not, Albany laughed. "I've been in on the foreign broadcasts. The air's full of chatter about Comrade Pregnesky. Rather distorted in parts, but in general fairly factual. The so-called Radio Free China is blatting about it. The funny thing is, they're insisting that our friend isn't Pregnesky, but General Malov."

Fallon offered no comment. Albany snapped on Fallon's desk set and tuned the dials. It was one of those irregular hours when the small instrument sometimes picked up distant stations, and after a moment Albany had Hongkong on the air. They waited out a musical interval and sat listening to a voice with cultured British intonations and a Cantonese accent presenting the news of the world. When he had disposed of the more pressing developments in the Korean truce, the voice's owner informed all listeners that Comrade General Andre Povich Malov, delegated by the People's Ministry to head a top-secret fact-finding mission in Southeast Asia, was making a fast recovery from an emergency brain operation in Shanghai, and would soon return to Moscow. He continued with biographical and current details of considerable accuracy. Albany turned the voice off.

"So you claim you didn't know who your patient was?" he said satirically. "Boy, what a chance for a guy like you to dig him good when you had the opportunity."

"What do you mean, for a guy like me?"

"You're not kidding me, Doc. You're sympathetic with these opposition groups that are always popping up like mushrooms. As subversives go, they're not very effective, but they have a lot of nuisance value. The dope on Pregnesky—or is it Malov?—probably went direct from here to Hongkong by the underground. It got around so fast they're obviously using radio. And where do they get the dope except from the horse's mouth?"

Fallon got up from his chair. "Who's the horse's mouth, Thorpe?"

Albany's face hardened. "I'm mistaken," he said. "I got the wrong part of the horse for you. How long do you think you're going to last in this job you've got with Li if you keep playing footsy with the malcontents? Kuo's as suspicious as I am, and almost as sharp. He isn't far behind. D'you think I didn't know you were giving that little tart from my office a rumble, before she took off? Hell, I saw you meeting her at least twice outside the hotel, and where else you met her I can guess. I know why you butted in that night I caught her prowling in Efremov's room. I'll lay ten to one you know exactly where she is right now, and that Tieh bird too, and it won't take Kuo long to figure that out himself. Not if I tip him."

Fallon hit him. Albany was caught off guard and off balance and went down. He had youth and weight but he had not expected the savage attack. He flung out an arm to save himself, caught the fringe of a runner on the desk, and jerked it, throwing the radio set to the floor. It bounced under his feet and he tripped, stumbled back and fell with a crash into the glass case in which Fallon kept his instruments. The glass shattered and Albany lay in the middle of it, sprayed with shards.

He did not move for a moment, but his heavy breathing grew uneven when he lifted his hands and saw the palms stained with crimson from welling cuts. A splinter had torn the skin above one eye and the blood ran into it. A thin keening of rage rose in his throat as he struggled to extricate himself from the wreckage. His pawing hand closed on one of the scalpels lying amid the broken glass; he clutched it and started to rise, the open eye glaring with a crazy fury.

Fallon experienced a mounting bitterness he had no desire to control.

He had been spoiling for this for a long time, knowing well enough that it could only result in a beating for himself, for he was no match for the agile and muscular Albany. But he saw the sharp knife Albany gripped and the wildness in his adversary. He stepped forward and kicked the hand; the scalpel was released and spun into a corner. And as Albany surged to his knees, Fallon brought his own knee hard into the other's face, feeling the crunching painful impact of nose and teeth against his bone. Albany sank again, supporting himself briefly with laboring hands and shoulders and then collapsing limply. He lay face down upon the floor, long gasps shaking his body.

The fight had lasted no more than two minutes and was now over, and bits of glass still tinkled in the silent room. Unbroken in the shambles lay a small bottle of ammonia from the medicine shelf. Fallon pulled the cork, tilted Albany's head to the side, and held it under the smashed and spouting nose. As he did so he heard the door open behind him and glanced over his shoulder.

Judith Markham stood in the doorway in her sleazy robe, the faded hair tumbled down one side of her white face. She raised a hand to her mouth to stifle a scream, and then advanced quickly to kneel beside Fallon and clutch Albany's dark head, lifting it to her lap. Her eyes were enormous in the lamplight.

"What is it?" she breathed. "Is he drunk again?"

"No," Fallon said ruefully, massaging his aching thigh. "I think he's got a broken nose. We had a little tiff."

She stared up at him, her mouth and the muscles of her cheeks tightening. "A fight? You mean you did this to him?"

"Well," Fallon said, handing her the ammonia bottle and rising, "let's call it an accident. We just had an argument."

Albany was coming around, but having difficulty with his breathing and his mouth gaped open, a thick rope of saliva trickling from the corner. Judith tried to wipe the blood from his eye.

"I heard a noise," she said wonderingly, "and there's no one else in the house, I suppose. I—I thought he'd been drinking and fell."

"He fell," said Fallon. "I guess we'd better get him to his room and I'll see what I can do about the nose. The cuts are minor."

Albany's legs wobbled but they got him on his feet and supported him, sagging, into his own quarters. As Fallon turned away from the bed, Judith said in a vicious tone, "I know what you were arguing about. You were trying to shut him up. He told me all about it this afternoon, what he suspected. You won't get away with this, you know."

She crouched on the edge of the ornate bed, cradling Albany's head in her arms, and tears of futile anger and near-hysteria coursed down

her raddled face. Fallon paused, his gaze on her speculative, and then he
went back down the hall to get bandages and disinfectant. He was picking what he needed out of the debris on the floor when he heard steps
in the room behind his back and looked around. Captain Kuo had
entered.

"What has happened?" he demanded. The odor of spilled medica-
tions was strong.

"Albany has had a collision with my cabinet," Fallon said. "I am giving
him first aid."

"The sound was loud, even in Major Huang's office. Is he badly
hurt?"

"Nothing serious."

"If he needs attention, the colonel's woman can take him to the hospital," Kuo said coldly. "I wish you to come with me."

"I can attend to him right here in a moment."

"Never mind Albany. I wish to talk to you."

"What about? We had a private fight, that's all."

"It is not about any fight. It is a graver matter. You are under arrest."

8

The West had built a city of tremendous spires on the river's bank that
dwarfed the ancient walled trading town, imposing watchtowers floating
on rafts of pilings over the mud flats and pointing brazen thumbs toward
the sky. One of the most massive of these was a formidable heap of
modern steel and concrete that had been erected as a prison and it em-
bodied all the best features of modern penal institutions, including a
gallows. It stood on Ward Road in the lower factory region along the
stream and was celebrated at one period in the past for having the largest
population of any known lockup in the world. That, of course, had
been during the benevolent and orderly reign of the great international
powers. It had been emptied by several amnesties at the time of the
Takeover. But one of the first acts of the New Order that inherited it
was to restore its effectiveness and fill it with prisoners, an infallible
mark of enlightened reform and change.

The new jailers were efficient but the warden was a whimsical man
with a taste for old and simple things. It was his conviction that a jail
should have a drum tower in the tested tradition, and he built one in the
middle of all that severe mass of Western planes and blocks. He put a
great circular signal drum in the top of it, a drum that had been used in

the times of Ch'ien Lung to sound the alarm against pirate fleets and barbarian forays, and he used it on all occasions to mark the watches. This medieval brick structure rising from the exercise yard was not very aesthetic, but the drum had a deep and powerful beat, one that jolted the inmates to the bottom of their empty and aching bellies, and it gave pleasure to the warden and the guards.

The prisoners were a mixed lot, notable for a lack among them of a properly criminal element. They were packed in misery and squalor in the cell blocks, a fair cross-section of the city's denizens, and most of them had in common a secret implacable hatred of the new regime. They were reactionaries: politicals, small men slow to obey strange decrees regarding property, a few captured bandits and thieves, but chiefly shop-keepers, money-changers, petty gentry and similar offenders. Some had lain in the blocks for a very long time. Some worked in the shops, some were sent to classes, most were too stubborn or stupid to merit attention.

There were additionally a few foreign wretches: expatriate Russian oldsters who had concealed valuables, homeless Jews who had known prisons such as this in Central Europe. The majority were despised Americans and the bulk of these were missionaries. This being in the fourth year of the Changeover, the earlier hue and cry for foreign blood had died in a fading din of great public trials and mass floggings, humili-ations, deportations and executions. Those who still survived in durance here were a hopeless and abandoned remnant, half-forgotten, with ash-gray faces and the sunken eyes of their soul agony and their living death.

Among them Paul Fallon languished.

He did not see the others, though sometimes at night he heard them screaming and cursing. He lay entirely alone in an iron cell-box, separated from the lesser fry who moaned unseen. The only ones he saw in this monumental prison were his guards and the interrogators. But he heard the drum in the warden's fine new drum tower. It tolled the hours just outside the narrow window-slit, reverberating resonantly upon the surrounding stone and metal, and Fallon concluded that this must be a refinement of the traditional water-drip torture. He found himself lying rigid on his filthy quilt, waiting for it to roar, as a man may wait in the dead of night for his neighbor's second shoe to drop.

He was still bewildered by the speed with which he had been arrested and transferred to this cell days before—how many days he was already no longer certain. He knew only that he had followed Captain Kuo down the stairs to the adjutant's office, and the captain had refrained from any threat or warning; he had scarcely spoken to Fallon again, or asked him a question, until the Security men came in, bound Fallon's elbows tightly behind his back until he thought his shoulder blades would break, and hustled him out to a waiting enclosed van. The van took him through the midnight streets to Ward Road, he was thrown into the cell, and that was the sum of it. Since then he had had no visitors, no explanations, no examination. He had been neither badly treated nor reviled. He had been left in a form of solitary confinement, interrupted only twice a day by his stolid and uncommunicative guards who brought the thin rice gruel and the cup of water.

Fallon did not know what to expect. If he had been quizzed or beaten or even tortured it would have followed an understandable and standard pattern. But nothing happened in his isolation. The guards had taken his shoelaces and his belt and had given him the cotton quilt, for the early autumn rains made the walls sweat in the cell. The cell was ten feet square with the high window-slit and a steel door, and a glass aperture in the door permitted the guards to stare at him, and in the high ceiling was a naked globe that glared down on him and was never turned off. Between the globe and the staring eyes and the constant banging and clanging of other steel doors along the corridor, the tramp of boots and the angry shouts and scuffles and the irregular yelling and the measured drum beat, there was little rest or sleep in the cell.

Fallon protested against the tasteless congee, and was surprised to receive a change of diet. Thereafter he was given a small wooden bucket of pickled cabbage and a tin pot of hot water. Once a day the guard took away his toilet pot, the only article of furniture in the cell.

The guards explained that they were not permitted to talk to him. But after several days when he went on his half-hearted hunger strike against the gruel, they came in and swore at him and threatened forced feeding with a tube, so he made no remarks about the cabbage. But they watched him closely after that for they greatly feared a suicide attempt, and constantly warned him against it. It was *tsing tze lu,* seeking the death way, and he had not thought about it before they talked so much. There was no way to accomplish it even had he been so inclined, but he saw that its threat was a weapon to force some sort of action before he dry-rotted, so he tried it again, through hunger.

They didn't use the tube. They took him down the corridor and stripped him and hung him up by his feet, head downward, and poured water into his nose. The usual water-cure was varied by the addition of a small amount of valuable gasoline to the liquid. They pressed cigarette stubs into the soles of his feet in the classic manner. This was effective and he thereafter ate his cabbage and got a very bad diarrhea. But everyone had that, even the guards, and it didn't matter, though it made the guards more work emptying the pot.

He began to get throbbing headaches because he had fallen into the firm habit of drinking large quantities of tea, of which he was now deprived, and because they wouldn't let him sleep enough. They refused to turn out the light, they yelled at him through the door, and the uproar in adjoining cells combined with the booming from the drum tower to keep him awake most of the time. He asked if he might write a letter to Colonel Li but it was not permitted. He wished to take a bath to rid his skin of the penetrating odor of cabbage and the sting of vermin, but it was not permitted.

After two weeks they handcuffed him from behind and led him barefoot down the corridor into a large room and sat him erect on a bench beneath a platform on which stood a long desk. Behind the desk on the wall hung the flags of the People's Republic and of Soviet Russia, and between them were three large framed portraits of Sun, Mao and Stalin. Fallon wondered vaguely how Sun had got into that rogues' gallery, and reflected that Mao was now the only survivor.

After a time three men entered and sat at the desk and looked down at him, and the one in the center, the chief investigator, smoked a cigarette while an orderly placed a teapot and bowl before him. He sat whiffling the tea through his front teeth, staring at Fallon curiously. Then he said that there was no need to explain to the prisoner why he was there, since he knew the reason very well. It was only necessary to cooperate and to confess his guilt, and that quickly. Fallon said he had nothing to confess. He asked if he would be permitted to have a lawyer for his defense, and was informed that he didn't need one because he had no defense to make.

"Do you insist that you have nothing to confess?"

"Yes," Fallon said.

"That," said the chairman of the investigation, "is a typically arrogant imperialist attitude. You will apologize."

"I have nothing to apologize for. I should like to talk to Colonel Li Han-tsen or to Captain Kuo Liang."

"Colonel Li has nothing to do with this case. Captain Kuo is fully informed and has no desire to see you at this time. Fah On I-sheng, you have been in this country several years and have been granted many special privileges. Your privileges are continuing here. If they were not, you would have already been executed for your crime. Return to your cell and reflect on wisdom."

9

The soldier in the midst of battle may know how the battle goes within a few hundred yards of his position but he is likely to be muddled by the Big Picture, though it may seem quite clear to complacent newspaper readers ten thousand miles away. Fallon, out of contact with reality and living in a fantastic world dominated by a drum beat, realized vaguely that he lay in the vortex of a sordid purge whereby the axiomatic inhumanity of man to fellow man was being monotonously demonstrated once again.

Outside his walls he was aware, in a sense, of torturous grillings and mock trials of innocent and inoffensive hordes, of mass enslavement and pillage and confiscation. He knew that large unruly masses of people were being systematically weeded out as a matter of cold policy. As a side issue, a minor digression in the atrocious upheaval, hundreds of foreign businessmen had already been harried out of the country, hundreds of churchmen had been imprisoned, many had been killed. But all that was still an abstraction, something outside the walls of the cell.

He began to dream, at intervals, that he was being throttled in a clump of brush, while close by on a busy street crowds walked past laughing and talking, unheeding his strangled screams. When he wakened, struggling in a bath of sweat, he knew the ultimate loneliness of one who faces cosmic violence and death without being able to pass on the horror of it to any other human person. His screaming and that of all the others was unheard, either by the guards or by anyone else in or out of the prison, in or out of the city or the country. The world passed by far away, and if it heard faint echoes of such screaming its face stiffened into dumbness with wonder and disbelief and its eyes assumed a glassy stare and it shook off the sound with a shrug of incredulity. The process of mass-killing went on in the prisons and labor centers and hostage camps and public streets as steadily as the regular drumming from the drum tower, but ears were stopped against it.

Fallon had not failed to perceive the grandeur and terror of the time into which he had been born and the place to which he had drifted, but now he fought to keep control of himself for he feared he might be becoming a little crazy, and might never be healthy and normal again. He strove to be matter-of-fact and unimaginative, but it was difficult, for he was finding that the stoic has a wider horizon than the fanatic. The limits of his awareness were expanding against his own wishes; focusing on a lump of reality in the clammy cell, he saw the trivial and the cosmic beginning to fuse.

He could see nothing through the tiny window-slit high above his head, but sounds penetrated from the central exercise yard. There was, inevitably, the sound of the watch drum. But he heard other things as well—the thud of blows, the bitter curse, the defiant howl, and once he heard the shuffle of roped prisoners' feet and the tramp of executioners, and presently the uneven bursts of a machine gun. Rumors passed through the prison by osmosis: there had been another mass execution of a group of deviationists. Fallon sat for some time thinking what it might be like to have a rope around his neck and stand against a wall to face the unprecise and capricious aim of a machine gun.

This was, naturally, what his interrogators had intended him to think. After he had been allowed to reflect for another week, they began leading him into the big room every night and haranguing him. Sometimes all three examiners were present, sometimes only the man who whiffled his tea. They knew that Fallon had been captured by the Japanese on Samar near the end of the war and had been interned in Cabanatuan. He was asked if he wished to spend another long period in prison.

There had once been forty-four nationalities living in the Settlement, and fifteen foreign powers had exercised extraterritorial rights there, but he was told that he must realize that such nationals were no longer the lords of the manor and the death blow had long since been delivered to their tenure. This was explained to Fallon as though he were a child, as though it were news to him that the roof had long since fallen in, as though he were unaware that special privilege had ended and the out-of-date undemocratic old treaties had been scrapped. Fallon pretended to listen, and sat thinking of the old days before economic chaos and frenzied financiers and the end of a way of life in a city that had gone soft, fat, frustrated and desperate. He had been here briefly in the time of the inflation and the rapid spread of panic and disorder. He had seen the great influx of refugees and the snarled traffic at the time of the Change-over and the dismay of the foreigners and the storm of forms, documents and affidavits that had hopelessly entangled their affairs.

Fallon was beginning to feel throughly browbeaten and sick from these nightly sessions. They ran into hours, during which he was not permitted to relax or stand up or smoke or drink water or even speak. The interrogators wished him to change his thinking. They wished him to confess. They demanded that he furnish information.

"We are always alert and vigilant for truth and justice," the chief interrogator told him in a friendly fashion. "All we want is for you to tell us what you know about this petty apparatus of which Chung Yin-kuei and Tieh Lao-hu are members, and we will return you to Colonel Li's headquarters."

"I don't know anything about it."

"Then how did news of Comrade Pregnesky's illness reach our enemies if you didn't pass word about it to the opposition?"

"I don't know of any opposition."

"But you have already said that such an apparatus exists and that you have collaborated with it."

"I said no such thing. I said such an apparatus may exist without my knowledge, and if I have collaborated with it I was not aware of the fact."

"But, Doctor, it is right here on the record."

"Then the record is deliberately incorrect. My answer was misinterpreted and twisted."

"We shall see about that!"

Finally the chairman declared that it was incomprehensible that Fallon had lived freely under the benefits of the People's Government for so long and had received no indoctrination. His ignorance was appalling. His hands were undoubtedly stained with the blood of the people because of his connivance with an apparatus, but the People's Government was merciful and would allow him to make amends.

There began a period of education in political and economic ideologies. Fallon was lectured. He listened to a series of evangelists who came into his cell and told him in nagging monotonous voices of the new salvation. They made him repeat his lessons without question or argument or back talk. Fallon was uninterested in doctrine but he pretended to listen. His instruction was a course under private tutors; he was not forced to attend the larger mass lectures and classes held daily in the prison for the general run of inmates. But he heard their chanting discussion groups. His tutors strove to emphasize the Truth. They told him about the nature of capitalism. He was informed that capitalism was very advanced, industrially, but that it needed a series of wars to prevent collapse. He was an American. American high standards of living came from the blood shed by people in other countries. American capitalism was dying and decaying; soon it would inevitably collapse of its own putrescent weight into economic ruin.

This was elementary; Fallon had heard little else for four years or more. He made rapid progress with his lessons in political science. He recognized that they were given on the principle of incessant bombardment. And dimly he knew that he was undergoing a form of the science of brain-washing. His examiners were frank about it. They called the process *hsi nao chin*, and he developed a great weariness with the fantastic and macabre proceedings. The statements dinned at him were familiarly ridiculous, and seemed no more reasonable after their hundredth repetition.

"What is the most reactionary government in the world today, Fah On?"

"The United States government, Comrade."

"Who profited by the imperialist war in Korea, Fah On?"

"Wall Street profited, Comrade. Big Business."

"Most Americans weren't interested in the aggression their leaders plotted and prosecuted in Korea, were they, or in the internal problems of the peoples of the democratic Eastern countries?"

"No."

"All most Americans wanted was to hear the last of the war and go on enjoying their luxuries at home, and their pleasures. Is it not true?"

"Yes."

"Well, have you read your assigned section in *Das Kapital* today?"

"Yes, Comrade. Also the last speech by Chairman Mao."

"Good. Now, where have you failed to make progress today, Fah On?"

"I accuse myself of inattention, Comrade. I couldn't get interested in the prompter's comments on Engels' social philosophy."

"That is bad. Now today we must return to self-analyzation. I wish you to write a complete autobiography and have it for me tomorrow. Please give all details on your family's struggles with that farm, on its forced sale to provide you with an education, and on the inability of your society to adapt your specialized medical knowledge to its needs and to integrate you. You were thrown aside, lacking money, and forced to take up a penniless wandering life, I believe."

"I have already written my autobiography with emphasis on those points three times, Comrade."

"Write it a fourth time, then, Fah On. Search your memories."

Eventually the indoctrination period ended. Fallon did not believe that his examiners had ordered it with any hope of real success, and had gone at it half-heartedly. They regarded him as a hard case. He had lived for four years under the aegis of Colonel Li and none of it had rubbed off on him, apparently. The proof was that he would furnish them with no definite information, which they were convinced he had. It roused them finally into great anger and then into a vicious calm.

One night the door of his cell opened and his four guards entered, followed by his chief prompter. Behind them was another. It was Captain Kuo Liang. Captain Kuo looked at Fallon impersonally, noting his face emaciated under the uncut beard and matted hair, the body disfigured by semistarvation, the wrists and ankles chafed and festering from rope and chain.

"You are a stiff-backed man, Doctor," Kuo said, staring at him with distaste. "You are fortunate you are still alive. They have not even hung you up by the thumbs yet, to pull the bones from the sockets. Perhaps you think these are idle threats and that such things do not happen?"

"I am certain now that they do happen," said Fallon.

Kuo glanced at the head guard and made a signal. The guards seized Fallon, who was too weakened to put up any resistance, hurled him to the floor of the cell and tore aside his shirt. A hypodermic was produced.

"This is the true-words medicine," Kuo said. "You are a physician and should know that it is effective. We will now find out what you really know."

The truth serum deprived Fallon of all thought and left him with only a peculiar sensation of free suspension. Through it he heard the prompter's chanting voice, ending in a blackout. When he recovered, Kuo was still there, sitting calmly on a stool and smoking cigarettes. Fallon's head was splitting. Kuo waved several sheets of paper he held in his hand, paper covered with typewritten lines.

"This is a transcript of your confession," the captain said. "It is complete, even to your signature. See?"

A signature was there. Fallon was not permitted to read the confession. He sat on the floor, holding his head between his hands. He did not believe in the truth serum. They had the stuff, probably, but whatever was turned out by their laboratories was not always reliable.

"That *cheng yen yao* is a fake," he said. "It's as phony as my signature. The confession is valueless. Anyway, I repudiate it."

"Your repudiation means nothing," Kuo said. "We have the signed statement."

But Fallon, lifting his eyes, saw that Kuo's face had gone bloodless with rage and he knew that whatever had been said in the statement was no betrayal of Yin Kuei and Tieh. He could only have parroted what he was told to say, and Kuo did not know what to tell him to repeat.

The Orientals had an unearned reputation for stolidity and control over their emotions. They were supposed to be dead-pan artists. It was a fallacy, of course, that Fallon had often seen exposed. They were highly emotional people, capable of veritable frenzies over trifles. This was no trifle to Captain Kuo. Fallon saw the venom at the edges of the captain's trembling mouth and the fury in his eyes.

10

Captain Kuo had a boundless contempt and an irreconcilable hatred for the Western world and all its spawn. He did not ordinarily display this face of his nature but it was there, the reverse of the hard metallic coin of an unchanging character. Those of his colleagues who were aware of it were puzzled, for his contact with foreigners had been extremely limited and so far as they knew he had suffered no indignity or slight, no blow or kick. His life had been spent in rural areas and in the Army, and Westerners were scarce in both environments. But Kuo was a student of history, like many of his contemporaries, and he followed Occidental reaction to the Oriental revolution with a morbid fascination. He knew that his creed was having its tremendous impact on the West, and that it would have an even greater one upon the East; he felt that he was directly involved in a duel to the death with Western degradation and corruption, and he accented the Marxist virtues and was merciless to his enemies. A scholarly policeman, he accepted Communist doctrine as Christians accepted the Sermon on the Mount, allowing himself the privilege of considerable latitude in its interpretation. But he blamed most of his country's travails upon the West, with its attitudes of superiority, its ignorance, its derisions and its rattle of arms. He fully expected the West to launch a military reconquest, though he was certain it would fail.

To Kuo, all foreigners were barbarous, including Russians, imperialists trying to reimpose enslavement and colonialism. They were gauche and uncouth, with abominable manners and weird customs, and he most deeply resented their color line. He had once asked Fallon, with a curl of his lip, "When is your country going to send its first Negro ambassador to an Asiatic nation?" It had been a good question, one Fallon obviously could not answer.

Kuo realized that all foreigners did not come from the same rat warren, just as here there were people who were rice eaters and those who ate noodles. Fallon was one type, the bigoted and hypocritical missionaries were another, the avaricious and criminal-minded businessmen were a third, and so on down the categories. In Kuo's youth on the Shantung farm, for example, a missionary had once come to discuss soils and fertilizers and demonstrate crop rotation, and had said practically nothing about Jesus Christ. But he lumped all foreigners together now. The Westerners had then been top dogs and the Easterners underdogs; the situation was currently reversed. He had once had an American oil company executive in this very cell, in the first year of the Takeover, and remembered clearly what the man had said. He had said: "Wait till our fleet and the marines come back in here again! We'll show you then we know how to handle Chinamen!" Kuo had no intention of being handled; he would do the handling himself. Rabid dogs and white men only got what was coming to them.

Now he sat on his stool in the cell, smoking and looking at Fallon, the deep flush gradually receding from his aquiline face. Fallon might not represent the direct focus of Kuo's hatred and contempt, but he would serve. He had lived a good and easy life thus far, enjoying the protection of Colonel Li, whom Kuo disliked. The dislike stemmed from the fact that Li was a soldier and fighting man, whereas Kuo was a policeman and disciplinarian. And from the vantage of Li's extended immunity, Fallon had virtually thumbed his nose at the Security Bureau.

The guards had bound Fallon's hands behind him. Kuo walked over, took the cigarette from his lips, and pressed the lighted end into Fallon's cheek.

"So you don't know where Yin Kuei is?" he asked mildly.

Fallon replied with a startled but crackling coolie oath. Kuo grasped him by the hair, banged his head against the wall, and pushed the cigarette end into his nostril.

"Where do you suppose she and Tieh are hiding?"

His victim tried to kick him away, and Kuo's heavy boot heel came down to crush the bare toes. The burning tip of the cigarette next went into Fallon's eyelid.

"You are working with them, aren't you?" he demanded, smiling.

Kuo looked around at the head guard. "Did a foreigner ever do you any harm?" he asked.

The man looked at him narrowly, grinned and said, "Often. And my family also. Once a British police constable beat my brother for violating the law against urinating in alleys."

"One should retaliate in kind," said Kuo. The guard's grin broadened, for this was an old game. He approached Fallon, fumbling with his uniform, and urinated on him, spraying his face.

"What about you?" Kuo asked the chief prompter.

"My father was once evicted from a mud-and-wattle hut in the western district to make room for a foreign taipan's expanding estate," the prompter muttered, and when Kuo nodded he ripped a bamboo splinter from the leg of the stool, seized Fallon's bound hand, and jammed it deep under the thumbnail.

"And you?" One of the guards, taken by surprise at this special attention, hesitated. Then he said, "Years ago, an Italian marine raped my young cousin in the French Consulate grounds."

"The rape of a girl or of a nation is a dreadful thing," said Kuo. "Beat him!"

The guards went methodically to work on Fallon with their boots, their gun butts, the rubber hoses and their horny palms, beating him bloody and pulpy. Each stunning blow was accompanied by a jeer: he would repudiate his confession, would he? The blows and the resonant voices both vibrated through him as he lay on the floor, propped against the wall with fire in his belly and throat and lungs and salty blood in his mouth. He dimly heard the repeated questions but could still manage to shake his head.

One of the questioners was most insistent and he forced open an eye, and saw Kuo's distorted face close to his own. He gathered the red saliva together in a glob on his tongue and spat it into the captain's face. Then his head shattered in a thousand swirling lights.

When Fallon next opened the eye, he saw Dr. Chu's chubby figure bending over him. The eye was glazed and sunken in a mass of livid bruised flesh that had been Fallon's face. His leg moved slowly, then his arm, and the smashed body convulsed in a crawling motion. He gasped at the hurt and the gasp pained the broken mouth, but his eye was still wide open as though his senses had been pulverized.

After a time he perceived a thinner figure behind Chu, and it was that of Colonel Li. The colonel's face was masklike; he stood holding the blood-streaked shirt that had been taken off Fallon. Beyond the colonel was a nurse, beyond the nurse was the wall of a room, a white hospital room. Fallon was home again.

"What do you say now?" the colonel asked Dr. Chu.

"I have seen worse cases," Chu said.

"Oh, certainly," said the colonel. "So have I. But he has suffered as keenly as any human or animal flesh can suffer. He bears it like a Chinese. There is a loose opinion that we are all stoics because pain and misery are our racial heritage. It's odd; he makes no outcry."

"He is in bad shape," Chu said. "His nose is packed with congealed blood. His ribs are cracked, but not broken. It is relatively bad."

Fallon lay in his own stench on the bed while Chu worked over him. He thought of what the colonel had said. He wondered if he'd let the dirty sods know they had hurt him so much. Presently he began to retch steadily, his bruised shoulders shaking until he could vomit no more. He assumed he was a little delirious. He heard himself disclaiming, through battered lips where the breath bubbled, that he knew anything at all about Yin Kuei.

Dr. Chu eased down the trousers and studied the blue marks of rifle butts across the stomach.

"Those are rather serious," he said to the colonel. "There have also been smashing blows across the kidneys. I suppose they have filled the cavity with blood and perhaps damaged the organs. When the time comes, he will probably have an agony to micturate. But I have seen worse. He will recover when the fever subsides. His mind will clear soon."

"It is clear now," Fallon managed to rasp. He turned his head aside and fell asleep.

Dr. Chu had a job; Fallon had had it, for a fact. Dr. Chu's assistant, the young man with the tic, spelled him, but the director got little rest because Colonel Li was always at him, biting and driving. Get Fallon well. Spare nothing to cure him. In a day or so Fallon was coming along so nicely that he could make a few weak jokes to the assistant. The colonel came to see him again.

"Your body is mending itself," Li said awkwardly. "You will be all right."

"How is Father Julien?" Fallon whispered.

"Eh? About the same, I am told. A little better, perhaps. Later on, I'll have his bed wheeled in here so that you can have company occasionally."

"And the comrade general?"

Li raised his eyebrows. The comrade general was far in the past, gone and nearly forgotten. Had it been so long that Fallon had been in that damned prison? "He has returned to Moscow, I believe. Anyway, we shipped him out of here for Peking in very good condition."

Fallon lay quietly. Then he asked, "Have I been released from prison, or am I to go back when I've recovered?"

He saw the colonel's mouth tighten until a white line appeared around its edges.

"You are not going back, I assure you. I didn't know you were there in the first place. You simply vanished. I am sorry to have doubted you, Fah On, but I was under the misapprehension for some time that you had escaped. I was told you had a quarrel with Albany and then disappeared. After all, you might have tried to escape, you know. I was not informed that you had been arrested and imprisoned. Captain Kuo said nothing to me about it."

Fallon tried to smile but his mouth was too sore. The colonel had supposed he'd gone over the hill, and all the time he'd been rotting in that cell under the drum tower, a mile distant.

Li saw the movement of the mouth, and went on in a low angry voice. "It was never officially reported to me what had happened to you. If I had known, I would have had you out of there immediately. It was a stupid brutal thing, and it accomplished nothing. Obviously you knew nothing about the underground apparatus."

Fallon's heart thudded. The confession had been false, as he suspected; the true-words medicine had been a ruse, a harmless narcotic.

"How did I get here then? Did Kuo release me?"

"No," Li said, frowning. "I released you. As soon as I learned of it, I rushed to the prison. The warden admitted that you were held, and I found you in your cell. Captain Kuo and his guards were still there. I arrived at a very embarrassing moment for him. I brought you here myself."

"I'm grateful," Fallon murmured. "But I don't understand how you learned about it."

The colonel glanced at him sideways. "Neither do I," he said. "An unknown river boatman left a written message for me with the sentry at the house one evening, and went away quickly. The sentry was going to destroy it but my orderly saw it. The message told me where to find you, and under what circumstances. It was not signed."

An attendant entered with a small glass, and Fallon drank the bitter medicine. He lay back.

"You apparently have friends who keep close track of you," Li said.

"Yes. It's baffling."

"It must also be comforting."

"Yes, it's comforting too, to have friends. I appreciate them."

When the colonel had departed, Fallon rested, twisting the thing over and around in his mind and smiling to himself. The assistant with the tic came in and sat beside the bed, taking his pulse. They had become friendly; the young man was forever talking with great wonder about the brain surgery it had been his fortune to watch.

"When you are in good health," he said slyly, "you must be quite a lady's man, Dr. Fallon."

"How's that?"

"A young woman comes here nearly every evening after Dr. Chu leaves the building and asks the attendants about you."

Fallon was alarmed, and his pulse jumped under the assistant's fingers.

"Please don't mention this to anyone," he said. "She is just a girl of the town I know, probably, but it isn't right that she should come here. Would you do me a favor?"

"Certainly, if I can."

"Have the attendants tell her not to come again. When I am discharged from here, I will come to see her."

"That won't be necessary, Doctor. I told her that myself, tonight. I noticed that she is a very pretty young woman. Not what one would expect to see from that class."

"No," said Fallon, relieved. "But beauty is only skin deep, you know. That's a saying of ours."

"Ours also. They are all alike, underneath, if you understand me."

They winked simultaneously.

Presently Fallon said, "The colonel indicates Father Julien is improving. I hope you are giving him good care."

"As much as Dr. Chu will permit," the assistant said. He leaned forward, his voice dropping. "I spend much time with the old man and I am glad your colonel is helping him. He is harmless and good and talks to me about many interesting things. I don't understand where he gets the strength but he draws on it and it holds him together."

"He has a faith," Fallon said after a moment's hesitation. "Nothing that happens to him can shake it, so he is tranquil in the strength we can't see. It isn't political, or a faith in science such as we know."

"Whatever it is, it is a good thing to have," the assistant said. "He isn't afraid to die. But I think he will live quite a while."

"Every man should have some belief that will make him unafraid and keep him living," Fallon said. "Father Julien is certain of the future. Perhaps that's it. Not many are certain of the future any more. It doesn't matter what you believe, as long as you are firm about it."

"I'll wheel him in here later tonight for a little while when it's quiet," the assistant said. "You will do each other good."

IV

The Iron Shadow Wall

The ebullient voice of Gregor Efremov thundered and echoed down the quiet halls and bounced through the open door of Fallon's hospital room. It roused him from a midmorning doze. The air from his window was cool; outside the fall day sparkled under a pouring sun, and the birds in the trees were going mad.

Efremov was loudly demanding admittance to see his poor friend Fallon, disregarding the protests of orderly and nurse that this was not the proper hour for visits. The Russian surged into the room, seeming suddenly to fill it with vigorous gesticulations, the essence of garlic sausage and an overpowering vitality.

"*Tovarish!* I scatter the barricades and invest the inner fortifications! Visiting hours are for the feeble in spirit to bother the feeble in body." He grasped Fallon's hand in both his own, engulfing it half to the elbow, and pumped it until the patient winced. "Ha! Here you lie, white and thin, a veritable lump! But you recover, no? From the way the colonel complains, one would think his physician is a corpse ready for the boneyard, but it isn't so. They can't kill us tough ones, eh?"

He dragged up a chair and sat beside the bed. "So?" he said, gazing at Fallon with appraising blue eyes under level and colorless brows. "They put you through the Lemon Factory, did they?"

"The Lemon Factory?" Fallon repeated.

"*Da!* The squeezer!" Efremov's immoderate laughter was infectious and Fallon grinned, though the movement hurt his healing mouth. "The more juice you got, the longer they keep you there." He put his finger beside his nose and looked up at the ceiling with an air of mystery. "I know. I've been in one, *tovarish*. Ekh, it comes to all of us. Long ago and nearly forgotten, but never quite."

He reached into the pocket of his old leather jacket and drew out a squat bottle. "From personal knowledge, I know that this is the best medicine for a man from the squeezer," he said, uncorking the vodka. "Take some, take some! If you will drink concoctions from that fat Dr. Chu, you can surely trust me."

Fallon managed to swallow without choking, and warmth spread rapidly in his belly and up through his limbs, tingling behind his eyes and fingertips. He raised himself and Efremov punched up the pillows behind him.

"Well, well," the agent said, "that Captain Kuo is the lump now, not you. Ho, *ho!* You should see how he skulks about, and scuttles away whenever he hears a footstep that sounds like the colonel's. He comes and sticks his nose into things, but he is not the man he was. The colonel almost spits on him when they meet, and has been to raise the devil with Kuo's superiors." He shrugged. "Of course, the colonel has great authority, but it is not so great that he can order the Security Bureau what to do. They listen and make polite noises and apologize and promise disciplinary action, but you know how it is with the *En-kay-vay-day*. Untouchable."

"I didn't expect anything would come of it," Fallon said. "It's enough that I'm out of the Factory."

"Yes, that is all one can wish, from what I hear of that place. The Chinese have little refinements that my own people have never yet imagined, though now that we are such good friends we are probably borrowing a few. Exchanging trade secrets. I suppose the captain was trying to find out if you are turncoat."

"One can't be a traitor when one doesn't belong in the first place."

"Well, it is the same thing. It is not easy to define ideological defection. He is still hunting for that girl; she is the real defector, of course." Efremov took a drink from the bottle he held on his knee and passed it to Fallon. "You look different, my friend. Your nose is as big as a potato. In fact, your nose and that of Comrade Albany's are almost identical." He laughed uproariously again. "Yes, I heard all about it, and it is a great pity I was not there to watch. It would have done me good. He went around for a time with a bandage on it, so sad! Madame Markham was his nurse and changed the dressing, and held his hand. Perhaps more —I do not pry. What a pair!"

"I remember that on the night of the incident an entente cordiale appeared to have developed."

"Well, what can you expect? She is English. She maintains relations with both the Chinese and Americans. She provides Li with a necessity and fights on the side of Albany. Personally, I think she would prefer to be Albany's lady friend now, but it would not be so diplomatic. Albany can give her nothing but love, like in your song, if he feels like giving her that, but Li can give her security. I am not so sure the colonel is even interested in that any more. He is cool; she suffers. I go to the colonel's suite to confer with him and see her sulking there, and she slips out to say sympathetic nothings to the poor fellow upstairs and the colonel laughs. He is more interested in an entertainer in a café in Kwangsi Road near the Louza Police Post. A singsong lady, very celebrated, called Jade of Evening. We may have Jade of Evening as a companion resident in Number 68 before long."

"That would be a little rough on Judith," Fallon said.

Efremov nodded. "Yes, but Madame Markham has seen rough times before. Oh yes, I know what she and the colonel say about her bad husband who abandoned her and fled to Hongkong. I know about the big home she managed, and the servants, and the parties and the clubs and the fine family in Malaya. But sometimes I think Madame Markham is a great dramatist. Sometimes I think maybe before we came she was an English singsong girl, like Jade of Evening."

"Sometimes I think you're an idle old woman with a clacking tongue," Fallon said. "The Russians are great talkers and gossips. You haven't enough work to do."

"I have so much work to do it would horrify you to face it." He chuckled. "Pregnesky's interrupted visit stirred up a hornet's nest."

"You mean Comrade General Malov."

"Eh, well, everyone knew it anyway. He is too significant a figure to pass incognito."

"And yet," said Fallon thoughtfully, "one hears on all sides that the party here is going it alone, as an ally but not a satellite. It doesn't need Russian help. But they send you and thousands like you, and they send Malov. And they keep on proclaiming that your country is chosen by some sort of mechanistic destiny to lead all the earth's dispossessed. That's something I read in your *Pravda*."

Efremov grunted, and looked at the bottle on his knee. "My friend,

Russia cannot afford to ignore what goes on here in the East. We cannot remain passive and watch the imperialists conquer this nation and make another strategic base from which to attack us. We have an historical affinity. We have always had a dominating influence on Eastern thought, and the impact of our ideology has been strong; it substitutes for their outmoded philosophies and religions. They worshiped Lenin. They saw Stalin as the greatest of all conquerors, the torchbearer of tradition and the possessor of the keys. Their own traditions have fallen and a hundred years from now most will have perished. The peasant is religious, and if his old gods fail he will seek new ones."

"Even if the new ones have Slavic faces?"

"They accepted a god with an Indian face, did they not? They only gave the Buddha classical Chinese features. No, Doctor, we are fighting a war for their minds now. Your people offer them only materialistic necessities, but we give them precise aims and objectives. Your country is a power vacuum, too rich and too contented. It has lost its youth and has acquired the habits of lazy old age. It has no policy. Fighting with weapons alone is a policy of bankruptcy. It is lazy work to fight a war. It is hard work to understand the minds of those we fight or woo."

"We've done that too, in the past," Fallon objected. "They've had all our literature. We've sent them missionaries and credos."

"I know," said Efremov indifferently. "But we don't need to bombard them with alien Christianity; we are their spiritual friends. They ally with us voluntarily. Their workers are the brothers of our workers, and all dream of world brotherhood. There is no racial prejudice in the class struggle."

"How can you ever wholly succeed with a race of individualists and their family system?"

Efremov smiled. "I do not come to the hospital to engage in polemics with you, Fallon. You are beyond conversion, you are lost. I come to comfort you, as you came to comfort me when I was dying of a jealous bazaar girl's subtle poisons."

"Colitis," said Fallon. "Nevertheless, I'm only saying that Soviet influence grows here daily, and why deny it?"

"I don't deny it. Why do you think Malov was sent on that mission? I will tell you why. It is because the revolt, not only of China but of all Southeast Asia, is the greatest single event in human history and we recognize it as such, while the West does not. It is part of the historic atmosphere of our times, just as much as airplanes and the atomic bomb, and it is as inevitable. A billion peasants have risen against the West's humiliations and oppressions, and they are forging a new way of life for themselves. It is a revolt against the old social order, against the past, against the cultural and economic domination of the West. The West strives desperately on the fringes to stem the tide, but these efforts will all fail. They can only delay it, with little dams at the frontiers. The leaders of the revolt are not fools, you know. They have the West's technical knowledge and our support. They are dividing the world in two parts—Asia and the West. And the center of gravity shifts from West to East."

Efremov pointed dramatically out of the window. "Over there is the Pacific—the new Middle Sea, the Twentieth Century Mediterranean—where all the power is concentrated. Man power on this side, machine power on the other. They must make a test of strength."

"What's the use?" Fallon said. He was remembering Malov's toast, *odin mir*, one peace. It might well have meant one world.

"The use?" Efremov's brows drew fiercely together. "We must fight exploitation, disease, illiteracy, the catastrophes of nature, the corruption of governments, starvation, the shelter of hovels, the lives of drudgery and toil. The indignities of the past must be righted, my friend. In your country democracy decays. Here it is being revived. So, from your viewpoint at least, the last war was not fought entirely in vain." An ironic grin twisted back his strange lips. He had been beating out his points with the vodka bottle on his knee.

Fallon lay silent. He had heard all this before, from the interrogators and brain-washers. The thing about it was, he knew some of it was true. But he did not actually believe that any Russian *diktat* could succeed in the face of Asian beliefs and customs. The leaders were too wise and too informed for that; they were scholars, not freebooters or storm troopers. They were men who wanted the West's skills and help—machines to replace the coolie lines, physicians like himself to replace the medicine men and practitioners of acupuncture. Colonel Li himself had once declared that if there could be peace, in ten years more books would be printed in Asia than in all the rest of the world together. There would be a renaissance.

"They can only get those things you speak of," he said at last, "if they stop this damned fighting among themselves and with everybody urging them on."

"They are only fighting with you," Efremov jeered. "Not with us. We are helping these peoples to spring overnight from the paleolithic age to the atomic age. We are advising them on decisions they must make, ones that in the next few years will determine the course of all history. History, you know, is no longer controlled by the powers of the West. The Asiatic Century is well under way."

He kicked back his chair and rose. "You lie here sick and remind me

that I have work to do. Take another drink, it will speed your recovery
so that you can come home soon."

"Home." Fallon had never really thought of 68 Soochow Road as home,
nor did he now. He took the bottle absently, sipped and handed it back.

"Certainly, home to the colonel's mansion." Efremov was grinning
again. "The colonel wishes to move this old Frenchman there also. This
priest, Vauzous. He is turning his house into a refuge for stray cats. You,
his propagandist, his defecting mistress, his bead-telling friend."

"And you, his most enthusiastic missionary."

"Yes, even the despised Russian. When you come home we will have
a party. Even Albany will come. But we won't invite the Angel Kuo.
Perhaps the colonel will bring his new delight, Jade of Evening. Huang
will supply food and I will supply drink. Hurry up! I feel the need of
relaxation; I cannot forever be settling the ills of Asia."

"Much more of that potato-peeling liquor and I'll leave this place in
the hearse," said Fallon. But he felt warmed and friendly, and filled
with strength he knew was false. Efremov's hearty slap on the shoulder
did not even hurt his numbed body. There was not much clarity left to
his thoughts after this bedside visit, but it was good to be welcomed
home.

2

They did have the party, and it was a notable one in a life of solemn
dedication to an austere task. The house at Number 68 may have seen
many more abandoned galas in its day, but none more fully appreciated
by the guests. For Efremov's party—it was his though the colonel footed
the bill—brought laughter, music and a measure of fellowship to a drab
and grim establishment that had known little of this since the time of
the Greek lady and her troupe; good wine flowed freely and the food
was provided by a caterer from a celebrated Canton Road restaurant, as
a relief from the series of uninspired rations served by the headquarters
cook.

It took no urging by Efremov to persuade the colonel to the project;
Li was usually on a diet and parties were no novelty to him since they
were part of his job, but he welcomed the diversion. It was another
opportunity to snub Captain Kuo, whom he did not invite. But he
made a point that the captain should hear about it, and learn that the
occasion was the return of the convalescent Dr. Fallon, his erstwhile
guest in Ward Road Jail. It was also pitched to welcome the colonel's

old friend, Father Julien, who was taking up residence in the house. Although the priest was still too ill to come from his new invalid quarters on the third floor to the mess hall where Li's staff made unaccustomed wassail, he had a constant stream of visitors through the festive evening. This information was broadcast for the captain's benefit also, and likewise for the annoyed Dr. Chu, who had urged for some time that the old foreign pauper be turned out of the ward. Colonel Li was in a thoroughly rebellious and flaunting mood.

Jade of the Evening did not appear, for the colonel still retained a certain discretion. Thus Judith Markham queened in solitary feminine triumph and enjoyed each vainglorious moment. She had little enough entertainment of this kind, as the colonel's duty parties were not for her; she had a new gown of crimson silk for the occasion, and a predinner hairdresser, for the colonel was in an expansive and reckless mood. He felt something of guilt for himself and pity for Judith. He had neglected her, they were all but estranged, and she made no secret of her attachment to Thorpe Albany. Her surreptitious visits to his room had been the pretense of an odd convention; she was nursing him, and now that he was recovered she had the excuse of trips to the third floor because of the presence there of Father Julien. Judith had no interest in or curiosity about the old man who had taken Major Huang's upstairs quarters, the adjutant having been moved down to his office where he was happier because more isolated from the strains and stresses of the house. But she volunteered to care for the priest and answer his infrequent calls, it was a good arrangement, and all were content. The colonel bore Albany no more animosity than usual; certainly Judith's deflection had little bearing on his attitude.

Indeed, the party planned and executed by Efremov was remarkably free of the normal tensions, bickerings and undercurrents of Li's establishment, as though an unspoken truce had been agreed for the evening. Fallon still felt rather shaky and moved with an uncertain step two days after leaving the hospital, but he braced himself and was much improved after one of Efremov's preliminary cocktails. They were drinking them in Efremov's room when Albany came along the hall and put his head in the door. Fallon had not seen him since the night of the arrest; the two regarded each other's discolorations with interest and both grinned. Albany came in and accepted a glass.

"Seems to me," he said, "you came off second best."

"There's no basis for comparison," Fallon replied. "I got mine from experts, yours was the result of an accident."

"Well, I just want you to know that despite what was said that night, I didn't repeat any of it to the colonel or to Kuo or anyone else. I recall that I thought Kuo was suspicious, and apparently he was sharper than I gave him credit for. Anyway, he did come up and question me later, but he didn't get anywhere."

"We might as well skip it," Fallon said. "Water over the dam."

"Down the hatch," said Albany.

The dinner was a luxurious spread after long months of commissary fare, though the colonel was the only one among them who took little pleasure in it. It reminded Fallon that the culinary art was one of many basic native accomplishments that could not be influenced by doctrinary shifts. The people retained a keen appreciation of the joys of the palate, and the caterer was a man in the old tradition of good living. He brought them mandarin duck, Yangchow shrimps, chicken with mushrooms and shoots, roast pork with steamed cabbage, soft bean curd with peppers, shredded ham and sea slugs, black fish-spawn, and a dish specially ordered by Li because he was convinced it was excellent for his household of invalids, pig marrow boiled in sheep's blood. None of the invalids tried more than a sample. The courses came and went in endless concert, the sweet and the sour, the hot and the cold, even to the gastronomic and now almost unobtainable shark-fin and bird's-nest soups, and ended on an extravagant note with a whole baked fish of noble proportion, swimming in a delicate sauce. Through it all flowed the finest yellow shaohsing, the fiery kaoliang made from millet, and the powerful Fenchow brandy; Efremov's vodka bottles towered among the bowls and steaming dishes, and Albany, in a moment of unusual goodwill, brought in one of his bottles of Scotch, distilled in Osaka.

The banquet began noisily, progressed in crescendo to the degree of hilarious semiriot that marked successful old-style gatherings of its kind, and gradually subsided through succeeding stages of repletion and somnolence. There were toasts, but if Fallon did not respond to all of them no one appeared to take offense, and his own unoriginal offer of *"odin mir"* brought vociferous approval from Efremov and all who understood it. Albany reeled off to bed unnoticed in the middle of the affair, and several of Li's officers were reminded of happier times, growing openly maudlin in the sanctuary of their own mess hall.

Judith, presiding in the role of hostess, assumed an exaggerated charm and graciousness that awed her nearest neighbors, and she did not succumb to any display of nostalgic sentiment that Fallon had expected as he watched her glass. But presently he saw that she too had vanished from the smoky scene, and if the colonel noticed he did not seem to mind. Major Huang had produced a gramophone and a stack of records, most of them native orchestrations but a few antiquated and scratchy melodies he had retrieved when participating in the takeover of an abandoned American air force barracks. Major Huang liked this music and had almost worn out the discs in the subsequent years. Efremov also preferred it to Eastern tintinnabulations; he repeatedly played a jerky version of the "Gypsy Lullaby," and explained to Fallon that while most Amerikanetz vocal and symphonic artists were a degenerate lot, he enjoyed Negro *dzhaz* bands.

A sleepy kitchen staff was beginning to clear the long table and finally Fallon slipped away, leaving Efremov and the colonel to the pumpkin seeds and wine and an argument over the relative merits of Slavic and Chinese music. He went to Father Julien's room and found the priest alone in a half-doze, an empty plate and tea glass on the floor beside his bed. The old man roused and took Fallon's hand in his blue-veined claw. His bearded sunken face was flushed with the excitement of visitors and faint music, unusual food and the realization that he had at last found a refuge in this house.

"I feel much better just since coming here from the hospital," he said. "It is a great relief to be away from it, and from Dr. Chu. Not that I complain, but he didn't want me there."

"You're much better off here," said Fallon, smiling. "We're just one big happy family in this place."

"Now you joke with me, Paul. But I am glad to be near you, just a step across the hall. I have lived alone so long, yet I am not self-sufficient, and the past few years have been especially trying. I have great faith in your powers of healing."

"I'm only good for attempts to heal the body, Father. You heal souls."

"Well," the priest said, "it is true that I was taught to believe the soul more important than the body, and I still believe it. But I have much respect for your science. I do not pretend to understand it, of course; it is not in my line. In my work I have come in contact with it only in matters of birth and death, and perhaps the marriage bed. My limitations are great. We have been credited by the Communists with dabbling in things both scientific and superstitious that are better left to others. Possibly it is true. I realize that I stand with one foot in the twentieth century and the other in the thirteenth." He paused and amusement gleamed in his eyes. "The straddle is often both painful and embarrassing."

Fallon laughed. "Don't pay any attention to what the Communists say. I've heard them, too. They've accused the missionaries of all kinds of things, like pretending special powers and supernatural benefits. They've said the priests are victims of a medieval system and are imprisoned in old beliefs, forced into the roles of good magicians. Well, that's what doctors are, too. Next time, ask them if they remember the Jesuits who set up the court observatories at Peking and Siccawei and taught them truths about winds and storms and stars."

"I don't argue with them," said Vauzous. "I have the patience but not the strength any longer, and it is pointless. They are strange and unpredictable people; they have imprisoned and executed and deported and harried all like me, and most of our unfortunate converts, yet they have not been unkind to me, and now I am in the best of hands. I thank God for this each time I pray to Him. I believe that He intends that the beauty of His Truth be revealed to them again, when He will warm them with the Love of His Sacred Heart."

Fallon had no answer to that. "Good night, Father," he said.

"One more thing, my son—a practical matter. Here is a message for you I have brought from the hospital. It was given to me there by one of the attendants, who asked I deliver it."

Fallon unfolded the paper and read it hastily; it was a greeting from Yin Kuei, a hope for an early reunion. He glanced up at Vauzous.

"You're nonchalant enough about carrying messages that might get you into serious trouble."

"Ah, I am accustomed to courier duties; it is little enough but all I am good for now." The priest's eyes suddenly sparkled. "I have been carrying such billets-doux for our friends about the country for the past three years, mostly in the north. Then I was sent here with certain bulky material that had to be delivered by hand, and later I became ill. I had no choice but seek the enemy's charity."

Fallon was dumbfounded; after a moment he began to smile. "How did you know about me?"

"Oh, they told me all about you before they sent me here, Paul. An efficient young man called Iron Tiger, and a lovely young lady, and others. I didn't dare mention it to you at the hospital; there are too many ears around. Our friends are too few but they seem to be strategically placed, eh? It is a comforting thing to know, in these times."

"It's a comforting thing to know that I'm not alone in this house, too," Fallon said.

"You are not alone," said Vauzous. "None of us is alone."

3

On the Rue du Consulat not far from the river there was a small jewel shop, one of those anachronistic luxury establishments that neither flourished nor wilted in the changing economic climate, for its stock was not very valuable and nearly all of it was secondhand. Destitute women came there to sell what they had left because the government had closed most of the pawnshops. It was a place Judith Markham frequented when she was in the neighborhood during her strolls. She had little money to spend but she ran a check on current merchandise and sometimes made a small purchase if the price was right, and had inexpensively acquired a number of good rings, brooches and bracelets.

Rain had fallen that day and the skies still wept softly and the gutters ran full when Judith stood in the shop door again, folding her oiled paper umbrella. She was wearing an oversized and dirty coat, an old one of the colonel's, and scuffed walking shoes that were soaked from the puddles, and from under the black kerchief she had tied over her head the lifeless fair hair straggled in damp tendrils. Judith never met anyone she knew on her solitary walks and she had dressed for the weather without care for appearance; the less noticeable a foreign woman was these days, she had learned, the better she got along. There were not so many stares, or so many police patrols demanding inspection of papers.

As she stood in the shelter of the arch, absently stamping water from her feet, a man went past not two yards away, hunched into a raincoat and with a soft felt hat pulled down to shield his face from the drizzle. Although she had only a glimpse of him in profile, she recognized Paul Fallon. Ironshod boot heels had crushed the toes of one foot recently and he had a distinct limp; she stared after him, wondering whatever the doctor could be doing over this far from the creek and the hospital and his normal circle of rounds, coming up from the Bund and walking as if he had a goal. Here in the old Concession, a stone's throw from the gates of Nantao, was not Fallon's beat.

Judith's curiosity flared, and her suspicions. Albany had told her that he had no doubt Fallon was in touch with that fugitive guttersnipe, the girl Yin Kuei whom the Security Bureau hunted so assiduously. Judith knew that Albany had made his own try for the little office messenger, but that was all past now; the girl had vanished, and good riddance. And so far as Judith was concerned, if the doctor was in contact with her, that was his own sordid affair. Judith had once entertained a notion that Fallon might be malleable, but he had quickly disabused her of it; the rebuff still rankled, though it was now assuaged by Thorpe's attentions. She narrowed her eyes after the tall receding figure with its distinguishable limp. Albany would be delighted to know where the little slut was hiding. So would certain others.

Without further reflection she unfurled the umbrella again and set out after Fallon, threading her way with the sureness of long practice through the crowds. She had no experience with shadowing, but it was not difficult to keep Fallon in sight for he stood head and shoulders above the average passer-by. And when he turned off into the narrow street leading to the Nantao gate the crowds grew even more dense so that Judith was well concealed under her sheltering umbrella. Fallon was evidently in a hurry; he walked fast and she was becoming a little breathless and kept bumping into people, but she pushed along until suddenly she realized that they had entered the Old City and were proceeding directly into its unknown labyrinth.

Judith had been in this district only once before, and then when well escorted and out for a look at the sights. She had been more uneasy than entertained with what she saw; the narrow streets, the overhanging balconies and signboards, the hordes of people and the hum and clatter had made her nervous and she hated the place with each step she took deeper into it. Now she was alone. And she knew that with white women so scarce as to be conspicuous in the heart of the former Settlement, they must be magnets for a million beady eyes here. Still, if anything should happen there was Fallon's angular figure limping on ahead and she could cry out to him. And it occurred to her that there were possibly a few of those dismal creatures, the hapless Russian exiled women, living in this miserable quarter. There were still a lot of them in the city. Her own appearance today was drab enough, and she might be able to pass as one of them. She jerked up the collar of her coat, pulled the kerchief further over her face, lowered her head and the umbrella over it, and stumbled on across the uneven paving stones with a rising disquiet. But anyone, she told herself, could get claustrophobia in such a horrible maze.

She could not read the street signs and Fallon continually made turnings, but Judith had a fairly good sense of direction and she thought that she could find her way back if they did not go too far. And eventually her determination was rewarded. She saw the doctor pause on a corner and she quickly stepped into the doorway of a vegetable stall as he turned to survey his surroundings and the crowds with a leisurely sweep. He looked as if he were unsure of his direction, but Judith, trembling with excitement, was certain that he was near his goal and was making a careless check for followers. Then he crossed the street and disappeared into a shop.

She waited for a time to see if he would emerge. The rain had begun to drum again on the roofs and cobbles and Judith was experiencing an unsettling mixture of panic and triumph. She was very proud of herself and her daring; she had seen enough flicks to know considerable about this bold and thrilling business of tailing a suspect and she felt a contempt for Fallon's bungles and amateurish attempts to cover his tracks. In fact, he had made practically no attempt. Ah, she thought, hugging herself under the umbrella, if she could just find her way out of here now without being spotted by the sinister lookouts of the underworld, and get to Thorpe Albany.

When Fallon did not show himself again she gathered up her courage and stepped out into the rain, mingling with the hurrying people, and passed the shop on the corner. From under the edge of the umbrella she got a vague impression of its dark interior, where a tremendously fat man was arranging jars on a shelf; then she was beyond and around the corner. But she was sure that Fallon had not come out of that hole; ergo, he was somewhere behind it and on the premises. She stopped again, making a hasty mental note of her position, and saw the towering mass of the nearby city temple. Nodding, Judith started back, avoiding a second passing of the shop, and her instinct took her in the right direction. Her rain-wet face was flushed and the lips were thinned and set in a firm line.

Fallon had moved quickly through the herb shop with a nod to the smiling proprietor, entered the reception room and gone on into the rear corridor. He, too, was excited; he had stolen the time for this detour from his duties and it must be cut short, but it was better than nothing. He had not been here for many weeks. He went down the corridor to Yin Kuei's rooms, unaware of a more perceptible limp because of the long walk, and knocked. He was shaking the water from his hat when she opened the door, stood for a moment staring up at him with widening eyes, and pulled him hastily inside. He drew her into his arms, and her eager lips were pressed to his wet face, covering the still ugly and discolored bruises.

"Paul, Paul," she murmured, beginning to cry against him. "It's been so long."

He held her while she shuddered out the sobs of her anxiety and relief against his breast, and kissed her again, and she put her fingers hesitantly to the swollen welts and the healing burn on the puffed eyelid, and touched his hair at the temples.

"I came as soon as I could," he said through the tightness in his throat. "It isn't very easy any more, because it's so dangerous for you."

"I am all right," she said, smiling tremulously and hurriedly wiping her eyes. "You must stop worrying about me. Here I have been, safe and unable to do anything, while all this time you—"

"It's over. I wish it were all over. I wish you were out of here entirely, away from this place. Away from the city. Yin Kuei, listen. Nothing is safe, and I want you to leave. There must be somewhere you can go, in the country, a village or anywhere away from these damned prying police."

"Away from you?" She shook her dark smooth hair so that it rippled and gleamed. "I couldn't do that, Paul. Not now. Besides, I am busy here and there is a great deal to do. I may not look it, dearest Paul, but I am really useful in this work." She smiled again, clinging to him. "And anyway, there is no place to go. All places are the same, and in a village, as you say, everyone wonders about the stranger."

"This organization of yours," he said uncertainly. "Can't it get you out somehow? I mean really out—out of the country entirely. Can't it pass you along, down the river by boat or any other way? Formosa or Hongkong, even Japan. Listen to me, Yin Kuei, I'm serious!"

"I am also serious," she said, pressing her full mouth against his.

"Yin Kuei," he said at last, "I'm not broke. I haven't any money here, and if I had there'd be no use for it. But I have money in Manila, in an account. I used to bank it when I was on the ships, and later on the plantation, and after the war it was credited to me and is still there. And I've not drawn much on it since. There's more than enough for you; you could live in Hongkong or Manila, with your friends or mine, and wait. This is bound to end some time."

"Yes," she said, "it must end some time."

"The colonel is friendly to me. It's possible that he can arrange to have me deported after a while—if I can convince him his ailments are largely imaginary."

"Are they? He thinks he needs you."

"Anyone can do for him what I do."

"The colonel has influence," she said, her lips tilting at the corners. "He wasted no time getting you out of that prison cell."

"How did you know where I was?"

"We didn't, at first. I was frantic! But one day Captain Kuo happened to be at the hospital on some business and he was talking to Dr. Chu there in the hall. And that old priest, Father Julien, you know? Your patient? He overheard them, and heard Kuo boasting about how he had you where he wanted you, in the prison. The priest, he's—"

"Yes," Fallon said gently. "I know, now. He's one of the—ah—the friends. You sent me a message by him."

"Well, yes. He was sent here by one of our groups in Peking to work with us, but he was sick when he arrived. So we simply passed him on to you. No need to endanger him with useless explanations, and the colonel did owe him something. Anyway, Father Julien got word out to us. We sent the note to the colonel immediately, and watched him rush to the prison in his car. We saw you brought to the hospital; we heard everything about you after that."

"You were very careless, asking for me as you did. You take chances. Kuo's relentless and he's still searching. Now that I know what he's capable of, I'm determined that you leave here. Surely you can be as valuable to this work, or more so, on the outside than by staying here. Ask your friends to send you out somewhere."

"I will think about it, Paul. Lao-hu wants to see you and perhaps you two can talk it over. There is something he is very concerned about, and he said when you came, to tell him. He's here somewhere now."

"Damn Tieh! I didn't come here to see him. And I have to go back soon."

"Very soon? You can stay with me a little while?"

"If I don't have to waste time on Tieh."

"Old Tung in the shop will have already told him you are here," she said, hastily rising. "But see—I can bar my door to all of them if I wish, I have a latch now. Now no one can get you away from me—Tung or Tieh or Kuo or anyone. This is our home for now."

"We'll have a fine home later, maybe in Manila."

"Isn't this good enough for the present, Paul?"

"Yes," he said. "It's good enough for the present."

4

Tieh's insistent rapping and the increasingly querulous note of his demands finally prevailed, and Yin Kuei's door was unbarred to him. Immediately he modulated both voice and attitude and came in quietly, shaking Fallon's hand and taking a stool in the corner where he would be out of the way. Yin Kuei, her cheeks flushed and her eyes bright, made a quick face at him and went into her small kitchen to brew tea. Tieh sat waiting, saying very little and not smiling as he usually did, though he saw many things at which to smile. He knew that neither appreciated his intrusion but he thought he had been very patient. He lit a cigarette and, holding it upright between thumb and first finger, studied the doctor through the curling smoke. He appraised the marks on the face, the limp, the slight favoring sag of a shoulder, and his bland expression did not change. He, like Dr. Chu, had seen worse.

When Yin Kuei brought the tea he took his tiny cup, sniffed its fragrance, and sipped, politely appreciative. He saw the momentary happiness in them both, the relaxation of Yin Kuei's worried tension, the new but smoothed-out lines in Fallon's lean cheeks. When Fallon commented on the efficiency of the apparatus in tracing him and indirectly effecting his release, and thanked him for it, Tieh made deprecating noises. He did not ask for details about prison life, either from delicacy or from surfeit with such grisly information. And he was silently attentive when Fallon began to talk in his grave and urgent way about the necessity of removing Yin Kuei far beyond the reach of the Security Police. Tieh nodded and looked thoughtful when Fallon spoke of the money in Manila, of personal friends both Western and Chinese in Hongkong, and of ways and means of travel by the underground.

"I understand Yin Kuei's devotion to this cause, and her loyalty to your group," Fallon said. "I have no doubt that you're doing a necessary work, something that has to be done wherever there's tyranny and persecution. With you, I believe that these efforts will eventually prevail. But you must consider Yin Kuei's personal position in all this, too. Of all of you, with the exception of yourself, she's the only one definitely known to the police and hunted by them. She's marked, and in danger every time she goes into the street. Even more than yourself. If they catch her, they'll have a treatment to extract information from her that will make my own experience pale in comparison. She's brave, too brave, but they'll learn things from her. Then you're finished, along with your work."

"I would tell them nothing, even if they caught me," Yin Kuei said with a toss of her head. "You knew where we are, but they didn't learn from you."

"They weren't certain I knew anything, so they didn't trouble with the finer methods. They were only angry and vindictive with me; Kuo hates me because the colonel has defied him in my case. With you, it would be different."

"There is some truth in what you say," Tieh said, not committing himself.

"Then you must send her away, it should be simple with your group. Every day ships and cargo junks leave the port and I understand the river police inspections are no longer very rigid. People escape to freedom all the time—it's easier for Chinese, of course, than for marked foreigners. I tried it once and failed, as you remember. But you have contacts for her. Or she could even travel overland to the south. Surely, Lao-hu, her work here isn't worth more than her life to you. She could work effectively on the outside; there's plenty to be done. Her life is worth everything to me."

"It is the other way," Yin Kuei said.

"I know this," Tieh said, nodding again. "I have seen it. And I agree with you, Fah On. Even though your own release might be long delayed, some day you would join her, and you would both be happy, and you could go to America to live, or to the many fine free places there are in the world. Or you could even stay close to us and help us from across the barriers. We will start to make a plan for her. Meanwhile, there is something I wish to tell you."

He rose from the stool and took another cigarette from the center table. "Doctor, Efremov has been doing a special work recently. Do you know its nature?"

Fallon shook his head impatiently. "I'll explain, then," said Tieh. "When Malov was here and became ill, his journey was interrupted. His mission was concerned with all the Southeast, all Nan Yang overseas, but in particular with the situation in Indo-China, just across the frontier. It is the key now. There are ambitious plans being made and already some have been translated into action. They have a strategic weight of great importance. Efremov, through the Bureau, is fully informed. When Malov was forced to return home, his aides arranged with Efremov to coordinate all the material and draw up a condensed report for the general, to be sent to him. That is what Efremov has been doing since then. His report is completed, and several copies have been made by translators in Russian and Chinese. We are very anxious to obtain one of the copies, or the original draft. We know that Efremov has the original. It would be simple to get it, just as we obtained that other material from his quarters, if it were not for the new security on the house. There is the guard at the door; no one enters now, you know, without permission. We had copies made of the two keys Albany took from Yin Kuei, but they are useless to us. We could, one supposes, burglarize the room, but a professional burglar would not know exactly what to look for and get it quickly. Do you see?"

Fallon shrugged. "Yes, I see," he said dryly. "You want me to do the job."

"That was our hope," Tieh said, his twisted smile flickering.

"It is not mine," said Yin Kuei emphatically. "The plan is good and the report is significant, but it is too hazardous for Paul to undertake. He is already suspect. Besides, you are asking him to do your assignment."

"I know," Tieh said, spreading his hands. "It is only that it would be so easy for him, while it is almost impossible for us. Fah On could open Efremov's outer window, muss things up, make it look like burglary. He could do it all in a moment. There would really be little danger."

"How do you know so much about this report?" Fallon demanded.

"We have friends in the translation office of the Information Bureau where the work has been done. Not the translators themselves, but others who saw enough of the work to recognize its value, and who heard it discussed. They told us that when the job was finished, Efremov took his original home. The copies are kept in a safe at the Bureau; no one can get at them. But the original is without doubt there in his room, in his file or his desk. It's true it would be too dangerous to try to return it, and pointless, as he would probably know immediately that it was gone. But—well, Fah On, here are the keys, if you will take them."

He held the keys out in his palm, and Fallon looked at them.

"Don't do it," Yin Kuei said earnestly.

"Do it," said Tieh, keeping his gaze on Fallon's face, "and Yin Kuei will be out of Shanghai in a week. In another week or two she will be over the border in Kowloon Territory, safe among our friends there, or perhaps among the Portuguese in Macao, or even in Manila. We have groups in those places, you know. It can, as you say, be done. Even if she objects a little." He flicked his smiling glance at the girl, who sat stiffly on the k'ang with clenched hands.

Fallon held out his own hand and the keys dropped into it. "That is a promise," he reminded Tieh.

"Paul," Yin Kuei said suddenly in English, "it isn't necessary to take this risk to make me leave. If you want me to go away, I'll go. Whatever you want me to do, I'll do. I love you, Paul, and I don't want to lose you. What Lao-hu is doing is bribing you. You can have what you want without paying such a price; I can get out of here without the organization's help if I must. I know the ways and the methods. It's even possible we could go together."

Fallon shook his head. "That's too much to hope for," he said. "We'll do it Tieh's way. After all, I'm not helping Tieh against my conscience. If it weren't for the color of my skin, I'd probably be a fugitive down here with the rest of you, working for the cause. Even Father Julien risked that."

He kissed her and followed Tieh out to the front shop. The rain had stopped, but its threat hung over the city, and the early autumn evening was sharp. Old Tung sat in the door, contemplative and huge.

"I don't know how soon this can be done," Fallon said to Tieh. "I'll bring the thing to you when I can."

He went off up the narrow street, limping in the dusk.

5

Fallon had not expected his opportunity to come for some time; instead, it came that same evening.

Walking home, he turned the project over carefully in his mind. He knew that the longer he must wait the less chance he would have to find what he wanted. If the report were as valuable as Tieh indicated, Efremov would not be fool enough to leave it unguarded in his room very long after he had finished it; he would either destroy the original or lock it away somewhere, but now he was probably holding it to check against final copies. Efremov himself had, of course, said nothing to Fallon about it. Neither had Colonel Li mentioned it, and Albany was doubtless in ignorance of the report. So Fallon must bide his time. He was determined to see it through. He had a natural aversion to becoming a guest again of Captain Kuo and undergoing his hospitality, but that must be risked. As Yin Kuei had said, it wasn't necessary, she would do what he had asked without this. But for all his mental leers at himself, he knew the thing was important, and he knew that he alone could carry it off where outsiders were almost sure to be caught.

He entered the dismal house as the others were finishing their dinners, and gratefully dined alone in the mess hall. He knew that he would have to set up a watch on Efremov's quarters if he were to seize the first chance. He decided he had a good excuse, for he could loiter with Father Julien. He went up to the priest's cubicle and found Judith Markham there with the invalid.

Fallon was unaware that Judith had reached home only two hours ahead of himself; he did not know that since then she had been haunting the upper floor in wait for Albany; he did not know that she was bursting with momentous news about himself. As he entered the patient's room he heard her querulous voice.

"But where has Thorpe gone, Father? Didn't he say when he'd be back?" And Vauzous' sigh. "He didn't confide in me, Judith. The young man comes in and out, in and out, and he has now gone out and I do not know where he has gone. He has many interests, you know. I heard him say something to the major about a demonstration, but that is all I know."

Judith caught sight of Fallon in the doorway and sucked in her breath, cutting off an impatient remark. She stared at the doctor, then suddenly smiled sweetly. The expression was rather remarkable, he thought, combining as it did open hostility and a large measure of triumph. She seemed almost to gloat; he was reminded of the cat that swallowed the canary. Her face was far from pleasant and it disturbed and puzzled him.

"Somebody missing?" he inquired innocently.

"Judith is anxious to find Mr. Albany," the old man said, unable to conceal a slight smile. "I'm afraid I am not of much help."

"He'll be back," Judith said. "What I have to tell him will keep." She still stared expectantly at Fallon, and added, "I'd forgotten the demonstration. We're all going, I'll see him there."

"Demonstration?"

"One of those howling torchlight parades at the Race Course," Judith said in the same peculiar tone. "Are you coming, Doctor?"

"I'll stay here and keep the father company."

"Do that," she said. "Perhaps Thorpe and the others will drop in on you when we come back." She turned on her heel and clattered off downstairs. Fallon pondered this enigmatic comment briefly, made no sense of it, and grinned at the priest.

His luck was in, he decided; this might be the night. He confirmed it when he went down to speak to Major Huang. They were all going, for the rain had stopped and the clouds had blown away. Yes, Efremov too. They would probably meet Albany at the Race Course. Fallon again declined the entertainment, pleading a headache.

He waited in his room while the group made preparations to depart, and though he was keyed up by the prospect of immediate action, a corner of his mind brooded on their anticipation of the spectacle. He had had all he ever wanted of parades and the drums of the Yangko dancers and the impassioned speeches and the shouted slogans of the multitude as it worked itself into another frenzy under a barrage of fireworks. Nowadays the exaltation seemed spurious, the fanatical denunciations of heretics forced. Crowds had changed in recent years. The people no longer entertained illusions of the communal way of life. They were reverting to their old and basic belief in the crookedness of all governments. They believed in that as firmly as they believed all persons past the age of forty were crooks.

When each man was a fortress, it was difficult to lay seige to a land in which conservatism was ingrained. The reaction had set in, the cooling of the fine ardor for sacrifice. It was all very well to shoot the rich merchants and landlords, and honesty among officials was too good to be true, but the ancient mistrusts were gaining a new foothold. They had only exchanged one brand of terror for another, a civil war for an imperialistic war, and the same old hunger and brutality prevailed.

Presently Fallon heard them all trooping out of the building. Some got into the colonel's car, others hailed pedicabs and drove off. The house fell silent. The kitchen staff had departed for its evening pleasures, only two or three of Li's staff lounged in their quarters in the far wing, and Father Julien slept. Fallon had no intention of bringing the priest into this, even though he was one of them; there was no need of it and he didn't want the guilt of knowledge to lie upon Vauzous.

He waited five minutes, then took a pair of fitted cotton gloves from a drawer and put them on and dropped a screw driver and flashlight into his pocket. He went confidently to Efremov's door, inserted the key in the lock and opened it. He knew, because Efremov had told him so, that the Russian had not thought it worth while to change his locks now that guards were on the house. But the guards rarely came upstairs.

The room was black as a pocket for the shade was drawn. He shut the door quietly and ran up the shade, letting in a slanting moonbeam. It fell across Efremov's desk; Fallon played the stronger flashlight beam over the scattered papers there and saw at a glance that they were not what he was after. There was no drawer in the desk.

He turned to a wooden filing cabinet, and the second key opened it without a squeak. It was filled with cardboard folders and heavy envelopes, classified alphabetically in Russian script. Fallon had no idea what classification to investigate; he began to hunt for something on Indo-China, found nothing of interest, searched for Laos with the same result, and suddenly discovered what he was looking for under the bold black label of Malov.

He drew out the thick folder and opened it on the desk, turning his light on it. His Russian lessons with Efremov now stood him in good stead, for while he could not read the man's script, he could read what had been written on a Russian typewriter, and Efremov had typed this report. He needed to struggle through only a few random lines on the first page to know that he had in his hand what Tieh sought. He doubled the folder in half and slid it into his jacket pocket. He closed the file and took out the screw driver, turning to the closed window.

The lower half of the window was on the latch. He found a bit of heavy cardboard, folded it, placed it on the sill and inserted the blade under the frame. Two springy efforts at prying brought a sharp crack as the latch above split the soft wood in which it was set and a piece of it fell to the floor. He ran up the window and looked out. It was quite feasible for an agile second-story man to scale the rear wall of the house, using the thick vines and ledges. Fallon jabbed the screw driver at an angle into the wood, leaving telltale marks of an outside jimmy; there were no marks inside. Then he forced the lock on the file with the same tool, breaking the wood. He was satisfied.

He snapped off the flashlight, returned to the door and opened it carefully. The hall was quiet, with only the dim bulb burning over the stair well and the light streaming out from the door of his own room. He could hear Father Julien's gentle snores. He stepped out, closed the door and locked it, and returned to his room. His watch showed that the group was just about now reaching the scene of the demonstration. The burglary had taken very little time, it was early, and this was the best chance he would have to reach Nantao.

He found that he was mildly perspiring. He wrapped the folder in an old newspaper, tied it with a string and put it under his buttoned jacket; even if he were stopped by a police patrol and the package examined, the language of the report would baffle them and he believed he could talk his way through. He put the flashlight away, for it was his, but the gloves and screw driver he kept in his pocket to toss up some alley. The keys he would return to Tieh.

Downstairs, he encountered the guard nodding in the areaway and told the man that he was going out for some air and might attend a theater. And as he walked away, he reflected that there was little more that he could have done: late tonight Efremov would return, find his window forced and his file burgled, and report to the colonel; the colonel would have to notify Captain Kuo. The guard would be questioned and would say that Fallon had gone out soon after the others. The suspicion would be strongly on Fallon, but the burden of proof would be on Kuo, and there was the jimmied window. It was the best that Fallon could contrive.

As soon as the lower entryway had closed behind Fallon, Thorpe Albany swung open his own door at the end of the third floor corridor and peered out. It had not been shut, as it appeared, but held to a crack, and there was no light in Albany's room behind it. Albany had been standing at the crack, waiting.

He had planned to attend the demonstration, and when he left the house for his office in midafternoon he had told Major Huang he would meet the others at the Course. But Albany had attended demonstrations before, their mechanical enthusiasms bored him and he foresaw a dull evening, only slightly more entertaining than staying at home and doing nothing. And he had remembered an unopened quart of Japanese-distilled rye in his room. That settled it: the rye was infinitely more appealing tonight than the stupefying thunder of the Holy War. He would not be missed.

When the guard admitted him he climbed the stairs silently, his steps muffled by a thick pile carpet. Albany always moved with unconscious stealth, a physical compulsion that made him very annoying to fellow workers and residents. He came into the upper hall, noticed Fallon's open door and light, and looked in as he quietly passed but saw no one there. He heard only the priest's snores; then, as he was reaching for the knob of his own door beyond, he heard something else. It was a faint brittle crack, followed by a metallic tinkle. It came from behind him, almost certainly from inside Efremov's closed room.

He froze in midstride, nerves tingling and skin prickling on the back of his neck. Then he noiselessly slid into his own dark quarters, pushed his door almost shut, and watched. This was something he had not actually expected, but it had been in the back of his consciousness since a very similar night not many weeks previously. Efremov's room and files had been ransacked once, and it could be done again, despite the guard below. And even before Efremov's door opened and Fallon appeared, Albany knew who would come out into the dim light. It could be no one else.

He waited, scarcely breathing, while Fallon locked the door and crossed the hall into his own room. He continued to wait, gaining control over his first impulse to yell an alarm and jump at the doctor. He heard Fallon moving about in his quarters for a few minutes, and he saw him leave, going purposefully down the stairs. Fallon had put the package under his coat so that the guard would not notice it, but its bulk was apparent to Albany in the hall light from behind. He drew a deep breath again.

He had the goods on the medico this time, he thought. The fellow was carrying off something of Efremov's. Albany knew nothing about the Malov report. But he knew that whatever it was, it was going direct to the people Captain Kuo so ardently hunted. Fallon knew the way, no doubt. All Albany had to do was follow.

For a moment longer he waited, without moving. He didn't want the doctor to be questioned and arrested again without good cause. It had been tough enough the first time; it would be hell the second, and though God knew Albany had no love for Fallon, he felt a jabbing sense of guilt whenever he saw the doctor's battered face and watched him limp. And after all, they were of the same race, or origins, or blood—whatever that was worth.

For that moment he did not know what to do. He could, of course, telephone Captain Kuo's office, tell the policeman what he had seen, and leave the rest up to the patrols. But Albany rejected this course almost as quickly as it occurred to him; he would make sure of the thing first, see where Fallon went if possible, then notify Colonel Li when the officer returned from the demonstration. That might give Fallon the benefit of the doubt, and certainly would give him the benefit of the colonel's protection and a fair hearing.

But it was almost too late to do anything at all, unless he moved fast. Albany ran down the stairs and the guard let him out. In the dark street he saw no sign of Fallon. He hurried to the corner. And dodged back, for just around the corner he had seen the doctor approaching a stand of pedicabs. When he looked again he saw one of them getting into motion, its red tail-reflector bobbing off down the street.

This, Albany reflected, was duck soup. He approached the stand, brushed aside the importuning hands of the first three or four drivers, and clambered into one manned by a husky fellow in a tattered T-shirt, wishing that there were still taxicabs available. He directed the pursuit;

the driver nodded his understanding that he was to follow but not overtake.

The vehicles bowled across town, and it gradually dawned on Albany that Fallon was heading for Nantao. He remembered that most pedicab pushers would not take fares past the Nantao gates, particularly at night. The alleyways beyond were too narrow and dark. A man going to Nantao left his cab at the old gates the French had erected to control rioting mobs.

He saw the leading cab stop before the gate, and Fallon's silhouette passing beyond the boundary street light. He paid off his driver and hurried after the figure. If that was not enough, the limp clinched its identity. Albany could have followed now with his eyes shut, by the uneven sound of the leather soles. He settled down to concentrate on the job of keeping his quarry in sight in the heavy enfolding gloom.

6

It began to occur to Albany that it was an odd thing to be following by ear a person in a throng of people. For the crowds were here, as always, compressed into the dark streets, endless streams flowing in every direction, going about their affairs in an unseen shuffle that made the most ordinary business seem mysterious. At first he was confused and he fought and bucked against the current until he discovered that by moving over a few feet he could be carried along by a countercurrent, one that flowed into and out across similar movements of humanity on diagonal lanes.

The darkness was profound, for by this hour the shop fronts had been shuttered and there were no street lights. But life throbbed behind the blank shutters, and up on the balconies yellow and blue gleams shone from family quarters. He heard all the sounds that had become familiar: the click of mahjong cubes, the clatter of dishes, the plaintive note of some gaffer's flute, and the constant buzz and hum of voices; and he smelled all the mingling odors. But his vision was obstructed by walls and the backs of men as though he were one of a column of ants gliding through a tunnel. His senses were tight-strung and when he heard the deep tone of a bell struck in the city temple ahead he almost jumped. Then he laughed at himself; for a moment he had recaptured the forgotten glamour he had so briefly known long before, but it was dispelled when he was brought up short at the crossing by a jogging hunchback under a bamboo hi-ho pole on which stinking buckets of offal swung.

So he went on following his ears; the harsh leather *clip-clop* on the stones ahead, sounding above the soft *slup-slop* of the multitude.

And presently the procession of two became a single file of three.

Tieh Lao-hu, returning home from a visit to his cell leader in the Rue Palikao, came down a side lane and saw, crossing the intersection ahead of him, the easily distinguishable figure of Fallon. He was now within a hundred yards of the herb shop. Tieh quickened his step, realizing what this glimpse of the doctor meant. But as he did so he saw another figure silhouetted against the blue light of the crossing, a light falling at an angle in the narrow lane from the climbing moon. And Tieh recognized Albany almost as soon as he had Fallon. Since they were twenty feet apart, the situation was apparent: the one was trailing the other. Tieh, greatly disturbed, fell in behind.

They had by now passed the bird market and it was too late, in this push, to intercept Fallon before he reached the shop and turned in there. His destination would inevitably be known to Albany—and that would be the end of Tieh's sanctuary. He worked his way closer, measuring Albany's broad shoulders with a calculating eye. Albany was big and powerful, but so was Tieh, a strong man for his race.

Fallon now came abreast of the shop and without a backward glance, because such precautions were useless in the dark, he crossed the lane and entered the door. The herb shop, unlike most others, was not yet shuttered; a lamp was lit inside, and the gargantuan proprietor sat in his usual place from which he could look out on the street. Fallon went through quickly to the inner room. And Albany halted, taken by surprise and uncertain of his next move. The shop light fell across him.

Old Tung saw him instantly. He lowered the hand in which he held a cigarette and grasped a cord beneath his stool, giving it four sharp tugs. The cord ran back through the corridor to the radio room and clattered a small brass bell there. On the fourth tug, the three operators gathered there rose and hurried along the corridor into the shop, grouping themselves behind Tung. He had not moved, but they saw the object of his intent stare. They also saw that Tieh had come up closer to stand directly behind Albany, who was about to proceed around the corner and take a precipitate leave.

Albany was feeling a sudden uneasiness that was developing into unreasoning panic. He didn't understand why the fat shopkeeper was looking at him so fixedly, and he was alarmed when three persons materialized beside the fellow. He turned on his heels to walk away, and as he did so Tieh stepped forward and swung his arm down in a hard chopping motion, striking Albany with the edge of his hand at the point where neck and shoulder joined and paralyzing the nerve. Albany staggered under the numbing blow, began to reel and tried to shout, and Tieh's arm clamped around his throat from behind, shutting off his wind and holding him up; otherwise he should have fallen on the paving stones.

The operators ran out from the shop, seized Albany by the arms and thighs, hoisted him up and rushed him in past Tung and through the rear door, with Tieh following. The abrupt swirl of activity in silence and semidarkness stunned a few passers-by; they paused, unsure if their eyes had deceived them, and then hurried on, collecting their wits enough to remember that this was no concern of theirs. One or two of them perhaps had noticed that the object of the frightening assault and abduction had been a foreigner, and it was better to forget the entire matter. Within two minutes the scene outside the shop was the same as before, and Old Tung squatted placidly on his stool, watching it and smoking his cigarette.

Albany was borne swiftly down the corridor and carried into one of the sleeping cubicles used by the operators and dropped on a cot. No words were spoken as a gag was thrust between his jaws and secured, his hands were wrenched behind him and fettered with a cord, and his ankles were bound for good measure. He lay on his stomach, his head turned to the side, and his wildly rolling eyes centered on the husky figure of Tieh, who stood supervising the job. He knew Tieh by sight, though he had not spoken a dozen words to him in the brief time the man had worked quietly at menial tasks around the offices of the Information Bureau.

The operators finished their work and left. They had lit a candle, and its flickerings revealed the tiny room's bareness. It was strangely aromatic with the scent of herbs, for Old Tung sometimes came here for a quiet nap. Tieh squatted on his heels, rolled and lit a cigarette, and looked at Albany reflectively.

In a moment the door was flung open again and a girl entered. Albany knew her very well, and despite the throb of pain in his shoulder and neck where the nerve was resuming its functions, he felt a quiver of exultation. Fallon had led him true to earth. This was definitely the place Captain Kuo's experts had hunted so long in vain.

"What is this?" Yin Kuei demanded fiercely. Tieh glanced up at her and lifted his palms.

"You can see for yourself," he murmured. "It is the propagandist. I came upon him in the street, and he was following Fah On here. A bold fellow, but not a very alert one. We took him."

"Why?"

Tieh's faint brows rose. "He saw where Fah On came. There was nothing else to do. If he had been left alone he would have gone directly back to his headquarters and informed the police. Did Fah On bring it?"

"Yes, he is in my rooms and has it. I hope you are satisfied!"

Albany was able to follow this conversation, carried on in the bastard local dialect. There was nothing cryptic about it. He made a choking sound of protest against the gag but Tieh did not remove it. The man got up and stamped out his cigarette.

"What are you going to do about this?" Yin Kuei persisted. She was angry.

"That depends. It is a serious problem, and I must report it and receive instructions. After that, we shall see. Meanwhile I will talk to Fah On."

He went out. Yin Kuei stood staring down at Albany, who struggled futilely against his bonds.

"If I remove the gag," she said finally, "do you promise not to make a big noise? It would do you no good even if you did, in this place."

Albany nodded with vigor, and after a moment's hesitation she untied the rag about his head and he spit out the wad. His face was mottled and his breathing was stertorous. Remarkably, he had retained his glasses intact and he glared through the thick lenses, rolling over on his side.

"You can't get away with this," he gasped, and realized how idle and empty the cliché sounded. They *had* got away with it, and just as they had kept out of the hands of the police indefinitely, so they could hold him as long as they liked. Or for that matter, do away with him. The thought had been under the surface but it now came to the top and his breathing quickened and the blood drained from his face. That devil Tieh, he thought, was fully capable of anything!

"Listen," he said. "Dr. Fallon is here. Can I see him?"

"I suppose so," Yin Kuei said. "He's probably been informed by now. I'll see."

She went to her rooms and found Fallon and Tieh seated there, talking in low voices. Fallon was distressed. He could not understand where he had slipped. He was certain Albany had left the house earlier in the day; then how had he managed to turn up suddenly here in the middle of Nantao, in Fallon's footsteps? The whole affair was disastrous. Like most things that cannot be explained, there was an element of malignant menace in it.

The Malov report lay neglected on the table. Tieh looked at it with suppressed eagerness, but the problem in hand was more pressing. When Yin Kuei said that Albany was ungagged and wanted to talk, Tieh frowned but Fallon went with her to the small room.

There was no need now for vituperation as Fallon looked down at

Albany, and both knew it. "How'd you do it, Thorpe?" Fallon asked, putting a cigarette to the other's lips and lighting it for him. Albany blew smoke and tried to grin, dropping the cigarette on the blanket, and Yin Kuei retrieved it.

"That wasn't so hard," he said, the accomplishment rising above his fear and chagrin. And he told how he had come back to the house, heard the noise in Efremov's room, and followed the doctor. "It was simple," he added. "I suspected you all along. But I gave you the breaks, Fallon, until tonight. I didn't want to see Kuo giving you the works again without some proof, but this was getting too raw. There's going to be hell to pay, you know. They'll be all over this joint like a ton of bricks."

"What makes you think so?"

"It figures," said Albany. But it didn't, and in his desperation, hoping to put the fear of God into the doctor, he cast about frantically for a threat. Anything would do if it would upset them. He said, "Wait till Judy leads Captain Kuo here. She came back to the house with me; she saw it all and knows I'm following you."

Fallon and Yin Kuei exchanged glances. Tieh had come in and was listening, and understood enough.

"She doesn't know where you are now," Fallon said.

"That's what you think!" Albany began to speak rapidly so that his words approached a babble. "As soon as we came into Nantao I stopped and found a phone in a shop along the street and called her. See? She'll know the general location, it's someplace near the temple, I said. It won't take the cops long to comb you out." Albany was sweating; his danger had sharpened his wits and he watched Fallon closely and saw the shadow of doubt that crossed the doctor's face.

The phone call sounded improbable to Fallon; service was bad and calls took time to put through. Albany would have lost the trail during the delay. But with luck he might have made it, hurrying later to overtake the doctor. Something of the same line of thought had passed through Tieh's mind, for Yin Kuei had been swiftly translating.

"If true, that is too bad for the lady, then," Tieh said flatly, and Fallon's troubled gaze swung to him, and back again.

"I'm afraid," he said to Albany, "you've stuck your neck out too far. You shouldn't have said that. Now something will have to be done about it." He saw the sudden flash of panic in Albany's eyes. "I don't know what it will be because it's out of my line."

Albany was silent, struck by the enormity of his error. Because of this impromptu fiction he had woven about a phone call, they might do him in right here and now. Or they might go after Judith too; they were wolves. Judith would never know what hit her, or why. And yet—there was a chance. If Fallon talked to Judith first, she might catch on. She was stupid, but it was the only hope.

"Look," he said, making a direct appeal to Fallon. "Go home and see Judy. She'll listen to reason. Tell her what's happened and calm her down—she's probably getting pretty jumpy by now. Lay it on thick, Fallon! She'll listen to you, she won't squawk." It was a long shot; Judith might be only bewildered, or she might take Fallon at his word and keep her mouth shut. But if she weren't too dumb, she also might run to the colonel.

Fallon glanced at his watch and saw that he had ample time to get back before the party returned from the demonstration.

"It might help," he said. "If she goes to Kuo, I can't guarantee your skin or hers either."

"You can't guarantee my skin anyway," Albany muttered.

"I think I can," Fallon said, looking at Tieh. "Nothing will happen to you if the police leave these people alone. Tieh takes his orders from higher-ups. This isn't a murder syndicate, you know."

But Albany was unconvinced, and a deep suffocating fear was creeping in his belly and throat. "Listen, Fallon," he said hoarsely, "I don't give a damn about Efremov's stuff, or anything else. I shouldn't have put my foot into this, but I did. Get 'em to let me go and I'll swear to keep my trap shut. I swear it!" He saw the blankness in Fallon's face. "Here's a better idea, Paul! Get 'em to put me on a boat, smuggle me out on a junk, anything. Ship me out of the country. That's all I want anyway. I'm fed to the teeth. I can't stand this mess any more. All I really want is out!"

Fallon turned away. That was all a lot of people wanted. "It isn't so simple," he said. He went up to Tieh. "You won't harm him? Just hold him?"

Tieh dropped his gaze. "Not unless the police come," he said. "Maybe not then; there would be no object in it. But he can't be released unless I am ordered to do so. I must send a runner to the group chief."

"See that he sticks to that," Fallon said to Yin Kuei, smiling for the first time. "I must hurry now."

He left her standing in the faint light of the front shop beside Old Tung. "I'll be back tomorrow," he promised. "If I can."

Yin Kuei said nothing. She felt the bitter welling of terror in her heart. But she would not speak of it. She could only smile with false courage.

7

When they had all gone and locked the door behind them, Thorpe Albany lay on the hard cot and stared at the candle set in a holder and left on a stool across the room. It burned with a clear and steady flame, and for a time it mesmerized him so that his breathing became light and he lay motionless. He did not feel the pain in his wrists and ankles from the binding cords; he heard no sound and though his position was cramped and awkward he was not very uncomfortable. The beat of his heart slowed as he calmed; the tremors went out of his stomach and diaphragm. There was really nothing to be afraid of.

It was inconceivable that they would harm him. They detained him for their own protection, that was all. They might detain him a long time. But they would not do anything worse, and eventually they would free him. Or he would be freed in a sudden blow by Kuo's patrols. Or he would free himself. It was best to relax and wait for that time.

On the wall behind the candle hung a long scroll. Although he did not know it, it was a treasure of Old Tung's, a memento of better days in Dr. Chung's home in Peking. Tung liked to come here, lie on the cot, smoke a meditative pipe holding a pinch of tobacco, and look at the scroll before he slept. Now Albany studied it without much curiosity, simply because it was there before his eyes.

It was a fine example of the calligraphic art, for which Albany had no appreciation; he preferred pictures. He could read the printed language but he could not read this, for it was grass-writing, the fastflowing or running hand that is almost indecipherable to one not familiar with it. The father of Yin Kuei had improvised on the scroll, as a musician composes, putting his own individualism into a form of shorthand through the soft hair-tip of a slender bamboo tube. One could see how the delicate brush had flown over the paper linking character to character with a rhythmic restraint, producing an abstract art form as cultivated as a painting and with the same regard for form and line.

It baffled Albany for it had no meaning to him beyond its obvious artistry and refinement. He had no concept of its natural inspiration: the plum branch, the dried vine with its hanging leaves, the springing leopard, the slim crane or the rugged pine. All he could see was that it had a sort of dynamic harmony and seemed to be a sketch in momentum, its swift sure strokes defying imitation or correction.

The scroll irritated him; it was only another of those incomprehensible

Chinese objects he collected and hung in his own room as a perversity. He began struggling against his bonds again and the sweat beaded his face and filmed his glasses. But it was no use, and he lay back panting, hating the scroll, wishing he could blow out the candle. But it was just too far, and the flame only wavered with his breath.

He heard a bell struck faintly in the nearby city temple, though whether it marked the hour or called the ragged Taoist monks and acolytes to heathen rites he did not know. He assumed it must now be close to midnight. Abruptly a strong rasping noise filled the room, a loud hum and irregular stabs of sound that quivered against every straining nerve-tip. He was so startled that his heart seemed to leap and try to burst his breast; the sweat poured anew. Then he understood what he was hearing: the powerful *gak-gak-gaaak-gak* of a radio transmitter. It came through the wall from the next room and he could feel it shivering in the cot.

As soon as he knew what it was he was calm again, his thoughts racing. Tieh's underground was grinding out a message on a schedule, and there could be no doubt what the message was about. It must be the gist of whatever Fallon had stolen from Efremov's files. Albany could not read it and supposed it was encoded anyway. He wondered at their daring; the noise was so raucous it must be apparent outside in the streets, unless the transmitter space were sealed tight. That could mean it was important enough to risk detection. It went on and on.

Then the door was unlocked and Yin Kuei came in, carrying a teapot and a cup and a small basket of rice cakes. She set them on the floor and looked at Albany uncertainly.

"I didn't think you were sleeping," she said with a sober tilt of her head toward the wall and the transmitter beyond. "At least we don't mean to be unnecessarily harsh."

"I could use the tea and a cigarette," Albany admitted. He saw that she was doubtful about how to proceed. "Can't you loosen a hand? The place must be full of locks and guards anyway."

She reflected, then suddenly bent over him and began working at the knot on his wrists. His hands parted and he brought them stiffly around and began chafing them together, slowly and painfully restoring the circulation. He accepted the cup she had filled and drank thirstily, and took the cigarette she lit, bolstering himself on an elbow. She refilled the cup.

His mind was working now to gain time. He nodded toward the scroll. "I've been admiring that," he said, putting his bound feet to the floor. "A beautiful job."

She glanced at the hanging, half-smiling. "My father did it. You can't read?"

"Not that sort."

"It has two parts and they don't have much in common, really. The upper block is an old proverb: 'Avoid the mean person, but do not make him your personal enemy.'"

"Fair enough. And the lower block?"

She hesitated, remembering a rainy night when she had first talked with Paul Fallon in his room. This scroll had been in her mind then, and she had referred to it.

"Fen chui jen ming tao," she said. "'The government is the wind, the people the grass; the wind blows and the grass must bend.' You have heard it?"

She had been looking at the scroll and did not see the blow coming at all. Albany's big fist hit her on the point of the fragile jaw, and he caught her as she slumped and lowered her noiselessly to the floor.

His numbed fingers became nimble again and he made short work of the cord knotted at his ankles. He blew out the candle and went quickly to the door. It opened without protest to his cautious touch and he looked out through the crack into the long corridor. He remembered only dimly how he had been carried to this room, but he had not been unconscious then and he knew that the transmitter was sputtering somewhere behind him. He stepped into the unlighted hall and went in the opposite direction.

Midway along the corridor he saw a crack of yellow light under a door and heard voices behind it. One of them, he was sure, was Tieh's; the man would probably be there with others translating or encoding the material Fallon had brought and sending it along to be put on the air, sheet by sheet. He slipped past on silent feet and entered the reception room from the rear, feeling his way through its darkness into the unlighted herb shop. The shutters had now been set in place, but one narrow panel had been left open and through it he could see moonlight in the street.

He started across the shop toward it and as he moved he heard a snort and a grunt of astonishment. Dimly he saw the bulk of the fat proprietor rising from a wooden bench where he had been reclining. Albany dove for the gaping hole and scraped through with the sound of Old Tung's roar of warning blasting his ears.

Outside, he tripped over an uneven paving block and sprawled full length on his stomach, and his glasses clattered away on the stones. He pawed for them frantically, for without them he was all but blind, and he lost a precious moment before his hand closed on them and assured

him that they were unbroken. Then he scrambled to his feet and started
to run.

The moon stood directly overhead, filling the streets with a thin bluish
haze shot with saffron, and in this ,diffused light he was thoroughly
confused. It seemed to filter down into the bottom of a deep network of
trenches. All streets looked the same and all looked strange; he had no
idea which way lay the river or which way the modern city. He ran
blindly, dodging past the occasional pedestrians still abroad. There
should be the bird market near by, he knew, but he saw nothing of it.
Instead, he saw the big gate of the city temple and swerved away, knowing it would be a trap.

He came to a corner and halted, sucking in his breath and trying
desperately to get his bearings. For here again he had a choice of three
ways to go. And then he heard the thud of running feet behind him, in
the alley from which he had just emerged, and an unintelligible shout,
and he knew they were in close pursuit.

He started off again at a new angle, not caring whether it was right
or wrong, and when he came to yet another crossing he turned once
more. But at a third intersection, where he was forced to stop for a moment because a large cart was being trundled across it, he glanced back
and saw a single figure approaching in the street at a dead run. To Albany, the thing was assuming the fantastic proportions of a nightmare.

He slipped behind the cart and forced his heavy legs into action again,
but he was beginning to give out. The labored breath sobbed and whistled, and the slamming of his heart seemed to echo between the shuttered walls of the lanes. He had come into one of those byways that
twisted and turned deceptively. For all he knew he was running in a
great circle and would wind up before the herb shop. The lane was
empty; no strollers came to this deserted corner between the temple and
the river, and the shops here were mean and dark and strongly barred.
It was not a place of refuge, and if people lay awake behind their shutters
and heard the feet outside pounding over the cobbles, they were not the
sort to interfere with such grim games.

But at the last turning, if any listened to the hurried stumble and the
tortured gasps passing by, they pricked up their ears, for this was a dead
end. Though Albany didn't know it. He made the turn in a final burst
of speed and ran full tilt into a high wall that barred the way, and
slipped to one knee at the base of it, stunned and blinded as his smashed
glasses fell in a tiny tinkling shower.

He had no time to struggle back to his feet before Tieh Lao-hu was
upon him.

Tieh had outdistanced the other pursuers and lost them behind in the labyrinth. He had followed with as firm a determination as he had ever felt in his life that Albany should not escape. It was all very well to move the transmitter in an emergency, but the transmitter could not be moved now. It was engaged in sending the Malov report, and the Malov report was far more important than Thorpe Albany.

Tieh had no weapon, a lack he was regretting with every bound of his hard body. For if he had carried a gun in his belt he might have dropped Albany long before, down one of those straight empty streets. But he had something else useful in his belt, a long piece of copper transmitter wire, and as he ran he twisted its ends together to form a loop, and he caught up a stick dropped in the lane to serve as a lever. It would do as well as a gun, and make no racket.

He landed almost squarely on Albany's back, the weight of the lunge driving him hard once more against the stone, and the gleaming loop flashed in the moonlight as Tieh swung it over the bowed head. The wire bit into Albany's taut throat when the lever was twisted, and Tieh, standing astraddle of him, continued to twist relentlessly until it was so tight it would turn no further.

There was no noise about it. The figure beneath him jerked and pitched spasmodically, clawing and scraping. But Tieh hung on, confident and no longer greatly impassioned. He waited it out as the struggler gradually subsided into a heap between his spread legs. Then he secured the wire in place and let go and turned his face up toward the moon to see where, at last, he stood.

The wall towered a dozen feet above the lane and six feet across the middle of it, leaving narrow passages on either side, and it was a solid block of dark stone carved with dragons. Tieh knew it, for he had been here once or twice, but had not realized until now where the chase had led. The people of the district called it the Wall of the Iron Shadow, and they gave the same name to the dead-end lane. In old times there had been a foundry here for the purpose of casting bells, and the wall had stood at the entrance to the foundry to prevent evil spirits from getting in and spoiling the castings. The smoke from the furnaces had impregnated the stone to a great depth, lending it the peculiar color of iron. The foundry was long since gone, but the wall remained.

Tieh looked around, but he was alone in this blue-lit silent place, except for the motionless huddle at his feet. He walked away as unobtrusively as he could.

8

At three o'clock in the morning, Fallon was permitted to retire to his quarters, exhausted, with a guard posted in the hall outside. The long grilling had been expertly conducted by Captain Kuo in person, and it had been intensive. But it had not yet resulted in his rearrest.

At six o'clock Fallon was roused from restless sleep and returned by the guard to Major Huang's office, where he was informed of the discovery by a patrol of a garroted body.

Fallon's watch had stood at eleven when he was admitted to the house by the drowsy sentry. Told by the man that the colonel's party had not yet returned from the evening festivities, he went up the stairs. The house was as still as it had been when he left it three hours before; there was no light under the colonel's door and no answer to his knock, though that was no proof that Judith Markham was not waiting inside for Li's arrival. Or perhaps after that phone call she had gone out to inform the colonel. He went to his room and sat down under the lamp after satisfying himself that Father Julien still slept.

Almost on the stroke of midnight he heard the colonel's car drive up and the group come into the entryway below. They were talkative and in a good humor; he heard the colonel's laughter and Efremov's deep voice. The colonel asked Efremov in for a nightcap and the Russian accepted, and Fallon suddenly heard Judith's high-pitched voice break in, saying that she would see how Father Julien had rested. Apparently there had been no alarm as yet. She came on up the stairs and her high heels rapped along the hall. Fallon went to his door, and seeing him standing there she stopped, irresolute.

"Father Julien is all right," Fallon said. "And if you're looking for Thorpe, he isn't here." When she turned her puzzled glance toward Albany's room he added, "Come in a minute, Judith. There's something I want to talk to you about."

She obeyed without answer, keeping a suddenly wary eye on him. He saw no evidence in her manner, however, that she knew of this night's affair; if she had returned to the house with Albany and witnessed his departure on Fallon's trail, she could not have concealed her knowledge very well. He shut the door and faced her.

"I haven't much time for this," he said. "Do you know where Thorpe went?"

She didn't reply but her face stiffened. He had no alternative but to plunge ahead.

"Did you come back here with him tonight? Did he phone you later?"

There was nothing in her silence to give him assurance one way or another. Albany's threat might be an empty one, a fabrication, but he couldn't take a chance on it.

"All right," he said. "If his life's worth a damn to you, keep still. Say nothing, no matter what's asked by anyone, and play dumb. Thorpe's been—he's been kidnapped, let's say, and he's being held as a sort of hostage against any trouble from the police. He says he phoned you and told you where he is. But if you mention it, or hint you know anything about it, the police will start raids and the people who have him may harm him. Do you understand?"

Her skin was gray, but her eyes didn't leave his face. This was the explanation, then, of Albany's failure to meet them at the Race Course. She had no idea what Fallon meant about a phone call, but she knew for a certainty now what had happened, and knew where Thorpe Albany was. If only she might have reached him in time, to tell him of that miserable hole in Nantao where she had seen Fallon only this afternoon. It was too late! She felt like screaming.

He looked steadily at her, attentive for the sound of anyone coming up the stairs, and pounded it home.

"You know the crowd that has him, it's the one Kuo has been looking for, and they're a rough lot. Albany came back here tonight for some reason—he says you were with him—and caught prowlers in Efremov's room again."

The conviction was growing in him that Judith knew nothing at all about this, that he had made a mistake, as Albany had intended him to do, in speaking to her of it. Now the cat was out of the bag; he would have to catch it and thrust it back, somehow. By luck or slyness she'd led him into the disclosure by simply saying nothing.

"Anyway, Judith, they're holding him," he said, pushing down the chagrin. "If you tell Kuo or anyone about it, or say that I know anything, the police won't worry about what happens to Albany. They'll start a big hunt for him and if they happen to alarm that crowd it'll get the wind up, and that's when Albany will be in danger. So for his own good, keep quiet. Have I made it clear?"

She nodded slowly, without speaking. A trace of color was returning to her waxy skin. Her hands began a nervous weaving between themselves and she thrust them into her coat pockets.

"I didn't meet Thorpe or come back here with him," she said in a voice that whispered. "I never got a phone call; I've been with the colonel all evening. I was worried about Thorpe. Now I know. I know where he is, too. I followed you myself to that awful place, just this afternoon. I was going to tell Thorpe about it tonight, but I didn't have the chance. I never saw him."

His disgust with himself rose again; he had no talent for this sort of thing. Even Judith Markham had traced him to the shop in Nantao.

"Have you said anything to anyone else about it?"

"No, I haven't yet."

"Then don't, Judith."

"You mean, if I pretend to know nothing at all, nothing, that will be best for Thorpe. Is that it?" She still whispered, her eyes large with shock.

"Yes. Pull yourself together and act casual. Keep out of the way and go to bed. The lid will blow off here as soon as Efremov discovers his burglary, but if anybody gets hurt, it'll probably be me. Go on now, Judith, and if Captain Kuo comes and questions you later, control yourself. Remember what it means to Thorpe."

She went out, walking dazedly, and he heard her go down to the suite. He sat under the lamp again with a book in his lap.

In a few minutes Efremov left the colonel's rooms with a jovial salute and stumped up to his own quarters. Fallon waited. There was no sound from across the hall for a quarter of an hour. Then Efremov came out and returned to Li's suite. Almost immediately Li's orderly clattered down to the entryway and called the guard, who reported to the colonel. Fallon could hear a mounting chorus of voices. Within another moment or so the orderly was running up to the third floor and pounding on Albany's door. When he got no answer, he came to Fallon's. The time had arrived.

Fallon followed him to the colonel's office. Li's tunic was unbuttoned as if he had started to undress. He sat now at his desk and raised angry bewildered eyes to the doctor. Efremov sat in a corner as though settled there for a long performance. The guard stood like a trembling ramrod by the desk. Judith was not present. The questioning began.

When the first dust had cleared, the colonel studied the notes he had been making. They told him a queer but apparently straightforward story. After the party left for the Race Course, Albany had arrived at the house and gone up to his room. Presently Dr. Fallon, unaware that Albany had come in, felt restless and had gone out for a walk. The walk ended at an open-air juggling exhibition in the theater district. Soon after the doctor left, Albany departed again. He had not thus far returned. But Fallon had come back about eleven. And sometime during the evening, Efremov's room had been entered, apparently by porch climbers from the outside and through the window, and the original of the confidential Malov report had been abstracted from the files.

The second raid on those files within a few weeks. It was insupportable!

"Tell Huang to phone Captain Kuo at the Central Station immediately," Li said to his orderly. "Inform the captain we have more trouble here and his presence is required." He looked again at Fallon, and his anger dissolved into weariness. "This is all beyond me," he said. "I am not a policeman; it's Kuo's job, unfortunately for everybody remotely concerned. Kuo won't be very amenable this time, I'm afraid. But I'm sure, Doctor, that you have little to fear from him; there'll be no more premature arrests of anyone under my jurisdiction."

He sighed, twiddling an ivory cigarette holder. "Captain Kuo doesn't care for any of us, and you in particular. You'll be the chief suspect, I suppose. But it's very strange that Albany is out so late. If he doesn't return soon, Kuo may find himself with a more likely suspect."

Captain Kuo was not, as Li morosely predicted, amenable. While his men swarmed through the headquarters and took it over from attic to cellar, he established himself in Major Huang's office and began a series of individual interrogations. The guard's testimony took a great deal of time; so did that of Efremov. Colonel Li was not exempted, nor were those members of his staff who had made the mistake of not accompanying him to the demonstration. Kuo even went up and talked to Father Julien, who had been aroused by the commotion, but it was plain that the priest was too weak to get out of bed, and too sincerely confused to know what was going on. Kuo came out of the room scowling; even the old man was not entirely cleared of suspicion.

Judith Markham had her quarter-hour on the stand. When she was dismissed and came with a dragging step up the stairs, Fallon stood at the top and their eyes met. Her bloodless lips forced a smile and her hand formed a circle of thumb and first finger perceptible only to him. He straightened his shoulders; all was well, and his turn was next.

With him, Kuo was icily correct. It was the first time they had met since that interesting occasion in a Ward Road cell, but neither referred to it. They reviewed the details of the current matter, point by infinitesimal point, but without any enlivening variations. After all, there was very little likelihood that anyone could check on Fallon's idle attendance at an outdoor juggling show. And it was quite reasonable that Albany could have returned to the house without Fallon's knowledge, even while Fallon was still at home.

When he was temporarily released at three, he went to bed. But the tramp of the Security men resounded through the house; their fingerprint people were everywhere; their burglary experts virtually took Efremov's window and locks apart and talked in loud voices in the garden beneath the vines. And Fallon's last sight of Kuo before retiring was of him pacing the lower areaway and checking the clock. Thorpe Albany had still not appeared. It was apparent that the captain had a new suspect, as Li had said he might.

Fallon had fallen onto his bed without removing his clothing. When he was wakened after daylight and taken to Kuo's office, he found it so crowded that it was difficult for him to enter. Fallon was reminded incongruously of an old comedy routine featuring the Marx Brothers where small rooms were always spilling over with people; he almost grinned. But he learned there was nothing really to grin about. An early morning police patrol on its rounds had found the body of Thorpe Albany an hour before, lying in a mean alley in the Nantao district, a place not far from the city temple called the Iron Shadow Wall Lane. The man had been dead several hours; he had been strangled with a piece of wire.

Fallon looked hastily around. Judith Markham was not visible. Colonel Li was there with the others who had been assembled; they reflected, variously, shock and fear and relief. Fallon did not know what to think or say, and was thankful no one addressed him at the moment. He would have faltered, he knew, and said something wrong. He wondered if Judith had been informed. He tried to imagine what could have happened behind the herb shop since he had left, but could make no immediate sense of it.

They had been brought together simply for the announcement and Kuo curtly sent them away again. Fallon ascended the stairs with Li.

"Does Judith know?" he asked.

Li glanced at him from under his lids. "Not yet. I will tell her."

"What do you think of it?"

"I am not expected to think in this case. That is the captain's function. But I will tell you what the captain is thinking. He is thinking that the same intruders who previously entered the house returned last night by Efremov's window and were seen by Albany. He followed them. Perhaps he found their base. They discovered him and killed him."

"It's quite possible."

"It's also possible—and Kuo is thinking this as well—that Albany was working with them all the time but became afraid about the Malov report and they executed him."

"That's possible too."

"There's still a third thought with Kuo, which concerns you. If you are very fond of that girl, I am sorry for you." He walked into his office.

9

There was breakfast in the mess hall but Fallon had no appetite and remained in his quarters, drinking tea brewed over his alcohol lamp. The day had come on gray again and rain was imminent. No one was permitted to leave the house. After a time he went into Father Julien's room and found the priest more composed than he had expected after the disturbances of the night. The excitement had rallied the missionary and he was full of questions that Fallon could not or did not want to answer. He administered to Vauzous' wants in an absent-minded fashion, still shocked by the cold-blooded disposal of Thorpe Albany and working vainly at its reasons.

Judith Markham made a sudden entrance. She usually visited the priest each morning and so had the excuse; she was still very pale, with a face untouched by cosmetics so that it was drawn and set and older. She performed a few unnecessary tasks, moving nervously about and not trying to conceal a rising emotion that combined both despair and anger.

Finally she turned to Fallon and, ignoring Vauzous' presence, said to him, "You knew it all the time, of course!"

He hesitated. "No, Judith, believe me. I told you the truth when I said that they were holding him only as a hostage. They had no intention then of—of harming him any more than that. They'd virtually promised me. I have no more idea than you do what has happened."

Her face crumpled and she buried it in her hands for a moment, but when she looked at him again her eyes were still dry and hard.

"All right, I suppose you didn't know, though I don't believe you told me all the truth—just the part you wanted to tell. It's that bitch you're protecting! Well, you may not have had anything to do with it directly— I don't say you did, with the killing and all. You're not that kind. But she is, and I'm not covering up for her. Or that lot of assassins! Now there's no one to protect by keeping still, like you said. I haven't told them yet— there hasn't been a chance—but I will!"

She whirled toward the door. "Wait, Judith," Fallon said. "There must be some explanation for why they did it. I'll know after a bit."

"Wait!" she said bitterly. "I waited too long. They didn't wait, did they? They didn't give him a chance. So what good are explanations?"

Father Julien's thin face was bewildered, but he held up a hand.

"I don't understand," he said. "Please don't try to tell me now. But Judith, if what you intend to do is only for revenge, think about it first.

Whatever it is, I feel it will make trouble and danger for Paul. Surely you don't want that!"

She paused, staring from Vauzous to Fallon and back again. She was distracted, with a wildness in her pale eyes. But a flush rose swiftly to her cheeks.

"No," she said at last. "I don't blame Paul. I should, but I don't." Her fingers twitched at her dress, and she dropped her gaze before the priest's steady regard. "I—you won't be brought into this, Paul. I've got to do something, but you won't be mentioned."

Before Vauzous could be permitted further words she slipped out and ran down the hall, and Fallon heard her heels clicking on the stairs as she descended to the adjutant's office.

"They've got to be warned," Fallon said to the old man. "It's the group, Father. Our friends. They're sitting ducks."

Without hesitation he followed her. But in the entryway he made straight for the outer door. Two guards posted there halted him.

"But I've got to go out," he protested. "I'm the doctor. I have sick patients that need my attention at the hospital. I can't stay in here doing nothing."

"No one may leave without a permit," a guard said. And Major Huang, coming out of the mess hall with quick steps, put his hand on Fallon's arm.

"The captain's strict orders," he muttered. He glanced apprehensively over his shoulder toward the closed office, and Fallon heard the high voice of Judith there, speaking rapidly. "Please don't make difficulties," the major added. "Your patients can wait."

Fallon returned slowly to his quarters; his chance to send a message to Yin Kuei had vanished.

Standing before Captain Kuo's desk, Judith said, "I *am* telling the truth now. I repeat that I'm sorry I didn't mention it last night, but I didn't really think it was important. I'm very dull. The fact I tell you now proves my good intentions, doesn't it?"

Kuo looked at her narrowly and tapped his long fingers on the desk. "You are very dull or very uncooperative," he said in his coldest tone. "Or very cunning. Now you come and say you saw this girl Yin Kuei on the street the other day, and followed her to Nantao. Then why didn't you report it to my bureau immediately? Why didn't you speak earlier this morning?"

"I've told you! The connection never occurred to me until now. I don't like that girl. Thorpe Albany used to be mixed up with her and I suppose I resented it. So when I happened to see her walking by, I just went after her to try to find where she was living. But she went down into that terrible part of the city and into a dark place and I was frightened. I thought, surely she can't be living here, she's just shopping. So I ran away, I didn't want her to see me. But now that they've . . . found him in that district, I suppose it must mean that the shop was where she was actually staying. And probably that's where he went. It's simple enough."

"You think Albany knew of this place and went there, eh?"

"Yes. I suppose that's how it was."

"Your unaccountable delay in reporting this significant fact may mean that she and her friends will have had plenty of opportunity to escape by now," Kuo said. "If they do, I may hold you responsible. Now again—describe the shop and the street. Here, take this pad and try to draw a map." He picked up the phone as Judith began, with a shaking hand, to sketch lines on the paper.

Fallon could not settle down in his room. It had begun to rain heavily. He paced until he was tired, then went below to the colonel's suite and asked permission to check over the medical supplies in the cabinet there. It was not wise to display so much concern, but he had to know. Li was at his desk, making a pretense of doing his own work, but he was haggard and snappish. From faint noises toward the rear, Fallon knew that Judith was at home, keeping out of sight. Occasionally Major Huang came in, acting in liaison.

The Security Bureau had thrown out a dragnet covering Nantao and was calling in the aid of the regular People's Police. Activity was centered on the district around the city temple, where streets were blocked and a house-to-house search was being made. Everyone was being screened. Judith's map was inaccurate; she had not been able to read street or shop signs and had only a general recollection of the crossing where the shop stood; she did not even know what kind of a shop it was, but only remembered rows of jars and a fat proprietor. There were scores of shops like that, and scores of fat men, even in lean times. Captain Kuo was bearing down on the radio monitors; their mobile units had been concentrated in the area. The chief of the monitoring service was under imminent threat of arrest. Kuo was raging at his inefficiency. For it had come to light that the service had known for some time that an illegal transmitter was operating somewhere in that maze, but its efforts to locate it had been unaccountably casual and unavailing.

"Perhaps," said Li, "that will take some of his pressure off our necks, anyway. A pox on these Security people! For all their boasts, they're great bags of wind!" The colonel had had no sleep.

"The captain is now inclined to the belief that there was no burglary at all by way of the window, from outside," Huang said. "His investigators tell him they think the window was forced from the inside as a ruse, and they can find no evidence of disturbance in the vines and no trace of prints in the grounds. They think entrance was made by the door with a key, and a key probably opened the files, just as before. Therefore the captain thinks it possible that Albany himself obtained the report and delivered it to subversive elements in Nantao, and they executed him to silence him."

"It requires no genius to reach such a likely conclusion," said Li. "In my opinion, and between ourselves here, Captain Kuo is a thick sack of donkey droppings. Go back and sit in a dark corner again and keep your ears open. Perhaps we shall benefit by more of the captain's sparkling gems of deduction."

But when Huang had gone, Li glanced at Fallon and added, "The captain doubtless holds with the equal possibility that it was you who committed the theft. However, there is a remarkable absence of fingerprints or other evidence. He has intimated that he would very much like to apply the screws to you to see if your account of yourself holds up, but I have assured him that I will not permit it. I advise you to cultivate tranquillity and retain trust in my ability to protect you from injustice."

Shortly after noon the adjutant burst in without knocking, and his eyes bulged.

"They have found the shop!" he said rapidly. "They have raided it and seized a powerful transmitter, and recovered the original of the report. There is, so far, no evidence that the report has yet been transmitted, but they have made two arrests and hope to know soon."

"Never mind minor details, Major," Li said impatiently. "Who were the captured?"

"Two radio operators, I understand. One person who resisted was shot and killed—I believe the fat man reputed to be the proprietor. It is a herb shop."

"Two operators. Then some of them escaped?"

"Unfortunately. Several made a successful escape through the rear and have thus far managed to elude the net. Whether they are still in the area is not certain. The search is continuing, of course."

"I take it," said Li, "that the woman Captain Kuo is so anxious to lay hands on is not among those taken?"

"No. She has vanished, and also the man the captain wants badly, the man called Tieh."

"Well, well," Colonel Li remarked, glancing rapidly at Fallon and away, "I am sure that Kuo's highly efficient organization will round them all up eventually. The operators will be persuaded to give information."

Huang looked at him uncertainly. "One was shot in the breast and is unconscious; he is dying. The other was shot in the throat and cannot speak; he will probably die. Captain Kuo is very upset about the marksmanship. He is also upset because the fugitives set fire to the premises and they are all but destroyed, with any fingerprints that may be there; the police were barely able to seize the document and the transmitter."

Li lit a cigarette. "The captain *should* be upset," he said. "And now I think I will get some sleep. A good idea for all of us, if the constabulary louse's eggs will move out of my headquarters and leave us in peace for a little while."

Fallon got up, finding his legs rigid with the numbness induced by tension, and glimpsed a quick movement in the living quarters beyond. He knew Judith had been listening, but she made no appearance. He climbed the stairs, went into his room and sat down. But presently he heard Father Julien's piping call and he entered the priest's cubicle. The old man stared up at him with bird-bright eyes.

"Something has happened," he said. "I sense it, I hear the excitement. What is it?"

Fallon stood beside the bed, wondering how much to tell the priest. He was far from strong.

"Albany is dead, and the police have caught some of our friends," he said finally. "Most escaped, however."

"But Albany was not—he was not one of us?"

"No."

"Did they catch that girl? The one you and Judith spoke about?"

"She got away."

"Ah." It was a sigh. Father Julien sank back against his pillows. His thin hand sought Fallon's. "I met that girl when I first came to this city. She was very kind; she sent me to you. You love her, yes? Go to your room, Paul, and pray to God. Thank Him for His help and mercy."

10

In the days that followed, Fallon was severely tried by uncertainty and inaction. He was under house arrest, with only brief visits permitted to the hospital, and those under guard. A depressing spell of dripping mid-autumn weather had set in and time hung very heavy. He found himself missing the sound of Albany's familiar inflections. He rarely saw Judith

Markham at all; she had become a wan wraith who scarcely ventured out of her quarters except to administer to Father Julien's needs. The priest talked to her a great deal in the seclusion of his room, when Fallon was not present. For Fallon her attitude was neither one of reproach nor forgiveness; she was apathetic.

Li had urged him to cultivate tranquillity, but he fretted. He spoke to Vauzous about it. Tranquillity, said the father, was an Eastern luxury, an attainment to some perfect goal at the rarefied levels of sages, scholars and hermit monks. The priest advised a most unorthodox course: seek the Great Ultimate, the cherished Void where all reality was denied and harmony reigned supreme in an aimless cycle through the four stages of Man. Fallon chided him. This did not sound like the teachings of the Church. Nor was it yet for an imperfect barbarian medico. They talked of many things together, passing time, and sometimes Judith listened quietly. It helped a little.

It was Gregor Efremov who brought the news that both operators captured in the raid had died without disclosing anything of importance to the police. He seemed privately amused by Captain Kuo's frustrations. As an official gesture, he had filed a complaint and a protest with the Security Bureau, and sent copies to Li and to his superiors in Peking. The police came around and changed the lock on his door and provided him with a steel cabinet. But he appeared to take the second pilfering of his files as something of a joke on himself. He displayed no change of attitude toward Fallon, no outward suspicion despite Kuo's frosty animosity for the doctor. And in a confidential session in Fallon's quarters one evening, he belittled the importance of the Malov report and declared that there would be no disciplinary orders from Moscow.

"Even if they succeeded in transmitting the gist of the document to their friends abroad," he said, "it would not be surprising news to our enemies. They know quite well already what are the goals of our program in all Southeast Asia. One must be realistic about it. I don't think much of the Malov report would amaze your intelligence agents. I don't underestimate them, you know."

No, Fallon thought, it would not do to underrate such agents, loitering just outside the fringes across the frontiers. He had a strong conviction that several of his former comrades, the people he had known in the old days of the Philippine liberation, were now employing their considerable talents at assessing such information as leaked out. He sat slumped in his chair, thinking of them. All the ones in a former life, now scattered near and far, each fulfilling his own destiny.

"Come, come," said Efremov, seeing his expression. "You brood too much. Get up and let us go and cheer an old man next door who has far greater reason to brood than you. We will go and jolly the little father. Wait, I will get some vodka I have; it will help him, maybe."

One morning as Fallon was passing through the hospital ward on his rounds, one of the attendants, a crooked-backed little man with a sly and leathery face who mopped and dusted and carried bedpans and slops, sidled up to him and leered in his comical way.

"I-sheng," he murmured, "I have something for you." He glanced about with exaggerated caution, though no one was paying them any attention. "Here it is. A man who sometimes comes to the rear to rest and smoke a pipe gave it to me and asked that you should receive it."

He pressed a small cloth-wrapped package into Fallon's hand and shuffled away. Fallon unrolled the object and the little tasseled cord with the queer knot woven in its end lay in his palm. He stared down at it a moment, then pushed it into his pocket and followed the sweeper down the aisle between the cots.

"Is this man still here?"

"He sits beside a tree outside, and has a clay pipe, I-sheng."

Fallon went out through the kitchens, noting that the guard assigned to accompany him each day was gossiping with a nurse in the main entrance hall. He found a man seated with his back to the building and when he turned around Fallon saw that it was the operator called the Buffalo.

"It is not wise to come here in daylight," Fallon said rapidly, smiling.

"It is not wise to do anything but obey the law," said the Buffalo. "I was asked to bring you a gift. You can trust the twisted sweeping man."

"She is all right, then?"

"Certainly. The work is going on as before, except that we must build a new transmitter. Meanwhile we use the smaller ones. We have a different cave now."

"I thought perhaps she had left the city. Tieh promised she would be sent away."

"I don't know about it," the Buffalo said. "Tieh does not tell me of personal matters. But she is still here, in the old Concession."

"What happened to the foreigner who was seized?"

"He escaped. Tieh overtook him before he could inform on us."

"I see. I heard the shopkeeper and others died also."

"Tung was shot when he saw the police coming and raised an alarm. It permitted some of us to flee in time, after starting the fire. We had already completed transmitting the long message. The Snake and the Carp—"

"Yes, I heard. Well, we mustn't linger here in the open. Thank you for coming. Will it be possible to see her?"

"I was instructed to tell you that while caution is necessary, it will be possible as soon as the restriction is eased on you."

"That may be some time. The police no longer trust me," Fallon said.

"She will wait, and she says she will be careful. The sweeping man can summon me when you wish." The Buffalo sauntered away through the back gate of the hospital yard.

When Fallon returned to the house that day, he went directly to the colonel's office and found Li there.

"How long must I endure this arrest and constant guarding?" he demanded. "It greatly interferes with my work at the hospital."

The colonel put down his writing brush and looked at Fallon quizzically. "There are a number of foreigners in this city," he said, "who have been under house arrest or worse for nearly four years. You have been fortunate."

"I know, and I'm grateful. Nevertheless—"

"Nevertheless, your restriction will be lifted soon. Captain Kuo has said so. And I will add a comment. From your standpoint, this is not a good sign."

"How so?"

"He could keep you restricted indefinitely, and has reason for doing it. The fact that he will return some freedom to you does not mean that he has become magnanimous. You will be closely watched. Without doubt the captain believes that you will make contact with that girl again as soon as possible." He sat turning the brush in his hands. "You can see that for yourself. I suppose you are thinking that this is a strange way for an officer to act, warning a prisoner against betraying his friends. So I don't offer you an explanation. I only say, don't be rash."

Fallon considered and said nothing. The colonel picked up the sheet of paper on which he had been writing and laid it down again.

"This is a report," he said. "It concerns preparations for a journey that I must soon make. It seems that my Department thinks I am the logical man to complete the inspection tour which Comrade Pregnesky could not finish." He made a wry face. "I don't like to travel any more. I am not a well man, as you know better than anyone. But my duty demands it. Pregnesky was going south to Canton, you know, so now I must go instead. He was traveling by air, but I must put up with the discomforts of rail transport. That is just one of many differences between a—a Russian General, shall we say, and a Chinese colonel doing the same job."

"A trip will do you good," said Fallon. "Canton is very pleasant at this time of year."

"Canton is never pleasant to me. I don't care for the Cantonese—they are too devious and intrigue-minded. I always become sick when I get into that hot damp climate. But that is now the center of my work and we have a new office there." He flipped his brush into the bamboo holder and raised his eyes to Fallon, a smile tugging at the corner of his mouth. "I hope you, at least, like the Cantonese and their climate, and will enjoy the trip. I am taking you with me."

Fallon blinked. "To Canton? What for? Besides, Kuo won't allow it."

"Kuo has nothing to say about it. You are my charge. And I need you on such a trying journey, to keep me on my feet and get my work done. Also, Fah On, a change of atmosphere may curb your recklessness and—ah—ardor, for your own good. The environment here is bad for you, and if I left you to your own devices, I should return to find you in jail again, and that girl also, probably. Kuo would certainly see to that."

"I have no choice, then?" Fallon asked, but already his mind was hurrying ahead, probing at the future.

"No. We will leave in a few days, so put a medical traveling kit together. I am also taking Efremov and an aide—probably Major Huang."

"What about Mrs. Markham?"

Li grimaced. "Judith remains here."

"She doesn't want to go?"

"Oddly enough, she doesn't. Says she has no interests in Canton. I thought perhaps the trip might divert her from her—ah—her troubles, but she has declined the invitation. You know, Fah On, I will never really understand the Western mind, and especially the Western woman's. It is inscrutable."

V

The Bo Tree

Where the exaggerated precautions taken by his friends had heretofore seemed extreme and a little silly to Paul Fallon, tonight he saw merit in it all and played the game with a grave concentration. There were mists and chill winds off the river, as if the evening had been made to order. That day he had told the hunched sweeping man that he wished to see the operator called the Buffalo again, and now the sweeper came up to him with a characteristic crablike scuttle and, in the dimness of the far ward, told him the pipe smoker was waiting behind the hospital kitchens. And, he whispered, so far as he could see there was no one loitering about the premises who might have any connection with Security.

Fallon took few chances on that. Ever since Captain Kuo had coolly informed him a week before that his house restriction had been lifted, he had felt the spine-prickle that he assumed was a signal he was being watched, though he had little experience in such matters and did nothing or went nowhere that would arouse curiosity. He saw the strategy as Colonel Li had outlined it. And he was determined not to expose Yin Kuei again.

As soon as the sweeper sidled away, Fallon put on an old white gown and informed the night duty nurse that he was going into the basement for an autopsy. The morgue was in the basement and this was no departure from his recent routine; there were usually bodies there and the place was deserted. He had deliberately arranged to do such work at night. But tonight he bolted the door and went on through the autopsy room and out past the row of cold-boxes, leaving a light on behind him and stripping off the gown. There was an outside delivery door here and a ramp for the carts, and beyond, in the dark wet grounds under the tree, he found the Buffalo waiting.

The man said nothing but immediately left the grounds by the rear gate with Fallon close behind, and turned up-creek along the shadowed embankment. They went past the post office and the apartment towers, and presently swung off from the water in the direction of Chapei, finally angling into what Fallon recognized from his drab surroundings as Tsepu Road in the northern reaches of the Settlement. This was a district not unlike Nantao and he tapped the Buffalo on the shoulder and asked, "Where do we go?"

"She told me to bring you to the house of the old woman she formerly lived with," the guide said calmly. "She does not live here now, but it is not good to take you to the new place, so she has come here to meet you."

Fallon had no desire to visit the relocated headquarters of Tieh and his associates; he had seared himself and the rest of them so that now he thought he knew how to avoid a hot stove. The Buffalo led him into an alley, waited a moment to assure himself that the street behind them was empty, and went down through the lane to a door where they entered. The house was actually a flat, one in a low-slung row of damp and gloomy dwellings no different from a thousand others in the neighborhood. But it was a warm sanctuary and a palace, this rendezvous, for Yin Kuei waited for him here.

She came into his arms, while the Buffalo hurried on into the kitchen where the old woman sat beside her oven. He held Yin Kuei a moment, his hands on her shoulders and feeling the spasm of trembling in the smooth firm body beneath the rough texture of her jacket. She had come here to meet him in the wide trousers, coat and kerchief of a peasant girl, with cloth slippers on her feet, and she looked small, like a wistful child, and he kissed her gently, wondering how it was that she could always banish his sense of isolation, establishing an uncomplicated bridge between them.

He saw the waiting tilt of her head, felt the wild and willing magic of her mouth beneath his own and the lithe body pressed to him and the strong slim arms about him. Until he had found Yin Kuei he had thought of the women of this race as cold, withdrawn, reluctant to express the surges of emotion and the delicate sexuality that was theirs. But they were strong and valid in her, only demonstrated more subtly, an abstraction that was strangely chaste. She murmured something to him he did not understand, touching him, and it was as if an intimate experience were recollected in mutual tenderness, rather than anticipated in the fever of warm desire. Her emphasis was preoccupied but no less demanding in its passion. It was like the art of her people, seemingly cool as silk, replete. And he thought, She knows rapture because it is the realization of love between us, while I only touch it in anticipation.

After a time, as he held her close, she sighed. "We are expected to grow up to be demure and modest," she murmured. "We're taught that love is a passive negative thing. But I don't want it that way, not now with you, Paul. I don't want to be sacrificing; I don't want the cold bed we're taught to expect."

They could not leave the house for the streets were unsafe for both, but there was a small flat roof a flight above, sheltered from the mist by a sloping mat canopy. From the balustrade they could see across the low plain of houses to the distant lights of the river and the towering buildings beyond, sparkling and luminous. Leaning on the balustrade with Yin Kuei drawn beneath the protective spread of his own coat, he felt the cold wet of the rain blown in against his face, dampening the heat of his flesh. Out there in the flickering lights from a galaxy of windows there were other lovers, he thought, each couple alone and self-contained in harmony. But not in this close harmony, this shared silence that seemed to glow in the dark; they couldn't be.

Love-making was for youth.

No, he rejected it! This sentiment, this enfolding and driving together that overwhelmed them now, it was not necessarily something that comes with the heyday of the blood. It was a divine and throbbing tenderness, but it was not reserved for the very young. Nor could he say that it was a last watch fire flaring up from the long-smoldering embers damped by stoic maturity. God knew, he sometimes felt as old and weary as the Flowery Kingdom, but that was because these last years had passed so slowly, without Yin Kuei. The passion was not measured by age but was a truth ever young and beautiful. He saw his life, with the defacements of its accidents and errors, but he did not shrink from it or grow melancholy. Around it now, here on this drab dim roof with Yin Kuei in his arms, the muses sang and roses bloomed, and yesterday was past grief.

He saw and felt the demonstration of love in both himself and her, and he thought he recognized the rapture for what it truly was. When he had first looked at it and realized what was happening, his inclination had been to put it resolutely aside as a thing which in all his life he had not really found and would never find. But the gleam pointed steadily into his eyes and closing them did no good. So he stood looking down into her bright still face, and it seemed natural to him that she should represent the human race for him, the melting cloud, the shining star, all in the world he had ever dreamed that was cunningly wrought into the texture of woman.

It was useless now to say that she was not for him, a folly to be rejected here before it did her injury. It was pointless to raise the rhetorical questions of disparate race, for race had nothing whatever to do with it. What could he ask and answer regarding such academic matters as the quality of love, the possibility of her infatuation, the likelihood of where this fancy—if such an inadequate term could be considered—would lead? Whoever dealt with such abstractions at this stage?

The future, they said, was already written; why argue with the record? What good would come of raising issues like roadblocks, issues of heritage and culture, interests and desires, the chances of sorrow and happiness? How few men or women ever did? Even the more immediate and concrete problems involving his status as a quasi-prisoner and hers as a fugitive were no longer important to him. These roadblocks were erected only to be crumpled by the invincible if illogical demands of their love.

"Paul, do you think I would make a poor wife for a foreigner?" Her voice was soft as the mist.

"No, I think you will make an excellent wife."

"I'm not like your girls at all, and I admire them so. They make good wives."

"You have a wife instinct," he said.

"No, I haven't, Paul. You see, a woman has a maternal instinct and she has a childish instinct. But she has no instinct of a wife. Her wife instinct is only a combination of the two."

"I'll trust your instincts."

They withdrew from the roof, returned to the warmth of the room below.

"But do you think we know each other too easily, Paul? My father used to say that men and women who do that are cheap lovers, just as those who make friends easily are never lifelong friends."

"You'll be my lifelong friend and lover, Yin Kuei."

"And after life? Do you believe in transmigration, Paul? There are so many things we don't know about each other yet."

"We'll learn," he said. "Sure I believe it. I'll survive in a hospital cockroach, and you'll be the kitchen cat who eats me."

She giggled, sitting beside him and braiding her black hair. He reached for his jacket, hung on a chair, and brought the silk tassel out of its pocket and handed it to her. "You should keep this knot with you. Don't go around giving it away to strange men like the Buffalo."

The old woman came in from the kitchen, bringing them a pot of tea and a small bottle of shaohsing. "The Buffalo sends the wine," she said, the crinkles in her brown face deepening. "He says not to linger too long over it, for there is a curfew to consider."

Yin Kuei poured the wine into the tiny cups. "I am going away soon," she said.

"I wanted to ask you about it," Fallon said. "What are the arrangements?"

"I haven't been told the details. But Lao-hu has promised, and his word is good. He is making the preparations."

"However you go or wherever you are, here's an address and a name," he said, writing on a scrap of paper. "These friends of mine will see that you're taken care of until I get there. Here is an address in Hongkong, and here is another in Manila. Will you have any money? They'll provide you with all you need when you get to them."

"Oh yes, Tieh has money for me. Not pay, you understand. But expenses. Anyway, we have many friends to whom I can go outside."

"Tieh is an impulsive fellow; you'll be better away from him."

"You mean Thorpe Albany? It was terrible. But Tieh says it was necessary."

Fallon set down his cup. "I have a little news, Yin Kuei. I'm going away myself for a while, with the colonel."

"Away?" Her eyes grew large. "He is releasing you?"

"Not quite that fast. It's just a trip to Canton and we may be back here within a month. But by that time I'm sure you'll be gone."

"Yes. Perhaps you can persuade the colonel it's time to let you go."

"I'm not that optimistic. But when I hear from Tieh that you're safe, then I'll make every effort. If Li doesn't listen to reason, perhaps Tieh can do something for me; maybe this underground railroad or whatever it is you're traveling on will take foreign passengers."

"It's possible, Paul. I'll talk to Lao-hu about it."

Fallon was turning the tassel in his hand, but she held the other end of the cord. He could think of nothing to say. He could tell her to be careful, but he would not draw a deep breath again until he heard that she was entirely out of this.

"I'm sorry about your friend Tung."

She nodded, her face quiet. "I shouldn't have escaped if it hadn't been for him. This old woman here—she was his wife, you know. She urges me to go away too. I don't like to run, but I'll do it for you. There's always our work to do outside. I'll go wherever you say and wait with as much patience as I can, because I love you."

The Buffalo coughed in the doorway. "You must stop this blowing on the cowskin," he rumbled. "Talk can go on forever, but the patrols are on the streets and there is a long way to travel for both of you."

"Patrols don't bother homely farm girls," Yin Kuei said. "You must conduct Paul back to the hospital."

"This autopsy has taken a long time," Fallon said. He rose and held Yin Kuei, and kissed her. "So long," he said roughly in English. "Take care of yourself."

"*Tsai hui*, Paul. We will meet again."

He went with the Buffalo out of the alleyway into the road and they walked toward the creek. The mist had thickened; street lights were bobbing globular masses of yellow fuzz in the wet wind and the pavement gleamed. Near the hospital's rear entrance they separated.

"Tell Tieh," Fallon said, "that if she is not gone by the time I return from Canton, there will be very serious trouble for him."

"Tieh thrives on trouble, I-sheng. But he wants no trouble with you. I am sure that she will be gone."

"Good luck, then."

He went down the ramp into the morgue, put on the white gown, and turned out the light. He stood for a moment in the black and silent room of the peaceful dead, rubbing the mist out of his hair with a towel, and then went up the stairs. The hospital was quiet; the duty nurse glanced at him from her desk and nodded absently and went on with her affairs. It was time to go home from his work.

2

The night train for Hangchow and Nanchang would leave the south station at sunset, and the colonel had told his driver to be at the house gate immediately after dinner. Fallon spent the morning at the hospital, turning his patients over to the care of Dr. Chu's assistant, and after lunch he went home to pack his bag and medical kit. His personal possessions were scanty and his clothing was getting threadbare but it was serviceable. He still retained worn tweeds that would do for travel, and he put his lightweight summer clothes in the bag, for Canton would be warm. When he had completed the brief task he looked around his room and was surprised that it appeared so unchanged; the removal of himself and his belongings would make little difference. In that respect it was like a hotel room, vacated and waiting for the next guest, except that in this case it would remain vacant until he himself returned. He had finally come to think of the room as home, but he would leave it with no regret.

He stood at the window, looking out at the gray October rain and filling his pipe, and recalled a score of rooms and ship's cabins strewn in his wake, each abandoned without sentimentality. Except, perhaps, that bungalow he had occupied on Samar, behind the plantation hospital. Attachments were a luxury one didn't afford in the life of a peripatetic doctor. He sometimes felt a little like the old wandering Dutchman, doomed to cruise in lonely seas forevermore, but today the parallel only raised in him a sardonic grunt. He tramped into the hall and almost collided with Judith Markham.

In recent days a subtle change had gradually become noticeable in Judith. Where before she had been either vivacious or sullen, ingeniously provocative or merely going about like a vacuous slattern, she had become subdued and seemed almost fragile, submissively caught in a routine of her own devising that centered around the well-being of Father Julien. A dozen times a day she climbed the stairs to the priest's room to bring him food, to change his bed and give him the medicines Fallon had brought; she had become his self-appointed nurse and worked serenely at the job, one that was often arduous and sapped her energy. Father Julien was deeply appreciative and Fallon was gratified though still dubious. Judith without her flamboyant air of sultry indolence, quiet and sublimated to the care of an old Frenchman, was both quaint and puzzling.

He had nearly upset the tray she was carrying and stepped back, but she murmured an apology and stood looking up at him.

"You are ready to leave?" she asked. When he nodded, she set down the tray and said, "The colonel is fussing about his medical supplies. I'm sure you have everything he needs."

"All he needs is his insulin and I have more of that. How's the father this afternoon?"

"About the same. He wishes he could go with you, he says."

"He'll never travel in the flesh beyond this point," Fallon said. "But he may hang on a long time. Judith, why don't you come with us? Li urged you to, I understand."

She shook her head. "Father Julien needs someone to care for him." But she could not meet his thoughtful gaze, and color began to flame in her face. Suddenly she raised her eyes and he saw a flash of the familiar smoldering defiance.

"What is it?" he asked quietly. "I can keep it to myself."

"Then it's just that I probably shan't see you again," she said in a tense rush, her words so low he could hardly hear them. "When you come back with Han-tsen, I'll be gone. But I'll leave instructions with the servants about the father's care."

"Gone? Gone where?"

"I don't know, Paul—just gone! Away from here, away from this empty house, from this horrible town if it's at all possible. There are still a few British people here like myself, remember—some of them I even used to know. There's one—he's a shipping man—well, I've seen him several times lately. He's—he offered to help."

Fallon's brow wrinkled. "How help, Judith? Take you in? Send you away?"

She lifted her chin. "It doesn't matter; there's nothing so bad about being taken in by a fellow countryman. Perhaps he can put me on one of the ships. What difference does it make? Everyone's gone—or is going. Even Father Julien."

"Well," Fallon said, trying to smile, "Captain Kuo can't very well interfere with that."

"I suppose you know Han-tsen had quite a row with the captain about taking you with him?" she said.

Fallon had heard about it. The Security officer had been bitter in his attempts to override the colonel's decision, but Li had prevailed with an arrogance that dimmed Kuo's. He must make this trip and he would go nowhere now without his physician, and that was an end to it.

"That man Kuo is hateful," Judith said. "Be very careful what you do."

She had regained her quiet composure. Fallon went into the priest's room behind her and Vauzous' eyes brightened. There was green tea on his tray, but he set it aside and made Fallon sit on the edge of his bed.

"You're getting better every day, Father."

"Ah," said the priest, "the blessings of health are only realized on the sickbed. Just as the blessings of a peaceful home are realized only when the peace is upset. It is quiet here these days, and Judith is very patient with me."

Fallon looked at him, a smile covering his thoughts. Father Julien had lost his home and his flock, and had become a transient courier on the hostile roads to aid a handful of rebels against established authority; if his absent bishop knew, he would have something to be truly scandalized about. He was a long-suffering and tolerant old man and now, bedfast in the stronghold of his persecutors, he gave new hope to Judith. She was not of his faith, a month ago she had regarded him as a nuisance, and with the renewed courage she drew from him she would presently depart and leave him to the indifferent care of orderlies. He knew his fate and was not dismayed.

"It's quieter now, at least, than when the police were staging such an uproar," Fallon said. "When we've gone, you and Judith will be almost alone."

"Something will be certain to divert us," the priest said with a twinkle. "This place is the same as an inn. It's not a very peaceful retreat. But you know, the Chinese say that the whole world is a great inn, and all its guests are, in effect, our relatives. So we may expect trouble from them any time."

Judith had stepped out of the room for a moment to change the water in Vauzous' pitcher. He leaned forward quickly and plucked at Fallon's sleeve.

"Paul, while you are gone I may be in a position to do some small services for our friends. That sweeper-attendant at the hospital is permitted to come to see me, and he will keep me in touch with them." He winked. "There is little I can do, of course, but give them poor advice and moral support."

Fallon was perturbed. "Don't take chances, Father. I'm afraid you let your fervor for humanity carry you past discretion."

"It's important to me. At least, I can keep them informed of what happens here, and of Captain Kuo's activities—Judith is an unwitting source of tidbits, poor girl. I do what I can regardless, because so many less fortunate than myself lie martyred and imprisoned."

He chuckled faintly. "There is little, really, that a missionary can do nowadays," he said, abruptly changing the subject as Judith returned with the brimming pitcher. "It is difficult to make a Christian of a man who profoundly believes that heaven should be high and the ruler should be far away—both of them the higher and farther the better. What must the people of this country think of us alien churchmen, after all, hearing us bickering and quarreling for years over petty trifles? Once when I was a young man in my first mission out here there was a great argument between Protestants and Catholics over which character should be used to translate the word for God!"

He glanced toward Judith and beckoned to her.

"There is something I want from the wooden chest there by the wall, daughter. The haversack I had when I came here the first time." While she went for it he added, "I brought very little from the north. Long ago I learned to travel light on the roads, for I walked a great deal in the country districts, you know." He winked again.

She brought the haversack and he rummaged through it, pulling out his wrinkled cassock and his boots, and finally withdrew a paper-wrapped package.

"This," he said, "is something I have been meaning to give you, Paul. It's just possible that I shan't see you again and I want you to have it. It's a little thing but I have treasured it. One of the communicants in my parish up in Kaihsien presented it to me some years ago, but you should have it more than I."

Fallon unwrapped it curiously and found a small yellowing scroll that he unrolled. It was a simple picture, little more than a silhouette of a gnarled tree something like a banyan, and beside it stood three characters. He read them slowly: *P'u T'i Shu.* But his expression was blank.

"It is the bodhi tree, the sacred pipal under which the Buddha sat on the night when he received supreme enlightenment," Father Julien said. "The bo tree is thus the Tree of Wisdom. I am told there is an old temple near Benares where the particular bo grew, but I have never gone to India. At any rate, it is really a fig, but symbolic. You have a great deal of wisdom, Paul, and the scroll should belong to you."

"I'm unworthy and overwhelmed," Fallon said gravely.

Father Julien laughed. "Don't talk like a polite mandarin! Perhaps I give it to you because I shouldn't want such a heathen fetish found in my poor effects after I die." He glanced at Judith slyly. "Don't you think we might expect to hear some pearl of wisdom fall from the doctor's lips, now that he has received his diploma?"

"Of course." She smiled.

"Well now," said Fallon. "You can't expect much from a medico. After all, he doesn't rate very high with the Chinese, either his science or his knowledge. They say that the doctor belongs with the soothsayer, or the astrologer. Also maybe with the dragonologist."

"Well, as for that," the priest retorted, "the dragonologist is highly esteemed by the people. I know, I've had controversy with them in the course of my work. In that first mission of mine that I just mentioned, I used to pit myself zealously against the geomancers and their scientific mumbo jumbo about that grotesque winged and horned reptile. But to no avail. I derided the marvelous tales my pseudo-parishioners whispered of its mysterious powers and terrible doings. I used to jeer at its universal use in their homes and temples. Once I even got into trouble with the police, because, after all, in those days it was the Imperial emblem and symbolic of the Emperor himself. How futile my efforts were—and how petty!"

He smiled, but his sunken eyes were thoughtful, and Fallon was reminded of Colonel Li's comment that this elderly wayfarer might be more of a Taoist than he cared to admit.

"Quite right," he said cheerfully. "Beliefs in such antediluvian wonders as five-clawed fire-breathing saurians floating through the clouds or
speaking as oracles in village fountains aren't so bad as other habits I
can think of. And they inspire some very interesting murals and amusing
spectacles in processions. Did you stop tilting against them?"

"I did, outwardly. Chiefly because I came to believe in them myself."
Vauzous' smile was still there. "Don't misunderstand me, Paul. Dragons
may make fanciful art and talk, and some may even seem benevolent, but
the hideous monsters are real enough. They represent the destructive
and anarchic principle, the physical power and untamed animal passion
that strives against human progress. Dragons must be destroyed, but it
requires heroes to do that, not bedridden old paupers. The beast vanished
with the Dragon Throne, but another appears in new form. He's still
the embodiment of the devil. Christ trod on the lion and the dragon,
you know, and both St. Michael and St. George fought him as the concept of sin and evil. He must inevitably be crushed under the feet of
dragon slayers, before the earth is strangled."

Fallon was silent for a moment. Then he said ruefully, "I know a
few dragon slayers, Father. But they're not cast in the mold of Hercules
or Beowulf."

"They are," said Vauzous, "but first they need a shield and sword."

3

He woke in a pale gold dawn to the rhythmic clicking of train wheels,
and lay for a moment staring through the compartment window at a
drifting blue line of hills beyond the gay patchwork of the fields. He was
stiff and chilled from a night stretched on leather upholstery, and the
air in the small swaying room was stale with tobacco smoke. But the
sight of the clear bright autumn morning spreading across an open
land unobstructed by the towers and writhing fogs of the city brought
an exultant pulse to his throat. He threw aside the blanket, swung his
legs to the floor and gazed avidly on the passing scene while fumbling
for his shoes.

On the long seat opposite, Efremov still snored resonantly. Major
Huang must have sat up most of the night in the narrow seat between
them but he was gone into the car's corridor now. The colonel had taken
two compartments on the southbound express and occupied the adjoining
one in solitary comfort. The new democracy had not, Fallon reflected,
yet eliminated the division of classes aboard the inland trains; they were

traveling in the old-style battered Continental firsts, trailing second-class coaches and hard thirds where the unbiquitous army personnel and petty officials were jammed. Stretching cramped muscles, he was glad for this hangover of bourgeois inequality.

A train attendant in a peaked cap slid back the door and set a tray on the compartment stand holding teapot and cups. Fallon absently scalded his mouth on the steaming green fluid and lit a cigarette, with his eyes still fixed on the slowly changing landscape. Morning expanded across the hills, throwing long shadows out from clumps of feathery bamboos where tiny thatched mud farmhouses crouched amid their geometric gardens of crops. The train curved along a canal for a short distance, and gaudy sails on cargo sampans caught the climbing light and a cormorant fisherman bobbed on his tiny boat amid his solemn birds. The calm water cast up the reflection of miles of gray mulberry thickets interspersed with cotton fields; a man in a wide straw hat trudged along the narrow wheelbarrow path beside the canal pushing his load of produce to market in some nearby village; a little girl with red ribbons in her black hair was herding a flock of ducks; a somnolent buffalo stood among the willows, watching the train roar past with great liquid eyes; farmers moved on the dikes between their paddies where the rice of the people flourished. All this was familiar and exhilarating to Fallon, but his gaze returned constantly to the mounting hills of Chekiang that broke the horizon to the west and south. They marked the limits of the flat delta, the boundaries of the Great Valley, and each double-click of the wheels took him farther from the city where he had been confined for more than four years.

It seemed incredible to him that he could have vegetated in the house beside the creek so long. He could not remember any time in his adult life that he had remained four years in any place. The engine hooted on the gently winding approach to the Wuyi Shan watershed, and Fallon was again grateful that the colonel had been obliged to travel by this slower and more crowded facility, rather than by plane. He pushed up the grimy window and drew in a deep breath of clean air blowing fresh from the hills, and watched a ponderous and deliberate water-wheel revolving beside a stream, hoisting water to moisten the tired land and force it to another season's effort.

Major Huang returned to the compartment, looking a little disheveled and weary. The colonel, he said, had had a restful night but was complaining again about the pain in his foot and leg. It was a raw blister he had worn from a tight new boot purchased for the trip, and though Fallon had cleaned and dressed it, the angry wound refused to close.

The colonel now limped gingerly, but refused to substitute a slipper for the boot.

"You and Efremov slept well," Huang said petulantly. "I suppose it was his vodka—these Russians are a savage race." He glanced at Efremov but the Slav snored on. "You saw nothing of Hangchow or the lake or the bay, and now we are well past Kinhwa. We shall be over the border into Kiangsi soon." His tone was a reproach.

"This isn't a pilgrimage." Fallon grinned. Major Huang's orderly mind demanded that the party for which he was responsible take due note of each stage in the excursion he had arranged. Soldiering was not Huang's forte. He was meticulous and made a good desk officer, but he would have made a better tour director under more peaceful circumstances. After leaving the Shanghai south station he had given Fallon and Efremov a briefing on the route ahead, emphasizing that while one could now travel all the way to Canton by rail, this was only a spur line. It ran westward deep into the country to link the coast with the main north-south trunk railway at Changsha, the great steel band that bound the nation together from Manchuria to the Tonkin frontiers.

"Our troop and goods trains are running with far greater efficiency now than ever they did when venal officials of the old regime were operating them and foreign investors reaped all the profits," Huang declared in his precise way. He sat down and looked out at the shifting view with eyes that saw little of its early morning beauty.

Fallon had no desire to listen to more of this in lieu of breakfast. He went down the corridor to the lavatory to wash soot from his face, and then called upon the colonel and found him propped up in his bunk, drinking tea and thumbing through a sheaf of papers from his portfolio. Fallon examined the foot and found the blistered area enlarged and moist, reddened and hot at the edges. He dressed it again, disturbed by its appearance but making no comment, and fed his patient a massive dose of vitamins. The colonel replied without interest to his questions, declaring that he felt all right except for the usual weakness and slight nausea, and submitted to another injection. He waved a handful of reports disgustedly at the physician.

"I must read this stuff," he said, "but it tells me nothing I don't know. The grand strategy is curiously simple and uninspiring when one is admitted to its secrets. Here is an analysis of why the Annamite peasant is in revolt against his French master. We have always known the reasons, and that is why we have had our own great revolts. Mencius explained it long ago. When a ruler treats his subjects like dirt, then it's right for the subjects to regard him as a bandit and their enemy. And the agent here wastes our time discussing bureaucratic interference in local affairs. Lao Tzu has said that a great state should be governed as a man would cook a small fish—the less it's disturbed the better."

"Does the new order here practice what you and Lao Tzu preach?" Fallon asked dryly.

Li shrugged. "Practice and theory are often difficult to reconcile. There has been a continual and merciless struggle in this land for centuries. Our tragedies are repeated over and over again by a blindness to reality in a long succession of rulers. It is often chilling to the soul, Fah On."

He turned his head to see the marching ranges at which Fallon was gazing, the unfolding panorama of hills, water and sky.

"Here," he said after a moment, "is the cradle of our endeavor. Nearly twenty years ago I was commanding a unit of the ragged and poorly armed peasant army in these Kiangsi valleys, south of the Poyang lake. The odds were desperate; the forces against us where overwhelming. But we survived. We launched the Long March from here. We were a a nation emigrating across wide rivers and high mountains and fighting a running battle as we went. We crossed the Tatu into Szechwan, and we crossed the grasslands of the Tibetan plateau into the sanctuary of the loess hills in the northwest. We marched six thousand miles in a dozen provinces, we fought ten successive armies trying to smash us, and twenty thousand of us got through. It was perhaps the greatest exploit in our history, and from it we triumphed, and now I return to look at the cradle again. It is unchanged. But sometimes I feel despair."

The train was moving slowly past a small town and Fallon saw the same blue-clad crowds on the station platform, the raggle-taggle soldiers in dirty green, the always fat officials and the always lean coolies. There was a big-drum player in an open space surrounded by a circle of spectators who watched a troupe of acrobats tumbling in the air while their employer peddled an elixir. Farther on, the crowd's attention was diverted by two embattled housewives shouting vituperations at each other before a market stall. Even before the train left them behind the quarrel was over and the amused watchers were scattering. One saw a great deal of incipient fighting and brawling in China, Fallon thought, but most often it was sound and fury ending short of blows. With this pragmatic people, arguments and compromise were more civilized than the final decision of violence.

The colonel had seen the satisfactory conclusion of the quarrel as well, and his mood lightened. He chuckled.

"Like our wars," he said, "these conflicts often tend to disintegrate if we leave them alone. I sometimes think we lack the ability to see them through. They seem to take on a fairylike quality—we laugh at them or walk away. They remind me of a play I once saw in a theater in Peking.

One of the actors took the part of a fierce tiger, and wore a gorgeous striped costume of yellow and black, with a mask. But he fell asleep backstage while waiting for the cue to chase the villain. The play changed, and in the next scene the Buddha was a young prince riding out on his proud white charger to become an ascetic monk. The tiger-actor awakened suddenly and savagely attacked. He ate the Buddha and the horse. It was a great success, I can tell you!"

Fallon went to the compartment door. "Stay in bed today and eat all the food I send to you," he said. "Keep off your foot. You don't want to be hobbling about your official duties in Canton."

The colonel frowned. "I never feel well when I go to Canton. I feel worse this time. It is my fate. A fortuneteller once told me, 'Destiny awaits you in the City of Rams.' Perhaps I should not have come on this journey."

Fallon left him shuffling his papers again in a quick return of his gloomy and protesting mood. A dust-flecked shaft of morning sunlight wheeled like a moving fan of gold across the rumpled bed.

4

The Hankow-Canton express, to which the colonel's ancient wagon-lit had been attached the previous day at the Changsha junction, stood on a siding along the main line above the turbulent Peh River. Green hills dropped precipitously into the gorge on both sides, and in the canopy of sky arching above the sun blazed down to fill the canyon with a heavy crawling heat. It radiated off the glittering tops of the motionless cars that lay like a twisted snake beside the waterway, the rails and the ballast were burning to the touch, and the compartments were stifling. Most of the troops and civilians from the lower class cars had abandoned them to seek shelter in the thin shade of overhanging trees and brush along the grade. A repair train from the north occupied the main line itself, standing parallel with the express, and wisps of steam and tendrils of smoke rose from the stationary locomotives. Both faced the bridgehead over the Peh, the center of an antlike scramble of coolies, a maelstrom of pounding, blasting, riveting and vocal clamor.

The workmen were part of a labor corps rushed up from Kukong to repair the railway bridge across the river. They were flanked by a unit of militia idly leaning about on their rifles, sent along as guards. But a detachment of regular army troops was due soon, according to the current rumor among passengers, workmen, soldiers and harried railway officials. When the troops arrived, a pursuit would be organized to round up the gang of desperadoes that had caused this disruption of service. Meanwhile the express must wait in the steaming valley along the Hunan-Kwangtung border. Nobody expected the troops to catch the bandits, who had completed their sabotage on a tight schedule less than an hour before the arrival of the express that morning, and were now doubtless a score of *li* away in some remote hill fastness. The wrecking had been done by experts with dynamite, but the iron span was not too seriously damaged. The labor corps commander estimated the temporary repairs would be completed by evening and the train could then cross and roll on into Kukong.

Major Huang brought back this latest intelligence from the bridge-head front. He bustled along the line of cars, pushing his way irritably through the throng of loitering passengers to the place where Fallon and Efremov sat on the wagon-lit step, observing the activity.

"This happens quite regularly, I'm told," Huang said. "These miserable bandits cut communications with impunity and are never captured."

"White guerrillas," Efremov corrected with a sardonic grin. "Deviationists. I couldn't have directed the job better myself." The Russian was stripped to the waist for coolness and wore only khaki shorts and sandals. His pale body was big and hairy and gleamed with sweat.

"Whatever you want to call them, it is a very serious matter—for you and for me and all of us. How is the colonel?"

"No special change," said Fallon. "And there's something I'd like to ask you, Major. The next time the colonel becomes ill, please consult me before you dose him with your own quack remedies. I found the stuff beside his bed, and if I read the label rightly, it comes from the Drug Hall of Propitious Munificence, and is called Pills of Transparent Efficacy. I doubt if it'll kill him, but if it does I'm going to note that in my certification."

Huang glowered. "Certainly it won't kill him! It contains ginseng, among other ingredients, and is very expensive. I purchased it near the station at Hengyang last night."

"Ginseng, so far as I'm aware, will not relieve a diabetic stupor such as the colonel was in at daylight today when you finally called me. His breathing is easier now and he has stopped vomiting, but the blood pressure is still very low and if we don't get him into a hospital pretty soon I can't guarantee anything. This is an emergency; he may go into a coma. And there's definitely gangrene in that leg."

"There's a military field hospital at Kukong," Huang said sullenly.

"Not good enough. If they get the bridge fixed and this train rolling again, we've got to take him on down to Canton. The leg condition is acute and very threatening."

He had not intended to go into such detail for Major Huang's benefit, but he was worried and angry. The major's stupidity annoyed him. Ginseng! Why not deer-horn shavings or silk-worm secretions or other panaceas of Eastern *materia medica*? Colonel Li's abrupt and unheralded relapse during the night after leaving Changsha alarmed and puzzled him. The colonel had been a diabetic for years and would always be one, but his condition had been kept under control by the usual valid remedies of strict diet and insulin and he had appeared no different at the start of this journey. Yesterday he had stayed in bed in his compartment as ordered and worked on his papers; today his symptoms were critical. Fallon had been giving him doses of insulin from the doctor's own kit and intravenous glucose injections; the man could keep little liquid on his stomach and had become very weakened.

Major Huang walked stiffly away. He had lost face and several passengers had overheard the doctor's sharp words. Efremov shifted his position on the step.

"What do you think, *tovarish?*"

"I think I'm not exaggerating," Fallon said, dropping his voice. His frown deepened. "I've taken away the insulin Li has and gives to himself, and I'm using my own solution. I wish I had a laboratory analysis of his stuff; apparently it's had no effect whatever for several days. It should also have some external checking reaction on the ulcer, but I've tried it and it doesn't. The thing's spreading rapidly."

"You think his medicine has been tampered with?"

"I don't know; I certainly don't know who could have done it. Frankly, I wouldn't put it past Kuo's agents. He's beginning to rally now. It's not the stupor that troubles me, it's the gangrene. That's one of the by-products of his condition, you know."

Efremov pondered this stolidly. "Do you mean he could die from it?"

"I mean unless we get him to a place where he can have proper treatment it could result in a need to amputate. The arteries below the knee are becoming occluded."

"Hmm. All from a little blister. Pah! These people have no vitality; they die like flies from a few bugs."

"The colonel's a strong fellow," Fallon said, "but his disposition to this is probably hereditary. He's been active but now he's sedentary, and I can't keep him off the rich food."

"You have done your best, I will testify to that!" Efremov lit a cigarette. "Did you know that Huang received a telegram when the train stopped at Chenhsien this morning from Captain Kuo? No? Hah! The excellent

Kuo inquires whether Huang may have noticed among other passengers
on this train anyone of special interest to Security. Meaning, of course,
that girl he is forever hunting. He suspects that you may have smuggled
her aboard, or that she is trailing you."

"He flatters me," said Fallon, feeling the sudden hard beat of the
pulse in his neck.

"Huang is now looking them over again," Efremov said. "He had me
look also. I saw nothing. That Kuo! That crazy Chinaman!" He considered the butt of his cigarette. "Mind you, I don't object to the Chinese.
My God! I've lived among them half my life. I've worked with the men
and played house with the women, and it isn't that Kuo is a Chinese.
I'm more of a Chinese than a white man myself, or even a Russian, I
sometimes think, and there are many who would agree with me. But I
have no use for policemen of any color. And damn them all!"

Fallon was forced to laugh. He slapped Efremov on the bare damp
shoulder and went up into the car again. In the compartment the shade
was drawn and the light was dim, and a fan whirred. The colonel was
tossing restlessly on his bed; he looked strangely emaciated and his
flushed face was dry and hot. The leg was a great bandaged lump. The
colonel was, however, rational.

"This is dangerous, I think," he said flatly as Fallon opened the wrap-
pings again. "Is it not? Don't lie to me, Fah On."

"Yes," Fallon said, "it could be dangerous. It wouldn't have been if
we'd gone straight through to Canton, probably. You'd have been in a
hospital by now. But this delay at the bridge—"

"I have seen legs like that many times before," Li said calmly. "Does it
mean that it might have to be cut off?"

"It could mean that. When people are ill with your trouble, the gangrene is very difficult to check."

Li was silent, looking up at the roof of the compartment. A fly buzzed
loudly in the heated room.

"There must be five million people in China with one leg, with all
our wars and diseases," he said finally. "It is not so great a loss. Now if
the gangrene were in the neck . . . But would an amputation save the
rest of me, Fah On?"

"Oh, yes. There is surgical refrigeration and all that, in modern hospitals. But don't let's anticipate this. The train will be moving soon."

"A thousand miles south of Shanghai," Li said absently, "and nearly
two hundred yet to go. What a damned nuisance these dissidents are
who go around blowing bridges!" He was still while Fallon repacked the
swollen and discolored leg, for the putrescence of it was strong in the
close space of the compartment.

"Doctor," he said, "I have no faith in the military hospitals at Canton, or in those ignorant gobble-tongued Cantonese surgeons. They are only butchers. And my position requires that I go to one, not to the civilian establishments. But they are no better. What is to be done?"

"Don't worry about it. I'll do any work that's necessary."

"Certainly you will. But the surroundings, the equipment . . . You can't even talk to those southern doctors there in their clacking dialect."

"I've usually managed to overcome the language barrier somehow," Fallon said dryly.

Colonel Li laughed; it was an odd sound. His manner toward Fallon had always been indulgent, proprietary and avuncular. Now he was very subdued.

"You must have had great trouble learning our anatomical terms when you first came," he said.

"I did, rather," Fallon said, smiling. "I had to learn them from attendants and nurses in country field hospitals in the northern villages, peasant girls mostly. They taught me the marketplace words for the genito-urinary tract and such because they didn't know any others. I used them on a missionary doctor later and he was fearfully shocked."

The colonel laughed again, and it was interrupted by the wail of the express locomotive. The repair train took up the piercing cry, the sound battering the canyon walls. Loungers outside the car shouted and ran. The car jerked and the colonel swore. Major Huang dashed in, beaming. One of the militia guards on the bridge fired his rifle in an unexpected salute. After a time the train began to roll southward again.

5

It had been many years since Fallon had seen this subtropical Kwangtung country, and as the train clanked across it at sunset, dropping down the winding Peh from the border highlands, he sat at the window of Li's compartment, marveling at its lush green and the profusion of its inland riches. It was a soft and luxuriant region of rice and sugar and tobacco fields, tea and fruit plantations, and the hills were veiled in a purple mist rising from the flooded paddies. The villages and farmsteads seemed old and more substantial than those of the north; the mountains and plain approaching the Pearl estuary lacked the barren brown harshness that made life in the north so rigorous and hence more torn by the strifes of man and nature. The province, though densely populated, did not seem so from the train rolling through it, except where lights had begun to twinkle among the fan-palm groves and under the spreading banyans. But the evidence of humanity's ancient, crowded and hazardous existence was everywhere: the land appeared, in the twilight, to be a vast and endless cemetery of gravemounds and flat stone mausoleums, with here and there a pagoda raising its black silhouette against the crimson west like a pontifical finger pointing toward heaven.

He had given the colonel a mild sedative after the express left Kukong and Li still slept, muttering a little with the fever that gripped him. Now and then Huang or Efremov looked in, but there was nothing for them to do. Huang had wired from Kukong for an ambulance to meet the train. Now Fallon saw the glow spreading across the horizon ahead where the city of Canton spraddled over the delta. By full dark the car was running through the outskirts of this tremendous human beehive; presently it was in an arc-lit purgatory of steam and glaring headlamps and shuttling goods trains and screeching switch engines, the huge marshaling yards. And in time it had crawled to a sighing halt under a thunderous arcade where the turmoil of an express arrival from the north numbed the senses.

Fallon remained in the compartment, avoiding the crush and confusion in the corridors and on the platform and leaving matters up to Huang. The colonel was awake again; Fallon bathed his face with cool water and answered a few languid questions. After some moments Huang opened the door and asked Fallon to step outside. Li roused up on his elbow and declared that there would be no whispered consultations; he was in full command of his faculties and wanted to know what was going on. Huang looked unhappy.

"They should have informed me at Kukong," he said bitterly. "But I suppose they didn't know, or more likely didn't care. I've only just learned about it from the ambulance attendant. It's waiting outside for you; we'll have a litter here and carriers in a moment."

"Learned about what?" Li demanded, a warning note entering his voice.

"The spot fever," the major said. "They say it's epidemic. The hospitals are all overflowing and they've got them in the halls and courtyards."

"For God's sake!" Fallon said aloud and to himself in English. "Typhus! Can anything else happen on this damned trip!"

Li sank back on the pillows, his bright dark eyes fixed unblinking on his adjutant. Then he said, "Spot fever is very contagious. Thousands die from it. I shan't go near any of their hospitals!" He looked at Fallon. "You hear me? Don't permit them to take me to one."

"They could hardly take you if you wished," Huang mumbled. "There seems to be very little room." He was shivering. The colonel's dread of disease had long since communicated itself to Huang and he had taken to dosing himself every time he got a twinge or a coating on the tongue. He was frightened and bewildered.

"There are only government hospitals here," Li said. "The mission establishments have been closed, of course, though I suppose their facilities are being used. Why did the ambulance people bother to answer your wire? What do they propose to do now?"

"The attendant suggested a hotel, sir."

"No," the colonel said. "They won't take in sick people. Huang, have them drive us to the Southeast Asia Bureau offices here, as we originally planned. Captain Wong is expecting us anyway. He's supposed to have accommodations for our party. We'll decide on the next step when we get there and learn more about the situation."

The litter bearers transferred Li from the compartment to the ambulance, the operation watched by a jam of curious idlers. Huang managed to find a taxi, and with Fallon and Efremov followed the big vehicle as it lumbered into the city. Fallon had only a vague recollection of the southern metropolis, and now he saw it by the distortions of a million glowing lights and his own disturbed thoughts. He recognized only White Cloud Road, a broad avenue leaving the railway terminal with a parkway down its center, and later he looked out on the Bund with its great stores, godowns, office buildings and municipal structures. Yellow and red lights gleamed on the sluggish water of the river, thick with shipping and its teeming, floating population, the boats and sampans so close-packed that they seemed like solid land far out from shore. The comb of the hive hummed from its countless cells, the ambulance pushed a ruthless path through the ever uproarious multitude, and eventually came to a stop before the doors of a modern business block on the edge of the avenues, where the old city began.

The Bureau offices were on the second floor and the bearers hoisted the litter up the stairs while Huang hurried on ahead to appraise Captain Wong of the approaching crisis. Wong, a roly-poly and cheerful fellow unabashed by superiors and capable in an emergency, immediately turned the three rooms of his office suite into a private hospital, with Li established in the small living quarters at the rear. The colonel had taken the ambulance ride quite well but told Fallon that he was in considerable pain from the leg, pain that was stabbing upward toward his groin.

The night was sweltering in such an enclosed space, for the building stood in the center of a crowded business district off the Bund, and with the windows flung open to catch a vagrant breeze, street noises below were all but deafening. The captain sent a messenger out for food at a nearby restaurant, and when it was delivered Huang and Efremov ate it. But Fallon had no hunger and he now made another examination of the growing area of inflammation. Li watched in patience.

"What now?" he asked quietly.

"Well," Fallon said, "it's acute but there's still a chance we can save it."

"What is necessary?"

"Certain drugs and equipment that are not available to me here, apparently."

"How long before an amputation may become urgent?"

"Difficult to say. The injections and packs seem to be holding it down pretty well. It's possible a separation may yet occur and the disorganized tissue would then begin to slough off. I've seen a cicatrix form on worse cases than this."

"You've operated under worse conditions than this also," Li said. "I've seen you do it, in an underground hole with shellbursts shaking down the dirt. But if possible, I don't want it done here. Neither do I want to go to a hospital and be exposed to a mob of typhus patients in a crowded ward."

"You're between the devil and the deep blue sea," Fallon said in English.

Li understood and nodded thoughtfully. "If I have choice, I take deep blue sea," he said. Lapsing back into the easier vernacular, he added, "It's only about ninety miles away, you know."

Fallon looked at him, uncomprehending, and then saw what he meant. "Hongkong? Well, yes—not too far. This leg is good for a while yet, I think. Modern hospitals there, of course." He stood beside the narrow bed, waiting.

"Good drugs, good facilities, excellent medical assistance," the colonel said. "We could be there by daylight if we started now—but we can't."

Fallon pulled at his lip. "You mean the matter of permits and passes and exit documents and all that, I imagine."

"Partly. I have the authority to cut through most of it. It could be arranged. It would take some time, but I can put Huang and the captain on it immediately and send them off to rout out the officials whose seals and signatures are required."

"How would you go—by boat or train?"

"That depends. Either way that's quickest. What do you think, Fah On?"

Fallon hesitated. "Well, this is beyond my professional limits, Colonel. After all, I'm interned, and over the Kowloon border is free territory." He stopped, glancing at Li, and the man on the bed smiled bleakly.

"Where free territory begins and ends is a matter of viewpoint, Fah On. But I know what you mean, naturally. Actually, it is in my jurisdiction to grant you a pass. To obtain your release, I have only to say that you have established merit by performing a useful service to us. You are still performing it and would continue to do so after we reach Hongkong."

He lay pondering the problem for a time, and another smile slowly spread across his thin face. "You know, Fah On, we Communists are dedicated to the defeat of three of China's greatest plagues—face, fate and favor. They have crippled us for thousands of years. To gain face we flatter and protect the powerful and seduce the rich and hypnotize the poor, we bribe and demoralize and paralyze justice. We're fatalistic and depend too much on our luck, and sometimes it brings us power. We often wield favor without justice. We prize these things. Now I will gain face by defying my fate and demanding the favor due me in my position. Ask Major Huang to step in here, please."

Huang was appalled. He agreed that the British would probably not turn away Colonel Li in such an emergency, and certainly they would admit Fallon. There was a steady, massive two-way traffic between Canton and Hongkong by land and sea. But Huang greatly distrusted the Crown Colony and all its implications. Would they permit the colonel to return? Might they not imprison him? This all required thought and conferences.

Li called in Efremov and the matter was explained in turn to him. He bared his big teeth in a humorless grin. "Go!" he said without a moment's hesitation.

"That is the decision," the colonel said to Huang. "Get the captain and obtain what permits are needed immediately. No delays! Move, Major!" The order was a roar.

6

When Huang had received instructions about Fallon's pass and other matters and had hurried out in the wake of the fat little captain, a waiting stillness fell over the suite. Fallon glanced at his wrist watch and was surprised that it still lacked a few minutes of eight o'clock; they had not yet been in the city two hours, but it seemed much longer. The colonel dozed again. He had roused out of the stupor on the train long before, and had been relatively alert after their arrival, but he was extremely weak. Fallon studied the leg in perplexity. Sometimes these diabetic gangrenes progressed with a terrible rapidity, and again they were retarded for no apparent reason. He had had little direct experience with them, though with gangrene itself he was all too familiar. He left the colonel in darkness and paced about the two adjoining rooms. Efremov had gone out for a stroll.

The Bureau offices were a dismal place to wait. Captain Wong used the front space for his small staff, now off duty, and the middle room as his own office, while the back cubicle was his residence. It contained only the bed on which his superior now lay and a few undecorative pieces of furniture. The captain's office contained an electric plate for brewing tea and a cupboard. A large tinted photograph of The Chairman gazed with fatherly benignity from the wall.

The phone shrilled in the outer office and Fallon answered. It was Captain Wong, reaffirming Fallon's impression that he was levelheaded and efficient. Using the national *kuo yu* speech because the doctor had no Cantonese, he said that he had first checked with the railway and harbor offices about transportation, and had learned that no fast vessel would be leaving for Hongkong before morning. But there was a passenger train, one of several that made the Kowloon run daily; it would depart from the station shortly after midnight. This was an owl express and normally carried few travelers down to the Territory border, but because of that it made the trip without many delays at checkpoints en route, and usually arrived at its destination about dawn. Wong would make every effort to put them on that train. He rang off abruptly.

Fallon's mind was filled with conflicting thoughts. One nagged: this was near the end of the line and he would not be returning to Shanghai again; the matter of Yin Kuei's escape was yet unsettled and she might be delayed there by Tieh indefinitely. And there was the question of his reception in the Colony. He still had his old passport—it was in the bottom of his personal bag—but he had never been registered at a consular office. They would probably regard him with considerable suspicion. He dug out his passport and looked at it. The photograph had been taken a decade and more before, and both it and the document were sadly out of date. He glanced at himself in Wong's mirror, comparing the lean face and deep-set eyes he saw there with the smooth and cheerful young countenance in the picture. Why, the officials could say with all sincerity that these were not the same man! They could repudiate him, they could say Dr. Paul Fallon did not exist, they could insist that they had testimony showing one Fallon was dead. They could clap him into jail. He threw the passport back into his bag, and it thumped against the paper-wrapped scroll Father Julien had given him. The scroll that honored him as a man of wisdom and knowledge! The man who had figuratively sat under the bo tree and received enlightenment.

After a while he composed himself, filled his pipe and lit it. Efremov returned, carrying a package; it contained two round stone bottles of the fiery Cantonese brandy.

"No vodka in the shops," Efremov shrugged. "Not many of my people here. I know some people in Canton but not vodka drinkers. This is a travel present. One for us to wait with, one for your bag. You must fortify yourself against the shock of disillusion when you return to the *bourzhuis!* The great capitalistic bastion will horrify you after so long in our pure air—you will stifle." He swiveled his mocking eyes around at Fallon as he filled two teacups.

"The devil!" he added, lifting his own cup in a toast. He savored the liquor, made a wry face, and sat down. "Paul, you are a good fellow. Do you know why I think so? Because that policeman Kuo hates you so much. I tell you, the man who is hated by the man you hate is a good person. Remember that." He gulped the brandy and winced. "One can hate without name-calling. That is childish. One side yells warmonger, filthy beast, noisome running-dog. The other shouts slant-eye bastard, dirty Red son of a bitch. Shame, for what? The agony and grandeur of revolution make such things silly. Nothing can stop the juggernaut; you have been here long enough to see that. You do not like it, no, but you see it before your eyes. In the few years you have been here, you have seen mighty changes, as if centuries of revolution had passed by instead of maybe only half a dozen years. Paul, when you get back to that degenerate world, you can be like old Marco Polo, when he lay dying in Venice. You can say, 'You may not believe me, sirs, but I have not even told you the half of what I saw there!' "

Fallon laughed. "One thing I can say is that most people here, most ordinary people, shrink from this upheaval; they think it's a form of immaturity and maybe insanity. They think the madmen have run amok—the asylum doors are open and the insane people are in the streets."

"Let them think what they like," Efremov said indulgently. "It does not make it true. Here is something to tell them when you go home, Paul. Half the people of the earth are in this upheaval, as you call it. Maybe ten times as many people in Asia alone as in your own country. After a little while all the Asians, all the Russians, all the Africans together—then what does that little pimple called Western Europe do, eh? Your country is alone; we dominate the world! There will be an ice age in every town in America!"

"I've heard it before," Fallon said. "You'll wake up some day. The Chinese say that the one who climbs a great mountain must come down the other side."

"Well, never mind all that." Efremov grinned, hoisting the bottle again. "What's the use of arguing, eh? You are going away and it doesn't matter."

He paused, listening. There were quick footsteps in the hall. The outer door opened and someone entered the front office, crossed it and stood in the inner arch. They sat staring up at Captain Kuo Liang.

The Security officer regarded them intently and his eyes swept the room and rested on the door beyond. He was in uniform and wore a side arm. His gaze returned to the two white men and the squat bottle between them and his thin lip curled as from a sour taste.

"Where is Colonel Li?" he asked shortly.

Fallon stood up. "He's ill and asleep."

"Yes, yes, I know he's ill. Major Huang wired me yesterday, and again today, from Kukong. Where is he—in there?"

"In there sleeping. Please don't disturb him."

Kuo looked at him with eyes as hard and dry as marbles. "Why isn't he in a military hospital then, if he's ill?"

"There's typhus in the city. The hospitals are filled. We brought him here. This is the Bureau office."

"Don't you think I know what this is? I came here directly by cab from the airport after the army transport landed, to learn to which hospital the colonel had been taken. Where are Major Huang and the Bureau's officer here?"

Kuo's back was turned to Efremov and Fallon caught the quick shake of the Russian's head. "They are out," Fallon said. "Out at a restaurant."

"What's the colonel's condition? Huang wired that he was critically ill."

"He's had a diabetic relapse, and there's an ulcerated leg. We are doing all we can for him. It isn't so serious that you needed to fly here all the way from Shanghai today. There's nothing you can do for him anyway."

Kuo moved into the room and leaned against a desk, folding his arms. "You needn't tell me what are my duties, Doctor," he said in the same rasping voice. "I didn't come here primarily because of the colonel's illness. I don't expect any information or cooperation from you, but I do from the colonel. I strongly suspect that the girl Chung Yin-kuei has come here with you—either with your knowledge and assistance or following secretly. I ask you now, both of you, officially, is that true, and if so, where is she?"

Fallon's cheeks felt stiff and his mouth was dry. "I know nothing about the girl. I haven't seen her or helped her, and I don't know where she is. Major Huang searched the train and found no one. So far as I would know, she's in Shanghai. If she's here, as you think, I have no knowledge of it. Does that satisfy you?"

"No," said Kuo. He looked at Efremov. "What have you to say?"

Efremov had not moved from his chair, and returned the captain's stare with contemptuous amusement.

"You have no authority to question me," he said. "And what I have to say, dear, is that you are a bigger fool than I had thought."

Kuo knew that Efremov directed the term at him in derision. His thin face paled with repressed fury.

"We will see who is the fool!" he said, starting for the bedroom door.

"There's no one hiding in that room," Fallon said. "The colonel is there alone, sleeping as I told you. Don't waken him."

Kuo whirled on his boot heel and struck him a stinging blow across the mouth, followed by a second with all the strength of his full-swinging arm. The slaps were like whipcracks in the small room. They staggered Fallon, and he tasted the salty blood on his tongue. Efremov came out of his chair with a rising growl of surprise and anger, and the captain quickly put his hand down and gripped the butt of his automatic, jerking it half out of its holster. Efremov saw the man's eyes and stopped in midlunge, catching himself up on the edge of the desk. The three stood poised in silence, then Kuo dropped the weapon back.

"Don't presume to give me orders!" he said to Fallon, the rage caged uncertainly in his throat. "You forget yourself. You are concealing something from me and I will see the colonel now." He was under control again but he kept his hand near his gun. "They say that everything new originates in Canton, and that this is the hatchery of plots. I intend to learn what is going on here."

He pulled the door open with a crash and stalked into the dark where the colonel lay.

7

The bare globe of an overhead light, snapped on in his face, roused Colonel Li and he heaved himself up in bed on his elbow, blinded and blinking. Then his eyes focused on the Security officer standing at the foot of the cot and he stared in complete astonishment. Fallon, coming to the door behind Captain Kuo, saw that Li was not so flushed, and a profuse sweat had broken out on his face, trickling down the dry yellowed skin.

"What is this?" Li asked, his voice a whisper. "Captain? Why are you here?" His recognition had been immediate and his mind was quite clear.

For a moment Kuo faltered and displayed an unusual trace of embarrassment, even apology. Then his gaze sharpened and his mouth tightened.

"I learned you were ill and I caught the first transport south, before noon," he said. "I just landed. Frankly, aside from your adjutant, I don't trust your companions on this journey. I told you so before you left and objected principally to this foreign doctor accompanying you. He has told me what has happened but I wish you to confirm it."

Li's eyes widened in amazement. "Do you doubt him? I am diabetic, as you well know, and I had a relapse on the train. Also I have a crippled leg. Did you fly all this way simply to ask me that?"

Kuo gripped the footboard of the cot and his knuckles grew white. "Your doctor had the impertinence to ask me the same thing, and this Russian jackal of yours called me a fool to my face. I assure you I am not such a fool as you imagine. How do you know that the doctor has not deliberately given you the wrong medicine to make you ill? Your adjutant wired me twice—he is an observant and dutiful officer—and told me something was odd about your medicine. He said also this doctor refused to allow you to be given a standard remedy purchased from a government shop in Hengyang. It is all very suspicious. Now your leg, too. You should be in a hospital, not lying here like a captive of these dogs."

The colonel had pulled himself up on the pillow. "This is absurd!" he said in a stronger voice. "What do you take me for? If you imply treachery by the doctor, then Efremov is correct—you are a great fool, and a turtle's louse besides! The doctor is a prisoner, but he is faithful and loyal to me in all matters pertaining to my health. I have told you this before and I have no intention of renewing the argument while I am sick. Get out of here, and go tell your troubles to your own Security people in the city!"

"I will inform the local Security branch of my arrival as soon as I have asked you what you know about that girl whom the doctor has protected," Kuo said angrily. "He denies that she is with him or that he knows where she is, but I have reason to believe she has left Shanghai, and that man Tieh as well. Both may have come here with you."

"Are you accusing me of conniving with the opposition?" Li demanded. "Is this a charge of collaboration? If so, make it formally, Captain Kuo, before witnesses, so that we can proceed from there."

"I don't say you are shielding them. I say they may be using you. My bureau conducted a series of raids in Shanghai the night after you left. We caught an old woman in a house on Tsepu Road, the widow of that fat herb-seller in Nantao, who was the front for the transmitter station.

A little persuasion produced information that the organization still exists. But Tieh and the girl have disappeared."

"What is all that to me? That's your affair. If that's all you came here for, you are wasting time for everyone. I think you are persecuting the doctor because of personal malice and not on any reasonable basis. That underground gang is not strong or important enough to warrant all this hounding, this raiding and arresting and a long trip by air. You have permitted petty animosity to blind you to justice or to your larger duties. At best, this is a job for one of your deputies, not for a man of your wide responsibilities, Captain Kuo!"

Kuo glowered at him. "Let me judge my own duties," he said. "There is more to this than one or two cockroaches. The cell operating in Shanghai has contact with a cell here, and another in Peking, and many others. This one in Canton may very well be the master group, and we are on its track, all trails lead to it. That is one reason why I think our cockroaches may have crawled south. Their friends may have known you were on the train and asked their allies in the hills to blow that bridge, if only to flaunt their intelligence system and their power."

"You see enemies of the State under every rock," Li said wearily. "You will never be anything but a policeman."

Fallon and Efremov had remained standing quietly in the back of the room during this acrimonious exchange. Now they all heard persons entering the front office and Fallon saw that the adjutant and Wong had returned. He glanced at Efremov, who was moving out to intercept them, but it was too late. Major Huang did not immediately notice Kuo.

"It is all arranged," Huang said, hurrying in. "We have the chops required, giving permission for the journey. We were fortunate to find the officials we sought. I still don't approve of it, but—" He had walked into the bedroom as he spoke and now perceived the Security officer. He stopped short.

"You don't approve of what?" Kuo asked coldly. "What journey do you mean?"

"Why—" said Huang, astounded, "why, to Hongkong, of course. The colonel is going there, isn't he? The train leaves in about an hour."

Colonel Li sighed, and Fallon, absorbing the jolt of this indiscretion, stole a surreptitious look at his watch. It was on eleven.

"I see," Kuo nodded with a thin smile. "The colonel is going to Hongkong, and has had his travel papers chopped within five hours of arrival here, although it is near the middle of the night. Will you explain this, Colonel?"

"I'll explain it," Fallon said suddenly. "I know how it looks to you, but you don't yet know the facts, and the adjutant whom you trust will support them, I think. The colonel has developed a gangrenous ulcer during the trip south, aggravated by his condition, and unless immediate action is taken his life is in danger. An amputation may be averted if we can get him into a proper hospital. But if operating is necessary, that is the only place it can be performed with safety. The hospitals here are jammed, and the colonel has decided to seek treatment in one of the institutions in Hongkong. I told you most of this, but I repeat it now."

Kuo turned on Major Huang. "Is that the case?"

"I don't know," Huang stammered. "I am no doctor. I only got the chops as the colonel ordered."

"This seems to be a very sudden decision, then," said Kuo. He looked at the fat Captain Wong, who only nodded in bewilderment.

But Efremov met his glance with the same jeering smile as before. "Remember what I told you," the Russian said warningly, and Kuo's jaw muscles tightened. He swung to the colonel.

"This is an obvious trick of the doctor's," he grated. "A trick to use you to assist him in escaping. You should have seen it. Or perhaps you did see it, and wish to go for your own private reasons. That is not for me to decide but for Bureau investigators. It is nonsense that you can't receive medical treatment in Canton in an emergency. There are plenty of excellent physicians here, and though I heard of an epidemic while on the plane, there can always be found room in a hospital for you. You have not even called another doctor, I presume, to consult and confirm this foreigner's report. He is probably exaggerating, and has fed your well-known fears. Everyone knows that Colonel Li, so brave on the field of battle, becomes a great coward in the face of any small ailment and cries out in panic!"

Li heard him out in grim silence, and when he was finished said, "We are going to Hongkong tonight, and if you think I have private reasons, be damned to you! Huang, if the papers are all in order now, call an ambulance to take me to the station."

"I have one waiting at the door, sir," the jolly Captain Wong said brightly.

"And I forbid it!" Kuo said. "I will remind you, Colonel, that your rank doesn't give you authority to overrule an order I may make in a Security case."

"Perhaps not," said the colonel, swinging his good leg off the cot, "but you'll have to enforce your orders and take the consequences."

Fallon moved forward quickly and pressed Li back against the pillow. "You can't take a step," he said. "Exertion may be fatal."

Kuo watched the colonel's subsiding struggle, his face expressionless. Then he said, "The order can be enforced. I will have Security men here in five minutes." He walked through the door toward the office desk and reached for the telephone.

As he did so, Gregor Efremov shifted from his position beside the door, came up behind the officer, and struck him a sharp blow in the back of the neck. Then he clamped a muscular arm around his throat, shutting off his strangled shout. The agent's other arm caught Kuo's hand as he clawed for his weapon, twisted it backward, and in a swift movement released it and grabbed the gun butt, sliding it from the holster.

Kuo hung powerless in the paralyzing embrace, his breathing throttled off and his face assuming a blotchy purplish hue. He squirmed and kicked vainly, but his energies rapidly drained. He began to sag, though Efremov held him up.

The only other person making any move was Major Huang. He stood gaping in horror for too long a moment and then launched a scrambling dash toward the outer door. He had to pass Efremov to get there, and as he tried to squeeze by the desk, the Russian swung the heavy automatic, raking Huang's head with the muzzle, and the adjutant stumbled and collapsed in a heap on the floor.

Captain Wong stood as though frozen, his smile plastered across the round pasty face. Colonel Li still lay on the bed, and Fallon was motionless beside him. Efremov felt the slack weight of the body in the circle of his arm and suddenly released it. Kuo fell across the flat desk like a sack and his head thumped as it struck the wood, and rolled loosely. But his shoulders and back labored, and they could hear the harsh choking gasp beginning as his lungs fought for air. It bubbled and hissed, bubbled and hissed.

"Like the water under a river dock," Efremov said reflectively. And he added, "It is a good comparison, eh? It puts a thought in my head." Then he looked at Fallon, the wide lipless mouth spreading in an ugly grin. "I have wanted to do this to the policeman for a long time. And he came a thousand miles to accommodate me."

8

Fallon came out of the colonel's room into the office and put his hand for a moment on Kuo's back, feeling the shudder and hearing the weird whistle of the breath. He looked down at the adjutant, who was beginning to stir; blood welled dark scarlet in the black bristles of hair on the side of his skull.

"Well," Fallon said finally, "that cuts it, I guess." He spoke in English and Efremov wrinkled his brow at the phrase.

"Only a small cut," he said with a deprecating gesture, the automatic still grasped in his hand. "I didn't want to hurt the little major too much. But he was being foolish."

"I think we're all a bit foolish," Fallon said. "What are we going to do about these fellows when they come out of it?"

Li could hear them talking from the bedroom and though he had not been able to see the action clearly, he comprehended it. "Come here," he called, and when they approached the door he said to Captain Wong, "Watch those two back there."

Wong seemed dumbfounded by the turmoil that had suddenly exploded in his once peaceful branch office. But he saluted the colonel with alacrity, went to his desk, shoved Kuo's leg aside so that he could open a drawer, and took out a big Mauser. Holding the ungainly weapon, he looked ridiculous and sensed it, but his effervescent humor reclaimed him and he chuckled. The colonel was the boss, and Wong had personal reasons, buried in the past, for not loving Security officers. He took up a position of fierce vigilance.

The colonel held a towel and was wiping perspiration from his face. "Despite all this," he said, "I feel a little better. Well enough to make a short train trip, anyway." He peered through the door. "Captain, do you have those travel papers?"

Wong pulled a sheaf from his tunic pocket and handed them to Fallon, and the colonel examined them. "Good," he said. "And the ambulance is waiting outside, I believe. Wong is a quick-witted man, and I should revise my opinion of the Cantonese. Captain, when we are gone you had better close the office for a little while. Perhaps go to the country and enjoy nature. I am sorry my first visit to you has been so irregular, but I will get in touch with you when I return."

He turned his attention to Efremov. "You have put yourself voluntarily in a delicate position. Kuo is not certain of his authority over persons with your status, but you have made it necessary for him to do something about you."

"Wrong," said Efremov. "He has made it necessary for me to do something about him! The matter will be settled after you have departed. And you had better leave immediately."

"What about you? You could come down to Hongkong by boat without all the usual formality of passports and entry papers. Any junk master will bring you for a price. Here is some money."

"I have plenty of money," Efremov said. "Don't trouble yourself about me. I am under an independent authority and what I do is not your problem. Perhaps I will join you in Hongkong—I can inquire at the hospitals."

"Probably the Queen Mary in Pokfulam," Fallon said. "Or the War Memorial on the Peak. Many conditions have changed there, I suppose. The Tsan Yuk used to be for Chinese only."

"I will find you if I come, don't worry," said Efremov. "Now I will go down and get the litter; the ambulance attendant mustn't come up here." He looked into the office where Huang was sitting on the floor, his knees drawn up and his head in his hands. Kuo had rolled sideways on the desk and Wong had lowered him into a chair but was standing back with the huge Mauser ready. "Your Captain Wong and I will see what is to be done about this pair after you are on your way. They must be isolated until you are across the border. Perhaps for longer," he added, his glance lingering on Kuo. He handed Kuo's automatic to Fallon and went out through the hall and down the stairs. Fallon put the gun in his jacket pocket and made a last hasty examination of the colonel's leg, but without removing the thick bandages. They were stained and the odor was very bad, but a repacking would have to wait until the train was rolling out for Kowloon.

Efremov reutrned with the litter and they lifted Li onto it. "The attendant cannot understand why he must wait below," the Russian grinned. "Now, Doctor, you at the front, I at the back, and we hoist, so. Wong, put our bags and the doctor's kit there in the corner on the foot of the litter. So! Now watch them, Captain Wong. When I return, we will use a little binding cord and some soft stuffing for their mouths."

Kuo seemed to be only barely recovering his faculties and took no notice of them as they went through the room with the litter. He was conscious but seemed stupefied, and his breathing was loud and hoarse. Major Huang raised his head from his hands and stared dazedly but did not move from the floor. They got the litter down the stairs without difficulty; at that hour of the night the office building was deserted and the ambulance had been backed up straight into the wide lobby door, blocking the walk. The attendant who was waiting took the front of the litter from Fallon and he went back past Efremov into the lobby. He was thinking uneasily of what the impulsive agent's intentions might be toward the Security officer, and climbed the stairs again to make certain nothing had been left behind.

As he reached the hall he heard a loud exclamation and the sounds of a sharp scuffle, accompanied by several solid blows. Someone was panting harshly, a boot sole scraped the tile floor, and there was a crash and a clatter as a chair went over. He stepped through the door into the light. Wong leaned against the far wall of the front office, disheveled and with a pencil of blood trickling from the corner of his mouth. Captain Kuo stood in the inner doorway, and held the ugly Mauser he had wrested from his guard's hand in the swift attack. Back of him, Huang sat where he had been before, tense and more watchful now.

"Soft fat men like you do not know how to handle weapons or prisoners," Kuo said to Wong. His voice was low and strained as if it hurt him to speak. He addressed Wong, but his olive-dark eyes were fixed on Fallon and there was a vaguely lopsided smile on his lips. Some of his color had returned.

Fallon remained where he was, just inside the door. He felt the weight of the automatic in his coat pocket, and remembered that it had been handed to him in the bedroom out of Kuo's view, and that nothing had been said about it.

"Well, I-sheng," the captain said. "It has been observed that predestined enemies will always meet in a narrow alleyway."

Fallon had no doubt that Kuo would have shot him then, and thus ended the matter. But Major Huang sat on the floor of the inner room, watching, and the disarmed Wong stood against the wall. Kuo glanced toward the front window, which had not been opened.

"Unfortunately," the Security chief added, "there are constables in the street who will come at a shouted summons, so the law must take its course."

He went to the window and with his free hand fumbled to raise it. The catch was obstinate. The heavy Mauser sank a trifle and Kuo frowned, turning his head toward the glass. Fallon reached into his pocket and pulled out the automatic, snapping off the safety. The rustle and click of the swift motion brought Kuo's eyes around. Light glinted on rising metal; then the Mauser wavered uncertainly.

"*Ching man i'tien,*" Kuo muttered. "Let's go a bit slower—"

The crash of the automatic bounded from wall to wall of the room, shattering the senses. Kuo leaned back against the window, lowering his arm gradually until his weapon pointed at the floor. He looked directly at Fallon and seemed now to have three eyes, the third having appeared just above the bridge of his nose, round and black and staring. Then his knees buckled and he slid gently to the floor and rolled over on his face.

Fallon put the automatic in his pocket again, battling sudden nausea, and noticed that his hand felt numb. He looked at the others; they remained where they were and said nothing. There were running steps on the stairs. Efremov burst through the door. He stopped, sniffed at the acrid odor, saw Kuo beneath the window, and his fair eyebrows lifted.

"Hmm," said Efremov. "You cheat me." He crossed the room, turned

Kuo's head a little with the toe of his shoe, and stared. "A healer did this? Very precise."

Major Huang was getting unsteadily to his feet and his face was gray, except where the blood had begun to clot. He did not take his frightened gaze from Fallon.

"I think," Fallon said to him, "that you had better come with the colonel and me, as we first planned. You'll probably be safer."

Efremov snorted. "I don't bother rabbits. But you are right, he will save me trouble if he goes, eh, Wong? We will just clean this place up a little and dispose of the rubbish somewhere and lock the door and go away ourselves. Doctor, you had better hurry or you will miss your train. Give me that gun; you don't want border searchers to find it on you."

They went down the stairs once more, the adjutant in front. There was a small crowd around the waiting ambulance, and Efremov grinned.

"I heard the shot because I was inside the lobby," he said. "Outside here it is too noisy with the traffic." He caught Huang's shoulder in a hard grip and spun him around. "Go and take care of your colonel, little man! On the train, obey the doctor and you are dumb, do you understand? Or shall I assure it by cutting out your tongue here?"

Huang hastily climbed into the ambulance and took the jump seat beside the litter.

Efremov shook Fallon's hand. "Go, go!" he growled. "What are you waiting for? The sunrise of a new day?"

Fallon sat with the driver and attendant but kept an eye on Huang through the cab window. The dial on his watch told him it was nearly midnight.

While the ambulance crew unloaded the litter at the station, Huang spoke for the first time.

"You needn't be concerned that I will try to slip away or talk to anyone," he murmured. "That would be very stupid for me. I have been stupid enough. Li is as much my patron as he is yours."

"Protégés together," Fallon said, leading the way.

There was no difficulty; the papers with the fresh red stamps and seals opened the gates and lanes through crowds, for Huang knew how to present them for maximum effect. As usual, there was one wagon-lit at the head of the line of cars. The compartments were already filled; Huang spoke sharply to the car chief, flashed his documents, pointed to the waiting litter, and a family of loudly protesting civilians was evicted from one of the private cubicles. Li had hardly been shifted from litter to lounge seat when the cars underwent their customary backbreaking series of jerks and the wheels were slowly turning. The ambulance crew fled shouting.

The colonel was fully awake, hardly a surprise to Fallon.

"We're on our way," the doctor said. "Do you have much pain?"

"*M'fatze*, never mind," said Li. "I have ordered the leg to mark time for a little longer. Give me a cigarette please, Major."

He did not ask any questions.

9

In the blackness across the unseen countryside of the delta, the train curved among endless rice paddies and the dimmed lights of the passing railway cars were reflected in still pools beside the roadbed. The engine hooted and wailed and sent up showers of sparks, the cars rocked on protesting wheels, the couplings and battered woodwork squealed and groaned. Everything was in constant motion: the dusty drapes on the compartment door, the carafe on gimbals filled with stale water that no one ever touched, the fruit rinds and litter on the floor left from the previous day's up-trip, the very dirt in the cracks of the splintered flooring. Most of the travelers who had boarded the Kowloon train had settled down among their boxes and bundles to try to rest a little, but there was a steady hum of voices through the cars, and a pet dog yapped untiringly.

The colonel occasionally dozed, stretched out on one of the wide seats, but sound sleep was unattainable. The car chief came solicitously to the door every hour. The ticket seller and the ticket taker arrived. Periodically a guard thrust his thick flat face through the curtain and stared at them. The tea dispenser brought tea and each half-hour came in with hot water to replenish the pot. A hawker of litchis, oranges, bananas and sweets sounded his *tic-tocs* in the swaying corridor. Another hawker of dough-balls, melon seeds, wine and cigarettes inquired optimistically after their desires. This was the short, crowded, ninety-mile night run to the border and official and unofficial personnel aboard made the most of each passing traveler.

The inspectors—three of them—took the longest and most leisurely time, and returned twice afterward. They read each separate paper down to the final printed line, studied chops and signatures, examined Fallon's passport and attached photo with interest, pursed their lips over his out-dated visa issued by a discredited regime, and listened to the major's prepared and repeated speech, and to the standard answers he gave to their questions. They gazed at the recumbent colonel, listened again as Fallon explained the nature of the ailment and wrinkled their broad noses at the mixed odor of decay and antiseptic. Eventually Huang went with them into the corridor and held a lengthy colloquy, and returned with a gesture of relief. The times had not changed so very much: palms were still buttered, ways were greased, and squeeze—the family virtue and the national kleptomania—still turned the wheels. This was a profitable train; its customers were all bound out of the country and quite willing to pay through the nose for the final privileges.

Then, when everything had been arranged and money matters had been settled, the inspectors returned as an afterthought and solemnly informed Huang that because of the typhus outbreak in Canton, there were reports that the border would be closed by morning for an indefinite period. The extent of the epidemic, one added, had been greatly exaggerated, but the British health authorities might quarantine travelers from the interior. This had happened before; all movement could be halted until inspection and special decontamination stations were set up on both sides. Meanwhile, passengers might experience considerable delay and inconvenience.

There was, however, nothing to be done about it now. The train, though billed as a fast express, made interminable stops at numerous points, the longest at the sleeping city of Sheklung, during which guards and passengers and officials tramped through the corridors and a babble arose outside and the engine alternately jerked the cars forward and smashed them back. There was really no hurry, the car chief said. No one could cross the border anyway before it was opened at daylight— if it were opened at all.

Li wakened during one of these noisy interludes. "So much idle talk!" he groaned. He drank a glass of tea and watched while Huang produced two suits of clothing he had purchased from a stall on the Sheklung platform. They had no civilian dress with them and it would not do to enter Hongkong in the uniforms of the Army of the People's Republic. Not that their credentials concealed their identities; on the contrary, they, were emphasized, though the colonel's exact duties were not mentioned. The colonel examined the cotton jackets and wide pantaloons and cloth slippers and nodded, and they made the change of costume.

"I wore clothing like this in the old days," Li said as they struggled with the trousers to get them over his reclining legs. "So did you, Huang. We are both of the people. When I first went into the service I did so for refuge. I'd only a pair of pants and a string to hold them up—I was broke." He laughed. He was exhilarated despite the pain and worry.

Like many of his countrymen, Li was a born raconteur, his tales mellow with unnumbered centuries of earthy living. At ease he was salty and satirical. He began to tell them of an old man named Sheng who once tilled the land in a poor valley among the bare hills of the north. The aged toiler and his sons hardly scratched a living from the stony ground and they despaired for the future of their growing clan of descendants. Then an itinerant monk told old Sheng that beneath the mountain of rubble across the valley there lay the richest earth within the Four Seas, land that would make his family wealthy forever if it could be uncovered. Sheng and his sons immediately went to work with mattocks and woven baskets to remove the mountain. As the years passed the family became the laughing stock of the region, because for all their labors they had made only a slight dent in the rubble.

"One day," Li said, "a high official happened to come that way with his retinue and was told about the Sheng family, and he stopped beside the neglected fields and asked the old man if he thought all this work was worth it. Old Sheng said it was. 'But it will never be finished,' the official protested. 'Certainly it will be finished!' the old man said. 'After us there will be more Shengs to do the work, and after them more Shengs, and more Shengs. There will always be Shengs, as there always have been Shengs. Eventually a Sheng will inherit the richest earth within the Four Seas and become wealthy.' "

But after a time Li grew silent and thoughtful, staring out of the compartment window. The first light was just beginning to creep on the ridges of the low hills to the north, outlining them, though the fields below still lay in darkness. Presently he stirred.

"This is a very old country," he said musingly. "It has stood aloof from the world. It is too large for the mind to encompass. It's both mystical and stupefying. You have seen it in chaos, Fah On—blood-soaked and fatalistic, groping for its destiny, and you think this destiny is simply to exist and survive despite endless war and pestilence. Perhaps you are right. This country is ancient and placid, and it seems insensible to misery and pain, like many of your patients—though not myself! Still, it is vital. And it is beyond sorrow and petty emotion, success or failure, calamity or death."

As the faint light of dawn spread down the slopes of the hills into the paddies, Li watched the changing colors and Fallon did not interrupt his thoughts.

"You are leaving this," Li said after a long silence, waving his hand toward the fields. "The future here doubtless has little true meaning to you. Our doctrines are only empty phrases to you, and spell only hopelessness and confusion. Well, you are not alone, of course. There are many who are disillusioned and who believe that ardor is cheap without wisdom and knowledge. Sometimes even the stoutest heart dies at the futility and incompetence, and thinks the changes that have been made are only superficial. I have heard many people say, and openly, that they were better off under the emperors or the warlords, because for all their faults there were periods of peace. These people have been the most misruled race on earth, and now they are caught in an eruption they can't understand. And with many of them it means merely a loss of restraint and decency and self-confidence. They fear unknown evils and follies and loosened passions."

"But in the face of all that, they remain patient," Fallon said.

"Yes. That is why I must come back when I can, even if I have only one leg."

The engine whistled for Shumchun.

Now, in the strengthening daylight, the last flurry and scramble began. The final inspections were made, the final offers of food and drink. There were goods trains standing along the sidings here and the mat roofs of godowns beyond, and a few concrete structures including pillboxes, and the train crawled to a sighing stop. The passengers poured out of the cars under the watchful eyes of soldiers and took up their bundles and formed up into weary queues. The car chief brought two train crewmen into the compartment with a litter and they moved Li out into the fresh morning air. The queues were shuffling forward, and the slow march started.

Fallon saw the high fences and the barbed wire above the crowd around the gate in the barrier. He saw the People's Police and the plainclothes men in black silk, revolvers bulging on their hips. The herd moved quietly ahead, channeling through the teams of searchers and prodders, the stampers of passes, the receivers of fees.

For a time Fallon stood bemused in line, staring at the scene of orderly confusion sharply etched in the early light, and then raised his eyes to the barren ranges of hills behind the boundary. They spread their sinuous course along the coast, and suddenly he was reminded that this protected district he approached so slowly, which the world miscalled Kowloon, was really Kau-lung to the people around him, the Nine Dragons. And indeed those hills above them lay like gigantic monsters, and this was the end of them.

He looked again at the gateway, nearer now, and though it did not gape wide there were teeth in it and he thought, We're being spewed out of the mouth of this damned beast, the serpent of which Father Julien warned me; I've come a long way out of the rotten belly into the gullet and up to the fangs, and I'll keep my fingers crossed that the jaws don't shut before I make it.

He was roused by the halting of the lines inside the barricades. And

Huang looked across the litter at him and said, "The quarantine is in force."

The robed men and trousered women carrying bags and baskets set up a wail and a great clamor of protest, the coolie gangs stopped their loading and unloading of trucks. But the police and the gray-clad guards were adamant. The British authorities controlled the other side of the barrier, and they were demanding the assurance of a healthy immigration.

Fallon and Huang pushed forward through the milling crowd and found a stolid Red officer to whom they explained their dilemma. He stared at the colonel on his stretcher, listened to the adjutant, fingered the papers, looked curiously at the foreign physician.

"You say you arrived in Canton by train from the north only last night?" He considered this, then left them and crossed the barrier and conferred with his opposite number there. A lengthy palaver followed. Eventually he returned, as stolid as before.

"They give special permission for you and your emergency case to pass," he said. "Since you were hardly in the city long enough to be exposed anyway. It is their risk, not ours."

Then suddenly Fallon had passed the wooden barriers and crossed the little trestle, and he looked up to see a red-mustached British police officer in helmet and shorts who stood two yards away, spraddle-legged, smoking a cigarette and gazing at him wonderingly. He was conscious then of his wrinkled and travel-stained clothing, his unshaven face and grimy hands. And he thought, They've seen hundreds of refugees like myself coming through this gate, native and foreign, people fleeing or people kicked out, the wretched and disinherited and dispossessed. And the hopeful, too.

The inspection on the Kowloon side was perfunctory, once the decision had been made. Li was passed without further inquiry when they saw his pallor; Huang was informed that a more formal checkup would be made later at the hospital. A uniformed man tapped Fallon's passport and remarked that he should hold himself ready to answer any subsequent police or consular inquiries. And they walked away from the surging and despondent crowd behind the wire.

Huang spurned the waiting shuttle service on to Kowloon. He found a cab, they placed the colonel across the back seat, and drove the last few miles down to the ferry in relaxed luxury. In the bustle at the ferry slip, coolies transferred the litter to the open deck and the boat slid out into the busy harbor toward the Victoria docks.

Fallon stood against the rail, with a cool morning breeze off the shimmering sea in his face. And watching the great rock rising ahead from the strait to a majestic peak, he was somehow reminded of New England again. The hills were broken on the island and softened by a floating gossamer mist; the city nestled at their feet and lifted in green terraces from the waterfront toward the sky, and about him lay warships and liners, stubby freighters and mat-sailed junks.

The colonel caught his glance and pulled a wry face. "A desolate view, eh?" he said lugubriously, and grinned.

"The stronghold of imperialism at its worst," Fallon agreed. "Shall we return immediately to Canton?"

"Oh, yes." Li nodded. "As soon as I have taken complete leave of my five wits."

10

When Fallon left surgery he passed a tall window in the hall and was astonished to discover that the afternoon was far advanced and was already shading deceptively into twilight. The window looked out on a small garden filled with broad shade trees, blooming shrubs and carefully tended flower beds, and beyond it was a white plaster wall to screen the hospital from the road. He was unfamiliar with the city, remembering it only in dimming recollections of past visits when a liner might have brought him to the port for a few days, and of the one transient stop he had made here seven years ago—no, eight now—on his way to the north. But he knew the hospital stood not far from the waterfront in the lower city and the deep bellow of a ship's warning seemed to come directly from across the wall, though he knew the sea was not quite that near. He was very tired, with virtually no sleep on the train last night, and his brain felt fuzzy.

When he went into the physician's lounge to get his street clothes he had another surprise; the old tweeds in the locker had been cleaned and pressed during the day, the worn shoes had been given a high polish, the hat had been blocked, the shirt washed and ironed. He dressed, feeling an unsteadiness in his legs which he took for a sign of weakness and probably hunger, but he thought he would rather have a stiff drink now than anything else.

In the lobby a man in a long gray linen gown rose to meet him and he had to look again to recognize Huang. He took the adjutant's arm and they walked down into the garden.

"Well?"

"We amputated," Fallon said. "It had gone much too long, of course. But he's doing very well, considering."

"Is there still danger?"

"No, Major, very little danger now."

"Just Huang, if you please. Mr. Huang."

The gravel crunched under their feet and Fallon smelled the salt cool coming up from the harbor, and the delicacy of folding flowers.

"I took two rooms for us," Mr. Huang said. "A small hotel just around the corner from here. It's Chinese, and perhaps you'd rather go to one of the larger places, the Gloucester or the Hongkong, where your people stay."

There was something odd and mixed up about that and Fallon paused, analyzing it. His people . . . "Well," he said, "that's all right. I'll want to be near the hospital for quite a while, you know. Is there a bar in our hotel?"

The bar was dark and quiet, not like bars should be at that time of evening before the dinner hour, and Fallon was relieved. He began to think ahead a little, for the first time. Tomorrow he must go to the Consulate and establish some sort of status, no matter how questionable, to get himself cleared up one way or another. And there was something about police registry that Huang was explaining; he gathered there had been a polite visit from an investigator sometime during the afternoon, but it was all right, Huang said. Nothing to worry about.

"The police want to know what we intend to do, that's all," Huang murmured. "They know why we're here and were very courteous. I told them the colonel and I would probably be returning to Canton, if he recovers."

"He'll recover," Fallon said.

And there was a matter of funds now, he thought practically. He would have to go to the bank and arrange a transfer from Manila. He was hazy about how such things were handled, but they would take care of it. And if at either the Consulate or the bank there arose any question of identity, there were two or three people he knew here—or had known, once. Former friends in another life.

Huang suggested dinner. Fallon looked at his watch and excused himself. There was something he must attend to first.

He left the hotel and walked from the narrow side street down into Queens Road and along it into the older and more crowded quarter. After a considerable search he found the address he wanted in Jervois Street. It was an unpretentious walkup office building, rather dingy and dark, but the right name was on the door of an attorney's office and he knocked and was admitted.

The man he asked for was a small and compact Cantonese in a linen business suit, who looked inquiringly at him through thick glasses and motioned him to a seat.

"Mr. Chao?" Fallon said, producing his wallet. "I am Dr. Paul Fallon— here are cards to identify me. I'm from Shanghai. A friend of Tieh Lao-hu."

The attorney peered at the cards and stared at Fallon with attention, then shook hands. "Dr. Fallon," he said slowly. "Yes, I have heard your name mentioned. Ah, I see . . ." He offered cigarettes.

"I just arrived here this morning," Fallon said. "By way of Canton. Tieh, or a friend of his, I should say, gave me this address."

"Yes," Chao said. "A friend. Would I know that name also?"

"Possibly. Miss Chung. Chung Yin-kuei."

Chao deposited cigarette ash in a tray. "Yes, I know of her." He seemed to be searching for words. "I—we, that is—we know quite a good deal about you, Doctor. We were informed of the—ah—the journey you were taking, though I hadn't expected to see you here quite so soon, if at all. It was problematic that you would be able to come. Well . . ."

He picked up a paper and laid it down again on the desk. "I doubt if you have heard. It was only two days ago, I gather. At any rate, Doctor, I regret we have so little information. But there has been another quite formidable police action up there, it seems, and we understand the organization has been temporarily scattered. Several were taken and several others were injured. I am really sorry to tell you this . . ." His voice dribbled off into silence.

Fallon said, "Yes?"

"The radio contact was broken soon after. This was the second time, you understand, that they've been raided. I am afraid Tieh was one of those—ah—who were injured."

"And Miss Chung?"

"No mention, Doctor, no mention. I am sorry." He looked at Fallon reflectively. "Well, perhaps we had better go out and have a drink and a little dinner and we can bring ourselves up to date on all this, eh? I realize it is rather a shock for you. We had heard . . ."

Sometime later in the evening—he didn't know how much later— Fallon found himself seated alone on a bench under a tree, a terraced and open space that looked out and down across a sea of twinkling and flashing lights in the lower city. For a moment he was entirely bewildered; he did not remember coming into the park at all. But he knew he wasn't drunk; he had had almost nothing to drink with Mr. Chao. He shrugged. He was growing absent-minded, probably early senility. He looked around curiously and decided this was somewhere along one of the winding paths in the botanical gardens where he must have wandered. He could pick out certain landmarks now, and the harbor was there below him, and the dark brooding hills of the mainland beyond.

A liner, no larger than a bathtub toy, lay at a pier down there, glittering with light. He watched it for several minutes. He could, he supposed, go home now. Get his papers, get his money, go aboard a ship like that and leave. It was not quite as simple as that, with Li to be considered, but Li could be left in good hands and it was not so complicated either. And he didn't have to consider Li any more. He didn't have to consider anybody but himself.

Eight years thrown away, and it was high time to pick up the pieces, if there were any, and be on the road. Like that fellow in Li Po's song, the leisurely vagrant who lay drunk and half-asleep in the sunny courtyard of a wayside temple, and woke to find that the spring was gone and he must hurry before night overtook him.

Old Li Po knew a thing or two, Fallon decided. There was another verse of his, something that went: "We are divided from one another and scattered. For a long time I shall be obliged to wander without intention; but we will keep our appointment in the far-off Cloudy River. . . ." Something like that, penned by a disreputable poet a thousand years ago.

But it wasn't easy to get up and go home when you were already there; it was impossible. When you'd been bitten by the idea of a people and a place, that was where you belonged, not in some distant and alien exile on the other side of the earth among strangers, just because your skin was the same color as theirs.

That would be more monstrous than running away. The thought was repellent. Better to be a dog in a village lane than a man in a dungeon.

Fallon raised his eyes from the brilliant little ship to the rolling range of black hills beyond it. No lights glowed there; no sound came across the water from them. They crouched under the stars, under the cloudy river. Behind them the struggle went on, unremitting, without quarter. And if one fell, like a flashing star through the darkness, who would miss it from the myriads, or mark its splendid brief passage, or remember it with yearning or regret? Who indeed could be reconciled, except the chance watcher who had followed its gleam with the clear steady gaze of love.

After a time Fallon rose, chilled by a little wind from the sea, and went down the path toward the descending necklace of lights in the streets. In the windings of this strange city he was lost, and how thoroughly lost, he was not yet prepared to say. But he was finding his way by instinct. And eventually it led to the door of the small hotel near the hospital.

The adjutant, looking queer and uncomfortable in his civilian gown, was sitting alone in the lobby.

"I waited for you, Fah On," he said. "Have you eaten rice?"

"I dined somewhere, Mr. Huang," the doctor said.

"Well, I didn't know what to do, so I waited."

"That is a good thing to do when you are uncertain," Fallon agreed. "You wait and work, or just wait. But working is better. Now for a while I'll be working with the colonel, and when he is able to travel again we must take the next step. But until that time comes, we don't have to decide on it, do we?"

"I suppose not," said Huang, giving him a peculiar glance.

"And meanwhile, if the bar here is still open," Fallon added, "I think it would be a good idea to emulate Li Po and drink a little wine. Don't you?"

"I suppose so, Fah On," said the adjutant. "I have great respect for your judgment."

Pierhead

The telephone buzzed. In the brilliant glare of early afternoon the hotel room overlooking Des Voeux Road was dim and soothing. When he lifted the instrument he heard the high precise voice of the Macanese desk clerk.

"A Mr. Keogh of your Consulate to see you, Doctor," the clerk said. "He says you are expecting him."

"All right," Fallon said. "Send him up to the roof garden; I'll meet him there. Will you send up the bar boy, too?"

"Yes, sir," the Macanese said. The receiver clicked. Fallon tossed his book on the bed, put on his jacket, and climbed one flight of stairs to the roof, hearing the lift whining in its well below. The garden was only a small enclosed space under an arbor, with a few round tables and chairs; in the heat of the day it was deserted. Later it would be filled with well-dressed and well-fed Chinese fugitives from Canton and prosperous exiles from the north and their svelte ladies, whiling away the time in the sanctuary of the Colony.

The lift door clicked, Keogh came into the arbor followed by the white-gowned boy, and they gave their order. They did not shake hands, for they had met like this three times in the past week. They had also known each other a long while, since the days of Cabanatuan and Santo Tomas. They were of an age and of a relative disposition.

"This isn't another official call," Keogh said, taking a seat. "Purely personal, no more questions for the record. I'm through with that and our report's already been mailed to Washington. The office and the Intelligence people apparently think they've pumped you dry, though I doubt it. You were never very garrulous, Paul."

"Garrulous enough," Fallon said. "I've been questioned so often by so many of you fellows in the past month I've got laryngitis. The Security Johns up north could take lessons in interrogation from experts here. I used to think they were tough."

"The local lads don't often get it as straight from the horse's mouth. But they think you're a hopeless case. They didn't really hear very much from you they didn't know or suspect already, except that bit about Albany."

"I don't know very much," said Fallon.

He looked out over the city on its firm shoulder of island, rounded and smoothed as though by gentle strokes of the tides, caressed by the sea. Above them the land fell down from tumbled mountains, paused on the cosmopolitan shore, and vanished into the waves. The harbor below flashed silver and emerald, swells surged up the channel under a warm winter sun, and on them a grotesque fishing junk did an elephantine minuet, light shaking from its broad patched sail. Beyond stood the coast, bare and brown and tortured in naked ridges rising from the distant surf, sweeping upward in sterile majesty against a blue ocean of air. It rolled away from sea to sky, the hard ranges of Asia, the battlements and rocky walls that guarded the secret land. But here sunlight glittered on the roofs of the safe and indolent city, and gulls wheeled above them, crying. There was the faint drift of music from the streets and the tinkling music of laughter, gay and without fear.

The boy brought glasses, put them on the table and departed.

"I hear that colonel, that fellow you brought here to saw off his leg, has gone back with his servant," Keogh said curiously.

"He was well enough to travel and their documents were in order." Fallon nodded. "He's probably on the northbound plane out of Canton today."

"Well, knock my ears down if I'm prying, but weren't you nearly of a mind to go with him, Paul? I gathered that earlier."

Fallon's regard was quiet, almost withdrawn. "I considered the notion, Tom. It wouldn't work. There's nothing I can accomplish there, though the colonel was willing to take me back in and vouch for me. It's easy enough to get in again, if I want to. It's not so easy to get out."

"What did you want to accomplish?"

"Too much, I'm afraid. When you clean up the germs, half the battle for the country up there is won. But it's a rough go. You can treat a peasant for beriberi, but that doesn't correct the malnutrition of the race. You can import food to relieve the hunger, but that doesn't correct the basic poverty that makes him hungry all his life."

"No solution for that," Keogh said, shaking his head.

"None but a fresh start," Fallon said. "I know some people who are working on it."

Keogh watched him thoughtfully. "What are their prospects?"

Fallon twirled his glass. "Not too good, not too bad, Tom. You've seen what happens when you put a foreign veneer on the native furniture? The coats crack off, the whole surface rots and breaks down and the old authentic structure emerges. The Slavic brand they've got now smells to heaven. These people are chipping at it. It offends the pride and dignity."

"No doubt, but what can they do about it except a bit of chipping?"

"Very little at first, I suppose. They need outside help of a special kind, and I think they'll get it. It's coming slowly. But you know, when a whole people has to get down and kiss the boss's feet and he has to get down and kiss his boss's feet, they get jumpy. When you get hundreds of millions of people jumpy you've got a problem. When you try to regiment them and make them think all alike, eventually they'll start laughing at themselves. And that'll be the damnedest noise you ever heard; everybody in Asia will listen to it, and it'll sound like the H-bomb in the Kremlin."

Keogh shrugged. "Laughs don't trigger revolutions."

"No, it takes a lot more than that. The stuff is being provided. They're stock-piling at the moment."

He was absently watching the progress through the crowded anchorage of a stolid iron cargo vessel that had trudged up the channel. He leaned forward, squinting at it as the ship maneuvered awkwardly with the aid of a puffing tug.

"What I really came around to say to you, Paul, is that there's a need for people like you here, trained ones. A bad need. The town's full of openings, you know. But I wondered if perhaps you were planning to go home. Or maybe back to Manila."

Fallon had risen to get a better view of the stubby freighter, now slowly being pushed in toward the pier that was the extension of the street beneath them. A wisp of greasy smoke rose straight from its rusted funnel in the still afternoon air.

"D'you see that?" he said, pointing. "I know that ship. I'll wager I know her skipper. He did me a favor once—he turned me down when I applied for passage. I'll bet he'd be delighted to see I made it anyway. Let's go down and shock him, Tom."

"Hell," Keogh said. "This is cool and comfortable. I asked you your plans, if it's not impertinent."

"No plans," said Fallon. "Stay here. Work. Lots of work out here. Like you said, there's a shortage of help. Come on, I'm restless—let's amble down there. I want to waggle my ears at the captain."

The street was hot and crowded, the wharf was hotter, reflecting the white light from godown walls and catching the sun's blast in its asphalt apron. But there were few persons on the pier to welcome this vessel, for she was only a coaster with no flair; she was dirty, she smelled, salt rime from the bucking Formosa Strait gleamed on her gray housing. Keogh grumbled as they pushed through the nondescript fan of longshoremen and shipping officials waiting for the lines to be secured. It had been only a five-minute walk from the hotel but he was perspiring, thinking of the beaded drink he hadn't finished, thinking of the job for his friend that he had in mind and wanted to talk about.

Fallon halted on the edge of the pier, head back, eyes under his shading hand peering up at the bridge wing. And a smile twitched at his mouth.

"There he is," he said to the disinterested Keogh. "The fat fellow there with the black mustache and red face. That's my boy! I want to see his expression when he spots me. Have to tell you about it sometime, Tom. He said he was going to quit this run, but he's still on it."

The freighter was being warped in gradually against the pilings. A row of shifting blobs, the heads of crew and a few passengers, lined the rail below and aft of the bridge.

"What's his name?" Keogh asked.

"Never heard. Wasn't introduced. Maybe he won't recognize me—he'd had a few that night."

Something plopped on the splintered planking of the wharf near Fallon's feet. He had not seen the object arching out from overhead and falling toward him, and did not hear it strike; he was intent on catching the eye of the master. Keogh bent and retrieved the small package, hastily assembled in the form of a rolled handkerchief. He unwrapped it, and held in his broad palm what appeared to be an old silk rag, some sort of tassel with a large and intricate knot woven in its end. He looked at it without comprehension.

"What's this?" he demanded.

Fallon glanced down and away, and back again. He reached out his hand and touched the thing, then took it carefully in his fingers.

Once more his face lifted, but not toward the bridge. A film of sweat stood on his forehead and Keogh, observing that he was starting to walk blindly forward and might go down between pier and hull, caught his arm. There was a haze obstructing Fallon's view, a confusing dazzle of fuzzy color at the rail above, but in a moment it cleared a little, enough to glimpse the flash of sunlight on a lifted bare arm, the violent flutter of a small hand. The hubbub around them all but drowned the clear voice calling.

"What's this?" Keogh repeated nervously.

Fallon was moving toward the point where the gangway was being run out. He moved faster, and Keogh swore, still gripping his sleeve. He began to run along the pier beside the ship and Keogh stumbled and perforce released him.

"Damn it!" Keogh shouted, suddenly furious. "What's the matter with you, you confounded idiot? Are you crazy?"

But Fallon didn't answer, didn't hear. The gangway was not yet secured but he had vaulted through the open cargo door at head level, and the last Keogh saw of him was the yellow glitter of the old rag in his hand.

A police constable, observing the peculiar action, stepped to Keogh's side.

"What's up?" he asked. "Anything wrong, sir?"

Keogh looked at him dazedly. "How should I know?" he muttered. "I think he's gone soft on the skipper!"